Dedalus Europe
General Editor: Timothy Lane

Slav Sisters:

The Dedalus Book of Russian Women's Literature

Slav Sisters:

The Dedalus Book of Russian Women's Literature

edited by Natasha Perova

Dedalus

This book has been selected to receive financial assistance from English PEN's "PEN Translates" programme, supported by Arts Council England. English PEN exists to promote literature and our understanding of it, to uphold writers' freedoms around the world, to campaign against the persecution and imprisonment of writers for stating their views, and to promote the friendly co-operation of writers and the exchange of ideas.

Published in the UK by Dedalus Limited
24-26, St Judith's Lane, Sawtry, Cambs, PE28 5XE
email: info@dedalusbooks.com
www.dedalusbooks.com

ISBN printed book 978 1 910213 75 9
ISBN ebook 978 1 910213 86 5

Dedalus is distributed in the USA & Canada by SCB Distributors
15608 South New Century Drive, Gardena, CA 90248
email: info@scbdistributors.com   web: www.scbdistributors.com

Dedalus is distributed in Australia by Peribo Pty Ltd
58, Beaumont Road, Mount Kuring-gai, N.S.W. 2080
email: info@peribo.com.au

First published by Dedalus in 2018
Introduction, Notes and Selection copyright © Natasha Perova 2018
Translations are copyright the translator and their name appears at the end of each text.
Texts which are in copyright are copyright their individual authors.

The right of Natasha Perova to be identified as the editor of this work has been asserted by her in accordance with the Copyright, Designs and Patents Act, 1988.

Printed and bound in Great Britain by Clays Ltd, Elcograf S.p.A.
Typeset by Marie Lane

The Editor

Natasha Perova is a translator, editor, publisher and literary agent. A philology graduate of Moscow University, she worked in publishing houses producing Russian books in English translation.

In 1991 she started the independent small press *Glas* to publish and promote new Russian writing in translation.

The Authors

Nadezhda Teffi (1872-1952) is regarded today as the foremost chronicler of Russian émigré life in Paris in the years following the 1917 Revolution, the most valuable creation of Russian émigré literature, a major writer in the Gogolian tradition. She was born Nadezhda Lokhvitskaya in St. Petersburg, into a distinguished gentry family. By the start of World War I Teffi was Russia's most famous female author. Liberal in her political beliefs, she drew the line at communism and settled in Paris in 1919, where she focused her acute powers of observation on her fellow émigrés. Almost all of her hundreds of sharply comic stories have been published in the last decade after a long neglect in her homeland. Three books of her prose came out in English translation recently.

Marina Tsvetaeva (1892-1941) ranks with Anna Akhmatova, Osip Mandelstam, and Boris Pasternak as one of Russia's greatest 20th-century poets. Her suicide at the age of forty-eight was the tragic culmination of a life beset by loss and hardship. In her diaries of 1917 to 1920, she describes the broad social, economic, and cultural chaos provoked by the Bolshevik Revolution. Events and individuals are seen through the lens of her personal experience – that of a destitute young woman of upper-class background with two small children, a missing husband, and no means of support.
"Is there prose more intimate, more piercing, more heroic, more astonishing than Tsvetaeva's? Was the truth of reckless feelings ever so naked? So accelerated? Voicing gut and brow, she is incomparable." – Susan Sontag

The Authors

Anna Akhmatova (born Anna Gorenko: 1889-1966) has long been recognised worldwide as one of the most important Russian poets. Her work ranges from short lyric poems to intricately structured cycles, such as *Requiem* and *Poem Without Hero*, her tragic masterpieces about the Stalinist terror. Her style, characterised by its economy and emotional restraint, is strikingly original and powerful. The strong and clear leading female voice marks both her poetry and her autobiographical prose. In 1964 she was awarded the Italian Etna-Taormina prize, and in 1965 she received an honorary doctorate from Oxford University. Her journeys to Sicily and England to receive these honours were her first trips outside her homeland since 1912. Akhmatova's works have been translated into most languages, and her international stature continues to grow.

Lydia Ginzburg (1902-1990) Russian literary scholar, writer, and memoirist, winner of the State Prize in 1988, graduated from the Institute of Art History in 1926. In her youth Lydia Ginzburg was close to the Formalists' art circles and the literary avant-garde. She was a friend of many famous cultural figures of the time, such as Mayakovsky, Mandelstam, Akhmatova, Shklovsky, and wrote perceptive memoirs about them. She is best known for her definitive monographs *On Lyrical Poetry* (1964) and *On Psychological Prose* (1971). Her *Notes on the Siege* has been translated into many languages including English, French, Spanish, Dutch and Swedish. Ginzburg considered her unique diaries of the 1920s through 1980s as "intermediary prose". It is only in the 2000s that the importance of Lydia Ginzburg's legacy and her role as a witness of the age were recognised and studied.

The Authors

Galina Scherbakova (1932-2010) grew up in Donetsk and began her career as a provincial teacher. Later she worked as a reporter on various papers (which she hated) and wrote children's stories (which she loved). It is only in her fifties that she finally managed to devote herself full-time to writing fiction which instantly brought her nationwide fame. Scherbakova created an impressive array of characters from all walks of life, old and young, rich and poor and she could write about love and human relationships with great insight and sympathy but without sentimentality. Her stories have been published in Germany, China, Hungary, Bulgaria and Finland. She left several short novels and more than thirty collections of short stories which have lost nothing of their relevance. Many of her stories have been adapted for films.

Ludmila Petrushevskaya (born in 1938) made a name in the 1970s with her sombre and unusual plays which were highly popular among dissident intellectuals. She has published fifteen works of fiction, including the *New York Times* bestseller *There Once Lived a Woman Who Tried to Kill Her Neighbour's Baby: Scary Fairy Tales*, which won a World Fantasy Award. In 1992 her novel *The Time Night* was shortlisted for the Russian Booker Prize and widely translated. Winner of many other literary prizes Petrushevskaya was awarded the prestigious Pushkin Prize by the Toepfer Foundation in Germany. For the animated cartoon *Tale of Tales*, directed by Yuri Norstein, she received several international prizes and the international jury of film critics called it "the best film in the archives of animation".

The Authors

Olga Slavnikova (born in 1957) in Yekaterinburg in the Urals, is one of the most important contemporary authors. She has a degree from the Urals University and worked on the *Urals* magazine before moving to Moscow in 2001 to coordinate the Debut Prize. In 1997, her novel *Dragonfly the Size of a Dog* was shortlisted for the Russian Booker Prize. In 1999, *Alone in Mirror* was awarded the *Novy Mir Prize* and the *Bazhov Prize*. Her novel *Immortal* (2001) was shortlisted for the *Bestseller Prize* and the *Belkin Prize* as well as receiving the *Critics Academy Prize* in 2002. In 2005, Slavnikova published her anti-utopia *2017* which won her the *Russian Booker Prize*, was short-listed for the *Big Book Prize* and was translated into English, French, Italian, Swedish, Chinese, Japanese, German, etc. In 2008, she published a collection of short stories, *Love on the Train*, shortlisted for the *Big Book Prize*. Slavnikova's latest novel, *Light-Headed*, has been shortlisted for the *Big Book Prize* and was published in English translation by Dedalus.

Ludmila Ulitskaya (born in 1943) is one of Russia's most popular and renowned literary figures. A former geneticist she is now the author of fourteen works of fiction, three children's books, and six plays that have been staged by a number of theatres in Russia and abroad. Her books won her almost thirty literary prizes in different countries, including the *Russian Booker Prize*, the *Big Book Prize*, the *Medicis Prize*, *Prix Simone de Beauvoir pour la liberté des femmes*. She was also shortlisted for the *Man Booker International Prize*. Her best known novels are: *Kukotsky Case, Sincerely Yours, Shurik, Daniel Stein, Interpreter, Imago/The Big Green Tent, Yakov's Ladder* and *Medea and Her Children*.

The Authors

Irina Muravyova (born in 1952) in Moscow, has lived in Boston since 1985. She is a prolific novelist with some of her novels and stories translated into English, French, Arabic, Serbian, Slovak, and Hungarian. She enjoys a reputation as one of the foremost Russian women writers, her books have been shortlisted for the *Russian Booker Prize* and the *Bunin Prize*, and her story "On the Edge", was included in *Women on the Case*, a collection of the best women's writing from around the world. She continues the tradition of the classical Russian novel, offering, as Oliver Ready writes, "A richly suggestive blend of prose and poetry, tirelessly jumping back and forth in time and place and begging multifold connections with the present that remain poignantly unclarified."

Svetlana Alexievich (born in 1948) to a family of school teachers was the 2015 Nobel laureate for literature. She studied journalism at Minsk University and later worked on various newspapers in Belorussia. For many years she collected materials for her first book, *War's Unwomanly Face* based on interviews with hundreds of women who participated in the Second World War. It was soon a worldwide success and became the first in Alexievich's cycle: *Voices of Utopia*, where life in the Soviet Union is depicted from the perspective of the individual. Published so far are *Voices from Chernobyl: Chronicle of the Future*; *Zinky Boys. Soviet Voices from a Forgotten War*; *Second-hand Time: The Demise of the Red (Wo)man*; and *Last Witnesses. Landscape of Loneliness* comes from her yet unfinished book on love Soviet style.

The Authors

Margarita Khemlin (1960-2015) was born in Chernigov, Ukraine, studied at the Literary Institute in Moscow, worked in the press and on television, and published her first work of fiction in 2005. She was a finalist for the *Big Book Prize* in 2008, won the *Russian Booker Prize* in 2010, and NOS in 2014. Her novel *Investigator* was shortlisted for the *Russian Booker Prize* in 2013 and translated into German and English. The Jewish world was her main theme which she treated in a highly original and evocative way. Her works are noted for their colourful language of the Jewish *shtetl*.

The Translators

Andrew Bromfield is the most popular and prolific translator of Russian fiction today. His list of published translations includes Leo Tolstoy, Victor Pelevin, Vladimir Voinovich, Boris Akunin and Svetlana Alexievich.

Robert & Elizabeth Chandler are best known for their translations of Andrey Platonov and Vasily Grossman. They have also translated Alexander Pushkin, Nikolay Leskov, Nadezhda Teffi and Hamid Ismailov. Robert Chandler is the editor and main translator of *Russian Short Stories from Pushkin to Buida* and *Russian Magic Tales from Pushkin to Platonov*. Together with Boris Dralyuk and Irina Mashinski he co-edited *The Penguin Book of Russian Poetry*. He runs regular translation workshops at Pushkin House in London.

Ilona Chavasse has been working in publishing for many years as a foreign rights executive while also translating from the Russian. Her literary translations include books by Yuri Rytkheu, Sergei Gandlevsky, and Dmitry Bortnikov.

John Dewey's published verse translations include a selection for the 15-volume *Complete Works of Pushkin,* and Pushkin's narrative poem *The Bronze Horseman* which was shortlisted for the John Dryden Translation Prize; also novels by Boris Yampolsky and Irina Muravyova. He is the author of *Mirror of the Soul. A Life of the Poet Fyodor Tyutchev.*

Boris Dralyuk is an award-winning translator and the Executive Editor of the *Los Angeles Review of Books*. He holds a PhD in Slavic Languages and Literatures from UCLA, where he taught Russian literature for a number of years. He is a co-editor of *The Penguin Book of Russian Poetry*, and has translated Isaac Babel's *Red Cavalry* and *Odessa Stories*, both of which are published by Pushkin Press.

Jamey Gambrell won a number of prizes for her work, but she is also a prolific journalist writing on Russian art and culture. Her many published translations include works by Joseph Brodsky, Tatyana Tolstaya, Daniil Kharms, Vladimir Sorokin, and Tsvetaeva's diaries and essays. In 2016 she won the *Thornton Prize for Translation* which recognises "a significant contribution to the art of literary translation".

Marian Schwartz is an award-winning translator of Russian classic and contemporary fiction, history, biography, criticism, and fine art, with over seventy published books to her name. She has done new translations for several Russian classics, including Leo Tolstoy's *Anna Karenina*. Contemporary authors she has translated include Nina Berberova, Leonid Yuzefovich, Olga Slavnikova, and Mikhail Shishkin.

Arch Tait studied Russian at Latymer Upper School, London; Trinity Hall, Cambridge, and Moscow State University. He has a PhD in Russian literature from Cambridge. From 1993 he was a co-editor of the *Glas New Russian Writing Translation Series*. To date he has translated thirty-five books by leading Russian authors of fiction and non-fiction, among them Ludmila Ulitskaya, Anna Politkovskaya, Mikhail Gorbachev and Vladimir Makanin.

Joanne Turnbull is best known for her prize-winning translations of Sigizmund Krzhizhanovsky, a rediscovered genius from the 1920s. As a co-editor of *Glas* she translated many contemporary authors such as Asar Eppel, Andrei Sinyavsky, Lev Rubinstein, Andrei Sergeev, and many others. She is the winner of the *AATSEEL Award for Best Literary Translation into English* and the *PEN Translation Prize*.

Contents

A century of women's writing in Russia

"I gave a voice to our womanhood…" Anna Akhmatova

Under the impact of turbulent Russian history the evolution
of women's writing in Russia differed from that in Western
countries. Although the earliest records of writing by women
date back to the eleventh century, none of those early literary
efforts have stood the test of time and today they are of interest
only to scholars. Women's presence in 19th-century Russian
literature was more conspicuous, but it was largely in the form
of memorable literary heroines: either idealised or demonised,
either angels or femmes fatales.

Only at the turn of the 20th century did women really make a
significant appearance on the literary scene. The fruitful period
of Russian modernism in the first decade of the 20th century
produced Anna Akhmatova, Marina Tsvetaeva, Nadezhda
Teffi, Zinaida Gippius, and some lesser known names, mostly
poets. However, this brief flowering of the Russian "Silver
Age" fell prey to the ravages of the revolutionary years and the
consequent tightening of state censorship. How was it possible
that women's writing, having made such a promising start,
soon ran into the sand and women had to keep a low profile
until the end of Soviet rule in the 1990s? Why was women's
writing regarded as subversive by the Soviets? It seems that in
conditions of totalitarian ideology anything unorthodox, even
not openly dissident, was an irritation to the authorities. When
women addressed topics from real life, such as their day-to-

day lives, family and child-rearing, abuse, alcoholism, suicide, depression, mental illness, and abortion, they were accused of being petty and sensationalist. Women were discouraged from writing about their personal problems and their low social status as these were an embarrassment to the state, while their inner world was of little interest to the male-dominated society.

With the ideological shackles gone after the collapse of the Soviet Union women's writing in Russia soon thrived. Initially its tone was plaintive and confessional as women tried to get their Soviet-era ordeals and grievances off their chests. A decade later their tone had a more vigorous and confident ring, reflecting increased self-awareness and the rise of feminist attitudes. Subsequently, stories by women were still focused on women's rights, often being straightforwardly autobiographical. Another decade later you could no longer tell male and female writing apart while women's rights were taken for granted. Currently, in the 21st century, young women authors increasingly tend to write under men's names to emphasise the fact that gender is irrelevant in real art.

Women's writing today immerses you in a world of basic human values such as love, children and family, but also looks at such problems as ageing, the generation gap, and violence against women. These stories reflect the current stage in the evolution of Russian women's fiction from its marginal position under the Soviets, through several stages of vigorous progress in the 1990s, to its current confident craftsmanship, wide thematic range, and high stylistic standards. Today Russian women have increasingly become a force in the world of letters. Under the Soviets the proclaimed gender equality was purely fictional: literary journals and anthologies would grudgingly include just one or two token women. Where in the past women were celebrated chiefly as literary widows

Introduction

or devoted wives, occasionally as poets or critics, and only very rarely as novelists, today they are beginning to dominate publishing lists in fiction and non-fiction alike.

During the early years of *perestroika*, a whole constellation of excellent women authors came on the scene, mostly authors banned from publication under the Soviets. Thus the interrupted tradition of women's writing in Russia was resurrected and allowed to develop normally. In conditions of a market economy women, as more practical creatures, have become particularly active in mass-market publishing whereas in Soviet times women's names, and gender problems as such, were practically absent in Russian literature. Today at least half of the authors in publishers' catalogues are women while in the past they would account for five to ten per cent. The current profusion of successful female authors, both in commercial and literary fiction, is a new feature of Russian book publishing.

In the present anthology the first half of the 20th century is represented by authors of unquestionable genius: Anna Akhmatova and Marina Tsvetayeva, who are internationally known as poets and whose prose is no less important and engaging; also by Nadezhda Teffi and Lydia Ginzburg, both fairly recently discovered by readers abroad. If not for the limits on the size of this book and the number of names I would also have included Zinaida Gippius, Nina Berberova, and Lydia Zinovyeva-Annibal. The highlights of the mid-century include Evgenia Ginzburg, Olga Berggoltz and Bela Akhmadulina, who might have also been in this collection.

The later decades are represented here by such recognised names as Ludmila Petrushevskaya, Svetlana Alexievich, Ludmila Ulitskaya, Galina Scherbakova, Margarita Khemlin, Irina Muravyova, and Olga Slavnikova. But mention should also be made of Svetlana Vasilenko, Nina Gabrielyan, Marina Palei, Nina Sadur, Maria Galina, Dina Rubina, Victoria Tokareva, and Tatiana Tolstaya – they are not included in this collection only for reasons of space or copyright.

The turn of the 21st century gave us some young talents such as Alisa Ganieva, Liza Alexandrova-Zorina, Maria Rybakova, Anna Starobinets, Marina Stepnova, to name just a few, who also deserve attention and translations into other languages.

Women's writing exists because there is a women's world which differs from the world of men whether people are aware of it or not. Women authors don't repudiate their gender or apologise for its weaknesses – that would be as futile as repudiating one's historical roots. But they view the world from a slightly different perspective and that should be of interest to men and women alike.

Female readers in the West will be surprised to find many more common issues than they expect – the setting is different but the issues and problems are essentially the same.

Natasha Perova

Kishmish
Nadezhda Teffi

Lent. Moscow.

In the distance, the muffled sound – between a hum and a boom – of a church bell. The even strokes of the clapper merge into a single, oppressive moan.

An open door, into murky pre-dawn gloom, allows one to glimpse a dim figure, rustling quietly and cautiously about the room. For a moment this shifting figure takes form – an uncertain patch of grey – and then it dissolves, merging into the gloom round about. The rustling quietens. The creak of a floorboard – and of a second floorboard, further away. Then silence. Nanny has left – on her way to church, to the early morning service.

She is observing Lent.

Now things get frightening.

The little girl curls up into a small ball in her bed, barely breathing. She listens and watches, listens and watches.

The distant hum is becoming sinister. The little girl is all alone and defenceless. If she calls, no one will come. But what can happen? Night must be ending now. Probably the cocks have crowed in the dawn and the ghosts are all back where they belong.

And they belong in cemeteries, in bogs, beneath solitary graves with simple crosses, at the crossings of forgotten roads on the outskirts of forests. Not one of them will dare touch a human being now; the liturgy is already being celebrated and

23

prayers are being said on behalf of all Orthodox Christians. What is there to be frightened of?

But an eight-year-old soul does not believe the arguments of reason. It shrinks into itself, trembles and quietly whimpers away. An eight-year-old soul does not believe that this is the sound of a bell. Later, in daytime, it will believe this, but now, alone, defenceless and in anguish, it does not know that this is a bell calling people to church. Who knows what this sound might be? It is something sinister. If anguish and fear could be translated into sound, this is the sound they would make. If anguish and fear could be translated into colour, then it would be this uncertain, murky grey.

And the impression made by this pre-dawn anguish will remain with this little creature for many years, for her entire life. This creature will continue to be woken at dawn by a fear and anguish beyond understanding. Doctors will prescribe sedatives; they will advise her to take evening walks, or to give up smoking, or to sleep in an unheated room, or with the window open, or with a hot water bottle on her liver. They will counsel many, many things – but nothing will erase from her soul the imprint of that pre-dawn despair.

*

The little girl's nickname was "Kishmish" – a word for a kind of very small raisin from the Caucasus. This was, no doubt, because she was so very small, with a small nose and small hands. Small fry, of small importance. Towards the age of thirteen she would suddenly shoot up. Her legs would grow long and everyone would forget that she had, once, been Kishmish.

But while she was still just a little kishmish, this offensive nickname caused her a great deal of pain. She was proud and she longed to distinguish herself in some way; she wanted, above all, to do something grand and unusual. To become, say, a famous strongman, someone who could bend horseshoes with their bare hands or stop a runaway troika in its tracks. She liked the idea of becoming a brigand or – still better, perhaps – an executioner. An executioner is more powerful than a brigand since, in the end, it is always he who has the last word. And could anyone have imagined, as they looked at this skinny little girl with shorn, flaxen hair, quietly threading beads into a ring – could anyone have imagined what terrible dreams of power were seething inside her head? There was, by the way, yet another dream – of becoming a terrible monster. Not just any old monster, but the kind of monster that really frightens people. Kishmish would go and stand by the mirror, cross her eyes, stretch the corners of her mouth apart and thrust her tongue out to one side. At the same time, she would say in a low voice, acting the part of an unknown gentleman standing behind her, unable to see her face and addressing the back of her head: "Do me the honour, Madame, of this quadrille."

She would then put on her special face, spin round on her heels and reply, "Very well – but first you must kiss my twisted cheek."

At this point the gentleman would run away in horror. "Hah!" she would call after him. "Scared, are you?"

Kishmish had begun her studies. To start with – just Scripture and Handwriting.

Each of one's tasks, she learned, should be prefaced with a prayer.

This was an idea she liked. But since she was still, amongst other things, considering the career of brigand, it also caused her alarm.

"What about brigands?" she asked. "Do they need to say a prayer before they go out briganding?"

She did not receive a clear answer – only the words, "Don't be silly." And Kishmish did not understand. Did this mean that brigands don't need to pray – or that it is essential for them to pray, and that this is so very obvious that it was silly even to be asking about it?

When Kishmish grew a little bigger and went for the first time to confession, she underwent a spiritual crisis. Gone now were the terrible dreams of power.

"Lord, Hear our Prayer" was, that Lent, being sung very beautifully.

Three young boys would step forward, stand beside the altar and sing in angelic voices. Listening to them, her soul grew humble and filled with tender emotion. These blessed sounds made a soul wish to be light, white, ethereal and transparent, to fly away in sounds and incense, right up to the cupola, to where the white dove of the Holy Spirit had spread its wings.

This was no place for a brigand. Nor was it the right place for an executioner, or even for a strongman. As for the monster, it would go and stand behind a door and cover its terrible face. A church was certainly not the right place to be frightening people. Oh, if only she could get to be a saint. How marvellous that would be! So beautiful, so fine and tender. To be a saint was above everything and everyone. Something more important than any teacher, headmistress or even provincial governor.

But how would she get to be a saint? She would have to do miracles – and Kishmish had not the slightest idea how to go about this. Still, miracles were not where you started. First, you had to lead a saintly life. You had to make yourself meek and kind, to give everything to the poor, to devote yourself to fasting and abstinence.

So, how would she give everything away to the poor? She had a new spring coat. That was what she should give first.

But how furious Mama would be. There would be an unholy row, the kind of row that didn't bear thinking about. And Mama would be upset, and saints were not supposed to hurt other people and make them upset. What if she gave her coat to a poor person but told Mama it had simply been stolen? But saints were not supposed to tell lies. What a predicament. Life was a lot easier for a brigand. A brigand could lie all he wanted – and just laugh his sly laugh. How, then, did these saints ever get to be saints? Simply, it seemed, because they were old – none of them under sixteen, and many of them real oldies. No question of any of them having to obey Mama. They could give away all their worldly goods just like that. No, this clearly wasn't the place to start – it was something to keep till the end. She should start with meekness and obedience. And abstinence. She should eat only black bread and salt, and drink only water straight from the tap. But here too lay trouble. Cook would tell on her. She would tell Mama that Kishmish had been drinking water that had not been boiled. There was typhus in the city and Mama did not allow her to drink water from the tap. But then, once Mama understood that Kishmish was a saint, perhaps she would stop putting obstacles in her way.

And then, how marvellous to be a saint. There were so few of them these days. Everyone she knew would be astonished.

"Why's there a halo over Kishmish?"

"What, didn't you know? She's been a saint for a long time now."

"Heavens! I don't believe it!"

"There she is. You can see for yourself."

And there Kishmish sat – smiling meekly as she ate her

black bread and salt.

Her mother's visitors would feel envious. Not one of them had saintly children.

"Maybe she's just pretending."

Fools! Couldn't they see her halo?

She wondered how soon the halo would begin. Probably in a few months. It would be there by autumn. God, how marvellous all this was. Next year she'd go along to confession. The priest would say in a severe voice, "What are your sins? You must repent."

And she would reply, "I don't have any. I'm a saint."

"No, no!" he would exclaim. "Surely not!"

"Ask Mama. Ask her friends. Everyone knows."

The priest would question her. Maybe there was, after all, some tiny little sin she'd committed?

"None at all!" Kishmish would reply. "Search all you like!"

She also wondered if she would still have to do her homework. If so, she was in trouble. Because saints can't be lazy. And they can't be disobedient. If she were told to study, then that's what she'd have to do. If only she could learn miracles straightaway! One miracle – and her teacher would take fright, fall to her knees and never mention homework again.

Next she imagined her face. She went up to the mirror, sucked in her cheeks, flared her nostrils and rolled her eyes to the heavens. Kishmish liked this face very much. A true saint's face. A little nauseating, but entirely saintly. No one else had a face anything like it. And so – off to the kitchen for some black bread!

As always before breakfast, Cook was cross and pre-occupied. Kishmish's visit was an unwelcome surprise: "And what's a young lady like you doing here in the kitchen?

There'll be words from your Mama!"

There was an enticing smell of fish, onions and mushrooms. Kishmish's nostrils twitched involuntarily. She wanted to retort, "That's none of your business!" but she remembered that she was a saint and said in a quiet voice, "Varvara, please cut me a slice of black bread."

She thought for a moment, then added, "A large slice."

Cook cut her some bread.

"And please sprinkle a little salt on it," she continued, looking up as if to the heavens.

She would have to eat the bread then and there. If she took it anywhere else, there would be misunderstandings. With unpleasant consequences.

The bread proved particularly tasty and Kishmish regretted having only asked for one slice. Then she went to the tap and drank some water from a jug. Just then the maid came in.

"I'll be telling your Mama," she exclaimed in horror, "that you've been drinking tap water!"

"She's just been eating a great chunk of bread," said Cook. "Bread and salt. So what do you expect? She's a growing girl."

The family was called in to breakfast. She couldn't not go. So she decided to go but not eat anything and be very meek.

For breakfast there was fish soup and pies. She sat there, looking blankly at the little pie on her plate.

"Why aren't you eating?"

In answer she smiled meekly and once again put on her saintly face – the face she had been practising before the mirror.

"Heavens, what's got into her?" exclaimed her astonished aunt. "Why's she pulling such a dreadful face?"

"And she's just eaten a great big chunk of black bread," said the telltale maid. "Just before breakfast – and she washed

29

it down with water straight from the tap."

"Whoever said you could go and eat bread in the kitchen?" shouted her mother. "And why were you drinking tap water?"

Kishmish rolled her eyes and flared her nostrils, finally perfecting her saintly face.

"What's got into her?"

"She's making fun of me!" squealed the aunt – and let out a sob.

"Out you go, you nasty little girl!" her mother said furiously. "Off to the nursery with you – and you can stay there for the rest of the day!"

"And the sooner she's packed off to boarding school, the better," said the aunt, still sobbing. "My nerves, my poor nerves. Literally, my every last nerve…"

*

Poor Kishmish.
And so she remained a sinner.

Translated by Robert and Elizabeth Chandler

Solovki

Nadezhda Teffi

for Ivan Bunin

The seagulls from the shore accompanied the steamer for a long time. After a while they grew tired and began coming down more often onto the water, barely touching it with one point of their breast, spinning – as if on the head of a screw – and then wearily gliding off again, leading first with one wing and then with the other, as if taking long strides.

From the stern, pilgrims threw them bread. Russians from inland, who had never seen the sea, were astonished by the gulls.

"What strong birds!"

"What great big birds!"

"But people say you can't eat them."

When the boat reached open sea and the shore it had left behind was no more than a low, narrow strip of pale blue, the gulls dispersed. Three last greedy birds took a few more strides, begged again for bread, veered off somewhere to the left, cried out to one another and disappeared.

The sea was now empty and free; in the sky shone diffuse areas of crimson. One that was not yet extinguished, still red hot from the departed sun – and one now catching fire from the rising sun. The steamer, lit by their silvery-pink light that cast no shadow, was cutting aslant through the waves; from the deck it appeared to be sailing sideways, skimming weightlessly over the water. And high in the air, fastened to the mast, swaying gently against the pink clouds, a golden cross marked out the boat's path.

"The Archangel Michael", a holy boat, was carrying pilgrims from Arkhangelsk to the Solovetsky Monastery.[1]

There were a lot of passengers. They sat about on benches, on steps and on the floor, conversing quietly and respectfully, and looking with awe at the golden cross in the sky, at the boat's steward – a monk in a faded, now greenish cassock – and at the gulls. They sighed, yawned and made the sign of the cross over their open mouths.

Up on the bridge a monk in a sheepskin coat and a black skullcap kept coughing hoarsely, calling out to the helmsman – his commands as abrupt as the cries of the gulls – and then bursting out coughing again.

Waves were beating rhythmically against the hull; the crimson glow had faded; the birds had flown away. The drama of departure was now over and the passengers began to settle down for the night.

Peasant women hitched up the calico skirts they had starched for the holiday and this unusual sea journey, and then lay down on the floor, tucking in their legs and their heavy, awkward feet. The menfolk were talking quietly in separate groups.

Red-haired, thickset Semyon Rubaev came down the ladder and joined the men. His wife remained alone, sitting on one of the steps. She didn't move. She didn't even turn

---

1 From the second half of the nineteenth century there was a huge increase in the number of pilgrims paying short visits to Solovki. The Archangel Michael, acquired in 1887, was one of three steam ships operated by the monastery. The journey from Arkhangelsk took 17 hours.

her head. She just gave him a sideways look, full of mistrust and malice.

Semyon was listening to the men. A tall curly-haired old man from White Lake was telling people about the smelt they now caught there: "We've a damage now. A damage. Engineers constructed it. They were needing earth for this damage. They took earth of mine."

"What damage? Ye're not making sense."

"For the damage… The da… For the dam." After correcting himself, the old man fell silent for a moment, then added, "I'm in my nineties, you know. Yes, that's how it is now."

Semyon didn't care in the least about the old man's age, nor about the smelt in the lake. He wanted to talk about his own concerns, but it was difficult to find the right moment, to find a way to slip these into the conversation. He looked around at his wife. She was sitting sideways to him, turning her broad face and the long, pale line of her mouth away from him.

And then nothing could hold him back – and off he went: "Well, we come from around Novgorod. From the Borovichy district. Penance, a church penance – that's why I'm taking her."

He stopped. But since no one asked him anything, he eventually began again: "Penance, confession and penance.[2] Varvara, yes, my wife. A serious matter, I had to take it to the district officer."

Varvara got up from the step. Baring her many white teeth like a vicious cat, she walked a little further away, then stood beside the rail, resting both elbows on it.

There was nowhere further to go. The pilgrims sitting on the deck were densely packed. She could hardly just step on

---

2 A penance would include going to all services, a prescribed number of bodily prostrations, and the repetition of additional prayers.

their heads.

Now at least she could no longer hear everything Semyon said. The odd word, however, still reached her.

"The whole village was complaining... There wasn't one woman that Vanya Tsyganov... The officer... My wife Varvara..."

Varvara hunched her shoulders and went on baring her teeth. But Semyon was still talking, talking, talking:

"Varvara, yes, Varvara... 'We just kissed,' she said... A court sentence wasn't possible. But a penance, a church penance..."

For ten months Semyon had been telling this story, over and over. And now, like clockwork, all through this journey. On the iron road, at every station their train had stopped at, in the pilgrims' hostel at Arkhangelsk, wherever there were ears to be filled, he had told this story. Since the day it had all begun, since Yerokhina their neighbour had come running back from the fields, pulled off her kerchief and wailed out that Tsyganov had wronged her – and then old Mitrofanikha had rushed out and yelled that her granddaughter Feklushka was being pestered by Tsyganov too, that Tsyganov wasn't giving the girl a moment's peace. Other women of all ages had appeared, every one of them white with fury, kerchiefs slipping off their heads, all cursing Tsyganov and threatening to make their complaints and drive him out of the village. And then Varka Lukina had caught sight of Varvara at her window and shouted out to everyone that she'd seen Varvara together with Tsyganov, out in the rye:

"Them two, walking side by side! Arms around each other!"

And that was it. From then on work had been forgotten. Semyon had done nothing but tell this story, over and over.

He had gone along as a witness for Yerokhina. He had told

the officer about Varvara. He had demanded she be brought
to trial and punished. He had dragged Varvara around with
him and wherever they went – on the road, in country inns, in
lodgings in towns – he had gone on and on telling this story.
At first he had been quite gentle, calling her "Varenka", just as
he always had done: "So, Varenka, tell me how all this came
to happen. All of the circumstances."

"How wot happened? Nowt happened."

Then he went purple all over, his red beard seeming to fill
with blood. Choking with fury, he said, "Bitch! Snake! How
dare you? How dare you speak so to your wedded husband!"

And all day long Varvara had busied herself around the
house, not exactly working, more just fussing about in one
corner after another – anything to get out of earshot, anything
not to hear Semyon.

Tsyganov was nowhere to be seen. He had gone off to
the city to work as a cab driver. The women began to calm
down. Only down by the river in the evening, when they were
beating the damp linen with their bats, would the young girls,
in their thin mosquito-like voices, sing a jokey song from St
Petersburg:

> *Vanka, Vanka, wot you done wi' yer conscience?*
> *Where be yer heart of hearts?*
> *– Wasted them both in the taverns*
> *for love of billiards and cards.*

As for Semyon, there was no end to his questions, his
interrogations, his story telling. And Varvara fell more and
more silent. When the officer questioned her about Yerokhina,
her only reply, reiterated with true Novgorod obstinacy, was
"Wot's it to do wiv me?"

And so life went on. In the daytime she hardly spoke. At night she kept thinking things over, reliving that day again and again. All over the village the women had been screaming. The devil, it seemed, had got into them; there was no escaping the women's white, maddened rage. And what a lot of them there had been. Even pockmarked Mavrushka had shouted out, as if bragging, "Think he didn't touch me? No, he touched me all right. Only I hold my tongue. But if all of you speak, then I'm speaking too!"

Her pockmarks, evidently, had not counted against her. The lads had jeered: "Oh Mavrushka, Mavrushka! And she's got the body of a bear!"

Yerokhina, for her part, had lamented, "Eight years, I believe, I've kept a hold of my honour – and then... Along comes this fiend – and snatches it from me!"

All shaking in jealous rage. All shouting, as if bragging: "Me too. Yes, me too!"

A sly fellow with the nickname "Tomcat" had smirked mischievously and said, "My good ladies, you seem most dreadfully angry. Why might that be? Eh?"

He seemed to have hit on something.

*

They reached Solovki as the bells were ringing for matins.

On the shore to meet them were monks and seagulls.

The monks were all thin, with severe faces. The gulls were large and stout, almost the size of geese. They waddled about proprietorially, exchanging preoccupied remarks.

Unloading and disembarkation took a long time. Some of the pilgrims were still packing their knapsacks when one old woman, the wife of the curly-haired fisherman, returned from the Holy Lake, having already bathed in its icy waters. She was wearing a clean linen shirt and smiling beatifically, her lips purple with cold.

The hosteller, a tall monk with a neatly combed beard, was organising the new arrivals, arranging who should sleep where. Since there were crowds of people and little space, the Rubaevs were put in what had once been the best room; with two windows and whitewashed walls, it was now divided into three by partitions. One part had been given to a teacher and his wife, and the biggest part, with three beds and a sofa, had been given to a party of four.

The head of this party was an Oriental-looking abbot. Handsome and well turned out, he had chosen, for convenience while travelling, to abandon his monastic dress for that of a priest: "People, I understand, have little love for monks, and they criticise them for everything: Why's he smoking? Why's he eating fish? Why's he got sugar in his tea? But how can a man observe the rule when he's on the road? Dress as a priest – and you don't tempt people to judge."

Together with the Father were a merchant, a lanky young gymnasium student – and a hypocritical old bigot of a public official. All three were family.

The remaining little cubicle, with no window, was allocated to the Rubaevs.

*

All that day the pilgrims were either attending church services, looking around the monastery, wandering about the forest or along the shore, walking down the long, musty corridor of the hostel – with its damp and grimy, finger-marked doors, weighted to slam shut – or visiting the little monastery shop and asking the price of icons, small cypress-wood crosses and belts for the deceased, with a prayer woven into them.[3]

Standing out amid this crowd was a young man who had come for healing. He was enormously tall, and finely dressed, with a new peaked cap and patent leather boots. He suffered from convulsions that repeatedly wrenched open his mouth; it was as if a vast, insuperable yawn were dragging at his jaw, pulling at his tongue, making him slobber all down his chin and neck. The fit would come to an end and his mouth would snap loudly shut, his teeth clicking together like those of a dog that has caught a fly.

The young man was accompanied by a rather short little fellow with a silver chain that hung across his round belly. He took pride in the young man's illness and behaved like the impresario of an exotic theatre troupe, always in a whirl, always bustling about and proffering explanations: "Keeps on yawning, he does. Several years now, yes indeed. He's the son of rich people. Make way, make way now, if you please!"

The monastery courtyard was full of seagulls. They were placid and round, like household geese. They sat between gravestones and on the track leading to the church. They had no fear of people and did not get out of the way for anyone – it was for you to walk round them. And on the back of almost every one of these gulls was a fledgling – like a fluffy, spotted egg standing on two thin little twigs.

The gulls called out to one another in quick, curt barks. They would begin loudly, then gradually quieten, despondent and hopeless. They sat crowded together about the monastery

3 During an Orthodox burial the deceased wears a belt, since he will need it when he is resurrected. Belts are symbolically important in Russian culture, suggesting order and dignity. And it was common, when on pilgrimage to a holy site, to buy items of clothing for one's burial.

and did not fly anywhere. It was too cold. The small rectangular Holy Lake was swollen with grey-blue water. One of the seagulls went down to the lake and looked for a long time, with one suspicious eye, at its violet ripples. Some way off, a fledgling was cheeping importantly, as if giving advice. The seagull stretched out one foot, touched the water, quickly withdrew the foot and twitched its head a little.

"Too cold, old girl?" asked a young monk.

Against the grey sky swayed one-sided trees; all their branches were on the side facing south, like arms outstretched towards the sun, towards a distant dream. The northern side, gnawed by cold breaths from the throat of the Arctic Ocean, stayed naked and sickly all summer, as in winter.

Down by the harbour some young lads, with faded skullcaps over thick strands of fair, curly hair, were throwing pebbles in the water and scuffling with one another. They were like puny young bear cubs, fighting clumsily and without anger. Pomors, from villages along the mainland coast, they had been brought to the monastery to labour for a year or two in fulfilment of vows made by their mothers: "Yes, the boy'll serve the Lord — and he'll earn his keep."[4]

And there were solitary monks wandering along the shore. Now and again they would stop and look at the water, as if waiting for something.

One after another the grey-blue waves uncoiled, splashing against the brown rocks, filling hearts with a sadness like lead.

Along with the other pilgrims, the Rubaevs went to the

---

4 Probably these women had prayed to the patron saints of the monastery and vowed to send their sons to Solovki (which did not accept women except as pilgrims on short visits) if their prayer was granted. The boys usually served as labourers but would also learn about spiritual matters.

church and then on into the forest. Monks in faded cassocks emerged from the chapel cells. They seemed to find it hard to understand even the simplest questions: "Which church is this?" – or "Which way?"

The monks would smile affably, then withdraw to gaze at the water.[5]

Outside the chapel of Saint Philaret, the pilgrims took it in turn to lift the long stone that had served Philaret as a pillow. They laid it on their heads and walked three times clockwise around the chapel – a cure for headaches.[6]

In the furthest of the little chapels, seven miles or so from the monastery, the pilgrims were met by the very oldest elders of all. They were barely able to put one foot in front of the other, barely still breathing.

"But how, good fathers, do you make your way to the main church?"

"We go, good people, but once a year. On Easter Sunday, yes, to Holy Matins. That's when we all meet together – from the cliffs, from the woods, from the open fields, from the bogs. Every one of us goes – and they count us up. As for food, we get by. They bring us our bread."

The hostel was no place to sit in for long. The Rubaevs' cubicle was dark and damp. Semyon would come in, sit down on the bed and, in a low voice, drone on yet again:

"Mind you tell everything. As God is your witness. Every circumstance. You must tell everything, or there'll be trouble."

---

5 Some recluse monks on Solovki, to this day, keep to a rule of complete silence; it appears that some of the pilgrims did not understand this. These elders were ascetics, living alone and devoting their lives to prayer, following the example of the ancient desert fathers.

6 Their walk echoes the Procession of the Cross around the outside of a church on Easter Eve and a number of other feast days.

Varvara did not reply.

Behind the partition the merchant and the gymnasium student were asking for samovars and drinking tea. The official was sighing piously.

Behind the other partition the teacher's wife was criticizing the ways of the monastery: "They just stand there, gazing at the water. Will that save their souls? And at table they defile themselves with mustard.[7] Will that save their souls?"

And then they would all wander along the shore again, or along the monastery corridors.

They looked at the paintings of the *Last Judgement* and the *Parables of Our Lord*. A huge beam planted in the eye of the sinner who so clearly beheld the mote in his brother's eye. And the temptation of beauty, illustrated by a devil – with a rather appealing canine muzzle, shaggy webbed paws, a curly tail and a modest brown apron tied around his belly[8] – and his charming legend: as the brothers were praying in church, this devil had moved unseen between them, handing out the pink flowers known as house lime. Whoever received a flower was unable to go on praying; charmed by the spring sun and grasses, he stole out to freedom[9] – until in the end the devil was caught by the Holy Elder. And ordeals and hardships of every kind, and sins and torments, sins and torments...

Towards evening they were called to the refectory. The women sat in a separate room.

To one side of Varvara was a woman all covered in scabs. Opposite her was an old woman with a nose like a duck's.

---

7 Mustard has long been considered an aphrodisiac.

8 Demons in Russian iconography were commonly depicted as shaggy, with webbed feet and twisting tails.

9 Being on the West wall, the *Last Judgement* was the last set of images a worshipper would see as he left the church; this makes the monks' surrender to temptation all the more ironical.

Before taking a scoop from the communal bowl, she would give her spoon a thorough licking with her long, flaccid, rag-like tongue. They drank insipid monastery kvas[10] with a faint taste of mint and ate salt-cod soup while a monk read aloud to them in a dismal drone: "Lechery, lechery, the devil..."

There was no night. The partitions did not reach the ceiling and the Rubaevs' windowless stall was lit by a wan light that cast no shadow.

*

The hypocrite official got up at cockcrow and began bowing and crossing himself before the icon, a living reproach to everyone else in the room. With loud sighs something between a whistle and a whisper he kept repeating, "Woe is me, O Lord, O Lord – for my loins are filled with mockings."[11]

The abbot awoke, shamefacedly put on his clothes and left the room. The merchant held out for a long time but was unable to get back to sleep. As if to the student, he said in a loud, clear voice, "You get some more sleep! Yes. It's early for church. Not even the monks have got up yet." He then repeated these words – intended, of course, for the hypocrite official, who was by then making more noise than ever.

The official finished praying, looked around him censoriously, sighed and turned away – as if to say that there were sights best not seen.

Varvara had had a bad night. There was no peace anywhere

10 A lightly fermented drink made from rye bread.

11 The official is quoting from Psalm 37, verse 45 (according to the Orthodox numbering of the Psalms), which is in the morning prayers for lay readers. The somewhat different translation of this verse in the King James Bible (Psalm 38, verse 7) is "For my loins are filled with a loathsome disease: and there is no soundness in my flesh."

and the seagulls were calling to one another, letting out dismal barks. Towards morning she dozed off. She saw a field of rye and a cart. There on the cart was Vanya Tsyganov, laughing:

"Here again, are you? Well, you won't get away this time."

He got down from the cart, took her by the shoulders and looked into her eyes.

"Why the shame? As if you're a maiden!"

Not a good dream, and it left her with a feeling of dread.

Once again everyone went off to the church or out into the forest. After the service, Semyon sat down beside the teacher, on a bench outside the hostel, and started up in his usual way. Varvara went back to the room. The student was alone there, sitting at the table and eating curd cheese from a large clay bowl with sly embarrassment.

"Want some?" he said to Varvara. "I got it from the dairy. I'm famished. All we get in the refectory is cabbage soup seasoned with holy relics." And he let out a little giggle.

"Thank you. But not for me."

The young lad stopped eating and looked at Varvara intently. Blushing, with an embarrassed smile, he said, "You're quite a woman, you know. As for your husband..." And he let out another snigger. "And your eyes are truly gorgeous. But sit yourself down, for the love of God."

Varvara looked straight into the young man's abashed but laughing eyes and suddenly had a sense of both warmth and horror, as if, rather than this lanky student, Vanya Tsyganov were now looking at her and there were no getting away from him.

"O Lord, O Lord! What is all this?"

She wanted to tear her hair and weep and wail.

Slowly, still looking him straight in the eye, Varvara backed towards her door.

"Is th-that where you s-sleep?" stammered the still

blushing student.

Varvara heard footsteps out in the corridor. She locked her door, sat down on the bed and listened to her heart trembling. The merchant and the official came back, caught sight of the curd cheese and were incensed with rage.

"Huh! Like that, is it? Can't even last three days![12] Well then, what's stopping you? Eat! You brought that cheese – so you eat it!"

"I've had all I want."

"No. Eat it now!"

Both men felt the same craving. And the stronger their craving, the fiercer their rage.

"Eat, I say! You brought it – so you eat it!" hissed the official.

"What's wrong with you?" the merchant chimed in. "If you know no shame, then eat all you like!"

They swallowed down their saliva, unable to take their eyes off the curd cheese.

*

During the afternoon a large-winged boat flew in, bringing Pomor women from the mainland coast. So high were the waves that no one even saw the boat come into the pier.

The women spilled out onto the shore. They were a bright, loquacious flock, in pink, green, lilac and pale blue dresses, with pearl rings on their headbands.

They had fair eyebrows and the eyes of seagulls or mermaids – round, yellow eyes with black rims and black dots

---

12 The length of time that these short-term visitors were allowed to stay. During these three days they were supposed to avoid meat and dairy products. They were then considered ready to receive communion.

for pupils.

The women chattered away and laughed. The pilgrims watched from a distance, the men twisting their beards between their fingers.

"Them Pomors are a rich lot. They catch fish, they shoot animals for their furs, they gather down from eider ducks. No wonder they go around in pearls."

A woman in a rose-lilac dress, with a yellow-eyed child on her back, was teasing a gull, holding out a piece of bread, then withdrawing it, repeating, "Bread for the gull-bird? Bread for the gully-bird?"

The gull, who also had a child on her back, stuck out her neck crossly.

The seagull and the woman – females of the same breed and with the same yellow-eyed children – both understood that this was a game.

"Mock away, mock away!" people called out. "But wait till she's up above your head – she'll show you what's what! Them gulls can get mighty cross."

Towards evening a ferocious gale blew up. As if down a funnel, it blew straight down the icy throat of the Arctic Ocean, shaking the trees, twisting skirts and cassocks around legs, stopping people in their tracks or knocking them to the ground, flinging sea foam right up to the hostel's windows. Flocking swiftly together, the Pomor women got on board and hoisted sail. Pink, lilac and pale blue dresses swirled in the wind. The boat had no thwarts and no gunnels – the women simply stood on the planking. Someone cast off. Two young lads got out their squeeze-boxes and began to play; pink, lilac and pale blue skirts swirled and danced, by the edge of the boat. The following wind filled out the sails, driving the boat on so fiercely that, for a moment, the entire stern rose up above the

45

waves. The wind interrupted the song, brought it back, carried it away again – and then blew everything into the sea, burying both boat and song under a huge, turbid wave that smelt of fish scales. A few minutes later the pilgrims were pointing to a tiny craft now rounding a distant headland:

"Look – already there! They're a desperate lot, these Pomors."

*

That evening in the refectory the old woman with the flaccid tongue licked her spoon again, and the monk with the nasal voice read the same words about lust, sin and the Devil. The yawning youth was again led through the yard. A new group of pilgrims appeared – old women in black, smelling of cod and incense.

The gulls in the yard seemed cross, and something was frightening them. The gale was getting under their feathers, making them stand up on end, and the fledglings were squealing shrill complaints.

After they had eaten, Semyon took Varvara to confession. And, just as when she'd been questioned by the officer, the whole of her soul closed up in blank, obstinate misery. Back then, to the officer, she had said, "Wot's it to do wiv me?"; now, in the church, she fastened her eyes on the copper clasp of the Gospels, repeated, "I have sinned, I have sinned," – and said no more.

No one in the room slept long that night – thanks to the hypocrite official, who chose to prolong his devotions until the second cockcrow. He groaned, prostrated himself and intoned his prayers in a noisy whisper: "Lord, Lord, who art present even in the uttermost depths of the sea. Even there thou art present." Seven beds, from seven corners, creaked angrily back.

The official overslept. He got up along with everyone else and sat down by the window, taking care not to catch anyone's eye. And then, still not looking at anyone, he sidled off to church.

The church was thronged with people. There was a smell of cod, sheepskin, melted wax and something sour. Candle flames swayed before the flat, dark faces on the ancient icons; where the saints' hands emerged from their gilt covering, the paint had long ago wrinkled and blistered from the touch of thousands upon thousands of lips. Beside the holy relics everyone looked with awe and horror at a deceased *skhimnik*, a monk who had observed the very strictest of the monastic rules: all that could be seen of him, poking out from a black shroud embroidered with pictures of bones, were the tip of a waxen nose, grey wisps of beard and two bony hands.

High above them all rose the head of the yawning youth, mouth gaping open with a groan and then snapping shut. The wind knocked at doors and windows, bursting into the church, howling when it withdrew. Now and again white wings soared past the windows – and a mermaid's round yellow eye would peep into the church.

In the alcoves the monks' silent, shadowy figures were barely stirring, their prayer beads as if frozen in their hands. A ripple passed through the congregation as people stepped back to let the communicants through. The choir had already begun the Cherubic Hymn,[13] the youngsters' high voices soaring right up to the cupola, when a woman's piercing voice began

---

13 This marks the beginning of the most solemn part of the Liturgy. It is sung as the clergy enter the sanctuary through the Holy Doors; the angels are believed to accompany them. It ends with the words, "Let us now lay aside all earthly care."

shrieking frenziedly, "Kuda-a-a! Ku-u-da-a-a! Ku-da-a-a!"[14]

Her shrieks grew ever louder, ever more violent.

"She's possessed," whispered the peasant women. "Possessed good and proper!"[15]

Then someone else let out a scream and a wail – and began to bark like a dog, not letting up.

Varvara clenched her hands tight. The chandeliers swayed, slid to one side – and she felt her legs and shoulders begin to shudder, swiftly, violently, while her whole face stretched as if clinging tight to her cheekbones, and her stomach swelled, climbing right up to her throat, and a wild scream flew out from the darkest depth of her body, twisting her whole body, tearing her body apart, smashing red lights against the crown of her head: "Ai-i-i! Da-a-a! Da-a-a!"[16]

A momentary thought: "Should I stop?"

But something made her tense herself more and more powerfully, forcing her to cry out more and more loudly, to clench her whole body, to will on the convulsions. The words didn't matter. The first sounds to burst out had been "A-i-i!" and "Da-a-a!" – and so she'd continued. What mattered was not to stop, to expend more and more of herself in the cry, to give herself to it more intensely, yes, more and more of herself: Oh, if only they didn't get in her way. Oh, if only they let her keep going... But it was so hard. Would she have the strength?

"A-a-a! A-a-a! If only... If only... How sweet... How

---

14 Teffi evidently chose this word both for its sound and for its meaning: "whither". In English it is impossible to reproduce both, so we have transliterated, reproducing the sound alone.

15 The celebration of Christ's Resurrection through the mystery of the Eucharist was believed to provoke fear among demons, which in turn could prompt fits among those in a state of demonic possession.

16 Varvara's "Ai-da!" echoes the first woman's "Ku-da!". It is also important that the Russian word "Da" means "Yes".

sweet that would be…"

Someone's feet, next to her cheek. A strip of rug, a flax rug.

"Am I lying down now? Oh, who cares? I can't keep going now. But another time. Another time, somehow…"

And suddenly she was being lifted up. She was being hoisted up, by hands under her shoulders – and there before her eyes was a vast golden chalice, vast as the world.

"Varvara," someone was saying beside her.

"Varvara," someone repeated.

And a pointed golden spoon, also vast, was parting her lips and knocking at her tightly clenched teeth.[17] Her teeth unclenched of their own accord, a gentle trembling passed through her arms and legs and her head fell forward; she could no longer hold it up. Small beads of sweat were cooling her forehead.

"How sweet! Oh, how sweet!"

And her whole body emptied. As if everything heavy, swollen and black had left with the scream.

*

They seated Varvara on a bench outside the hostel. She had grown suddenly thinner. She had thrown back her head, her hair uncovered, and she was smiling with a look of exhausted bliss.

---

17 Varvara would not have normally have received communion until she had completed her penance. To Orthodox understanding, however, she is at present possessed by demons and so not considered responsible for her state. In the words of John Chrysostom, "They that be possest in that they are tormented of the devil are blameless and will never be punished with torment for that: but they who approach unworthily the holy Mysteries shall be given over to everlasting torments." (Quoted in R. W. Blackmore, *The Doctrine of the Russian Church* (Aberdeen, 1845), p. 223 n.) And so Varvara is being given communion: a small piece of bread dipped in wine.

Not daring to approach her, the other pilgrim women were looking at her in fear and awe, just as they had looked at the deceased *skhimnik* in the church. Semyon was also looking at her in fear and awe, not saying a word. And Varvara was saying in a delirious voice, her words coming out in fits and starts, "Oh my darlings! All of you! What sweetness! Lord God! My dearest Semyon! And now – a long, long journey, on foot, to Saint Tikhon of Zadonsk.[18] How dear the sky is. Sweet sky, bright sky. And the gulls… the dear gulls…"

Translated by Robert and Elizabeth Chandler
with thanks to Christine Worobec for her help with
regard to religious matters.

---

18 Saint Tikhon of Zadonsk (1724–1783) was born – like Varvara and her husband – in the region of Novgorod. After serving for seven years as a bishop, he retired to the monastery of Zadonsk, beyond the river Don, because of poor health. Eighty years after his death, he was canonised as a saint. Varvara evidently imagines herself and Semyon walking to Zadonsk, as pilgrims, stopping at other holy sites on the way. This would probably be a distance of around 1200 miles.

My Jobs
Marina Tsvetaeva

Prologue
Moscow, November 11, 1918

"Marina Ivanovna, do you want a job?"

My lodger flew in, X, a communist, the gentlest and most ardent.

"You see, there are two: at the bank and at Narkomnats... and actually (snapping of the fingers), for my part, I would recommend that you..."

"But what do you have to do? I don't know how to do anything."

"Oh, everybody says that!"

"Everybody says it, I do it."

"In short, as you see fit! The first job is on Nikolskaya St., the second right here, in the first Cheka building."

I: "?!"

He, wounded: "Don't worry! No one is going to make you execute anybody. You'll only be making lists."

"Making lists of the executions?"

He, irritated: "Oh, you don't want to understand! As if I were inviting you to join the Cheka! People like you aren't needed there..."

I: "We're harmful."

He: "It's the Cheka building, the Cheka has left. You probably know it, on the corner of Povarskaya and Kudrinskaya streets, in Leo Tolstoi it was (a snap of the fingers)... the house of...

I: "The Rostovs' house. I accept. What's the name of the institution?"

He: "Narkomnats. The People's Commissariat of Nationalities."

I: "What do you mean, nationalities when it's supposed to be international?"

He, almost boastfully: "Oh, more so than in tsarist times, I assure you!... So then, it's the Information Section of the Commissariat. If you agree, I'll talk to the director right away, today." (Suddenly doubtful): "Though, actually..."

I: "Just a moment, it isn't anything against the Whites, is it? You understand..."

He: "No, no, it's completely mechanical. Only, I must warn you, there are no rations."

I: "No, of course not. How could there be in a respectable institution?"

He: "But there will be trips, perhaps they'll raise the pay... And you definitely don't want the bank job? Because in the bank..."

I: "But I don't know how to count."

He, thoughtfully: "And Alya, does she know how?"[19]

I: "Alya doesn't know how either."

He: "Yes, then the bank is hopeless... What did you call that building?"

I: "The Rostovs' house."

He: "Perhaps you have *War and Peace*? I would love to... Though actually..."

I'm already flying down the staircase at breakneck speed. A dark corrridor, the former dining room, another dark corridor,

---

19 My daughter Alya is four and a half years old.

the former nursery, the cabinet with the lions… I grab the first volume of *War and Peace*, knock over the second volume nearby, open it at random, forget everything, become oblivious to everything…

***

"Marina, X left! Just after you went out! He said that he reads three newspapers before bed and also some tabloids and that he won't have time for *War and Peace*, and for you to call him tomorrow at the bank at 9 o'clock. And also, Marina," (a blissful face) "he gave me four lumps of sugar and – just imagine – a piece of white bread!"

She lays them out.

"Did he say anything else, Alechka?"

"Just a moment…" (she wrinkles her brow) "…yes, yes, yes! sa-bo-tage… And he also asked about Papa, if there's been any letters. And he made such a face, Marina, a grimacing one! As if he wanted to get mad on purpose…"

***

The 13th of November (a good day to start!) Povarskaya St., the house of Count Sollogub, "Information Section of the Commissariat of Nationalities."

Latvians, Jews, Georgians, Estonians, "Moslems", some sort of "Mara-Maras", "En-Dunyas" – and all these are men and women in short, fur-lined rustic jackets, with inhuman (ethnic) noses and mouths.

And me, who has always felt unworthy of these hearths (shrines!) of clans.

(I'm talking about houses with migrants and my fear of them.)

***

November 14th, the second day of my job.

Strange job! You arrive, set your elbows on the table (fists against cheekbones) and rack your brains: what to do to make the time pass? When I ask the director for work, I note a certain hostility in him.

***

I'm writing in the pink hall – pink all over.

There are marble window bays, two huge muslin-covered chandeliers. Small things (like furniture!) have disappeared.

***

November 15th, the third day of my job.

I'm compiling an archive of newspaper clippings. That is: I rephrase in my own words Steklov, Kerzhentsev, reports about prisoners of war, the movements of the Red Army, and so forth. I rephrase them once, I rephrase them twice (I copy from the "journal of newspaper clippings" onto "cards"), then I glue these clippings onto enormous sheets. The newspapers are delicate, the type barely visible, then add captions in lilac-coloured pencil, and then the glue – it's utterly pointless and will return to ashes even before it's all burned.

There are different desks here: Estonian, Latvian, Finnish, Moldavian, Moslem, Jewish and several entirely unpronounceable ones. In the morning each desk receives its share of clippings, which it then processes over the course of the day. I see all this clipping, labelling and pasting as endless, convoluted variations on one and the same, very meagre, theme. As though a composer had it in him to invent only one musical phrase, and he had to fill about thirty reams of musical notation paper – so he "variates": and we variate.

I forgot to mention the Polish and Bessarabian desks. I, not without justification, am the "Russian" desk (the assistant of either the secretary or perhaps of the director).

Each desk is grotesque.

To my left are two dirty, doleful Jewesses, ageless, like herring. Further on, a red, fair-haired Latvian woman, also ugly, like a person turned into a sausage: "I knew khim, such a svcetie. Khe partissipated in ze plot, und now zey haf zentenced khim to be shot. Chik-chik." ...And she giggles with excitement. Wears a red shawl. The fat, bright-pink display of her neck.

The Jewess says: "Pskov is taken!" I have the tormenting thought: "By whom?!!"

To my right – two people (the Oriental table). One has a nose and no chin, the other has a chin and no nose. (Who is Abkhazia and who is Azerbaijan?)

Behind me sits a seventeen-year-old child, pink, healthy, curly-headed (a white Negro), easy thinking and easy loving, a real live Atenais from Anatole France's *The Gods Will Have Blood*, the one who arranged her skirts so carefully in that fateful carriage – "*fière de mourir comme une Reine de France.*"

Also – a type of a boarding school mistress ("an inveterate theatre-goer"), also – a greasy, obese Armenian woman (chin resting on chest, impossible to say what's where), a mongrel in student uniform, also an Estonian doctor, sleepy and a born drunk... Also (a special breed!) a doleful Latvian woman, all sucked dry. Also...

***

(I'm writing at work)

A typographical error:

"If foreign governments would leave the Russian people *in piece*," and so forth.

The Herald of Poverty, Nov. 27, No. XXX11.

I, in the margins: "Don't worry! They'll wait a bit and they'll do just that!"

***

In the performance of my duties I paraphrase, in my own words, a newspaper clipping on the necessity of having literate people on duty in train stations:

"Day and night, literate people should be on duty in train stations in order to explain the difference between the old order and the new order to those arriving and departing."

The difference between the old and new orders:

The old order: "A soldier came by"… "We made pancakes"… "Our grandmother died".

Soldiers still come, grandmothers die, only no one makes pancakes anymore.

***

An encounter.

I'm running to the Commissariat. Supposed to be there at nine – it's already eleven: I lined up for milk on Kudrinskaya St., for dried fish on Povarskaya St., for hemp-seed oil on the Arbat.

There's a lady in front of me: ragged, skinny, with a shopping bag. I come up alongside her. The bag is heavy, her shoulder bowed, I feel the tension of her arm.

"Excuse me, ma'am. May I help you?"

Frightened glance:

"Oh, no…"

"I'd be glad to carry it, don't worry, we'll walk together."

She gives in. The bag really is hellish.

"Do you have far to go?"

"To Butyrki prison, I'm bringing a package."

"Has he been in long?"

"Quite a few months."

"No one to vouch?"

"All Moscow would vouch for him – that's why they won't let him out."

"Young?"

"No, middle-aged… Perhaps you've heard of him? The former governor, Dzhunkovsky."

***

I had the following encounter with D-sky. I was fifteen and cheeky. Asya[20] was thirteen and insolent. We were visiting a grown-up friend. There were lots of people. Father was there. Suddenly, the doorbell: D-sky. (And the answering ring: "Well, D-sky, just you wait!")

We are introduced. He's kind, charming. I'm taken for a grown-up, and asked whether I like music. And father, remembering my antediluuvian wunderkindness:

"What do you mean, why of course! She's been playing since she was five!"

D-sky, politely:

---

20 My sister. (*M.Ts.*)

"Perhaps you'd play something?"

I, putting on a show:

"I've really forgotten everything. I'm afraid you'll be disappointed…"

D-sky's courtesy, the guests' persuasion, father's insistence, the friend's fright, my acquiescence.

"But first, if you don't mind, let me play four hands with my sister to work up my courage."

"Oh, of course."

I go up to Asya and whisper in my own language:

"Wi(pi)rwe(pe)erde(pe)nTo(po)nlei(pei)te(pe)rspi(pi)…"

Asya can't take it.

Father: "What are you up to, you little imps?'

I – to Asya: "Scales backwards!"

To my father: "Asya's being shy."

***

We begin. My right hand is on re, the left on do (I'm playing bass). Asya's left hand is on re, her right on do. We start toward each other (I – from left to right, she – from right to left). At each note a thunderous double-voiced count: One and two and three and… Deathly silence. After about ten seconds, father's uncertain voice:

"Ladies, why so… monotonous? How about something a bit more lively?"

Without stopping, in unison: "This is just the beginning."

Finally my right and Asya's left hand meet.

We rise with gleeful faces.

Father – to D-sky: "Well, what do you think?"

And D-sky, rising in turn: "I thank you. It was extremely clear."

***

I tell the story. At her request I give my name. We laugh. "Oh, he wasn't only tolerant of jokes. All Moscow ..." We say good-bye on the corner of Sadovaya. Once again her shoulder bows under the weight of the bag.

"Your father died?"

"Before the war."

"You don't know any more whether to be sorry or envious."

"Live. And try to keep others alive. God be with you!"

"Thank you. The same to you."

***

The Institute.

Did I ever think that after so many schools, boarding schools and grammar schools, I would be handed over to an Institute as well?! For I'm in an Institute, and have in fact been handed over (by X).

I arrive between 11 and 12 o'clock; each time my heart stands still: the Director and I have the same habits (ministerial ones!) I'm talking about the head Director – M-r; my own director, Ivanov, I write with a lowercase letter.

Once we met at the coat rack – it was all right. A Pole: courteous. And then, I'm also Polish on my grandmother's side.

But more terrifying than the director are the doormen. The former ones. They seem disdainful. In any event, they don't greet you first, and I'm shy. After the doormen, my main worry is not to mix up the rooms. (My idiocy for places.) I'm ashamed to ask, it's my second month here. Enormous idols stand in the hall – knights-in-armour. Left for their uselessness... to everyone but me. I need them, just as I, the only one here, am akin to them. I ask for protection with a glance. From beneath their visors they answer. If no one's watching, I quietly stroke a forged leg. (Three times taller than I am.)

The hall.

I enter, awkward and timid. In a mousy man's jersey – like a mouse. I'm dressed worse than everyone here, and that's not reassuring. Shoes tied with strings. There may even be some shoe laces somewhere, but... who cares?

The main thing is to understand from the first second of the Revolution: all is lost! Then – everything is easy.

I steal by. The director (my own, the lowercase one) – from his seat:

"Were you waiting in line, Comrade Efron?"

"In three lines."

"What did they have?"

"They didn't have anything, they had salt."

"Yes, well, salt sure isn't sugar!"

A heap of clippings. Some are quite long, some only a line. I look for ones about the White Guards. The pen scratches. The stove crackles.

"Comrade Efron, we have horse meat for lunch today. I suggest you sign up."

"No money. Did you sign up?"

"Certainly not!"

"Well then, we'll drink tea. Shall I bring you some?"

***

The corridors are empty and clean. The click of typewriters behind doors. Pink walls, in the windows, columns and snow.

My Jobs

My pink, blessed Institute for the gentry! Wandering about, I come upon the stairs leading down to the kitchen: the descent of the Virgin into hell or of Orpheus into Hades. Stone tiles, worn by human feet. Sloping, nothing to hold on to, the steps twist and turn, in one place they fly headlong. The serfs' feet certainly did their work! And to think, in indoor homemade shoes! It's as though they've been gnawed by teeth! Yes, the tooth of the only old man with any bite! The tooth of Chronos!

Natasha Rostova! Did you ever walk here? My ballroom Psyche! Why wasn't it you – later, at some point – who met Pushkin? Even the name is the same! Literary historians wouldn't have had to relearn anything. Pushkin instead of Pierre, and Parnassus instead of nappies. To become a fertility goddess, having been Psyche – Natasha Rostova, isn't that a sin?

It would have been like this. He would have come to call. Having heard so much about the poet and the Moor, you would have turned up your pointed, bright-eyed little face – and laughing at something, already feeling a pang... Oh, the flounce of a pink gown against the column!

The column overflows with heavenly foam! And your lyrical foot – Aphrodite's, Natasha's, Psyche's – on the slippery serfs' stones.

Actually, you were only flying down the stairs to the kitchen for bread!

***

But everything comes to an end: Natasha, serfdom, and the staircase (they say eventually, even Time!). By the way, the stairs are not that long – only twenty-two steps in all. It's just that I walked down them for so long (1818-1918).

Firm. (I almost said: firmament. I was younger and there was the monarchy – and I didn't understand why the heavenly firmament. The revolution and my own soul have taught me.) Potholes, pitfalls, cave-ins. Groping hands grip wet walls. Close over my head, the vault. It smells of damp and Bonivard. Methinks chains are clanking. Ah, no, it's the clang of pots and pans from the kitchen! I go toward the lantern.

**

The kitchen is a crater. So red and hot it's obvious: hell. A huge, six-and-a-half metre stove spews forth fire and foam. "The seething cauldrons boil, they sharpen their knives of steel, they ready the goat for slaughter…" And I am the goat.

The queue for the kettle. They scoop ladlesful straight from the boiler. The tea is wood pulp, some say from bark, others from buds, I just lie – from roots. Not glass – but a burn. I pour two glasses. I wrap them in a flap of my jersey. On the threshold I inhale horse flesh with a slight movement of the nostrils: I can't stay here – I have no friends.

**

"Well then, comrade Efron, now we can goof off a bit!"

(I arrive with the glasses.)

"With saccharine or without?"

"Pour on the saccharine!"

"They say it affects your kidneys. But you know, I…"

"Yes, you know, I too…

My director is an Esperantist (that is, a Communist from Philology). An Esperantist from Ryazan. When he talks about Esperanto, a quiet madness glimmers in his eyes. The eyes are light and small, like the ancient saints' or like Pan in the Tretyakov Gallery. See-through. A touch of the lecher. But it's not the lechery of the flesh, some other kind – if it weren't for the absurdity of the association, I'd say: otherworldly. (If it's possible to love Eternity, then it's also possible to lust after her! And the lusters – philologists – are more numerous than the silent lovers!)

Dark blond. Something under the nose and chin. The face is puffy, proggy. A drunkard, I imagine.

He writes in the new style – in anticipation of worldwide Esperanto. Has no political convictions. Here, where every-one's a communist, even this is a blessing. Doesn't distinguish Reds from Whites. Doesn't distinguish right from left. Doesn't distinguish men from women. Thus his camerarderie is completely sincere, and I willingly pay him in the same coin. After work he goes somewhere on Tverskaya St., where on the left side (if you're heading down toward Okhotny) there's an Esperanto shop. They closed the shop, the shopfront window remained: fly-blown postcards Esperantists have sent one another from all corners of the earth. He looks and lusts. He works here because it offers a wide field for propaganda, all nations. But he's already beginning to despair.

"I'm afraid, Comrade Efron, that here there are more and more..." (in a whisper) "Jews and Latvians. It wasn't even worth applying: Moscow's full of these goods! I was counting on Chinese, on Indians. They say that Indians readily absorb foreign cultures."

I: "Not those Indians – American Indians."

He: "Redskins?"

I: "That's right, with feathers. They'll slit your throat – and absorb you all in one piece. If you're wearing a jacket, then jacket and all, in a tuxedo – tuxedo and all. But Indians – just the opposite: terribly dense. Won't swallow anything foreign, neither ideology nor foodstuffs." (Becoming inspired): "Do you want a formula? The American Indian absorbs (the European), the Indian disgorges (Europe). And rightly so."

He, embarrassed: "Now, really, you're… I, by the way… I've heard more from the communists, they are also counting on India…" (Becoming inspired in his turn): "I thought – I'll up and esperanto them all!" (Subsiding): "No rations – and not one Indian. Not one Negro! Not even a Chinaman!… And these" (a circular glance at the empty hall) "don't want to hear of it! I tell them: Esperanto, and they say: 'the International!'" (Frightened by his own outcry.) "I've nothing against it, but first Esperanto, and then… The word first.

I, falling in: "And then the deed. Of course. In the beginning was the word and the word was…"

He, in another outburst: "And that Mara-Mara! What is it? Where did he come from? Not only haven't I heard a word from him: I haven't even heard a sound! He's just a deaf mute. Or an idiot. Doesn't get any clippings – only his salary. I don't begrudge it. To hell with him, but why does he come? The fool, he comes in every day. Sits here till four, the idiot. He should just come on the 20th, for payday."

I, craftily: "Poor thing, maybe be keeps hoping? I'll come in and on my desk there'll be a newspaper cutting about my Mara-Mara?"

He, irritated: "Oh, Comrade Efron, really! What cuttings? Who's going to write about that Mara-Mara? Where is it? What is it? Who needs it?"

I, thoughtfully: "It isn't in geography…" (Pause). "And it isn't in history… What if it doesn't exist at all? They just made it up – to show off. Like, we have all nations. And they dressed this guy up… But he's mute." (Confidentially): "They chose a deaf mute on purpose, so he wouldn't give himself away in Russian…"

He, gulping down the last bit of cold tea with a shudder: "Who the d-d-devil knows!"

***

Clatter and crash. It's the nationalities returning from their feed. Fortified with horse flesh, it's on to the cutting files (on to filet cutlets would be better, eh? By the way, before the Revolution, cross my heart, I not only couldn't tell filet from tripe – I couldn't tell groats from flour! And I don't regret it in the least.)

Comrade Ivanov, anxiously: "Comrade Efron, Comrade M-r might drop in, let's get rid of our mess quickly, eh?" (He rakes it in.) "'The Red Army's Advance'… Steklov's articles… 'The Liquidation of Illiteracy'… 'Down with the White Guard Scum' – that's for you. 'The Bourgeoisie Schemes'… You again… 'All to the Red Front'… mine… 'Trotsky's Address to the Troops'… mine… 'The White-liners and the White Guard'… yours… 'Kolchak's Lackeys'… yours… 'The Whites' Atrocities'… yours"

I'm drowning in whiteness. At my elbow – Mamontov, on my knees – Denikin, near my heart – Kolchak.

Greetings, my "White Guard Scum!"

I write with relish.

"What's going on, Comrade Efron, why haven't you finished? The paper, number, date, who, what – no details! I was that way at first, filled sheets full, then M-r admonished me: 'You're using up a lot of paper.'"

"Does M-r believe in it?"

"What's here to believe! You copy, you clip, you glue…"

"And into the Lethe – boom! Like in Pushkin."

"Yes, but M-r's a very educated person, I still haven't lost hope…"

"You don't say! You know, I thought so too. I ran into him not long ago at the hangings… ay, good Lord… at the coat hangers: I've got all those 'White Guard atrocities' in my head… A quarter past twelve! It was all right, he even looked at me rather intelligently… So, you have hope?"

"Somehow I'll manage to get him to the Esperanto club one of these evenings."

"An aspirant to the Esperantists?"

Espère, enfant, demain! Et puis demain encore…
Et puis toujours demain. Croyons en l'avenir.
Espère! Et chaque fois que se lève l'aurore
Soyons la pour prier comme Dieu pour nous bénir
Pêut-etre…

Lamartine's poetry. Do you understand French?"

"No, but fancy that, it's very pleasant to listen. Oh, what an Esperantist we could make of you, Comrade Efron…"

'Then I'll recite some more. I wrote a composition about this in sixth grade: '*A une jeune fille qui avait raconté son rêve.*'

Un baiser… sur le front! Un baiser – même en rêve!
Mais de mon triste front, le frais baiser s'enfuit…
Mais de l'été jamais ne reviendra la sève,
Mais l'aurore jamais n'eteindrera la nuit –

"Do you like it?" (And, not allowing him to answer) "Then I'll continue:

Un baiser sur le front! Tout mon être frisonne,
On dirait que mon sang va remonter son cours…
Enfant! – ne dites plus vos rêves à personne
Et ne rêvez jamais… ou bien – rêvez toujours!

It's piercing, isn't it? The French teacher I wrote the composition for – he was a little in love with... Actually, I'm wrong: it was a French lady, and I was a little in love with..."

"Comrade Efron!" (A whisper almost in my ear.) I jump. My "white negro" is standing behind me, and she's all red. There's bread in her hand.

"You didn't have lunch. Perhaps you'd like this? Only I warn you, it's made with bran..."

"But you yourself, I'm so embarrassed..."

"Do you think... (an ardent face, a challenge in every sheep's curl) I bought it at Smolensky? Filimovich from the Eastern desk gave it to me – it's from his rations, he doesn't eat it himself. I ate half, half's for you. He promised more tomorrow. But I still won't kiss him!"

(Illumination: Tomorrow I'll give her a ring – that slender one with the almandine. Almandine – Aladdin – Almanzor – Alhambra... with an almandine. She's pretty, and she needs it. And I won't know how to sell it anyway.)

***

Don. Don. Not the river Don, a ringing gong. Two o'clock. And – a further illumination: I'll think up some emergency and I'll leave right away. I'll finish up the White Guards – and I'll leave. Quickly and without any more lyrical digressions (I myself am just such a digression!) I shower the gray official paper with the pearls of my script and the vipers of my heart. But that counterrevolutionary old letter 'Ѣ' keeps popping up like a church cupola. Yat'!!! "Comrade Kerzhentsev ends his article by wishing General Denikin a good and speedy hanging: we, in turn, wish the same for Comrade Kerzhentsev..."

"Saccharine! Saccharine! They're signing up for saccharine!" Everyone jumps up. I must take advantage of other people's sweet cravings to satisfy my own freedom craving. Ingratiatingly and impudently I slip Ivanov my clippings. I cover them with half of the white negro's bread. (The other half is for the children.)

"Comrade Ivanov, I'm leaving now. If M-r asks, say that I'm in the kitchen getting a drink of water."

"Go on, go on."

I rake up the draft of Casanova, a purse with a pound of salt... and sidling, sidling...

"Comrade Efron!" – he catches up with me near the knights. "I won't be coming in at all tomorrow. I'd really appreciate it if you'd come – well – at least by 10:30. And then the day after tomorrow, don't come at all. You'll really help me out. All right?"

"Yes sir!"

There and then, in front of the perplexed doormen, a dashing salute, and I rush off – rush through the White Guard colonnade, over the snowy flowerbed, leaving behind me nationalities and saccharine and Esperanto and Natasha Rostova – to my house, to Alya, to Casanova: homeward!

***

From *Izvestia*:

"Sovereignty of the water is sovereignty of the world!"

(I'm enraptured, as if it were poetry.)

***

9/23 of January (Central Executive Committee News, "The Heir")

Someone reads: "Kornilov's son, Georgy, a minor, was

appointed a constable in Odessa."

I, through the general mocking laughter, innocently:

"Why a constable? His father didn't serve in the police!"

(But in my chest everything seethes.)

The reader: "Well, you know, they're all gendarmes there!"

(What is most touching is that at that moment neither the communist nor I even suspected the existence of the Cossack constables.)

***

In our Narkomnats there's a private chapel – Sollogub's, of course. Near my pink hall. The "white negro" and I stole in there not long ago. Dark, sparkling, cellar air. We stood in the choir gallery. The "white negro" crossed herself, and I was thinking more about ancestors (ghosts). In church I feel like praying only when there's singing. But I don't feel God inside buildings at all.

Love – and God. How do they manage to combine them? (Love as the element of loving, the earthly Eros). I glance at my "white negro": she's praying; innocent eyes. Those very same innocent eyes, those praying lips...

If I were a believer and loved men, these things would fight in me like vicious dogs.

My "white negro's" father works as a doorman in one of the houses (palaces) where Lenin often comes (the Kremlin). And my "white negro," who often visits her father at work, sees Lenin all the time. "So humble, wears a cap."

My "white negro" is a White Guard, in the sense, not to confuse things: she loves white flour, sugar and all earthly blessings. And what's even more serious, she is passionately and profoundly devout.

"He walks by me, M.I., and I say 'Good day, Vladimir

Ilich!'– while I think to myself" (a boldly cautious look around), "I'd like to shoot you right now, you so and so, with a revolver. Don't rob churches!" (Flaring up). "And you know, M.I., it would be so simple – pull a revolver out of my muff and finish him off!" (Pause.) "Only I don't know how to shoot, you see… And they'd shoot Papa then."

If my negro were to fall into the right hands, hands that know how to shoot and how to teach shooting, and, more important, they know how to destroy and know no regret---
---e-ekh!

***

There's an old spinster in the Commissariat, gaunt, with a ribbon, who's in love with her overgrown doctor-brothers, she gets them chocolate with children's ration cards. A finagler, a conniver, who knows languages, by the way ("that sort of family"), etc. As soon as she hears that someone's ill, she diagnoses, with unshakable certainty, as if pounding a gavel: "He's caught it," or "She's caught it," depending on whether she's talking about a person of the male or female sex.

Typhus or sciatica – it's all syphilis to her.

Spinster psychosis.

***

But there's another one – plump, raw, a grandmother's pet, friend of my "white negro", a provincial lass. A very poignant young girl. She arrived only recently from the town of Rybinsk. Her grandmother and little brother remain at home. A twofold, inexhaustible mine of bliss.

"That's just the way our grandmother is: she can't stand little children. She won't go near an infant: they smell, she says, and they're trouble. But when they get bigger – well, all

70

right then. She'll dress them, teach them. Me she raised from the age of six, 'Do you want to eat?' 'Yes.' 'Well, then, go to the kitchen and watch how dinner's made.' So by ten I already knew how to do absolutely everything (animatedly): not just your pies and cutlets but patés and aspics and cakes... The same for sewing: 'You, little one, you'll be a woman one day, a housewife, with children and a husband to sew for.' I'd want to run around, she takes my hand and sits me down on the bench: 'hem those handkerchiefs, embroider initials on those towels.' And when the war started I did it for the wounded. Cut patterns myself, sewed myself. Then Papa got married – I'm an orphan – and little brother came along, I made his whole layette myself... All the nappies with embroidered initials, with satin-stitch... And his little blanket, clothes to take him out in, all sewn with my lace, four-fingers wide, cream-coloured..." (Blissfully): "You know, grandmother taught me to knit and satin-stitch... She ordered an embroidery hoop for me. We lived well! But she did everything by herself! Grandmother made things herself, I made things myself... I can't stand for my hands to lie idle!"

I look at her hands. Golden hands! Small, plump, well-shaped, tapered fingers. A tiny ring with a tiny turquoise. There was a fiancé, shot by a firing squad not long ago in Kiev.

"His friend wrote to me, he's a student too – a medical student. My Kolya left the house, hadn't gone two feet – shots rang out. And a man fell right at his feet. All bloody. And Kolya's a doctor, he couldn't leave someone who's wounded. He looked around: no one in sight. So he took him, dragged him into his own house and looked after him for three days. He turned out to be a White officer. And on the fourth day they came, took them both, and shot them together."

She dresses in mourning. Her face a sallow gray amid the

71

blackness. Not enough food, not enough sleep, loneliness. Tedious, incomprehensible, unfamiliar work in the Commissariat. Her fiancé's ghost . Homelessness.

Poor middle-class Turgenevian girl! The epic orphan of Russian fairy tales! In no one do I feel the great orphanhood of 1919 Moscow as I do in her. Not even in myself,

She dropped by to see me recently, stood over my untidy trunks: a student uniform, officer's jacket, boots, riding breeches – epaulets, epaulets, epaulets…

"Marina Ivanovna, you should shut them. Shut them and put a lock on. Dust builds up, moths will eat them in the summer… He might still return…

And, pensively smoothing a helpless sleeve:

"I couldn't. Just like a living man… I'm still crying…"

***

We went to an operetta recently: she, the "white negro" and I (for the first time in my life). The tunes were nice, the verses bad. Dry and harsh is the Russian tongue on Polish lips. But… a sort of love, but… beyond herring and heavy bags, but… light, laughter, gesture!

Mediocrity? For me the worse – the better. "Genuine art." It would offend me right now. All my requirements would arise: "I'm not cattle!"

But this way – a fake for a fake: after the Soviet farce – a juvenile farce.

***

A few more words about my "bride." With eyes (marvellous, dark-brown eyes) tear-stained and puffy from crying over her fiancé, she goes on plaintively for hours, wearing out herself and everyone around her: "I just so love everything fatty and sweet... I used to be much plumper. I can't live without butter... I just can't swallow frozen potatoes..."

O thee, sole provision
Of the Communist nation!

(A poem about dried fish in the Menshevik paper *Forever Onward*.)

***

My assistant.

Our desk has been enhanced by a new co-worker (co-idler would be more exact). A ripe, red-blooded Hercules from the Volga region. Perpetually and bestially hungry. At lunch he despairingly asks for more: the silently proffered plate meekly and doggedly pleads. He eats everything.

Handsome. Eighteen-years old, so ruddy-cheeked that you get hot sitting next to him: a furnace! No beard and no moustache. Timid. Afraid to move – knows he'll break something. Afraid to cough – knows he'll deafen everyone. The timidity and gentleness of a giant. I feel tenderness for him, as for a huge calf: hopeless tenderness, because I've nothing to give.

Seeing him for the first time at the desk – a huge bear from the Urals leaning over the lace of *Izvestia* clippings, Ivanov and I grinned simultaneously. I don't know what Ivanov was thinking, but right away I knew: "I won't come in tomorrow, or the day after tomorrow, or the day after the day after tomorrow. I'm going to wash clothes and write."

I didn't come in for six days, not three. On the seventh I showed up. The desk is neat – not one clipping: licked clean.

Not a sign of Ivanov. The bear, leaning on his elbows, rules alone.

I, distraught: "But where's Ivanov? Where are the clippings?"

The bear, beaming: "I haven't seen hide nor hair of Ivanov since then! I've been in charge here alone for a whole week."

I, horrified: "But the clippings?! Did you keep up the journal?"

He, blissfully: "What journal! Everything's in the basket! I gave it a try – the pen was bad, the paper crumbling, I write – can't read it myself. And I get so sleepy… It must mean spring's coming."

(I, mentally: "Wrong, bear, it means winter!")

He, continuing: "Well, I thought, what will be will be! I collected them up, the sheets, that is, and into the basket with them. In the morning when I come – it's empty. The cleaning woman must have burned them. The same thing every day. The little ones are all in one piece, I saved them for you."

He opens a drawer: a swarm of snow-white butterflies!

And I, captivated by the line and already taking off, think to myself:

"A swarm of snow-white butterflies! One, two… four"…
(– no! –)
A swarm of snow-white maidens! One, two… four…
A swarm of snow-white maidens! But no – in the air
A swarm of snow-white butterflies! A charming swarm
Of little Grand Princesses…

and, breaking off, to my "co-worker":

"We'll reconstruct all this right now…" (mentally: except the Grand Princesses!) "Sort them out chronologically."

He: "How's that?"

I: "By dates. You know, the 5th of February. The Roman

II – that's February, do you see? I is January, II is February…

He doesn't breathe or blink.

"Then, wait a minute… Just write a letter home. Take a pen and write: 'Dear Mama, I'm very bored and hungry here'… Something like that, or the other way around: 'I'm very happy and well fed here.' Because otherwise, she'll be upset. And I'm going to reconstruct Steklov's and Kerzhentsev's articles."

He, admiringly: "From your head?!"

I: "Not from my heart!"

And, in a trice: In his article of February 5th, 1919, "White Guardism and the White Elephant,"[21] Comrade Kerzhentsev claims…

***

We decamp to another hearth and home – from the Rostovs' house to the Jerusalem town house. It takes a whole ten days to sort ourselves out. We make off with the remains of the Rostov-Sollogub belongings. I take a plate with a coat of arms as a souvenir. In a brick-red field – a *borzoi*. A lyrical theft, even chivalrous: the plate isn't deep or small, by current standards it's obviously for salted fish stew, but in my home the inkwell will stand in it.

Those poor Sollogubian Elzevirs! In open boxes! In the rain! Parchment bindings, ornate French type… They carry them away by the cartloads. The library commission is headed by Briusov.

They take away: sofas, chests of drawers, chandeliers. My knights remain. So do the portraits painted on the wall, it seems. Right on the spot – the divvy. The jealous dispute of the "desks."

---

21 Which never existed. (M.Ts.)

"That's for our director!"

"No, for ours."

"We already have the Karelian birch table, and the armchair goes with it."

"That's precisely why. You have the table, we get the armchair."

"But you can't break the set!"

I, sententiously:

"Only heads can be broken!"

The "desks" are disinterested – we won't get anything anyway. Everything goes into the directors' offices. In flies my "white negro":

"Comrade Efron! If you only knew how wonderful it is at Ts-ler's! A redwood writing desk, a rug, bronze sconces! Just like in the old days! Do you want to take a look?"

We ran through the floors. Room Number... Section such and such... The director's office. We enter. My "negro", triumphantly: "Well?"

"Just add a cushion under foot and a lapdog..."

"A cat would be enough!"

In her eyes, a joyful demon.

"Comrade Efron! Let's catch a cat for him! There's one in apartment 18. What do you say?"

I, hypocritically:

"But he'll dirty everything here."

"That's exactly what I want! Darn thugs!"

Three minutes later the cat is nabbed and shut in. "Work" is over. We fly down all six flights, forgetting everything.

"Comrade Efron! The raspberry ottoman, eh?"

"And the countess's rugs, no?"

The diabolic meowing of the avenger pursues us.

My Jobs

***

The three vital Ms.
"So, how'd you carry the potatoes back?"
"It wasn't too bad. My old man met me."
"You know, to make meal you have to mix 2/3 potatoes with 1/3 flour."
"Really? I'll have to tell my mother."
I have neither mother, nor man, nor meal.

***

Frozen potatoes.
"Comrade Efron! They've brought potatoes! Frozen!"
I, of course, find out later than everyone, but bad news – always too soon.
Some of "our people" went on an expedition, promised sugar deposits and motherlodes of lard, travelled about for two months and brought back... frozen potatoes! Three poods a head. First thought: how to get them home? Second: how to eat them? The three poods of rot.
The potatoes are in the cellar, in a deep, pitch-dark crypt. The potatoes croaked and were buried, and we, the jackals, are going to dig them up and eat them. They say they arrived healthy, but then someone suddenly "prohibited" them, and by the time the prohibition was lifted, the potatoes, having first frozen and then thawed out, had rotted. They sat at the train station for three weeks.
I run home for sacks and the sledge. The sledge is Alya's, a child's sledge, with little bells and blue reins – my gift to her from Rostov in the Vladimir region. Spacious wickerwork like they use for baskets, the back upholstered with a handmade

77

rug. Just hitch up two dogs – and mush! – off to the Northern Lights…

But it was I who served as the dog, and the Northern Lights stayed behind: her eyes! She was two years old then, and she was regal. ("Marina, give me the Kremlin!" pointing at the towers.) Oh, Alya! Oh, the sledge along midday lanes! My tiger-fur coat (Leopard? Snow leopard?) that Mandelstam, having fallen in love with Moscow, stubbornly designated Boyaresque. Snow leopard! Sleigh bells!

There's a long line to the basement. The frostbitten steps of the staircase. Cold at your back: how to lug them? My own hands – I believe in these marvels, but 100 pounds upstairs! Up thirty leaning, pushing steps! Besides which, one of the runners is broken. Besides which, I'm not sure the sacks will hold. Besides all of which, I seem so cheerful that – even if I died – no one would help.

They let us in groups: ten at a time. Everyone's in pairs – husbands have run over from their jobs, mothers have dragged themselves over. Lively negotiations, plans: one will barter, another will dry two poods, a third will put them through the meat grinder (100 pounds?!) – obviously, I am the only one who intends to eat them.

"Comrade Efron, are you going to take the supplement? A half pood for every family member. Do you have a certificate for the children?"

Someone:

"I wouldn't! There's only slime left."

Someone else:

"You can sell it!"

We forge ahead. Grunts and sighs, occasionally laughter: someone's hands have met in the darkness: a man's and a woman's (man's and man's – isn't funny). Apropos, whence this jollying effect of Eros on the simple people? Defiance? Self-defence? Impoverished means of expression? Timidity under the guise of levity. After all, when they're afraid, children often laugh as well. "*L'amour n'est ni joyeux ni tendre.*"

But maybe – more likely – no *amour*, just surprise: men's hands – cursing, a man's and a woman's – laughter. Surprise and impunity.

There's talk of an impending trial for our co-workers – they presented huge bills for both purchases and expenses. Lodging, supplies carts, drivers…

They brought a lot of everything for themselves, of course.

"Did you notice how so-and-so has fattened up?"

"And so-and-so? His cheeks are about to burst!"

They let us in. We run into a crazed string of sledges. Runners over feet. Shouts. Darkness. We go through puddles. The smell is truly putrid.

"Move aside, will you!!!"

"Comrades! Comrades! The bag broke!"

Squish. Squelch. The feet disappear up to the ankles. Someone, braking the entire team, furiously removes his footwear: his felt boots are soaked through! I stopped feeling my feet a long time ago.

"Hey! Is there ever going to be any light?!"

"Comrades! I lost my identification! In the name of all that's holy – light a match!"

It sputters. Someone on their knees, in the water, is helplessly raking aside the slime.

"You should look in your pockets!"

"Could you have left it at home?"

"How do you think you'll find it here?"

"Move along! Move along!"

"Comrades, there's another group coming this way!

Watch out!!!"

And – a crater and a waterfall. A square hole in the ceiling, through which rain and light fall. It gushes, as if from a dozen pipes. We'll drown! Leaps and jumps, someone lost their sack, someone else's sledge got stuck in the passageway. Lord Almighty!

***

The potatoes are on the floor: they take up three hallways. At the far end they're more protected, less rotten. But there's no way to get to them except over them. And so: with our feet, our boots. Like climbing over a mountain of jellyfish. You have to scoop them with your hands: one hundred pounds. The unthawed ones have stuck together in monstrous clusters. I don't have a knife, So, in despair (I can't feel my hands) – I grab whatever kind comes my way: squashed, frozen, thawed... The sack won't hold any more. My hands, numb through and through, can't tie it. Taking advantage of the darkness I start to cry, but then and there I stop:

"To the scales! To the scales! Who's ready for the scales?!"

I hoist and haul.

Two Armenians are doing the weighing, one in a student uniform, the other in Caucasian dress. The snow-white felt cloak looks like a spotted hyena. Just like an archangel of the Communist Last Judgment! (The scales undoubtedly lie!)

"Comrade Meess! Don't hold up the public!"

Quarrelling, kicking. Those in back push. I've blocked the entire passageway. Finally, the Caucasian, taking pity – or growing angry – shoves my sack forward with his foot. Poorly tied, the sack spills open. Slip. Slobbber. I gather them up patiently, taking my time.

***

The return route with the potatoes. (I only took two poods, the third I stashed away.) First through raging hallways, then up a resistant stairway – whether it's tears or sweat on my face I can't tell.

And I know not whether it be tears or rain
That burn my face...

Maybe it was rain! That's not the point! The runner is very weak, it's split in the middle, it's unlikely we'll make it back. (It's not I who pulls the sledge, we pull together. The sledge is my comrade-in-woe, and the potatoes are the woe. We carry our own woe!

I'm scared of the plazas. The Arbat can't be avoided. I could have gone by the Prechistenka lanes, but would have gotten lost there. Neither snow, nor ice: I'm sliding on water, and in some places – on dry ground. I admire the cobblestones pensively, some are already pink...

"Oh how I loved all this!"

I remember Stakhovich. If he could see me now, I would indubitably become the object of his loathing. Everything, even my face, is dripping. I am no better than my own sack. The potatoes and I are now one and the same.

"Where the hellrya goin? Canya like that – right into people?! Tailless bourgeoise!"

"Of course I've no tail – only devils have tails!"

Laughter all around. The soldier, not assuaged:

"Some hat yer decked out in! And that mug could use a washing...

I, in the same tone, pointing to his leg wrappings:

"Some rags you're decked out in!"

The laughter grows. Not wanting to relinquish the dialogue,

81

I stop, and pretend to adjust the sack.

The soldier, working himself up;

"The upper classes they call 'em! Huh! Intellygents! Can't wash our face without a servant, can we?!"

A simple woman, shrilly:

"You'll give her some soap then, will you? Who's slipped off with all the soap, tell me? What's soap going for at Sukharevka, d'ya know?" Someone from the crowd:

"How would he know? He gets it for free! And you, Miss, you've got potatoes there?"

"Frozen. From my job."

"Of course they're frozen – they need the good ones for themselves! Give you a hand, then?"

He gives a push, the reins grow taut, I'm off. Behind me the woman's voice – to the soldier:

"So what, she wears a hat, so she's not a human being?"

The ver-r-r-dict!

***

The day's outcome: two tubs of potatoes. We all eat: Alya, Nadya, Irina, I.

Nadya – to Irina, slyly:

"Eat, Irina, it's sweet, with sugar."

Irina, stubbornly, lowering her head: "Nnnnnoooo…"

***

March 20th.

Instead of Monplenbezh, lost in thought, I write "Monplesir" (Monplaisir) – something like a small Versailles of the 18th century.

Annunciation 1919,

Prices:
1 lb. flour – 35 roubles.
1 lb. potatoes – 10 roubles.
1 lb. carrots – 7.50 roubles.
1 lb. onions –15 roubles.
Herring – 25 roubles.
(Salary – our raises haven't gone through yet – 775 roubles a month.)

***

April 25, 1919.
I quit the Commissariat. I quit because I can't put together a classification. I tried, I racked my brains – nothing. I don't understand. I don't understand what they want from me: "Compile, compare, sort... In each section – a subsection." As if they'd rehearsed it. I asked everyone: from the department director to the eleven-year-old messenger boy. "It's very simple." And the main thing is that no one believes that I don't understand. They laugh.

Finally, I sat down at the desk, dipped my pen in ink, and wrote: "Classification." Then, having thought a bit: "Section." Then, having thought a bit more: "Subsection." On the right and on the left. Then I froze.

***

I've worked for 5 and 1/2 months, two more weeks – and vacation (with salary). But I can't take it. And the last three months of clippings aren't pasted up. And they're starting to give heed to my ѣ. "Come on, comrade, haven't you gotten used to the new spelling yet?"... The classification has to be presented by the 28th. At the very latest. I have to be fair –

communists are trusting and patient. An old regime institution would have taken one look at me, and fired me immediately. Here, I myself resign.

The director, M-r, reading my letter of resignation, briefly:
"Better conditions?"

"Military rations and discounted meals for all family members."

(Spontaneous and brazen invention.)

"Then I couldn't possibly keep you. But be careful: those kinds of institutions can fall apart quickly."

"I'm an executive."

"On whose recommendation?"

"Two pre-October Party members."

"What's your position?"

"Translator."

"Translators are needed, I wish you success."

I leave. I'm already at the door – and he calls out:

"Comrade Efron, you'll be presenting the classification, of course?"

I, pleading:

"All the materials are there... My assistant will have no problem... Or just deduct it from my salary!"

***

They didn't deduct it. No, hand on heart, I can say that to this day I, personally, haven't seen communists do anything bad (maybe I haven't seen any bad communists!) And it isn't them I hate, but communism (for two years now all I've heard everywhere is: "Communism is wonderful, but communists are horrid!" I'm sick and tired of it!)

But, to return to the classification. (Illumination: isn't

this the entire essence of communism?!) Its exactly the same as with algebra when I was 15, with arithmetic when I was seven! Full eyes and an empty page. It's the same with cutting patterns – I don't understand, I don't understand: what's left, what's right, my temples whirl, there's a lead weight on my brow. It used to be the same with selling at the market, in the old days with hiring servants, with all of my Antaean load of earthly life: I don't understand, I can't stand it, it doesn't work out.

I think that if others were forced to write *Fortuna*, they would feel the same.

***

I go to work at Monplenbezh – in the card file division.

April 26th, 1919.

I've only just returned, and I've made a momentous vow: I'm not going to work at a job. Never. Even if it kills me.

It happened this way. Smolensky Boulevard, a building in the garden. I enter. The room is like a coffin. The walls are made of index cards: not a ray of light. The air is paper (not noble, like book paper, but ashen. Thus, the difference between a library and a card catalogue file: there you breathe the air of refuge, here of refuse!) Frighteningly elegant ladies (co-workers). In bows and "booties," They look you over – and scorn you. I sit opposite a grill-covered window, the Russian alphabet in my hands. The cards have to be separated by letters. Everything starting with A, everything with B, then by the second letters, i.e., Abrikosov, Adeyev, then by the third letters. From 9 in the morning until 5:30 in the evening. Lunch is expensive, I won't eat. Previously, they gave you this and that, now they don't give you anything. I missed the Easter rations. The directress is a short-legged, ungainly, forty-year-old cuttlefish in a corset and in spectacles – terrifying. I smell a former inspectress and a current prison guard. With caustic frankness she's astounded at my slowness: "We average two hundred cards a day. You obviously aren't familiar with this work…"

I cry. A stony face and tears like cobblestones. It probably looks more like a tin idol melting than a woman weeping. No one sees because no one raises an eyebrow: they're competing for speed.

"I've done this many cards!"

"I've done this many!"

And suddenly, I don't know why, I stand up, collect my belongings, and walk up to the directress:

"I didn't sign up for lunch today, may I run home?"

A perspicacious, bespectacled look:

"Do you live far away?"

"Nearby."

"But be back here in half an hour. This sort of thing isn't done here."

"Oh, of course."

I leave – still a statue. At Smolensky market, tears – a torrent. Some woman, frightened:

"They've robbed you, have they, Miss?"

And suddenly – laughter! Exultation! Sun full on my face! It's over. Nowhere. Never.

It wasn't I who left the card file: my legs carried me. From soul to legs: without going through the mind. This is what instinct is.

EPILOGUE
July 7, 1919.
Yesterday I gave a reading of *Fortuna* in the "Palace of Arts" (52 Povarskaya St., Sollogub's house, my former job). Of all the readers, I alone was well received – with applause (a measure not of me, but of the audience.)

In addition to me the readers were: Lunacharsky – from the Swiss poet Karl Muller, a translation; a certain Dir Tumanny – his own poems, that is, Mayakovsky – there are lots of Dir Tumannys – and it's all Mayakovsky!

Lunacharsky I saw for the first time. Jolly, ruddy, uniformly and proportionately protruding from a foppish jacket. The face of a middle-brow intellectual, the impossibility of evil. A fairly round figure, but of a "light plumpness" (like Anna Karenina). Kind of lightweightish.

He listened well, as I was told, even shushed when someone moved. But the audience wasn't bad.

I chose *Fortuna* because of the monologue at the end:

...So that serves you right, the triple lie
Of Liberty, Equality and Fraternity!

I have never read so distinctly:

And I, Lauzun, with a hand as white as snow
Raised my glass, the mob to flatter.
And I, Lauzun, claimed nobleman and woodcutter
Equal to each other in the sun's fair glow!

I have never breathed with such a sense of responsibility. (Responsibility! Responsibility! What delight can compare

87

with thee? And what glory?! A nobleman's soliloquy – to a commissar's face. That's living! Only too bad that it was addressed to Lunacharsky and not – I wanted to write "'Lenin," but Lenin wouldn't have understood anything – and not the whole of No. 2 Lubianka!)

I prefaced the reading with a kind of introduction: who Lauzun was, what he became and why he died.

At the end I stood alone, with a few casual acquaintances. If they hadn't come up I would have been completely alone. Here I'm as much a stranger as I am among the lodgers of the house where I've lived five years, as I am at work, as I once was in all seven of the Russian and foreign boarding schools and primary schools where I studied, as I have always been – everywhere.

***

I read in the same pink hall where I had once worked. The chandelier was shining (before, it had been covered up). The furniture had resurfaced. The grandmothers on the walls had recovered their sight. (The chandeliers, and the furniture, and the great-grandmothers, and the luxury items, and the utensils – down to the dishes – everything had been reclaimed from Narkomnats by the "Palace of Arts." Weep directors!)

In one of the halls – a charming marble Psyche. The guardedness of the soul and of a bather. A lot of bronze and a lot of darkness. The rooms are sated. Then, in December, they were starving and stark. This sort of house needs things. Here things are least of all materiality. A thing that is not for sale is already a sign. And behind the sign – inevitably – is a meaning. In such a house things are meanings.

***

I caressed my knights.

***

July 14, 1919.

Three days later I found out from Balmont that the director of the "Palace of Arts," Rukavishnikov, appraised my reading of *Fortuna* – an original play, never read anywhere, the reading of which lasted 45 minutes, maybe more – at 60 roubles.

I decided to refuse them – publicly – in the following words: "Take these 60 roubles for yourself – for 3 lbs. of potatoes (maybe you'll still be able to find some at 20 roub!) – or for three pounds of raspberries – or for 6 boxes of matches; and I, with my own 60 roubles, will go light a candle at the Iverskaya Virgin for the end of the regime that thus values labour."

Moscow, 1918-19

Translated by Jamey Gambrell

Autobiographical Sketches
Anna Akhmatova

The Cabin

I was born in the same year as Charlie Chaplin, Tolstoy's *Kreutzer Sonata*, the Eiffel Tower and, I think, T. S. Eliot. That summer Paris celebrated the hundredth anniversary of the fall of the Bastille in 1889. The night of my birth was, and still is, St. John Baptist's Day, the 23rd June (Midsummer Night). I was named Anna in honour of my grandmother, Anna Yegorovna Motovilova. Her mother was a descendant of Genghis Khan, the Tatar princess Akhmatova, whose surname I took as my pen-name before I realised that I intended to be a Russian poet. I was born in the dacha of Sarakini (Bolshoi Fontan was the small steam-engine's eleventh stop) not far from Odessa. This dacha (or rather, hut) stood right at the bottom of a narrow plot of land that ran downhill – beside the post office. The seashore there is very steep, and the rails of the steam railway ran along its edge.

When I was fifteen and we were living at the dacha in Lustdorf, we happened to be passing this place and my mother suggested that I should get off and take a look at the Sarakini's dacha, which I had never seen. At the entrance to the hut I said, "Some day there will be a memorial plaque here." I was not being vain. It was simply a stupid joke. My mother was upset. "Good grief, how badly I've raised you," she said.

1957

***

90

... No matter how far you looked, no one in our family had ever written poetry, there was only Anna Bunina, the first Russian poetess, who was my grandfather Erasmus Ivanovich Stogov's aunt. The Stogovs were modest landowners in the Mozhaisk district of the Moscow province, who had been exiled there for taking part in the rebellion of Marfa Posadnitsa. In Novgorod they had been richer and more notable. My forebear, the Khan Akhmat, was killed at night in his tent by a hired Russian assassin and this, as Karamzin relates, put an end to the Tatar yoke in Rus. There used to be a Procession of the Cross in commemoration of this happy day, starting out from the Sretensky Monastery in Moscow. This Akhmat is known to have been one of Genghis Khan's descendants.

One of the Akhmatova princesses, Praskovya Yegorovna, was married in the eighteenth century to the wealthy Simbirsk noble and landowner Motovilov. Yegor Motovilov was my great grandfather. His daughter Anna Yegorovna was my grandmother. She died when my mother was nine years old, and I was named Anna in her honour.

Several diamond rings and one emerald ring were made from her coronet, but I could not get her thimble on, even though I had slender fingers.

Shukhardina's House

The house was a hundred years old. It belonged to the merchant's widow Yevdokia Ivanovna Shukhardina, who looked like a lynx. I admired her strange way of dressing up when I was a child. The house stood on the corner of Shirokaya Street and Bezymyanny Lane (which was the second from the station). They said that before the railway, the house was some kind of tavern or inn which was the final halt on the way into town. I tore off the wallpaper in my yellow room (layer by layer) and the last layer was a wonderful bright red. That was the wallpaper in the inn a hundred years ago, I thought. There was a cobbler, Nevolin, living in the basement: It would all be a shot in a *mise-en-scène* in a historical film nowadays.

This house has more memories for me than all the other houses in the world. My childhood was spent here (on the lower floor), and my early youth (on the upper floor). About half of my dreams are set here. We left the house in the spring of 1905. Then it was rebuilt and it lost its old appearance. It has been gone for a long time now and they have laid out a station park or something of the kind on the site. (I was last in Tsarskoye Selo in June 1944.) The Turs' dacha is gone too ("Delight" or "New Chersonese") – it used to be three versts from Sevastopol, and I lived there every summer from the age of seven to thirteen and I earned the nick-name of "the wild girl". The Slepnyovo of 1911-17 is gone too, there is nothing left of it now but the word at the end of my poems in *White Flock* and *Plantain*, but that is probably all in the nature of things...

1957

***

...From time to time an incredibly magnificent funeral procession would make its way along Shirokaya Street from the station or towards the station: the choir (boys) sang with the voices of angels and the coffin was hidden under living greenery and flowers dying in the frost. They carried lighted lanterns, the priests swung censers, the blinkered horses trod slowly and solemnly. Behind the coffin walked guards officers, who always somehow reminded me of Vronsky's brother, that is, they had "drunken, open faces", and gentlemen in top hats. In the coaches which followed the hearse there sat grand old women and their hangers-on, as though they were waiting their own turn, and everything was like the description of the countess's funeral in *The Queen of Spades*.

And it always seemed to me (afterwards, when I used to recall these sights) that they were part of some immense funeral for the whole of the nineteenth century. This was the way they buried the last of Pushkin's younger contemporaries in the 1890s. In the blinding snow and the brilliant sunshine of Tsarskoe Selo, this was a magnificent sight, but in the yellow light of those days and the thick darkness which crept up from all sides it could also appear quite terrible, even infernal.

***

I was ten, and we were living (for one winter) in Daudel's house (on the corner of Srednyaya and Leontyev Streets in Tsarskoe Selo). A hussar officer who lived somewhere nearby used to drive out in his red, barbarous-looking automobile and ride for a block or two – then his machine would break down and the cabman would tow it home ignominiously. Nobody then believed that transport by automobile was possible, let alone by air.

***

I first tried writing my autobiography when I was eleven years old, in mama's red book with the ruled lines for recording the household expenses (1900). When I showed my notes to the grown-ups they said that I could remember when I was scarcely more than two (Pavlovsk Park, the puppy Ralph, and so on).

***

The smells of Pavlovsk Station. I am condemned to remember them for the rest of my life, like some blind deaf-mute. The first is the smoke from the antedeluvian locomotive which had brought me there – Tyarlevo, the park, the *salon de musique* (which we called in Russian "*solyony muzhik*"– the pickled peasant), the second is the polished parquet-flooring, and then there is a smell from the hairdresser's, the third is the strawberries in the station shop (Pavlovsk strawberries!), the fourth is mignonette and roses (a coolness in the stuffy heat) in the fresh, damp buttonholes that were on sale in the flower kiosk (on the left), then cigars and greasy food from the restaurant. And then there was Nastasya Filippovna's ghost (from *The Idiot*). Tsarskoe Selo was always weekdays, because it was home. Pavlovsk was always holidays, because we had to go there, because it was a long way from home.

***

People of my generation are in no danger of being saddened by returning to the scenes of our past – we have nowhere to return to… Occasionally it seems as though I could take a car and go off to see the festivities for the opening of Pavlovsk Station (when the parks were so deserted and fragrant), to the places where the shade yearns for me inconsolably, but then I begin to realise that it is impossible, that I should not try to force my way into the mansions of my memory (especially, of all things, in a petrol-driven tin-box), that I will find nothing to see and will only succeed in effacing what I see so clearly now.

An Imaginary Biography

Tsarskoe Selo in winter, the Crimea (the Turs' dacha) in summer, but it is quite impossible to convince anyone, because they all think I am Ukrainian. Firstly, because my father's name is Gorenko, secondly, because I was born in Odessa and graduated from the Fundukleyev Grammar School, thirdly, and most importantly, because Gumilyov wrote: "From the city of Kiev,/ From the Dragon's lair,/ I took not a wife, but a witch." (1910)

But I have lived less time in Kiev than in Tashkent (1941-44, when we were evacuated). One winter, when I was preparing to graduate from the Fundukleyev School, and two winters when I attended the Higher Courses for Women. But people's ability to ignore what others say knows no bounds, and the reader of this book must become accustomed to the fact that everything happened differently, at a different time and in a different place from the way he imagines it. It is a terrible thing to say, but people only see what they want to see, and only hear what they want to hear. "On the whole" they talk to themselves and almost always answer themselves, without listening to the person they are talking to. This characteristic of human nature is the basis for ninety per cent of all monstrous rumours, false reputations and piously preserved gossip. (To this day we still preserve Poletika's vicious serpentine whisperings about Pushkin!!!) I only ask those who disagree with me to recall the things they have heard about themselves.

The Wild Girl

A pagan childhood. In the neighbourhood of the dacha ("Delight" on Streletsky Bay, Chersonese) I was dubbed "the wild girl", because I went barefoot, wandered about without a hat and so forth, I dived into the open sea from the boat, went swimming during a storm and sunbathed until my skin peeled, and all this shocked the good provincial ladies of Sevastopol.

***

My childhood is as unique and magnificent as the childhood of all children everywhere…

It is both easy and difficult to speak of one's childhood. Since it is static, it is easy to describe, but this description is too frequently tainted with a sickly sweetness which is quite alien to such an important period of life as childhood. Furthermore, some people wish to appear too unhappy in their childhood, and others wish to appear too happy. In most cases both are nonsense. Children don't know enough to compare. They simply don't know if they are happy or not. As soon as a person acquires consciousness he or she enters a completely ready-made and unchanging world, and it is the most natural thing possible not to believe that this world was ever different. This initial picture remains forever in a person's soul, and there are some people who believe in it alone, but somehow manage to conceal this peculiarity. Others, in contrast, have no belief at all in the picture's reality and they also seem rather absurd when they constantly ask, "Could that really have been me?"

…At about fifty the whole of a person's life comes back to them. This accounts for some of my poems from 1940 "The Willow", "Fifteen-Year-Old Hands" which, as everyone knows, led to my being reproached with a yearning for the past.

***

Anna's room: the window looking out onto Bezymyanny Lane... which in winter was buried deep in snow, and in summer was overgrown with weeds – agrimony, luxuriant nettles and gigantic burdocks... A bed, a desk for studying, a book-stand. A candle in a brass candlestick (there was no electricity yet). In the corner – an icon. No attempt to soften the harshness of the surroundings with trinkets, embroidery or picture postcards.

***

In Tsarskoe Selo she did everything that a well brought-up young lady was supposed to do. She knew how to fold her arms in the correct formal manner, how to curtsey, how to answer an old lady's question courteously and briefly in French, she fasted and prayed during Holy Week at the school's church. Occasionally her father would take her to the opera with him (in her school dress), to the Mariinsky Theatre (a box). She visited the Hermitage and the Alexander III Museum[22]. In spring and autumn she went to Pavlovsk for the music. The Station... the museums and the art exhibitions... In winter she often skated in the park.

The parks at Tsarskoe Selo were also full of antiquity, but a quite different kind (statues). She constantly read a great deal. She was (I think) strongly influenced by the great intellectual force of the time, Knut Hamsun (*Enigmas and Mystery*): less by *Pan* and *Victoria*. The other dominant influence was Ibsen... She was a poor student in the younger classes, but later a good one. She always found the school irksome (she had few friends).

***

---

22 Now The Russian Museum.

97

I wrote my first poem when I was eleven (it was monstrous), but even before that for some reason my father used to call me a "decadent poetess"... I did not graduate from the Tsarskoe Selo Grammar School (because my family moved to the south), but from the one in Kiev (the Fundukleyev School), where I only studied for one year. Then I studied for two years at the Kiev Higher Courses for Women... All this time (with rather lengthy interruptions) I continued writing poetry, and for some unknown purpose I numbered each poem. As a curious fact I can say that, according to the manuscript, which has been preserved, "Song of the Final Meeting" was my two-hundredth poetic composition.

***

I returned north in June 1910. After Paris Tsarskoe Selo seemed quite dead. There is nothing surprising in that. But where had the life that I had known in Tsarskoe Selo vanished to in five short years? I could not find a single fellow-pupil from the school, and I did not enter the door of a single house in Tsarskoe Selo. A new life began in St. Petersburg. In September Gumilyov went away to Africa. In the winter of 1910 to 1911 I wrote the poems that made up the book *Evening*. On the 25th March Gumilyov returned from Africa and I showed him the poems...

***

For some reason these meagre verses by an empty-headed young girl are now being reprinted for the thirteenth time (if I have seen all the pirated editions). Some of them have also appeared in foreign languages. The girl herself (as far as I can recall) did not anticipate such a life for them and she hid the first copies of the journals in which they were printed "in order not to upset herself". Her distress at the appearance of *Evening* even drove her to depart for Italy (spring 1912), and sitting in the tram she would look at the other passengers and think: "How lucky they are – they're not having a book published."

Slepnyovo

At that time I used to wear a green malachite necklace and a cap of fine lace. A large icon hung in my room (the north wall) – *Christ imprisoned*. The narrow sofa was so hard that I would wake in the night and sit up for a long time before I could relax... Above the sofa hung a small portrait of Nicholas I, not the kind the snobs in St. Petersburg had, but a simple, serious portrait in the *Eugene Onegin* style ("Portraits of tsars hung on the wall"). I don't know if there was a mirror in the room, I've forgotten. The bookcase held the remains of an old library, even *Northern Flowers* and Baron Brambeus[23], and Rousseau. I was there when the war started in 1914, and I spent the last summer there (1917).

...The trace horse gave a sideways glance and arched its neck in a classical pose. The lines of verse ran along with a light and easy stride. I was waiting for a letter that did not come, that never came. I have often seen this letter in my dreams: I tore open the envelope, but either the letter is written in an unintelligible language, or I go blind...

The peasant-women went out to work in homespun sarafans, and then the old women and the uncouth country girls seemed more graceful than antique statues.

In 1911 I arrived in Slepnyovo straight from Paris, and the hunchbacked female servant in the ladies' room at the

---

23 Pen-name of Russian writer O. I. Senkovsky (1800-1858).

station in Bezhetsk, who had known everyone in Slepnyovo for ages, refused to recognise me as one of the Russian ladies and told someone there, "There's a Frenchwoman to see the Slepnyovo gentlefolk," and the Zemstvo chief Ivan Yakovlevich Dyorin – a bumpkin in glasses and a beard – could think of nothing better to say, when he found himself dying of embarrassment beside me at the dinner table, than to ask, "I expect you find it very cold here after Egypt, don't you?" The point was that he had heard the name that the local youth had given me (because I was so fabulously thin and, so it seemed to them, mysterious): the famous London mummy, which brought misfortune to all who encountered it.

Gumilyov could not endure Slepnyovo. He yawned in boredom and went off on trips without explaining where he was going. He wrote "these boring, far from golden, old world ways", and filled the Kuzmin-Karavayevs' album with mediocre verses. But nonetheless he did learn something new from it all.

I did not ride and I did not play tennis, and I only gathered mushrooms in the two orchards at Slepnyovo, and behind me Paris still blazed in its final sunset (1911)...

I was only once in Slepnyovo in winter. It was magnificent. Everything seemed to have shifted back into the nineteenth century, almost back as far as Pushkin's time. Sleighs, felt boots, bearskin rugs, immense fur-coats, the ringing silence, the snowdrifts, the diamond-brilliant snow. I met the new year of 1917 there. After the gloomy military town of Sevastopol, where I had been choking with asthma and freezing in a cold rented room, I thought I had suddenly entered the promised land. And in St. Petersburg Rasputin had already been murdered and they were expecting the revolution that had been set for 20th January (that day I dined at Nathan Altman's[24]. He

---

24 Nathan Altman (1889-1970), artist, author of the famous portrait of Akhmatova.

gave me a drawing and wrote on it: "On the day of the Russian Revolution". On another drawing (still extant) he wrote: "To the soldier's wife Gumilyova from the draughtsman Altman").

Slepnyovo for me is like an archway in architecture... At first it is small, then it grows bigger and bigger, until finally there is total freedom (if you actually go out through it).

***

In essence, no one really knows which era they live in. We did not know that after 1910 we were living on the eve of the first European war and the October Revolution.

1910 and After

1910 was the year of the crisis of Symbolism, the year Lev Tolstoy and Komissarzhevskaya died. 1911 was the year of the Chinese revolution, which changed the face of Asia, and the year of Blok's notebooks, filled with foreboding... *The Cypress Casket*... Someone recently said in my presence: "1910 and the following years were a most drab period." That is probably the way one is supposed to speak now, but anyway I replied: "Apart from anything else, that was the time of Stravinsky and Blok, Pavlova and Scriabin, Rostovtsev and Chaliapin, Meyerhold and Diaghilev."

Of course, there were a lot of people without taste then, as there are at any time (for instance, Severyanin)... By comparison with the coarse first decade of the century, the second was composed and elegant. Fate cropped the head of its second half and spilled a lot of blood in the process (the 1914 war)...

***

The twentieth century began in autumn 1914, at the same time as the war, just as the nineteenth century began with the Congress of Vienna. The calendar dates mean nothing. There is no doubt that Symbolism is a nineteenth-century phenomenon. Our revolt against Symbolism is entirely justified, because we felt that we belonged to the twentieth century and did not want to linger in the previous one...

The City

The "beauty" of St. Petersburg was a conjecture of the "World of Art" group who also, as a matter of fact, discovered mahogany furniture. I can recall St. Petersburg from a very early time – the nineties. It is essentially Dostoevsky's St. Petersburg. It is pre-tram St. Petersburg, mounted, horse-drawn, rumbling and squeaking, boating, hung from head to foot with signboards which pitilessly obscured the architecture of the buildings. Its impression was particularly fresh and sharp after the quiet, fragrant Tsarskoe Selo. Clouds of pigeons inside the Gostiny Dvor[25], with large icons in gilt frames and icon-lamps permanently lit in the corner niches of the galleries. The Neva covered with ships and boats. A lot of foreign voices on the streets.

A lot of the buildings painted red (like the Winter Palace), crimson or pink and none of these beige and grey colours that nowadays merge so dismally with the frosty mist or the Leningrad twilight.

At that time there were still a lot of magnificent wooden houses (mansions of the gentry) on Kamennostrovsky Avenue and around the Tsarskoe Selo station. They were pulled down for firewood in 1919. Even finer were the two-storey

---

25 A big department store.

nineteenth-century mansions, some of them built by great architects. "Fate dealt with them badly"[26] – they were built over and extended in the 20s. But then there was almost no greenery in the St. Petersburg of the 90s. When my mother came to visit me for the last time in 1927, then her populist reminiscences of the "Narodnaya Volya" organisation brought back memories of St. Petersburg, not in the 90s, but in the 70s (her youth), and she was astonished beyond measure at the amount of greenery. And that was only the beginning! In the nineteenth century there was granite and water.

***

I have just been astonished to read in the journal *Zvezda* (an article by Lev Uspensky) that Empress Maria Fyodorovna rode in a golden carriage. What gibberish! – There were golden carriages, but they were only supposed to appear on great occasions – coronations, weddings, christenings, the first reception of an ambassador. Maria Fyodorovna's equipage was distinguished only by the medals on the coachman's chest. How strange that such nonsense can be invented after only forty years. What will happen after a hundred?

1957

More on the City

It is hard to believe your eyes when you read that the stairways of St. Petersburg always smelt of burnt coffee. They often had tall mirrors, and sometimes carpets. Not a single St. Petersburg stairway smelt of anything but the scent of the ladies who had passed by and the cigars of the gentlemen. Probably the person had in mind the so-called "tradesman's entrance"

---

26 A line from *Borodino* by Lermontov.

(which is nowadays, by and large, the only one) – that could certainly smell of anything at all, because the doors of all the kitchens opened onto it. For instance, pancakes at Shrovetide, mushrooms and vegetable oil at Lent, Neva smelt in May. When they were preparing something with a strong smell, the cooks would leave open the doors onto the back staircase –"to let the fumes out" (that is what they called it), but nevertheless, the back staircases smelt most frequently, alas, of cats.

The sounds of the St. Petersburg yards. In the first place, the sound of firewood thrown into the cellar. Organ grinders ("Sing, swallow, sing and calm my heart..."), knife grinders ("Knives and scissors to grind!"), old-clothes men ("Old robes, old robes!") who were always Tatars. Tinsmiths. "Get your Vyborg rolls here!" The wells of the yards had a fine echo.

Thin mist over the roofs. St. Petersburg's Dutch stoves. St. Petersburg's fireplaces were a futile endeavour. Fires in St. Petersburg during heavy frosts. The ringing of bells drowned by the sounds of the city. The beat of the drum that always summoned up the idea of an execution. Sleighs swinging against posts on the humpbacked bridges, which are now almost no longer humpbacked. The final branch on the islands always reminded me of Japanese prints. A horse's face encrusted with icicles almost resting on your shoulder. And then what a smell of wet leather there was in a horse-cab with the top up when it rained. I composed almost all of *Rosary* in these surroundings, and all I did at home was write down the finished verses...

***

...And two windows in the Mikhailovsky palace, which were still the same as they were in 1801, and it seemed as though Pavel was still being murdered behind them, and the

Semyonovsky barracks, and the Semyonovsky parade ground, where Dostoevsky waited for death, and Fontanka house – a whole symphony of horrors… "The Sheremetyev lime trees, the calls of the house spirits…"

The Summer Gardens… First – fragrant and frozen in the immobility of July, and second – under water in 1924, and the Summer Gardens again, cut to pieces by the foul-smelling slit-trenches (1941), and the Field of Mars – the parade ground where they trained the new recruits in 1915 (the drum), and the Field of Mars – an allotment already dug up and half-overgrown (1921), "beneath a cloud of crows' wings", and the gates through which they took the members of the Narodnaya Volya group out to execution.

And not far from them, Muruzi's house (the corner of Liteiny Street) where I saw Gumilyov for the last time in my life (the day that Annenkov drew my portrait). This is all my Leningrad.

***

In the 1920s Tsarskoe Selo was a messy sight. All the fences had been burnt. Rusty bedsteads from First World War infirmaries stood over the open manholes of the water mains, grass was growing in the streets, cocks and goats wandered about crowing and bleating loudly. For some reason the goats were all called Tamara. On the gates of the recently magnificent home of Count Stenbock-Fermor hung a huge, resplendent sign: "Mating Station". But in the autumns on Shirokaya Street there was the same sharp scent from the oaks that had witnessed my youth, and the crows on the cathedral crosses still shouted to me the same message that I had heard as I crossed Cathedral Square on my way to the school, and the statues in Tsarskoe Selo's parks still looked at me as they had during the previous decade. Sometimes I would recognise natives of Tsarskoe Selo in the tattered and terrible little figures I saw. The Gostiny Dvor Department Store was closed…

***

…In 1936 I begin writing again, but my manner has changed, my voice sounds different. And life leads up by the bridle a Pegasus that somehow resembles the Pale Horse of the Apocalypse or the Black Horse of verses still not written at that time. (…) There can be no return to the first manner. What is better and what is worse, it is not for me to judge. 1940 is the apogee. The verses come continuously, stepping on each other's toes in their breathless hurry and sometimes, probably, not good.

From a Letter to ***
(In place of a foreword)
In the first half of March 1940 verses totally unrelated to anything else began to appear in the margins of my drafts. This was particularly the case with the drafts of the poem "The Vision", which I wrote the night that Vyborg was stormed and the armistice was announced.

The meaning of these lines was obscure to me at the time, even, if you like, strange, for quite a long time they showed no promise of forming into a unified whole and seemed to be quite ordinary stray lines, their hour had not yet struck and they had not yet been cast into the furnace from which they emerged as you see them here.

In the autumn of that same year I wrote another three non-lyrical pieces, and at first I wanted to link them with *The Woman of Kitezh*, to write a book called *Little Narrative*

Poems, but one of them, *Poem Without a Hero*, broke loose, ceased to be little, and most importantly, became absolutely intolerant of company: two others – Dostoevsky's "Russia" and "Fifteen-Year-Old Hands" suffered a different fate: they apparently perished in the siege of Leningrad, and what I have restored from memory here in Tashkent is hopelessly incomplete. Therefore *The Woman of Kitezh* remained, as our fathers used to say, in proud isolation.

***

In Tashkent the melancholy of "evacuation sickness" led me to write "The House Was a Hundred Years Old". In Tashkent, in the delirium of typhoid fever, I kept listening to my heels clattering across Tsarskoe Selo's Gostiny Dvor Department Store – I was on my way to school. The snow around the cathedral had turned dark, the ravens were calling, the bells were ringing, they were burying someone.

***

I have started to write a biography on several occasions, but with varying degrees of success, as they say. The last time was in 1946... As far as I recall, it was not very detailed, but it included my 1944 impressions – Post-Siege Leningrad, The Three Lilac Trees – of Tsarskoe Selo and a description of a trip at the end of July to the front at Terioki, to read my poetry to the soldiers. It is difficult for me to recall them now. But all the rest has hardened into stone in my memory, it will only disappear when I do.

***

How long ago it all is now... The first day of the war, which until quite recently was so very close, and Victory Day, which only yesterday seemed to be just behind us, and 14th August 1946... And now it is all history. Just recently there were translations that I finished and those I was still doing, there was my stay at Zamoskvorechye[27], and the young pines that are now swaying furiously against the backdrop of the white night.

"It is very northerly here – and I have chosen autumn to be my friend this year," I wrote last year, and how far away it already is, and I was just about to describe the 1890s!

1957

***

On the book which I shall never write, but which already exists anyway, and which people deserve to have. At first I wanted to write it all, now I have decided to insert a few pieces of it into the tale of my own life and the destiny of my generation. This book was conceived a long time ago, and some of its sub-plots are known to my friends.

***

Who would have believed that I was meant to last so long, and why did I not know it? My memory has become incredibly acute. The past presses in on me, demanding something. What? The dear shades of the distant past almost speak to me. Perhaps this is the last chance for the felicity which people call oblivion to pass them by. From somewhere words emerge that were spoken half a century ago and which I have never once recalled throughout those fifty years. It would be strange to explain all this simply by my summer solitude and my

---

27 Ardov's house where Akhmatova usually stayed when in Moscow.

108

nearness to nature, which has long ceased to remind me of anything but death...

***

For so many days now I have been tinkering with this biography. I am beginning to realise how very boring it is to write about oneself and how very interesting it is to write about people and things (St. Petersburg, the smell of Pavlovsk Station, the sailboats at Hungerburg. The port of Odessa at the end of the forty-day strike). One has to put in as little of oneself as possible. Definitely the 9th January[28] and Tsushima[29] were a shock that would last a lifetime, and as the first shock, particularly terrible.

***

... I am afraid that everything I am writing belongs to that dismal genre, *Faust's Daughter* (cf. Daudet's *Jack*), that is, quite simply, none of it really exists. And the more people praise this wretched, barren mumbling, the less I believe them. This is because I myself see and hear so much behind these words that it entirely blots out the words themselves.

22nd November 1957, Moscow

***

To manage to write down a hundredth part of one's thoughts would be true happiness.

---

28 "The Bloody Sunday" of 1905, when a peaceful crowd of people were shot down in front of the Winter Palace.
29 The scene of the Russian Navy defeat in the Russian-Japanese war.

***

However, a book, the cousin to *Safe Conduct*[30] and *The Noise of Time*[31], is bound to appear. I am afraid that in comparison with its resplendent cousins it will seem a sloven, a simpleton, a Cinderella, etc.

Both of them (Boris and Osip) wrote their books when they had scarcely reached maturity, when everything they recall was not so fantastically distant. But it is almost impossible not to feel dizzy when looking down on the 1890s from the elevation of the mid-twentieth century.

***

I have not the slightest intention of reviving the genre of the "physiological essay" and burdening the book with an infinite number of unimportant details.

***

As far as memoirs in general are concerned, I wish to caution the reader that in any case twenty per cent of memoirs are fraudulent. The wilful introduction of direct speech should be declared a criminal act, because it migrates with ease from memoirs to respectable works of criticism and biography. Continuity is another deception. The human memory is constructed like a searchlight, so that it illuminates separate moments while leaving all around in impenetrable darkness. Even a person with a magnificent memory may and should forget some things.

---

30 Boris Pasternak's *Autobiography* (1931).
31 Osip Mandelshtam's *Autobiography* (1925).

***

It makes no difference where one starts from, the middle, the end or the beginning. For instance, I want to start now from the fact that when I was in the Fifth Soviet Hospital (Moscow) in 1951 after a heart attack, and was probably under sedation, I constantly saw before my (closed) eyes these little green houses with the glass-fronted terraces (I live in one of them). These houses did not yet exist then – they were built in 1955, but when I saw them, I instantly recalled where I had seen them before. That is why I wrote in Epilogue:

I live in a strange house I have dreamed, Where, perhaps, I have died...

"*Pro domo mea*"[32] I can say that I have never left Poetry, never, either flown or crawled away – from it, although I have repeatedly been invited to sink by heavy blows of the oars on my numb hands clutching the side of the boat. I confess that at times the air around me has lost all its moisture and become quite impervious to sound, that instead of a joyous splash, the bucket lowered into the well has given out a dry clang as it struck stone, and in general a suffocation could last for years. "Acquainting words", "colliding words"– nowadays that is all quite ordinary. Thirty years later an act of daring sounds like a banality. There is another way – precision – and even more important, to make each word to stand in its own place in the line as though it has been there for a thousand years, but the reader hears it for the very first time. This way is very difficult, but when it is successful, people say: "This is about me, it is as though I had written it myself." I myself (very rarely) experience this feeling when reading or listening to other people's poetry. It is like a kind of jealousy, but a noble one.

---

32 About myself (Lat.)

X asked me whether it was difficult or easy to write poetry. I answered that either someone dictates it, and then it is very easy, or they do not dictate – and it is simply impossible.
1959

***

A poet has his own secret attitude to everything that he has ever written, and it often contradicts what the reader thinks about one or another poem.

For instance, the lines I really like now from my first book *Evening* (1912) are:

Intoxicated by a voice
That sounds like yours.

I even think that a lot of my poetry has grown out of these lines.

On the other hand, I like very much a poem that was never continued in any way, the obscure and quite untypical: "I have come to take your place, sister… " – I love the lines:

The tambourine's beat has long been stilled.
And I know that you fear the silence.

But the things the critics still frequently mention, even today, leave me absolutely indifferent.

Poems are still divided (for the author) into those which the poet can remember writing, and those which appear to have generated themselves. In the first the author is doomed to hear the voice of the violin which once helped him to write them, and in the second the rumble of the railway carriage that hindered him. Poems may be associated with the smells of scent and flowers. The sweetbrier in the cycle *The Sweetbrier Blossoms* actually did smell cloyingly sweet at a particular moment associated with this cycle.

However, this does not only apply to my own poetry. In

Pushkin I hear the waterfalls of Tsarskoe Selo ("these living waters"), which I saw in the final days of their existence.

From My Diary
24th December 1959 (European Christmas Eve)

... A light snowstorm. A calm, very quiet evening. T. left early – I have been alone all the time, the telephone has not rung. The poems come constantly and I, as always, drive them away until I hear a genuine line. The whole of December was a month of composition, despite a constant pain in my heart and frequent attacks, but "Michal" still will not come right, that is, I can only glimpse the less important things. But I will master it, nevertheless.

Attempts to write my memoirs summon up unexpectedly deep layers of the past, my memory grows almost painfully acute: voices, sounds, smells, people, a brass cross on a pine tree in Pavlovsk Park, and so on without end. For instance, I remembered what Vyacheslav Ivanov said when I first read him my poetry, and that was in 1910, i.e. fifty years ago.

The poetry has to be protected from all this.

In recent days I also have the feeling that somewhere something is happening to me. In connection with what is still unclear. Either in Moscow or somewhere else, something is drawing me in, like the hot air of some immense oven or a ship's propeller.

On the 29th Irina and I are going to the Writers' Retreat in Komarovo – only for ten days. Perhaps I shall get my breath back, most likely not.

... Everyone knows there are people who feel spring coming on from Christmas. Today it seems to me that I felt it, even though it was not winter yet. This is such a marvellous and joyful feeling that I am afraid to spoil it by telling anyone.

And it seems to me that I am connected with my Korean rose, my demoniac hydrangea and the silent, black life of their roots. Are they cold now? Is there enough snow? Does the moon look down on them? All this is vitally important to me, and even in sleep I do not forget them.

The Birches
In the first place, no one has ever seen such birches. It frightens me to remember them. It is an obsession. Something menacing and tragic, like "The Pergamum Altar", magnificent and quite inimitable. I think there should be ravens. And there is nothing better on earth than these birches, huge, mighty, ancient like druids, but still more ancient. Three months have gone by and I still cannot come to my senses, like yesterday, and in any case I do not want this to be a dream. I need them to be real.
1959-1961

***

It is well known that anyone who has ever left Russia has taken his final day with him. I recently had occasion to verify this when I was reading Di Sarra's article about me. He writes that all of my verse derives from the poetry of Mikhail Kuzmin. No one has thought that for about forty-five years. But Vyacheslav Ivanov, who left St. Petersburg forever in 1912, took with him an idea of me which was somehow linked with Kuzmin, simply because Kuzmin wrote the foreword to my *Evening* (1912). It was the last thing that Vyacheslav Ivanov could recall and of course, when they asked him about me abroad, he presented me as Kuzmin's follower. In this way I have acquired a wraith-like double or werewolf figure who has dwelt peacefully in someone's idea of things all these decades, never coming into contact with me, my real life, etc.

The question which automatically arises is how many of

114

these doubles or werewolves are at large in the world, and what will be their final role?

***

Of all these (none-too honest) devices one stands out: the desire to single out from all that I have written my first book (*Rosary*), declare it my *Livre de chevet*[33] and instantly trample the rest under foot, i.e. to make of me a mixture of Sergei Gorodetsky (Yar), i.e. a poet without any artistic history – and Francoise Sagan – a "sweet, honest" little girl.

The point is that *Rosary* came out in March 1914 and it only had a life of two and a half months. At that time the literary season closed at the end of May. When we returned from the country we were met by war. A second edition of about a thousand copies was required about a year later.

The case of *White Flock* was more or less the same. It came out in September 1917 and because there was no transport it was not even sent to Moscow. However, a second edition was required a year later, just as in the case of *Rosary*. A third edition was printed by Alyansky[34] in 1922. Then one appeared in Berlin (the fourth). That was the last, because after my trip to Moscow and Kharkov in 1924 (...) they stopped printing my work. And that went on until 1939 (...)

The two volume editions (Petrograd) that had been printed by Hessen's publishing house, was destroyed, the abuse ceased to be episodic and became systematic and planned (Lelevich in the journal *On Guard*, Pertsov in *The Life of Art*, etc.), reaching force twelve at times, i.e. a lethal gale. They would

---

33 Favourite book.
34 S. M. Alyansky (1891-1974) – in the 1920s director of Alkonost Publishers.

not give me any translations (apart from the letters of Rubens, 1930). However, my first Pushkin work (*Pushkin's Final Folktale*) was published in *Zvezda*. The ban only applied to verse.

That is the naked truth. And this is what I now learn about myself from the foreign press: apparently after the Revolution I completely stopped writing poetry, and did not write any until 1940. But why were my books not republished and my name never mentioned without being accompanied by foul language? Evidently the desire to immure me in the second decade of the century is irresistible, and possesses some allure which I fail to understand.

***

I listened to the Dragon-fly waltz from Shostakovich's ballet suite. It is a marvel. The very spirit of elegance dances in it. Is it possible to do with words what he does with sounds?
November 1961

***

And if in the twentieth century Poetry is destined to flourish here, in my native land, then I may make bold to state that I have always been a joyful and trustworthy witness... And I am sure that we still are not fully aware of what a magical choir of poets we possess, that the Russian language is young and supple, that we have only been writing poetry for a very short time as yet, that we love it and believe in it.

A Talk on Leningrad Radio in Late September 1941

Dear fellow-citizens, mothers, wives and sisters of Leningrad:

For more than a month now the enemy has been threatening to overrun our city and inflict upon it mortal wounds. The enemy threatens the city of Peter the Great, the city of Lenin, the city of Pushkin, Dostoevsky and Blok – our city, with its great tradition of culture and labour – with death and disgrace. Like all Leningraders, I am horror-struck at the thought that our city, my city, may be trampled into the dirt. My entire life has been linked with Leningrad – it was in Leningrad that I became a poet, Leningrad is the very air that my verses breathe...

At this moment, like all of you, I cling to the unshakeable faith that Leningrad shall never belong to the fascists. And I feel my faith strengthened when I see the women of Leningrad defending their city with simple courage and maintaining its normal human life...

Our descendants will pay honour to every mother who lived during this Patriotic War, but their gaze will be drawn as by a magnet, to the women of Leningrad, who stood on the roofs as the bombs fell, holding their hooks and tongs, ready to defend the city against the threat of fire; the women of the Leningrad civil-defence corps, who went to the help of the wounded while the ruined buildings blazed around them...

No, a city which has bred women like these cannot be defeated. We Leningraders may be suffering hardship and danger, but we know that the entire country and everyone in it is with us. We sense their alarm at our plight, their love, their efforts to help and support us. We thank them and we promise always to stand firm and never to lose heart...

September 1941

Translated by Andrew Bromfield

Delusion of the Will
Lydia Ginzburg

In Lieu of a Foreword

There is a type of consciousness, a mode of perception, which may be termed immanent. People of this stamp are free of unconditional, external values. Their values (for a person cannot act without values) are either the rules imposed on them by society or derive from their own inclinations and abilities. We find this type of consciousness all around the globe, and so the question of moral victory or defeat in the struggle against its ruinous incoherence is a global one.

This immanent consciousness finds it nearly impossible to reject the crude spatial conception of time against which Bergson had fought. Inner life, as it perceives it, is not a coherent chain of interpenetrating elements, but a set of solitary moments automatically partitioned by time. In fact, this conception of time cannot even serve the purposes of hedonism, because the moment it regards as a unit has either yet to emerge or has already elapsed; no moment is ever accessible to empathy. Ultimately, then, this conception rejects the very pleasure in the present for which it had rejected everything else. But man, who is never satisfied, is dissatisfied even with the knowledge that oblivion will relieve his pain. There is something even more offensive in the transience, the pointlessness of suffering than in the momentary nature of gratification – a kind of disrespect for mankind.

The immanent consciousness cannot link up the elements of life – yet it fares no better when confronted with death. If empiricism wishes to be honest but, at the same time, resist howling in fear, its only option is to say, with Epicurus: "Death does not concern us, because as long as we exist, death is not here. And when it does come, we no longer exist."

The immanent consciousness cannot comprehend pleasure, which falls through the crack between the past and the present – yet it finds no more sense in suffering, which passes without a trace. It cannot relate to death, because death does not concern it. It is always empty – like a sieve placed under running water.

The basic facts of social life – domestic, legal, moral – are facts of connection, which presuppose the reality of the past. This alone can justify guilt, retribution, indelible offence, honour and the loss of honour, merit, and duty...

Hedonism may cast out the concept of connection – but this concept will return to it from the other end, mercilessly proving its veracity. And if the egoistic consciousness can sometimes do without a sense of duty or honour, it will not manage to avoid remorse...

The objects of remorse, like the subjects of history or of art, belong at once to the present and to the past. (If they were not admitted into the present, remorse would not be so painful; if they did not belong to the past, it would not be so irreparable.) Remorse is one of the most powerful mechanisms of imagination and memory, generating representations that are detailed, unalterable, and horrifying precisely because it had once been in our power to alter what they represent. Indeed, remorse is inseparable from the sense of unexercised power over reality. It is the guilt and tragedy of the will. Schopenhauer conceived of remorse as the torture of a will that has failed to act as it wished. Comprehending its unity with others, the deep-seated will has failed to recognise itself. It has been led astray by the superficial desires of spite, greed, vanity, cowardice, and laziness. One of the formulations of remorse is Eugene Onegin's "I'd curbed myself of that sweet habit." Why, why had he curbed himself? In order to buy time – to understand his desire just a little bit more clearly. No aspect of remorse is more heart-rending than these little bits, these almosts.

The life and death of someone close to us is the very best food for remorse. This owes to the fact that our attitude towards that person – our indifference, irritation, confusion – could not have been the true expression of our will, but only its error. It also owes to the fact that we had undeniable power over this person's life – the life of someone who had loved us. The contours of their life could have been altered, had we only directed our will correctly... It's like a precious object that we'd held in our hands but tossed aside out of sheer ignorance. The structure of their lamentable life is now paralleled by a second structure, replete with imaginary, unrealised amendments. The person is no longer here, but both structures – the one that was and the one that should have been – continue their incomprehensible coexistence within us, and perhaps even beyond us. We bear the guilt for all we would have liked to correct but had not corrected, as a creator bears guilt for what remains uncreated.

Below is the story of one such guilt – the guilt of a man we'll call N.

Whenever this subject occurred to him, it came in a long current of broken thoughts. And it was never clear whether this was a new current or the very same current that had buzzed in his head during those first few days after his father's death.

Each time, for some reason, the buzz would start with the inrush of the neighbouring house's light yellow walls (he was standing on the other side of the yard in the suburb where all this had transpired), and then the rest would follow: a swarm of representations, the only point of which was to make him suffer. Two forces directed this current – remorse (when the representations began their work, they painfully penetrated deeper and deeper), and logical, dull self-justification.

Yes, of course, there were objective reasons for his neglect: fatigue – due to poverty, to various failures, to miserable family nonsense. And then that love (it all came together so inconveniently…), that love – that attempt at real, honest-to-goodness life. By that time, of course, this attempt was already succumbing to disaster. He kept shattering everything, then clutching at the wreckage as it swam away; and anything that threatened to distract him from this activity was unbearably irritating.

"Ah, yes!" says remorse. "You were irritated… You acted like all abstract, fanciful people, who, deep down, don't believe in the reality of another's life. You accepted responsibilities without understanding their everyday implications. You dragged the old man away from the place he'd grown accustomed to, from work, in order to calm your own delicate nerves. Your nerves couldn't stand worrying at a distance. And then, after you made such a mess of his life, you still wanted to live entirely for yourself – so you began to squeeze him out, to ignore him, to grow bitter. Oh, the lamentable delusion of egoists! 'I'm so close that I can, at any moment, stop the pain I'm causing…' A criminal illusion of correctability."

"But," self-justification responds in a dull voice, "a man – a very lonely man – has the right to build something for himself, to build the semblance of marital life… He had taken so little for himself, in the narrow sense of the word. There were days when he hadn't had enough to eat. (Once he showed up there, hungry, when his aunt was paying the old man a visit; the two of them were having coffee and some kind of delicious vegetable stew, and this contrast relieved his conscience in the most pleasant way.) He even rubbed the nail off his big toe; his painful shoes just wouldn't wear out, and he couldn't bring himself to throw them away."

But remorse isn't so easily deterred; it wants to sink deeper and deeper. It replies: what's all this illiterate talk about yourself in the narrow sense of the word? Don't try to impress me with the generosity of a man who went hungry in the narrow sense and, at the same time, bought chocolate that was, in the broad sense, for himself.

It all comes down to one of those eternal clashes: on the one hand, a person – close but no longer necessary; on the other, the loved one – and whatever you do for her, you do for yourself (therein lies the broad sense). This is the age-old struggle between duty and feeling, in which feeling secures its victory by employing irritation – by entangling all the objects of duty in irritation. But retribution, in this case, is also standard. When accounts are being settled, it turns out that once the loved one has ceased to be loved, her fate no longer concerns the lover in the slightest; for him, heavy, immediate objectivity now lies only in the state of the unnecessary close one, because he himself had created that state, and nothing, no trick in the world, will free him of it. And when the fog of selfishness and cowardice finally lifts – always too late – a person discovers within himself the toxic source of pity.

Suffering doesn't always inspire pity. It may inspire disgust, horror, or awe. Pity should not be confused with the healthy, active principle of compassion. It is instead a particular experience of another's humiliation secretly applied to oneself. Therein lies the individual and shameful sense of pity, which forces a chaste person to shudder. Pity can verge on disgust or contempt, if one believes that its object has lost all value (a pitiful person). When it comes to an object we truly love, such a notion is simply unacceptable; it is replaced by the notion that the object's value has been unjustly depreciated, and it is now our duty to restore and protect that value. In these cases, pity verges on tenderness – and as an exercise in erotic tenderness, it may even be pleasant. The common folk have a saying about this: to pity is to love.

Like the tragic, the comic, and the sublime, the pitiful refashions the material of reality for its own purposes, employing explicitly aesthetic devices. Pity makes use of selection, symbols, analogies, and, in particular, detail – a wrinkled neck, a missing tooth, a hole in the clothes... Consider anthropomorphic pity for the trampled flower, with its delicate sullied petals and the cloudy drop oozing from its torn stem... Or the verbal symbolism of a felled tree – its sap that drips like tears and blood, its dead branches. Or the tragedy of a bitch whose puppies have been drowned, which is developed into an analogue of a human mother's tragedy, obscuring the fact that, in a couple of days, the dog will have forgotten all about its puppies.

Pity is not determined by the empirical, logical content of its object, but by its expressiveness; the decisive – and, from the logical point of view, entirely meaningless – factors are spatial and temporal proximity, detail, and clarity. It is impossible to sympathise in full measure with the suffering of those who lived in Egypt under the pharaohs, or even with the suffering of our contemporaries in New Zealand. But when we learn that someone was crushed by a tram on Liteyny Avenue last night, we receive the news as an emotional fact, although that unknown someone is, for us, logically equivalent to any victim of Egyptian tyranny. And if that unknown someone should be hit by a tram in front of our very eyes – our sympathy materialises to an unrecognisable degree. But pity may require additional factors; in order for us to feel the characteristic sting of pity in the muddle of horror, disgust, and pain, it is perhaps necessary that the person hit by the tram should have been carrying home a bag of apples; that the paper bag should have been soaked with blood and that an apple should have crunched under the boot of the approaching policeman.

If the source of pity happens to be an artistic fact, the effect loses none of its intensity – on the contrary... And this reveals the particularly contemplative and fruitless nature of pity. Art expresses and excites pity with such perfection because only art can measure off the necessary materials and then freeze the situation. Turgenev, who failed at many things, succeeded in depicting the elderly Bazarov couple at their son's grave. But could he have afforded to show the elderly Bazarovs at home afterwards, drinking tea and squabbling with their household? Hundreds of pitiful literary endings are based on the false stabilisation of a given moment. The true tragedy of reality, which few authors aside from Tolstoy and Proust seem to have understood, is that sorrow is no more lasting than joy... If the elderly couple that have lost their son were to have tea, or even go to the cinema, this wouldn't interfere with our sense of compassion, which is healthy and aspires to help. But pity is another matter... Pity relies on an eternal tear, half-dried in a senile wrinkle.

Pity that hasn't been purified by art is an excitation of the nerves and the imagination; this feeling, with its aesthetic shamelessness, can arise in very foolish, selfish, and even cruel people.

But pity isn't only an emotion; it is a social fact. And as a social fact it requires two conditions: the sense of distance and the sense of responsibility. In order to sympathise painfully with another's deficiency, one must, at that moment, be free of this deficiency. A legless person who meets another legless person might feel any number of things – ranging from anger to active compassion – but never pity, which always entails some degree of surprise, of incomprehension, of a view from the outside. It may be that each experience of pity contains a bit of that pain aroused by the sight of a blind, shivering human stump lying on the sidewalk next to a plate for donations; we pass by it, unable to comprehend how it lives and perceives the world – not daring, not wanting to comprehend – consoling ourselves with the thought that it must live and perceive the world in a manner wholly different from ours... We can pity someone who suffers from the same deficiency as us only if we sense a real or imagined distance from them. On a sinking ship or in prison the strong man pities the weak because he believes that the latter has it worse; the lover pities the beloved, because, for him, the beloved's value is greater than his own, and in her deficiency he finds a suffering separate from his own torment. Pity for oneself is always partly a metaphor or a game, a paradoxical posture of regarding oneself from the outside.

As we approach another, we often lose our sense of pity. We lose our incomprehension, lose the distance created by the aesthetic work of pity, which builds itself an object and cares nothing for facts that do not fit its design. Pity is imposed from without, like a form, on empirical chaos. From within, one sees too many things. Where we had expected to find the pitiful, we suddenly find indifference, anger, resistance, or inappropriate contentment (pitiful people may be completely unaware that they are pitiful). We have come too close and are surrounded by the empirical diversity of the inner life, which isn't subject to contemplative selection, which lacks subtle concreteness and detail – those age-old stimuli of pity.

If a man driving by in a car sees a row of prisoners trudging along under guard, he pities them momentarily and, at the same time, tries to dismiss the situation as impossible for himself personally and for life in general. But say the circumstances change and the man finds himself among those prisoners; it turns out that he can go on living, and can even have certain goals in life, certain interests. Having lost the sense of disparity, he loses his pity for those like him. His own suffering neutralises his conscience; the man considers himself free of the onerous obligation to pity.

But distance between the subject and object is, in itself, insufficient for the development of pity. Another, almost converse, condition is required: the object, which is remote from the subject, must nonetheless have some relation to it. No one would waste emotion on an entirely alien object.

Responsibility can take different forms. The responsibility of power often leads not to pity, but to cruelty. This is because power generalises people; for those in power, the boundaries between individual existences dissolve. The development of pity requires something else: not power as a social reality, with its practically unavoidable cruelty, but power as a psychological possibility, with its characteristic fantasies of generosity.

The rich pitied the poor because they could share their property with them. The strong pitied the weak because they had the power to fight for social justice. The wise pitied the foolish... The ability to help became the duty to help, just as the opportunity to create becomes the irresistible need to do so.

People of the nineteenth century wished to have some relation to everything in the world. They believed it possible to correct social ills by social means; this conviction endowed them with a sense of duty and, above all, a sense of guilt. Oh, how they could pity! In French romanticism, their pity reached the level of hysteria, and in Russian populism, the level of martyrdom. The wider the gap between the pitying and the pitied, the more feverish the attempts of the pitying to fill that gap with penance. Did the pitied always profit by this? Regardless, the pitying always gained the sense of moral adequacy, which separated them from the unpitying, who were ignorant of their social guilt.

The new century brought with it new people – fragile, unhappy, unable to distance themselves from misfortune.

They knew that they were prey to anything that could possibly befall a human being. Many of them were pitiless, because they related to nothing. They could not be of help and, therefore, felt no desire to help. They were already punished and, therefore, no longer considered themselves guilty.

Pity is not proportional to the number of misfortunes; if anything, it is inversely proportional. We can only absorb a limited amount of another's suffering. Anything beyond that amount (perhaps this is a protective reflex of the spirit) only dulls the senses. Blood, war, thousands of deaths, deep-rooted fear, catastrophe – this is the school of indifference; the suffering of those nearby is converted into a mere statistic, like a story of life under the Egyptian pharaohs.

And don't repeat the old formula in a new form: what are you writing and shedding tears about when the world is on the verge of unimaginable disasters?

The theme of war is not only the theme of death infinitely

multiplied, the horror of war is not only an amplified fear of death, and the heroism of war is not only an intensified effort to overcome this fear. War encompasses a multitude of elements other than death. It encompasses almost all of reality, which it transfigures, but not beyond recognition. However, this is a different topic, which, unfortunately, still lies ahead.

We must remember that a thousand deaths is a figure. The death of a single person is concrete. A thousand deaths are horrifying precisely because a single person's death is repeated a thousand times.

Through the usual catastrophe, through the fortitude of those who have adapted themselves to it, through the round figures of newspaper reports, we must return to a single death, rich in detail, drawn out – the death of Ivan Ilych – either because the death of a single person is clear in its concreteness, or because only this death is incomprehensible.

For many months N was besieged by the cruel operations of memory. It all came together – piling up, one on top of the other: his responsibility for a life he had the power to alter, but chose not to alter, and the expressiveness of this pitiful life.

Some people are possessed of a tremendous life-force. Just as a healthy body expels all substances that are harmful to its existence, so too do these people's psyches isolate and eject all that might destroy them. These are not always hard, strong-willed people; at the lowest level, they are simply tenacious (there are many women of this sort), endowed with a naïve, indiscriminate desire to live, and to live as well as possible. They distort and dissemble, lie in order to hide their hurt, and boast irrepressibly. Do not disdain boasting – it's the expression of an assertive, optimistic life principle; at worst, it's a show of resistance.

N's aunt (the old man's sister) happens to be an excellent

example of this type. After paying someone a visit, she'll tell you how warmly she was greeted by the maid, the host's child, the cat, the wife of the building manager; but as to how she was treated by the hosts themselves – by her own friends – that she won't say, because it goes without saying. Coming back from the club, which she attends on her son's pass, she'll tell you that the doorman bowed to her and gave her a broad smile – doubtful, since she only tips him fifteen kopecks, but that's how she sees things. When she heads to the public baths after a three-day break, she sees the nurse and the two bath attendants nod to her and hears them say, "Why did you stay away so long?" In her passionate self-assertion, she sees things smiling at her, encouraging her, making way for her. But if she should meet with anything hurtful, anything bad – be it a communal kitchen squabble or her son's evident disregard of her existence – she won't say a word; the gossipy old dame, whose loose talk always causes trouble for her nearest and dearest, won't say a word. She will stubbornly, warily conceal her humiliation.

That's why the aunt was offended and irritated by everything her brother said. The first thing the old man would have noticed was that the doorman despised him, because he'd only tipped him fifteen kopecks – but he simply didn't have any more to give. This is typical of people with a weak life-current. Such people are slow and hesitant, because only strong impulses can motivate one to choose, quickly and accurately, among a multitude of objects; they are unsociable, because they lack the will to attain influence and power, which attracts others; and they are stingy, because they fear the future and are unsure of their ability to cope with it. In their ideal form, they are bachelors, because family responsibilities are the strongest motivation to fight, to act, to make decisions.

The old man once had a wife, but the marriage didn't last long; their only son went to live with her and would only pay his father visits. (She died when the son was still a young man.) The son loved his father, loved the man's strange bachelor existence and the atmosphere of camaraderie and male trust the two had established between themselves. The father had settled into a way of life that suited him particularly well: it allowed him to avoid both utter loneliness and the fullness of everyday responsibility. In later years the father grew somewhat eccentric – he relished this reputation – a little peevish and suspicious, with an increasingly marked penchant for stinginess, a bit selfish and occupied with the minutiae of his daily routine. He liked to philosophise, because, among people of his type, philosophising flourishes in the void that would otherwise be filled by a strong will and sensitivity.

His philosophising fed on the general intellectual premises and recollections of his youth – his materialistic-atheistic-democratic youth in the 1880s. These recollections coloured his sated being with a vague love for the people, and caused him to regard his own aloofness – natural for a man of weak character – as withdrawal from the vulgar bourgeois crowd. He lived well (and could even contemplate buying a car), but his motivations were feeble and he never sank his teeth into great wealth. Still, his philosophising furnished him with a pleasant sense of superiority over his successful acquaintances – the engineers and the doctors – and enabled him to conjure and dwell in an atmosphere of old intelligentsia democracy. And so it went. But then came the Revolution, destroying his comfortable combination of socialist sympathies and a little money in the bank. Yet his desires were so limited, and his habit of populist penance so strong, that he never allowed himself to resist internally. He might consider the Revolution cruel, but he could not consider it anything other than just. In addition, he was a specialist in his field, and so things turned out all right. It was only when he quit his job (his son thought it was getting to be too much for him), only when he lost the support of external, habitual obligations that everything went to pieces.

It turned out he simply had no capacity for internal resistance. Such weak-willed people commit an irreparable crime with terrible ease – they begin to see themselves as pitiful. They no longer fear humiliation, no longer resist it; on the contrary, they insist on humiliation. And everything around the old man helped him in this regard. Every aspect of the rough, straightforward life of the time kept insisting, in a range of voices, that he had lost all value to society. This found expression, for example, in his being given a pension of sixty roubles and then, all of a sudden, having this pension withdrawn (it was restored after three months of pleading, petitioning, and needless headaches).

Among other expressions of the rough, straightforward life of the early '30s were the Tenants' Cooperative Associations. These devices were adapted to serve as constant reminders that one should not be able to live the way one wished to live, and that one always had more than one deserved. They were devices for denying human rights – the rights to space, to air, to a toilet; this denial, of course, was theoretical – a denial in principle, as an ideal – because, in practice, a building manager was forced to endure his empirical tenant, who occupied a certain amount of space. But 'cooperative' thinking simply could not assimilate the notion that an old pensioner should take up a good sunny room all by himself. The manager threatened him with eviction, roommates, and resettlement – tried to bully him, fool him, sent in people with briefcases.

All of this was illegal, absurd, and impractical. But, at some point, these acts of cruelty and rudeness encountered the old man's sense of humiliation and fear. Regardless of all real-life and legal evidence to the contrary, the threats of roommates and resettlement convinced him. In his heart he believed, right along with the building manager, that he didn't deserve to occupy the sunny room. And N, downtrodden by his father's conviction, stupidly went to the Office of the Public Prosecutor to explain matters.

The way of life N had established for his father fed and renewed the old man's humiliation and fear. This was a lonely (the aunt only paid an occasional visit), old woman's way of life – with the primus stove and the walks to the market, where one had to count out kopecks... Theoretically, yes – theoretically there's nothing wrong when an old man, having nothing to do, cooks his own favourite vegetable stew. Not a thing wrong... But each of these things bore its own special meaning, and these meanings slowly emerged like toxic secretions. His dicing a pink swede into little cubes meant, in itself, that he was no longer a member of society, no longer a man... Oh, what wilful ignorance, what stupidity – N's self-justifying thoughts about the old man having a minimum of human comforts, which was more then he could say for himself... N had overlooked it, had misunderstood the very principle of human life, its prime mover: the conviction in one's own worth. As the old man stirred his diced carrot and swede in a saucepan with an unsteady hand, this conviction slowly evaporated.

N would lie on the old man's bed, reflecting crudely on human comforts and on the fact that he himself was less well provided for. He would come over there and lie on the bed, thinking himself overworked, and would allow the old man to wait on him. There was that time with the bath... He had allowed the old man to heat the bath for him; this wasn't hard, of course – just a matter of lighting a few pieces of firewood. But they wouldn't light. They only sent up smoke and kept going out. This really got to him, and he lost his temper; he felt suffocated by the whole atmosphere of endless difficulties. All he had ever wanted was a fenced-off life, even a dog's life, but an easy one, so that you wouldn't even notice it... And here, in this house, everything was desperately noticeable: each piece of firewood, each swede, each utility bill represented difficulty and humiliation. And the old man not only failed to resist difficulty and humiliation, he actively sought them out at every opportunity.

N had burst into the room after this abortive bath (he'd been fantasising about lowering his tired body into the warm water), muttered that no one could do anything right in this place (referring to the aunt as well), no one gave anything any thought... and then went out to walk the wooded streets of the suburb, trampling the dirty snow. He knew that the old man was sitting by the water-heater, terribly upset; he had so wanted to treat his hardworking son to a bath. N walked and walked until dusk, dwelling on his victimhood, but not entirely ignoring the fact that he was a son of a bitch. Back in the house, the old man was still sitting by the water-heater in his old summer coat, felt boots, and colourful skullcap, holding a piece of firewood in his pale hands, with their swollen sclerotic veins. He was pleased: he'd proved more stubborn than the water-heater. N took his bath – though it was only lukewarm, because they had to keep the door open a long time in order to disperse all the smoke.

Remembering this was hard work morally. Could all this have happened because he'd failed, simply failed to understand the principle of life – by virtue of which the old man refused to recognise that he would never again be able to work?

At the house the assumption had been that the old man was merely taking a break from work; regular service would, of course, have been too onerous, but he'd still manage to write something concerning his specialty, make contacts with certain publishers. Several times he had given N lists of books and journals to obtain. N hated obtaining things... One day he took the old man to the Public Library, and this turned out to be pure torture. The old man was utterly lost; he couldn't understand what the librarian told him, couldn't make heads or tails of the card index. N would recall this scene with great rancour every time the old man gave him a new list of specialised literature. He would say, 'Yes, yes,' shoving the little list in his pocket or in a drawer and forgetting about it instantly, for good.

On several occasions the old man had gently chided him for ignoring his needs. Once they had an unpleasant conversation on some unrelated topic – N couldn't remember what, exactly. But he had suddenly lost control and said something to the effect that he had his own problems to deal with, reminding the old man about the Library. In the end, he said something like, "It's too difficult for you, too tiring..." This was a stab in the back – the lowest, meanest insult. The old man's pain was frighteningly evident; he got all fired up, said it wasn't true... Yes, this was his lowest, meanest act – and, moreover, one expressed in words.

N had generally been able to keep his words in check, but sooner or later this was bound to happen, because too many bad thoughts had accumulated in his head, all linking up in one formula: idle, emotionally parasitic old age was an enormous burden.

This formulation didn't come easily to N. It amounted to a

recognition of one of his personal catastrophes. As a student
– lonely (despite his academic elation), cold, half-starved –
he had dreamt of the resurrection of home. Even back then,
this dream appeared to him in the guise of a bachelor's
existence. In point of fact, what he desired wasn't a 'home'
built by an exertion of strength, but a 'home' some distance
away, excluded from the structure of life, which would remain
stable as life changed – outside of life, as it were. His father
would live there, his aunt would keep house, and he would
come visit when he felt tired. Ideally, this home would be
somewhere outside of town. He would come there on snowy,
fluffy, sparkling evenings. There would be a white tablecloth,
a lamp, a kettle – and he'd be at the table, his heart and weary
head comforted by the kettle, by the white tablecloth.

Old dreams, which one nurses for years and which fuse
with one's will, have a strange property – they almost always
come true; and this is terribly unfortunate. N's dream of a
country home coincided with reality to a surprising degree,
down to his visits on snowy, sparkling evenings. The only
element of his dream that didn't materialise was love. Love
had been a natural prerequisite of N's youthful schemes. He
had assumed that the love which had once bound an ageing,
somewhat eccentric, philosophising man to a somewhat
wild boy, who was even then looking to establish himself in
life, would simply continue unabated. This love had been a
friendship, with walks, rowing, mischief, and loud debates
about everything under the sun, in the heat of which the boy
would grow angry at the stupidity of the intelligentsia, at the
pacifism or misapprehension of pre-Revolutionary poets like
Alexander Blok. But by the time they met again years later –
everything had changed. The father was no longer an ageing
eccentric who loved modest comfort, debates, and rowing,

but an old man accustomed to being pitiful, whose world kept shrinking and shrinking, funnelling ever more quickly down to indifference; there was no longer any space in this microscopic world for his son, for his son's interests.

And N met the abstractedness of a dimming mind with his own abstractedness. He was now a tired man with bad nerves and a muddled fate, occupied with his own thoughts and generally indifferent to things and people. He was also occupied with something other than his thoughts – a confused and doomed attempt to arrange his own human happiness. These two men met again, expecting, out of habit, to be greeted with kindness; instead, they surprised each other with selfishness. The younger one, who now had the upper hand, felt how difficult it was to be kind. And the older man grew scared... "You're yelling at me," he said once, sounding hurt. This meant: "You never spoke to me like this before, when I was strong..." This happened when they quarrelled about fixing the Dutch oven in the old man's room. The old man said it couldn't be done, that it was too expensive, and cited all kinds of other complications. N said it had to be done, that he'd find the money, and lost his temper – not only was it going to be expensive and difficult, but, as always, the old man insisted on complicating matters. And precisely because he was, as he saw it, being magnanimous in this quarrel (I don't care about the money...), he gave free rein to his rudeness and exasperation, which immediately rose to the surface. Or maybe this happened on a different occasion, during one of their theoretical disputes, when he grew angry at "old-intelligentsia foolishness" – "You're yelling at me..." – how, how, how could he have allowed it to happen...

Yet most oppressive of all was the scene with the liverwurst. One time the old man had paid him a visit and they'd enjoyed a good breakfast. Then N left the room; stepping back in, he caught the old man picking at the remnants of liverwurst on his plate with his knife. N had come in without warning, and the old man had twitched slightly and quickly pulled away from his plate. He'd been ashamed to show that he had wanted seconds. That was a blow to N's heart. Pain washed over him, bringing to mind an image from long ago: of himself, as a boy, in the old man's study. He saw himself sitting on the couch, cross-legged, and before him lay plates of his beloved Chinese pine nuts and tangerines... The blow had been so sharp that, for a moment, it had promised to dispel the fog of cowardice and cruelty... But N felt that the pain's first wave had been too strong – that it had heralded an infinite expansion of pain. Pushing away everything that could have dispelled the fog, he instead unleashed disgust – the vilest reaction with which he could have responded to the scene with the liverwurst.

N had already been irritated by everything that emanated from there – and most of all by the deprivation the old man suffered. The Dutch oven had broken in the old man's room, so it was always cold. And N would say angrily that he couldn't come any longer, that his insides would freeze; and indeed, in the winter, he'd stay away for a full two months. But the old man had to live there. He'd heat the room with kerosene stoves, which poisoned the air; when he warmed his hands at them, his skin would stretch unpleasantly. The old man would insist that he was used to it, that he wasn't cold; and he had, in fact, got used to it – got used to wearing a skullcap, felt boots, and a woollen coat in his home. The kerosene situation was bad. One had to bring it in from the city, but doing that was forbidden – and very reasonably – as a fire-prevention measure (the fine was a hundred roubles). The old man would wrap the kerosene bottles in paper and pack them deep in his basket. Once, in the train, he had an accident – the kerosene leaked, forming a puddle on the floor (a hundred-rouble fine!). A soldier on the neighbouring bench took pity on him: He gave him a newspaper to cover the puddle – 'tent it, so it doesn't soak through'; and he sat down beside him, blocking him from view. The old man told the story anxiously, and kept praising the soldier with the kind face.

Due to the difficulties with the kerosene, the old man had once caught a terrible cold and had to move in with N for ten days. This coincided precisely with the period when Liza was coming over almost daily, with the express purpose of having it out with N. The old man's presence in the next room interfered with their quarrelling, and, what's worse, their making up. Towards the end, N could hardly conceal his impatience: He'd examine the thermometer with a grim face – 37.3 – of course, with a temperature, he shouldn't leave... One time the old man suddenly said, in a disappointed tone, "I'm not bothering you..." N was lacerated with shame; he began to explain something or other, attempting to blot out his rudeness. The old man finally left. He set off for the tram stop, with the ever-present grocery bag in his hand. N walked him to the tram with a clenched heart, an obscure shame, an obscure desire to go back and do it differently. But if they had, in fact, been forced to return home together (say, if a blizzard had struck and the trams had stopped running), this desire would have immediately given way to anger at everything that prevented him from living his own life. At the tram stop, he kissed the old man's worn face, speaking softly, helping him into his seat, and handing him the bag. Then he walked away, feeling very tired.

With an effort, one could, in fact, recall things in a different light. The old man had had a good room, good neighbours.

138

The air in the suburb was clean; there was a quiet main street, where he had liked to sit and read his newspapers. He'd even said that his digestion had improved after the move. Once N had some people over, and one of the guests – one of the women – had noted that his father was looking well, younger and younger, which had pleased the old man very much.

No, these sorts of memories simply don't stick; they are dull, forced. The structural work of remorse forcefully sweeps aside anything it cannot use. Remorse found much use, on the other hand, in what the old man once said, not to him, but to this aunt – though surely intending her to pass it on: it would be better, he said, for N to give him a certain amount per month – not a little here, a little there, as the mood struck him. It would be better – meaning, more like a pension or a salary; in any case, it wouldn't be so degrading... How, how could he have permitted this degradation...

That last summer N had gone off to the country with Liza, to work on his subject, psychology. The aunt had also gone off, to visit relatives. For two months, the old man was alone. And then he did something he had never done before. Despite his propensity to feel pitiful, he had never complained to N about life directly, as a whole; perhaps he had wanted to spare him, or had simply felt shy. Either way, he had left N a loophole of incomprehension. But now he suddenly wrote to him, saying, in no uncertain terms, that he didn't have enough money, that he was lonely and bored... N had known all this, of course, but he had somehow hoped that the old man himself didn't know – didn't know, for instance, that he was bored. Having passed through the old man's consciousness, having found expression in words and been committed to paper, the complaint pierced N's heart. He was anguished, especially because he was far away; he desperately wanted to change

139

everything, that very minute. He was far away, and so the usual irritations couldn't destroy his anguish. He immediately wrote a letter (a "warm response", for which the old man later thanked him); essentially, he explained that he himself had no money and lived a very meagre existence. He didn't write this in order to rebuff the old man – on the contrary, he immediately scraped together some money and sent it – but in order to beg forgiveness and console himself. He twitched for another day or two, and then, as always, pushed it away. Pushing it away proved all the easier, because he had never actually dared, had never really forced himself to understand what the old man had said, to understand his boredom: the repetitive days of reading the paper on the main street, of walks to the market, of the primus stove, of the unyiedling sadness stalled in the calcifying brain. The days were very quiet, because there was no one to talk to; and the nights were half-sleepless – like most old men, he slept poorly – and filled with night-time thoughts, which could only be thoughts of loneliness, of worthlessness and death, of the fact that they'd asked more for the eggs at the market again, and that his leg seemed to be hurting again.

They really did happen – those protracted old-man's nights, with their thoughts of worthlessness, of the pained leg, of death. There was no way to remove that link from the chain of remorse, to eliminate those days and nights and thoughts. Imagining them clearly as having happened was enough to make one want to slam one's head on the edge of the table.

There's no solution for the tragedy of desire – for the eternal contradiction between what one desires and what one manages to accomplish – but the senile desire for peace may, at times, be achievable. People grow old differently. Ideal old age – a natural and resigned diminution of strength – is rare. More common is lachrymose old age, which doesn't wish to resign itself; it's hard to help this old age, almost as hard as it is to help youth. But an old age that has lost its aspirations, an old age with a steadily dimming consciousness – that old age can be helped by simple material means. It's a deformed state of mind, which can indeed take peace and comfort as its objects of desire. But this has to do with the drama's social aspect.

The elderly used to prosper when they avoided losing power over life and youth after losing their positions in the workplace – when they maintained their power by means of custodians, guarantors of worldly comforts; or when their children, confident and well fed, gladly performed their filial duty, providing comfort to old age, paying it respect. Among the poverty-stricken, on the other hand, the elderly have always been useless and tragic. And the irritation that these young, tormented people experienced when they faced those obsolete observers of life finally penetrated the world of the intellectuals; it overcame the intellectuals' faintheartedness and was dubbed the problem of "psychological parasitism". In the absence of an innate, lifelong place in the hierarchy, in the context of a cramped and disorderly domestic life, stripped of all conventional goals and fictions (cf. the clubs, charities, sinecures, affectation of honour – all that the social summits of the pre-Revolutionary world could offer a secure old age), the claims of the elderly appear illegitimate.

"Why do parents wish so badly to be entertained?" a woman says in an exasperated tone – a woman who is still beautiful, but who no longer has the time to be beautiful. "They want our lives to serve as their entertainment… They latch onto our work, our relationships, our boredom. Even those of us who've managed to put up with every sort of material hardship can't put up with this."

One of the saddest laws of life is the so-called ingratitude of children. This is the law of discrepancy between the values that parents and children place on each other. For parents, children are their creation and realisation, the overcoming of loneliness and the promise of immortality. For children, parents are the objects of debt, or of pity, or, at best, of unselfish and hence disinterested affection. N passively and apathetically sacrificed everything he had. But when it turned out that this wasn't enough – that he also had to overturn his way of life, sacrifice his time, and expend his mental energy – he couldn't bear it, he refused. And all the while he had held in his hands the threads of a tragedy that could have been mended by the simplest of means.

N had never believed in money; that is, he couldn't believe in money's actual power over a man's life and death. Absent-minded, indifferent to material blessings, occupied with his own thoughts, he didn't even notice that he was impoverished; he wore his poverty lightly and would never have thought of calling himself a poor man. Now, the sight of this acknowledged, avowed, shameless poverty – which had become not only his own poverty but also his guilt – proved unbearable. The most characteristic aspect of grey quotidian poverty isn't physical suffering. Rather, it is a complex of oppression, dependence, a deep-rooted lack of self-respect, and fear. It manifests itself, for example, in the conviction that it is necessary, that it is perfectly natural to stand for four hours in the waiting room of a free clinic, so as not to go to a clinic where one would have to shell out a rouble; it expresses itself in sentiments like, "What am I, a queen, that I should go to an upper-class bathhouse?" This complex involves, above all, the sense that all the things of this world are difficult and latently hostile. For the poor person – as for the artist – nothing in life can remain unnoticed. The poor man walks in the knowledge that he is wearing out the soles of his boots; he gets on the tram in the knowledge that he must pay a certain number of kopecks; when he prepares a letter, he is aware of affixing the stamp. He is deprived of automatic gestures. Nothing in his surroundings is pliant and submissive. And N, holding the threads in his hands, unravelled the tragedy of poverty...

This constitutes a minor episode in the eternal struggle of the weak against the strong, in which the strong are defeated in advance by remorse. The weak have an all-powerful weapon: the shamelessness with which they expose everything that has rendered them pitiful. The weak torment the strong with familial humiliation, which the strong mirror with remarkable exactness. In order to go on living, the strong grow embittered, pushing away and ignoring what is plainly visible to everyone else. But then, when the strong are finally made to see – all too late – they are defeated and punished, and a festering wound opens in their heart. Nothing – not work, not passion, not fatigue – can help them justify themselves.

One often behaves especially badly towards one's close relations – not only because one doesn't fear them, but because one sustains the irrational belief that it is never too late to right the wrongs done to them: "I'm like a balm that can, at any moment, soothe the pain I myself have caused." The physical proximity of one's close relations reinforces this delusion. He's right there – I can breathe easy; he's here, I'm here – so I'll certainly have the opportunity to right my wrongs. But if he should leave the house, if he should step out to visit a shop even for half an hour, the equilibrium is disturbed. What if something happens? What if it's already happened? Then my most recent wrong, my latest cruelty, will turn out to be the last...

No one is more prone to familial anxiety and panic than

143

rude domestic despots.

The old man had been ailing. Then N was told that things had taken a turn for the worse and he suddenly began to fret. He decided he needed to improve the old man's diet. He spent all the money he had on a chicken, oranges, and cream. He trembled with impatience as he made the purchases; he needed to hurry, hurry and get over there – to supplant the experience of poverty with chicken and oranges. He walked across the courtyard in the dark, the bags tugging at his fingers, and stumbled because his eyes were on the windows. He thought that if the windows were lighted, as always, then it could not have happened... He just had to make it in time – to nullify, with love and chicken, all that had come before. Standing at the threshold, his face contorted, he asked: 'Well, how do you feel?' It turned out nothing had changed. Then the old man told him that cream was bad for him, that he had plenty of milk, and that chicken soup was also no good, as the doctor had prescribed a vegetarian diet. Everything had been purchased in vain, and the fear with which he had purchased it had also been in vain. The fear of irreparability, which had instantly changed the balance of all the elements, passed; N sat there, numb, downcast, listlessly answering questions. He wanted to plunge headlong into solitude, as into water.

Only now did he realise what he had failed to realise back then. He should have stopped that deadly transience... He now sees clearly what had failed to happen. He sees himself sitting next to the old man. He places his palm on the back of the old man's hand, which is resting on a knee. He strokes the hand, running his finger down the swollen sclerotic veins (a gesture he had performed as a child but had forgotten in his rough and hurried life). He fosters a strange illusion of permanence, as though it were no longer possible for the man sitting beside him to pass away. This illusion is like a precious object that you hold as tightly as possible, so that no one can take it away from you. He squeezes the hand more and more firmly, holding on to the fleeting moment with all his strength. Let it erase all past wrongs – let the future end seem unreal by comparison. He thinks: "I'm doing precisely what people talk about when they look back: Why didn't I do that... why didn't I understand... why didn't I stop it? I'm deepening the present." But it didn't happen that way. The will had not manifested itself in the necessary gesture. His consciousness returns to the empirical chaos of broken and equal moments, which crowd each other senselessly, correcting each other. Until the irreparable appears.

Death violently drags a part of existence out of the darkness. In order to avoid pain, we keep ourselves from understanding the life of those close to us. But the pain caused by death is so powerful that it fears no other pain and rends the veil. We seek to focus the pain, because we feel that a loved one's death is our fault and calls for internal punishment. This is how death dredges up remorse. Remorse, for its part, loves details and has the power to re-establish lost connections.

How did it all happen – everything that later became this death? It all began with N's telephone, which stopped working. Actually, it all began with the party his aunt had thrown at her flat in the city. The old man was invited – and didn't come. The ladies were eating sweet cakes. N went to his aunt's and ate cakes. He couldn't stop worrying – why hadn't the old man come? And, as always, all of this irritated him, even more than usual, because he had to give a lecture in a few days and really needed a clear head.

Total silence, a telephone hanging idle with its useless buttons – all this was later assimilated into the experience of death. The old man fell ill – that is, his leg began to hurt – the day he was to visit the aunt's flat. He asked a neighbour (she worked in the city) to call his son and tell him to come. But the telephone didn't work. The neighbour couldn't reach him; nobody came. That day the old man went to fetch an armful of firewood from the shed all by himself. A neighbour met him on the stairs and helped him carry the wood up to the flat. The old man had already developed a cough. Had the telephone worked, maybe none of it would have happened…

The next day the old man's neighbour stopped by after work (had she come earlier, perhaps none of this would have happened…). N's response was habitual – he bawled out his aunt. He went to her flat and shouted that her neglect of the old man was disgraceful, that he was too busy, had a lecture to give, but if this was how things stood, he'd quit everything and go over there himself… He didn't – but he did manage to get the aunt to go. His lecture went over well – a bigger success than anything he'd experienced since his student years. He had his colleagues over in the evening for a few drinks. In recent years N had accepted the position of a loser – not an embittered loser (that would have been indecent), but, in any case, a sceptical loser, who never complained about his fate. And now this success roused within him the long-repressed desires of his youth. He was excited, fatigued. He didn't want to work – he wanted to talk, relax, sense the lightness of life.

Liza stopped by the next morning, before work. Despite her tendency towards obstinacy, she somehow succumbed to the atmosphere of success and agreed to share it. This was an unexpected and important element of his triumph. They talked, and N himself was surprised at how freely they spoke. In the afternoon, at about two o'clock, they got a call from there (the telephone had been fixed). It turned out that the old man was in very bad shape, and had been for several days. They hadn't wanted to tell N and upset him before he gave his lecture. He said, "Yes... right away... of course..." His heart sank. He feared for the old man, and, as always, feared the onset of remorse. It came as a sudden blow. He had to buy food and go – go now – instead of experiencing his triumph. Worst of all, he had to leave Liza, who had so unexpectedly agreed to share his triumph. He went.

And so, the telephone, the aunt's guests, and the lecture had set in motion a chain of events that lasted for two weeks, until the end: train journeys to the suburb and back, every other day or so. N was very busy (he'd been asked to write an article on the subject of his lecture, on a very tight deadline); these journeys left him feeling numb and dull. Although it was still February, the thaw had begun, and the weather was irritating. The commuter train was always half-dark. N could never make anything out through its wet windows. Sometimes it was especially cold, because the carriage was empty; sometimes he had to stand, his face brushing against his neighbours' disgustingly damp collars. He would walk from the station across the thawing snow, his hands weighed down by bags full of groceries; he would dwell on his sense of dullness and torpor: "This is the way it's going to be from now on..." But when he stayed home, he was relentlessly tormented by anxiety and the desire to change everything immediately. Then he would take off for the suburb. And that's why he made the journey every other day or so: one day he'd suffer remorse, fearing even greater remorse, and the next he'd feel himself a victim and grow angry. It was a kind of trap.

He would take off, desiring to set everything straight, including himself, and regretting that he no longer felt love; this regret was so strong that it bordered on love... On the way, he'd imagine telling the old man about his successes, or his projects, or some funny incident; but once there, he felt cold, too lazy to utter a word, and it seemed to him that his father wasn't at all interested in what he had to say. He would sit with him – cold, bored, downcast – wondering when he could leave, and whether he could still keep his date with Liza later. One time, shivering near the half-cold stove, he began to examine the things in the room (decent, tasteless odds and ends from his father's old bourgeois flat); he gazed at the table, at the chairs, and at the old man, who lay on his back, quietly chewing his lips, on the modern couch with a mirror set awkwardly into its high back. He thought about the fact that – quite possibly – the old man would die, and that he would have to clear out the flat, move all these things… what a terrible bother, dealing with the building management office, the removal men. Better get rid of as much as I can… that… that… I'll take that black one there… What will I feel when he dies?… Perhaps – nothing… I have to try to imagine it… maybe – nothing… I don't think I feel anything now…

Fool!

But worse than all these cynical thoughts was his constant cowardly haste. He felt cold and bored, and couldn't wait for his evening with Liza, which was supposed to reward and soothe him (though it always turned out quite differently), and he would suddenly grow rudely restless. He knew that the sick man's room was in complete disarray, that it was poorly heated, that they needed to hire a woman to keep house. He'd get angry and demand that action be taken; flattering his conscience, he'd leave behind the last of his money, but he never did the one thing he should have done – he didn't stay and take matters into his own hands. He knew that he should have talked to the doctor, but he would have had to wait nine or ten hours for the doctor to arrive – and then his evening would have been lost.

That last time before the beginning of the end, saying goodbye and taking the money out of his wallet, N said:

"I'll be back in a few days."

"Your visits are a great comfort to me," the old man told him. He had always been so shy and reserved in N's company. And now that pitiful word – 'comfort' – resounded with such terrible clarity. This was just as intolerably unpleasant as the old man's loud groans from the ache in his leg; N wanted to put a stop to this as quickly as possible. Hastily blocking the pain borne by that word – "comfort" – N said, with a cruelty he himself hadn't expected:

"It isn't easy for me to come so often. I'm very busy these days."

His heart grew heavy at his own words. He put more money on the table than he had initially planned. Almost all of it…

"I'll be going now. You get better, you hear?"

The old man was looking at him from his high-backed modern couch with its mirror.

"I'll try," he said, and didn't smile at parting.

That was their last conversation.

On the eve of the decisive day N called his father's neighbour at work, wanting to know how things were over there. The neighbour answered rather sharply.

"Not very good, in my opinion. You should speak to the doctor yourself…"

N took offence at the neighbour's intrusion into his affairs. He stayed home that day. The next day, before taking the train, he met with Liza; they went to the store together, to buy the sick man oranges. Liza said:

"You mean all three hundred roubles are gone? Goodness!"

"Of course," he said, and immediately felt himself a victim. At the same time, he felt satisfied – such extravagance soothes one's conscience

During the journey, he thought of practically nothing. That must have been because he had made the journey so many times, languishing in the train, approaching the house and staring in fear at the lighted windows – hoping, hoping it hadn't yet happened... And many times they had opened the door for him, after fumbling with the locks. And indeed, nothing had happened; and the fear had receded, giving way to irritation and boredom. This sequence of psychic transitions had become habitual. After fumbling with the locks, N's aunt opened the door. Startled, as always, by the opening door (another phase in the fixed series of psychic transitions), he asked, breathlessly: how is he?

"Weak," the aunt answered, going back to the kitchen. "Had a fever last night."

She said nothing else, but he didn't get the impression that he usually got – the impression that nothing had happened.

N entered the room. The old man looked at him from the couch with light, blank, and attentive eyes. Confronted with this gaze, N felt overcome by an unpleasant wave of lethargy. He greeted the old man; the old man didn't respond. But N wasn't ready to comprehend what was happening; he put his bag on the table and opened it, took out an orange, peeled back its skin into a kind of rosette, and brought it forward on his palm, timidly asking the silent man on the couch: "Want an orange?" The old man stared at him with a strange expression. He stretched a slightly trembling hand towards the orange without shifting his gaze. N brought the orange closer. The old man groped for the orange as if he were blind (he continued to stare at his son's face), found it, squeezed it with his fingers, tore a segment from the peel, brought it to his mouth, and began to chew it very slowly; then he reached for a second segment. His movements grew slower and slower, as if every motion, no matter how small, demanded a rest. N stood there, sinking into torpor. Then he placed the orange on a chair and left the room without looking back. In the kitchen, his aunt was boiling milk.

"Why doesn't he talk?" N asked his aunt, unable to shake off his torpor. 'Has he been like this long?'

"Don't know – he was talking a half hour ago. I said: 'Why isn't he here? Probably isn't coming.' He said: 'Well, he has to get ready...'"

N interrupted her:

"Take a look..."

They went to the room together. The old man was lying flat on his back and staring directly at the arm of the couch. The aunt spoke to him; he didn't respond. It was no longer possible not to comprehend.

"What is this?" N asked. He didn't dare speak loudly and began to shake. Horror swept off his torpor. And he immediately began to act – systematically, with a kind of mechanical efficiency.

The old man's doctor was back at the hospital. N bursts into the downstairs flat and grabs the idiotic telephone with the rotating handle. They connect him to the wrong department at the hospital – he turns the handle; they connect him to the right department, but the doctor is out – he turns the handle. Now everything is focused on the desire to reach the doctor. All the downstairs tenants gather around the telephone; they don't even think of concealing their curiosity. The doctor informs him, through the orderly, that he himself won't be able to come until the evening, but that he's sending over an assistant to administer an injection.

Upstairs, the old man, his condition unchanged, lay quietly. The aunt told N in a low voice: he had had to relieve himself during the night, she had helped him, and they'd spilled a little on the sheet... And he'd said to her: "I'm as weak as a fly..." The doctor had come earlier that night and told them that there was no need for injections, but he had prescribed camphor internally.

"And he's taking the camphor?"

"I didn't have time to buy it."

Yes, she didn't have time... It's true – she didn't, and he wasn't there to go out and get it. And he immediately thought that if he hadn't spent so much time chatting with Liza on the way to the station, he would have arrived an hour earlier. The old man would have still been conscious. He would have seen the old man's delight at the sight of the orange. And they would have had one more chance – their last chance – to talk.

N went to get the camphor. At the pharmacy, the gleam of the glass medicine bottles, the colourfully, skilfully packaged sanitary and hygiene items filled him with disgust and fear. The cashier was particularly disgusting, tapping out receipts as if this were a grocery store. By the time he got back, the assistant had arrived – a tall languid woman with syringes. Two women from the downstairs flat had made their way into the room behind her. The sick man's son had used their phone – now they had the right to enter the man's home. N understood – the smell of death frees people from their inhibitions: doors open and walls collapse. In the hours of death, people celebrate their victory over the shyness of those who are used to locking their doors.

The assistant seemed somewhat piqued. The doctor must have instructed her not to treat the old man, just to give him the injection. But she was a doctor, after all, not a nurse. And so, before administering the injection, she got the patient to sit upright, supporting him with her hand, and lifted his shirt to listen to his heart, thereby baring his yellow belly, covered in grey hair. The neighbours looked on with great interest.

"Would you please step out?" N said. "He might prefer a little privacy…"

The neighbours stepped out, exchanging surprised glances: the man was clearly unconscious – how could he prefer anything?

N followed the assistant out of the room.

"Well? What do you think?"

"I can't say anything," she responded in an offended tone. "I haven't auscultated the patient."

"Examine him, please," the aunt suggested, always eager to please strangers.

"No," N said. "Let's not bother him. But tell me – what do you think?"

"I don't know… It's serious…"

She dropped the professional-offended tone, and her voice took on a note of human embarrassment.

"Yes, a serious situation…"

And so someone had finally come out and said what was happening in that room.

The doctor came in the evening, and one of the aunt's friends, also a doctor, happened to stop by as well. The two of them seemed to be trying not to lose face in front of each other. They examined the old man – he now lay with his eyes closed – and spoke rather loudly. They said that he was in a bad way, that he appeared to be paralysed on his right side; pulling back the blanket, they lifted and dropped his right leg, which fell as if it were lifeless. The old man breathed loudly the whole time, but his face was calm. It occurred to N that, maybe – he had been told these things happened – the old man could hear and understand every word they said, so that perhaps the doctors should lower their voices. But he felt shamefully timid before these self-assured people, and he said nothing.

The doctor opened a transparent yellow vial; the aunt's acquaintance and he injected the old man with camphor, saying it was of no use. N's life – with its writings and its setbacks, with Liza – withdrew far, far into the distance, became completely foreign to this new sphere, this unprecedented sphere rotating around the body on the couch. And the body, too, was something indescribable; it wasn't a living person, because all that constitutes a person's essence had already fled from it, and whatever remained was clearly hurtling towards final oblivion. Nor was the body a corpse, because, as long as it breathed, one couldn't believe in the immutability of what was coming – because it required care and inspired the mad desire to keep it on this side of oblivion.

N did small chores, taking on as many tasks as he could. He no longer feared work or pain; on the contrary, he sought them out as a remedy against the only thing he did fear – remorse. He wanted to do everything he could in this narrowing sphere of death, but he failed to acquire the strangers' confidence in dealing with the body that lay on the couch, breathing loudly and evenly.

The aunt's acquaintance, leaning over the couch, kept repeating:

"Do you recognise me? Do you recognise me? Answer me."

Some kind of movement passed over the old man's face, and, in a strange plaintive tone, he muttered her surname. A glimmer of consciousness. Why hadn't he come over to the old man himself, leaned over him, called out to him? Why hadn't he spoken words of love and comfort – why hadn't he taken advantage of that last moment of consciousness? He could have pulled a chair up to the couch, sat down face to face with the old man, taken his hand. Instead he had stood frozen behind the old man's head. N felt shy – he himself didn't know why – and his shyness kept growing. It was either the gravity of what was happening or his sympathy with the old man – his sense of the humiliation and powerlessness of a dying person being dealt with by strangers; or perhaps it seemed tactless to turn to the old man with an expression of emotion, demanding a response; after all, the old man might also feel shy about his emotion, and about the fact that he was dying.

In short, it was a complete tangle of ideas, and this larger tangle also swept up all sorts of trifles. It suddenly occurred to N that the old man had craved oranges so badly, and now it appeared N had brought them in vain. He was thrilled when the doctor said that they still needed to feed the old man and ordered them to make orange juice with sugar. They fed the old man with a spoon; he swallowed without opening his eyes, and everyone was happy that he had managed to swallow so much orange juice. But N thought – he still doesn't realise that he's eating the oranges he had craved. And then it turned out the whole thing was in vain: the old man belched and the pink juice flowed down his chin, trickling onto his shirt and the blanket.

It was getting late. They couldn't find a sick-nurse to watch the old man through the night and administer the injections. The aunt's acquaintance refused to stay. Before leaving, she gave him one last injection and insisted that his pulse had steadied. All they needed to do, she said, was monitor his pulse through the night. She'd come back in the morning, and the nurse would come even earlier to administer another injection.

They were alone, the three of them – N, the aunt, and the body on the couch. The aunt huddled on her bed, with her clothes on, and peered out anxiously. N didn't undress either; he lay down on the daybed. It seemed to him that he kept falling asleep and waking right back up. He'd listen closely – the old man was breathing loudly and evenly. Then N would fall asleep again and wake up with a ready-made terror. He'd jump up to check the old man's pulse. The left arm, the one that wasn't paralysed, kept slipping down from the narrow couch; moist and pale, it would dangle as if it were full of lead. That, for some reason, proved to be especially memorable; for months afterwards, when his own arm would slip off the bed in his sleep, N would pull it up, horror-stricken. N would catch hold of the sick man's dangling arm and awkwardly grope for the pulse. Every time, it would seem to him that there was no pulse, and his own heart would stop. A moment later his thumb, roving in confusion over the cold, clammy wrist, would feel a throb. The mysterious vein of life would throb with uncanny clarity beneath the thumb, in deep rhythmic spurts. And N – pressing it down with his fingers, so that it didn't escape – would take the pulse, occasionally losing count. He understood nothing, save this: that blood, that life itself kept beating and battling in the motionless body. He would lie down to sleep and then wake up again, as if roused by some smooth-running mechanism.

Towards morning he drifted off for an hour or two. He awoke in the half-light of dawn. The old man was still lying there in his skullcap; the hand that N had lifted so many times and placed on the blanket was hanging down again. N's back ached. The morning sleep had calmed him a little, and now he wasn't so scared. After all, they'd told him that the pulse was steadier. Before making the effort to get up, he dwelled on the fact that he'd need to go to the market, stop by the pharmacy along the way, tend to all sorts of other matters; this was the start of a hopelessly long existence in the sphere of illness; the pulse was steadier, the woman had said.

It wasn't long before the aunt's acquaintance arrived.

"No, the pulse is weak again..." She shook her head. "Why hadn't the nurse given him the injection when she stopped by earlier? Her job isn't to argue – it's to do what she's told."

The woman picked up the syringe with an embarrassed look (they had begged her to stay the night). N stood there, grim and silent; he knew that the nurse had argued because she was afraid of being late for work. The aunt's acquaintance left and then the doctor came. He stood for a while, then sat, then looked the old man over, touched him, and then suddenly declared, in a low voice... Yes, he's in a very bad way, the right side is paralysed, haemorrhaging, a matter of hours – strange, that: there hadn't been any dangerous indications in the course of the illness...

N went over to the window, turned away, and began to cry. The aunt wept loudly behind his back.

Their artificial uncertainty had collapsed, and everything they did now could be done only in anticipation of death, as preparation, as an attempt to lessen the suffering; from now on, everything that was done here, everything that happened, was death. In connection with this death, there arose certain questions of housing, of the aunt's things, etc., and these questions would brook no delay. He would have to go into town, secure the necessary papers. N didn't seem to mind – it was easier to spend a few hours travelling than to stand next to this couch. But as soon as he reached the platform and stood under the big dial, he grew anxious. The suburban train, the two stations and the two trams, the chain of anticipations

– although each brief – stretched time beyond measure. A complicated space and time formed between him and the body on the couch. What was he afraid of? What was left to fear? That his father would die without him – that he wouldn't be there to witness his death?'

In the city he saw to everything, secured the papers, made calls about getting a sick-nurse. He did it all with numb outward attention, possessed of a single unrelenting desire – to get back as soon as possible, as if that would grant him relief.

His neighbours asked him over for lunch (they had pancakes). He realised that he hadn't really eaten that morning. But at the table he immediately felt that it was impossible to stay. If they had served cutlets, he might have finished, but pancakes with caviar – it turned his stomach.

N made his way back, pushing through time, sucking in the space that lay between him and death. No, death had not yet arrived. Now he could be sure that he wouldn't miss it.

In his absence, a new, near-death way of life had taken root. A woman had shown up to help; the nurse had sent her. She was silent and looked rather slovenly herself, but she had tidied the place up. As the unconscious, dying man came closer and closer to the moment when all his desires would cease, the things he had desired in life but could never acquire began to appear all around him.

They heated up the stove, and the room was warm – for the first time that winter, as far as N could recall; it turned out all they had needed to do was keep the stove heated. They washed the body on the couch and dressed it.

"Why have you got him all wrapped up like that?" the woman helper asked. "You're making this hard for him."

Everyone took great care not to make things hard for him, although they all insisted that he didn't feel a thing. The doctor kept sending a nurse from the hospital to administer injections (of course, he had admitted that morning that the injections were useless) and to help the patient relieve himself.

The aunt's mood brightened slightly. She was proud that they had managed to organise his dying so well. N thought: "Why did we do everything so well now, when he's indifferent – and will only grow more indifferent? His face looks so calm... Why didn't I come a half hour earlier that day? Why did I waste time looking for those oranges?"

That night they found a sick-nurse, though now everyone realised she was unnecessary. The woman was cheerful, ate heartily, kept going out into the hallway to smoke, and treated the dying man with kindness, as she did everyone else. She didn't bother N. He smoked with her in the hallway, and they'd exchange a few words now and again. There was no rudeness, no fear in her attitude towards death. And the professionalism of this attitude was tempered by the age-old decorum of Russian peasants in the face of death.

There was absolutely nothing for her to do; she ate, smoked, and slept in the daybed, which she had pushed up close to the couch. That night the old man's breathing took on a new sound; the air would enter with a protracted, rhythmically steady rattle. This breathing was not an expression of suffering, but N found each long, slightly gurgling inhalation dreadful; as soon as one was done, the next would begin. N had placed a pillow on the big chest in the hallway. He would fall asleep, wake up, glance into the room, go to fetch some water in the kitchen... The nurse would step out to smoke.

In the morning the old man still lay motionless on his back, eyes half-closed (as though the mechanism of his eyelids had broken), and still breathed hoarsely and evenly, but his face had changed. It had fallen; his cheeks were sunk, and his lips had collapsed into his toothless mouth. It was a foreign face, not quite angry, not quite surprised. Only the forehead had stayed the same – the characteristic forehead, with the two round bony ridges over the eyebrows, between which sat a little soft wart. Standing behind the old man's head, N saw only the forehead, ending in those two prominences – as a child, he had called them "knobs" and had loved to trace them with his finger; the forehead was very calm. The nurse said he would die in a couple of hours. The doctor came and half said, half asked:

"No point torturing him with camphor…"

And N said:

"I don't know… No point, I suppose…"

Now there was nothing left – no strangers, no tasks, no doubt. Only death. A clean, empty – resoundingly empty – anticipation of death. Only time, transparent, as in prison. The body on the couch was in agony. In order to ease its suffering, they removed the warm sheet and blanket and flung open its shirt; the yellow, grey-haired chest rose and fell with a wheeze. N led his aunt out of the room. He closed the door behind her and stayed with the sick-nurse. He knew he had to endure the pain to the end. And at the very end it seemed to him that he had grown completely numb, that the pain could no longer penetrate; in fact, he was absorbing this death with such spiritual force that he would have enough material for years of dreams, in which this death would appear in various guises. Things proceeded on their usual course: the dying man hiccupped, his temperature – which they measured, with medicinal dullness, every fifteen minutes – started at 39 degrees and kept plummeting until its number was an unquestionable indicator of death.

"What a heart, I tell you. Keeps fighting!" the nurse said.

The body was putting up a fight; the chest fought, wheezing ever more briefly and frequently; the veins fought, throbbing on the neck so insistently that the pulse could be taken by sight. But the face remained impassive, as if alien to everything going on inside the body.

"You'll see," the nurse said, "when the sorrowful tears come, that'll be the end."

N was now sitting right next to the couch, so as not to let a single breath slip by. He was struck by what the nurse had said about the sorrowful tears; he sat there, repeating her words to himself – anticipating their materialisation. But afterwards, he could never remember whether he had actually seen tears on the dying man's face. The face fell even further, then suddenly grew shorter. It fell and grew shorter rhythmically, joining the near-death struggle. There wasn't a glimmer of conscious suffering in this agony, yet the torments of senseless matter tore at its witness's heart. And in a final fit of selfishness, he kept repeating: "If he were suffering... I don't know if I could take it..."

Death did not strike and did not thunder. One of the sighs and sobs simply turned out to be the last. And the nurse said with relief: "It's over." N got up and leaned over the couch, testing himself; he didn't know whether he'd feel fear when touching the dead body. He felt no fear. He stroked and kissed the calm forehead with its knobs, which hadn't changed in the slightest.

Everything that followed – which all had to do with the liquidation of this body, this life – was, for N, tinged with falsity. He discussed the material for the coffin with the head of the funeral home, inquired at the cemetery about springtime flooding, and listened to his aunt deliberate as to whether the old man should be buried in a jacket or a blazer. He did everything he was supposed to do: he went to the registry office, where they crossed out the first page in the old man's passport; talked to the building manager; borrowed money. He arranged for relative decorum, but he himself was alien to this decorum – because for him the question of death and oblivion had little to do with graves and coffins, or even with this body. Perhaps that was why the moment he closed the dead man's eyes and gave him another kiss on the forehead was tinged with falsity. Several times during the day N had lifted the sheet off the couch. The old man lay there in his underwear – very small, shrivelled up, not at all frightening, with grey bristle on his cheeks. But all this had almost no relation to what already sat atop N's heart, like a bud that would soon unfold, filling his existence. It could well be that in the hours of the funeral, when N was occupied with the final arrangements for the dead body, he was calmer and more distracted than he would be for many months to come.

The funeral was a quiet one, without guests. When the coffin was lowered into the ground, the aunt suddenly began to cry, very piteously; holding a handkerchief to her lips, she kept repeating:

"Why so deep, why dig so deep?…"

N realised that she was thinking about her own impending death.

N sent the aunt home by cab, paid the cemetery workers for carrying the coffin and the spruce branches with which they had laid out the grave, and walked away across the snowy field. He knew that now, at last, he would start thinking – and it was easier to start thinking on the go, in the frosty, sunny wind.

And so began what would continue for a very long time: a constant rotation, a current of broken thoughts, which were senseless in their repetitiveness. Their only meaning lay in the fact that they provided indestructible material for remorse. The old man was waiting for him, waiting for the oranges – but he was half an hour late. He was talking with Liza... There was no one to send out for camphor – if they had gone out for camphor... Of course, all these treatments were useless, but if his mind hadn't gone blank, if he had managed to call a nurse out from the city to administer the injections, or if he had persuaded the aunt's acquaintance to stay the night... But he hadn't persevered – he'd been too shy, too treacherously shy. And then he thought that they hadn't paid the sick-nurse enough – that was really shameful. And then he thought that he had mishandled an entire life, a life that had been entrusted to him, and that all of this would revolve in his mind for an infinitely long time...

Father Goriot is a very false book. Have any children ever refused to see their dying father because of a dinner party? The truth is much worse, much simpler: children always go to see their dying father, hurry to their dying father, after having ruined his life.

Liza will understand this – she's like that herself. Liza had once told him:

"Have you ever noticed that people who really love their parents react fairly calmly to their deaths? Only the selfish torment themselves. Instead of thinking about the deceased, they fixate on their own guilt."

The aberrant belief in the possibility of rectification – the naive concept of an isolated act, free from the correlation of sin and retribution – is among the indications of an immanent consciousness, a consciousness devoid of common goals.

For this consciousness, existence is either an empirical muddle of moments, equal in their senselessness, or a dull sequence of moments, each one cancelling out the other. And the last moment is death, which cancels all.

Such is the logic of extreme individualism. But existential practice is more powerful than logic. It demands that people, whose lives are fleeting, live as if their actions made up an infinite historical chain. It insists on the irrevocable bonds of co-existence, of love and creation, of pity and guilt.

Translated by Boris Dralyuk

The Lady with the Dog
Galina Scherbakova

It was the sound of the door slamming shut that woke her. Soon after, she heard the rumble of a car moving off. No, not again! What made her think that this time would be any different? That this time the two of them would wake side by side, and have their morning tea together, and then she would kiss him good-bye and make the sign of the cross at his retreating back as he went from the door. And when she came back inside, there would not be this acrid reek of the escaping male. Surely, someone – some day – must stay, and linger to see her waking? Yet no one had… How many times had she listened to that slamming door, or even caught a glimpse from her window of the same hurried jog to the bus stop, pulling on jackets as they go? She was no undiscriminating slut, not what they call an easy lay. She only ever did it for love, properly, with flowers and chocolates, and outings to the theatre, or exhibitions of samurai armour. And she had dreamed up, like an incantation: "The one who doesn't wake first will be the one who stays forever after". God almighty, how she longed for that accursed ever after!

So for the umpteenth time she makes the customary trip to the mirror and considers her dishevelled hair – not terrible hair, not at all – no, she has good hair, thick and smooth, even first thing in the morning it lies on her head like a neat cap. Her eyes are dark brown, almost black, her brows arch naturally, without the use of a pencil.

Her nose isn't perfect, that's true enough – just a bit too long. Not beaky, mind, but with a round, soft little button on the end, over a full mouth. A sexy mouth, you could say, one that men like very much. And everything below just as it should be, a dimple in her chin, a long neck, rounded sloping shoulders, and as for her breasts – well, a perfect pair: full and high, not a bit of drooping.

All right, that's enough of singing the self-praise. Meanwhile, she's so heartsick, she could almost walk out of the window. She is desperate to have a man for keeps, to sleep by her side permanently, whatever her girlfriends may say about their husbands, the "randy old goats". Randy old goats they may be, but kept close to home nonetheless; just try looking twice in that direction, you'll get a heap of trouble. She never had anything to do with any of her friends' husbands, no. She only went with men from outside their circle. Or men from work, sometimes – she worked for a giant chemical-industrial planning bureau in charge of all the synthetics production in the region (they jokingly referred to it as the chem-chron-pharmatron). There were heaps of them over on secondment, not to mention a very adequate male contingent on the permanent staff. She had spent over fifteen years there, straight out of college, and seen at least twenty-seven weddings. Bored to death of them, she hadn't even gone to the latest one, making up some excuse. But she never had a wedding of her own – no, not even close. Not even a relationship that fizzled out before it got that far.

The ache she feels now, at the predictable sound of the slamming door, is the same ache of remembering that boy from school, when they were both sixteen and mad for each other, desperate to get married!

Naturally, what they were both mad for was sex... they

were right queasy with horniness. But times were so different then – it would never have occurred to either to just find a way, some secret place… They did kiss and paw at each other, however, until they were both giddy with it. And then he and his school valedictorian medal went off to Moscow. And that was it. As though it had never been. He was her first, really, the first to slam the door as he went out of her life. Granted, he had offered to marry her straight after graduation. Insisted, even. "I don't need to study for the exams," he'd say to her, "to hell with the medal (he had been working towards it for years), we can just fool around all summer long."

"Well, I won't pass without studying," she'd reply.

"You don't need to pass – I'll be a professor soon, and you can stay home and be a professor's wife!"

But this was all so unconventional that you couldn't even joke about it to your parents, or believe it could be true.

And by the way, the boy did become a professor in the end. And his wife doesn't work at all. They come back to visit annually, and she'd even crossed paths with them a few times. The first time, she felt all her insides clenching, while he shied violently away from her, muttering something vague and non-committal like "see you around, then".

Has anyone ever seen the place that love goes when it's run its course? Maybe it isn't a place at all, maybe love dissipates into molecules and atoms inside one's own body, and the most searing of the passions turns into a horny toenail? Or maybe it all scatters like ashes, so there's no use looking for any trace of those hungering, searching hands, or the ardent lips that kissed yours until pleasure mingled with pain. Scattered, like the white bloom of apple trees.

And so it seemed that in her life, each new encounter repeated the one before.

She walks the length of her apartment, searching for answers. The first answer comes, but it couldn't be more stupid: she's not to let any man near her, unless they've both come straight from the registry office. But where is she supposed to find such a paragon, at her age, which is firmly in the neighbourhood of forty? And heading for fifty in the blink of an eye.

Cunningly, these men – whether rumpled, crumpled, kippered or raw – dock atop her body, seeking refuge from their monotonous marriages, and muttering tomorrow's shopping lists as they drift off to sleep. Then there are the curious, who come to tea when invited, and drink their tea patiently, and drop biscuit crumbs. Then they go to the toilet, and on the way back, in the corridor, grope you impatiently - down there. And it turns out that was what you'd been waiting for all along.

There were all kinds. Old acquaintances and men she's just met. The middle-aged, no longer so sure of themselves, but also delivery boys, randy and clumsy. It wasn't that there were multitudes exactly, but one a month as a rule. She never got pregnant because she had an underdeveloped womb. This was her great good luck. There was a simple reason why she'd never wanted children: she had never seen a happy mother. Children were a pain, a cross to bear, they were a punishment to every woman who had torn up her guts for their sake.

She had no idea that at work, they all said: "Well, she's nice enough, but she sleeps around without a shred of sense, and she will never find a husband like that."

That's just how life can be. She herself thought otherwise. She was intelligent and good-looking, and good at her job, and she would find a husband eventually. He just hadn't come her way yet. She wasn't going to settle for just anybody, though the somebodies were few and far between. Even the papers said the same thing – men aren't what they used to be, the male stock is dwindling.

Her widowed neighbour came by that evening. Lina Pavlovna had always found this woman oddly irritating. First of all, the way she carried her widowhood like a banner, head held high, when everyone knew that a widow's head was supposed to droop until her chin touched her clavicle, instead of pointing up. Secondly, her going off into extraordinary raptures about the life she'd spent with her departed husband – as though Lina was deaf as a post and had never had to listen to the breaking crockery next door. Every so often, something less breakable would thump against her wall, right above where she knew the couple's bed was, and so Lina Pavlovna always suspected that it was the wife's head.

Comparing herself with her neighbours made Lina Pavlovna feel a particular kind of pride, which had something in it of the government's quality assurance stamp – you know, the kind with the stupidly outstretched wings, or something, the one we used to be snobbish about. Lina Pavlovna's pride was a feeling kindred to that snobbery. And lately things had taken a ridiculous turn. A suitor had begun calling. They would go out together, walking another thing that irritated Lina Pavlovna: a dog – a dachshund – called Gemma.

So then. The neighbour dropped in and, clasping her hands beseechingly to her bosom, said:

"Lina Pavlovna! I beg you, would you take my Gemma for three days? She's docile and clever. You just need to walk her in the morning and in the evening, and feed her. It won't be hard. She knows you, and she loves you."

Had the neighbour stopped there, she would have been resoundingly and definitively refused. But instead, she wrung her hands even harder and uttered something astonishing:

"My friend Nikolai Petrovich and I must go and see his

169

parents. It wouldn't be right to get married without their blessing."

"You're getting married?" croaked Lina Pavlovna, trying to add up through her feeling of dismay whether it was six or eight months that had elapsed from the death of the first husband.

"It was actually Gemma who brought us together, you know. She and I were out for a walk, and then she just started to follow him."

Here the widow omitted to mention the fresh liver that had been in the man's shopping bag at the time.

"So that's how we met. He's a wonderful man. A dentist. He's all alone, and I'm all alone. We have such a nice time together. Igor, as he lay dying, he told me: "If you meet a worthy man, don't think twice." But I'm hesitating. I want to see what his parents are like. I'm begging you, take my Gemma in. If not, tell me straight out, so I have time to find someone else... But I hope you can..."

"I'll do it," Lina Pavlovna replied.

She herself was surprised at the unhesitating answer. There was something strange at work inside her, a kind of transmigration of her organs: her heart had slipped out from its place and was fluttering in the pit of her stomach, while her brain was pressing down on her eyes, squeezing out tears. Two thoughts duelled, like musketeers, inside her head. The first: that's all you're good for now, walking other people's dogs. The other thought, the dashing d'Artagnan of the two, was more specific: if a man could be persuaded to follow a loser-widow's dog into a happy ever-after, Lina Pavlovna herself would certainly look to her full advantage with a little dog in tow. She would float next to the dog like a swannee.

Anyone could say swan – but that was how the voice inside

170

her said it: a swannee.

And so it was decided.

"I'll bring over the dog food," said the neighbour, "so it's all easy. We leave tomorrow night, but we'll have time to all walk the dog together, so she can get used to you. We'll be back on Saturday evening, in time for her walk, so you'll only have Thursday evening, Friday and the Saturday morning to do. We'll leave you the phone number, just in case. We're only going to Azov, it's not far. We'll bring you back the freshest fish, and some gooseberry jam. It's their speciality over there."

Lina Pavlovna was so shaken by the widow's story that she completely forgot that she didn't much like dogs, or cats, or any kind of animals really. In her mind's eye, she was expanding upon the swannee theme, and imagining how she would walk along the embankment with the little dog, looking all slim and bright. For some reason she kept seeing a small dainty hat perched on her head, with an elegant little veil. And kid gloves, naturally. It wouldn't be *comme-il-faut*, somehow, to hold the lead in her bare hand. She did have a pair of gloves, a touch mended along the seams, but who was to notice that? She could buy the hat tomorrow. She would tell them at work that she had business at the regional office, and no one would question it.

She took a volume of Chekhov to bed with her.

Her books had once belonged to her parents, those crazed bibliophiles who in their days had braved all-night queues to put their name down for new book subscriptions. She had sold their library as a job lot to a friend of her mother's, whose apartment was an unholy mess. They were so dusty, all those books! She had kept just enough of them to fill two little shelves under the lintel in her room. One of them happened to be a single volume edition of Chekhov, who was, in her

171

opinion, the most boring writer of a boring bunch. She could only remember one thing, and that from school: the phrase "Come, Pava, perform!" from the short story "Ionych".

The teacher had read that part most amusingly.

Lina Pavlovna would trot out the phrase whenever something incongruous occurred, and was even thought of as a bit of an intellectual because of it. "It's from Chekhov's 'Ionych'," she'd explain, acknowledging the approbation of those present.

She had never actually read 'The Lady with the Dog.' She had seen a boring film of it. All she could remember was the mother character, from whom the father character was trying to escape, making their children learn declensions. They were declining something stupid, some random word like wash-stand.

There was another thing she remembered from the film: the dog in it was a spitz. It was a shame that the neighbour's dog was a dachshund and not a spitz. There was something disconcerting about it. She read the short story before bed, persevering even though it bored her rigid. All she could glean from it was that the lady with the spitz was similarly out on the embankment to catch a man. Similarly with a dog for bait. What else could you use, if a dog was all you had? Cats didn't seem suitable somehow. Anyway, a cat is just a mousetrap, nothing more.

She was ready to drop the book, when she saw this phrase, out the corner of one sleepy eye: "...something stirred in his heart; and he perceived that there was no one in the world who was as close, dear and vital to him as she, lost though she was in the provincial crowd; this small, unremarkable woman holding a vulgar lorgnette in her hand, was the meaning of all his life now, his despair, his joy, the only happiness he could now wish for himself…"

There was the sweetness of a lover's caress in those words, and it made her swoon. "This small woman was the meaning of his life now": the words seared themselves onto her heart like a visa stamp in a passport. The lorgnette had vanished like the insignificant detail it was. The main thing was to think of it just like that, in those very words. It would happen, just like that, when she went walking with the little dog. Her old granny had liked to say: "Nothing happens out of nowhere. It all comes from God." Gemma had not come out of nowhere. Gemma was a sign.

And Lina Pavlovna burst into tears, weeping like that sensitive man from the short story. It was for her that he had wept. It was for him that she wept now. And her heart softened and grew pliable, it stilled momentarily, only to startle and beat once more, to fresh tears.

…She had found a hat straightaway. As soon as she laid her eyes on it, she had known that was the one. She adjusted the veil as she thought fit, ignoring the saleswoman's advice to "gather and pinch" it into shape. She didn't wear it on her way back home, nor on the evening's group excursion with the widow, the suitor and Gemma, who didn't seem to notice her at all as she trotted next to her mistress. Stretchy and short-legged, she didn't look like a Gemma at all, and most importantly, she was not a spitz. This was greatly to the detriment of Lina Pavlovna's plan, but the bridges had been burned, the hat had been purchased, the gloves winkled out of the accessories bag. She would try with the gloves, and without.

She made the morning sortie wearing nothing special, just her usual work clothes. There was hardly anybody on the embankment in the mornings. Gemma behaved with dignity, didn't try to wrench the leash, did her business under a bush, shook herself off and went home happily. She squealed a bit in front of her own apartment door, but consented to walk through another door, too. The first sortie had established that the dog would not be any trouble.

Lina Pavlovna prepared for the evening walk the way Natasha Rostova prepared for her first ball. She wore a beige suit comprised of a split skirt and a jacket featuring sharply tailored lapels and large decorative buttons. Her blouse was a complementary shade of yellow and frothed winningly around her neck. She had put on the Viennese-heeled shoes (at least that's what they used to call them, but she wouldn't know about now), as these were comfortable. The gloves looked nice on their own, but didn't go with the worn leash. She had to tuck them into her pocket, fanning the ends out attractively. The hat, on the other hand, was a poem and a song all by itself. Gemma was certainly not worth such splendour, and Lina Pavlovna did consider swapping it for her old hat, wide-brimmed with a moiré ribbon, ultimately she couldn't resist the beauty of the new – so she didn't even try the old one on.

The evening was fine, the river calm. The embankment had only a Thursday's-worth of people promenading, rather than Saturday or Sunday's. Lina Pavlovna felt that men and women were looking at her, but fleetingly, without much care. "It takes time," she admonished herself. "It takes time." She stopped to look at a theatre poster, she hadn't been in ages. Who would she go with, her girlfriends? That would be pitiful. She had similarly lost the knack of going to the cinema. Well, occasionally... Very occasionally she'd go to a matinee of something especially touted. The last thing she saw was *Moulin Rouge* and it didn't leave much of an impression. All right, so it was bright, and pretty, but it didn't make her throb with emotion... No, not in the slightest. Anyway she had a

174

good television set, she'd treated herself to a satellite dish. She had all the movies at home now.

"Are you a fan of the circus?" Oh. Gemma must have pulled her right over to the circus poster.

It was Him, standing by her side. There could be no doubt. Middle-aged, tall, and a bit unshaven – just the way she likes them. What's more, in a naval captain's uniform. Quite a big deal in Rostov, which was after all a port city.

"Just loitering," she answered. "I haven't been to the circus in ages, and I can't say I wish to go. I'd be lying." How perfectly lightly, how casually it tripped off her tongue. She even took a few steps after Gemma, who was pulling at the leash. He would follow – of that she was certain. And already she was feeling the beginnings of a rising heat, and she wanted to unbutton her jacket, and her frothy blouse too.

In her mind's-eye she can already see how, when she wakes first and starts to rise, his strong arm will hold her back, and they will lie together in silence, and then he will say: "I think I might want to stay here forever." That's almost like becoming someone's despair, joy and only happiness, isn't it?

Big, tall, unshaven, he was an exact match for her dream, her aching hope.

"I had a dachshund too," he said. "She died of heartbreak, I can be away for so long, you understand."

"It seems to me rather selfish, if you'll forgive me, to have a dog if you're never home."

"That's why I don't have one anymore," he said sadly, and that was the end of that topic.

They walked together in silence. She gazed at the pair of them fondly, as though from afar. A beautiful lady with a dog, a handsome captain, just now on shore leave…

"I've lived in Rostov all my life," she said, "but I've never known any sailors. Very much a land-lubber, I'm afraid."

"And what kind of work do you do?"

She was tempted to say chemchronpharmatron – the word was already bubbling and fizzing on the tip of her tongue – but instead said simply:

"I'm a chemist." This, despite being only a lab technician. They were chemists too, though, weren't they? "I really love my profession," she added. "It's not exactly lucrative, but it's not all about money, is it? Do you agree? You have to feel interested in what you do, fulfilled…"

Some inchoate instinct told her this was not a good topic of conversation. Feverishly, she began to search for something clever to say, but her head was filled with tomorrow morning and his heavy hand upon her breast.

"Are sailors well-paid?" Her tone was casual, if a shade apologetic.

"Don't make me laugh. It just about pays for socks and ciggies."

The conversation was straying quite far now from the daydream with the strong manly arm. This was the way labourers spoke at their places of work. But she wasn't fond of labourers. Nor was she fond of peasants. She saw herself in a quite different light, as someone above considerations of money. Obviously there wasn't anything above considerations of money nowadays – not really – not art, not literature, not family nor love… What else have we got to show for existing in a world where everything can be bought and sold?

Just to be on the safe side, she twitched the lead, as if to go home. Gemma refused to turn. Maybe it really was too early to go.

"How old is your little dog?"

This conversational gambit was even worse. How was she

to know how old the stupid dog is? And how long do dogs live, at any rate?

"Three," she said, quite at random, "or thereabouts. I'm not sure because she was my neighbour's, who died suddenly of a stroke."

Wasn't lying a bitch. As soon as you lied once, another lie, then another was sure to follow. It wasn't a big deal for a chance encounter, but it had come straight from Chekhov, from those words now imprinted in her very being. This was getting too specific. Talk of money and earning a crust –it was all anathema to her fantasies of tomorrow morning. And now the dog's age, to boot! She's meant to be this guy's "lady with the dog", and here she is without the faintest idea about dogs.

"She lived with me after the neighbour died," she is making this all up on the spot, "but now a relative has appeared, who wants the apartment and the dog. She's got some difficulties with the move, so she's between here and Kamensk, and so I look after Gemma sometimes. I'm happy to. I live on my own. Gemma loves me…"

That was more like it. She thought she had got them back on to the right path now, but she was wrong.

"Why, is the relative young and feisty? Keen to inherit?" asked the captain.

"That's the thing, she isn't really. She's still a kid. You have to show her everything, teach her what to do. And anyway, there isn't anything to inherit besides the apartment and the dog."

"An apartment is a big thing these days," the sailor said. "The base of operations. You can rent it out, you can sell it. And every apartment has something in it, for sure… some little wooden dresser, from the old days. And inside, a savings book, worn out little thing. Just the ticket for a young woman…"

Lina Pavlovna was anxiously trying to recall the particulars of the neighbour's flat, and also feeling that she didn't like the thrust of his questions somehow. They were sort of inessential, leading somewhere off the path. They made her vaguely nervous.

"Oh, the apartment is nothing special. I must say I haven't poked around in her savings-books. As that's none of my business," she said pointedly. "My business is Gemma." And at that moment she did really love the dog, like it was her own dog, like an ally against something frightening.

"I know what you mean," said the captain. "If you're doing good, you're not stopping to count someone else's money. It's apples and hoo-ranges, so to say."

The "hoo-ranges" seemed off too. And something – not doubt exactly, but a kind of impotent dislike – seemed to take root in her. Lina Pavlovna twitched the leash again, away from the captain. But she had clearly been unfair to him, because he now took her arm. He told her she was the best-looking woman on the whole of the embankment. He said he could sense the dog was tiring. "The short-legged kind tire quickly," he said. And then they were going up the hill, up the narrow street where she lived, and Lina Pavlovna's heart beat faster and faster, it let go of dislike and fear, bringing her back to what she had dreamed. Because tomorrow would be Friday, and so there was barely any time left at all. Now she was worried about something else: her lies. How would she explain everything after? How could she? Where's the kid, he would ask, when he saw the neighbour with her beau. If everything went according to Chekhov, the captain would be certain to meet them both. And the inevitability of their love would crash into the implacability of the truth.

Now she is thinking, "I still have time – there's still time.

I'll think of something!"

There's the whole of tomorrow, and a lot can happen. They will have breakfast together, and lunch, and lie down for a rest in the afternoon. And he will tell her that he would like to stay forever. And then she will whisper to him: "I lied to you, but our meeting was worth it, don't you think? Does it really matter after everything that's happened between us?"

And he will embrace her and say: "My clever little fibber! Everything is just fine. I would have approached you with or without the dog."

And she will embrace him and they'll have mad sex, and the dog will be nothing to do with any of it.

In the meantime, they had come inside the building and then inside the apartment, and the captain hung his cap on the hook by the door, but when he raised his arm Lina Pavlovna caught a whiff of sweat. She knew that men generally don't smell of roses, but this smell was, well, how could you put it… But once in the living room, everything came all right again. There was a man sitting gracefully in her armchair, lightly for all his size. His raised trouser turn-ups revealed quite decent socks and shoes. If you looked side on, though, you could see that the heels were quite worn. Gemma was rattling her bowl, the sun had almost set, a little longer and the sultry southern evening would be upon them – with all that it entails…

"Lina Pavlovna, have you ever been married?" he asked directly, and somewhat tactlessly. "It's just that there are no traces of a man in your home. Are you a widow? Divorced?"

No one had ever questioned her in such a crass way. All her lovers had met her at the technical college, or had been neighbours, or co-workers at the chemchromepharma. They'd all known everything about her, and she had never been with any man who hadn't. How stupid not to have prepared some

179

answers in advance? Just in case she met a man who would stay forever, instead of rushing away. A man who would wish to know about her life before him.

"My husband drowned on the day after our wedding. Please don't ask me again. I don't like talking about it…"

Why had these words, precisely, this pitiful little story, escaped her? At least this one was a sailor, he wouldn't just go and drown…

He seemed to sense her – well, not confusion exactly – but a sort of shyness, and gallantly threw her a lifeline.

"God forbid," he said. "I wouldn't pry in someone's affairs. I don't need to know everything. It's just… You could find yourself going to pay a visit to a lady with a dog, smitten, so to say, by her charms… and here's her husband, come home suddenly from a work trip. How would that be, now…"

Could this really be what he thought of her? That she was one of those women, with their husbands away on a work trip?

"Why, does that often happen to you?" she asked, voice cracking.

"Not once! But there's something mysterious about you, or maybe it's not you, but the dog… or perhaps it's the sun, lying on the ground now like a hot meat pie, the kind that calls out for a shot of vodka. I don't suppose you've got any?"

She did have some, as it happened, but she was supposed to offer it to him herself, and not just a bare shot of vodka, but with a proper accompaniment of salted pork and horseradish, with boiled shrimps and tiny, freshly pickled cherry tomatoes.

"I'm sorry, I don't have any. Shall I put on some music?"

"Nah," said the captain abruptly, and rose to his feet. "Where's your lav?"

This bald "nah" and "lav" really were rude. Especially from him, who had seemed so respectable, with his long fingers and

180

The Lady with the Dog

his large clever eyes, without a hint of the lout in them.

But that's exactly how he was. He perceived her disappointment, and was almost tender when he said:

"How about we have some tea, then?"

She replied joyfully, "On the double!" and raced to the kitchen, with him following. She really did have everything to go with tea. A little cake, a small package of chocolate truffles, and even a liqueur miniature left over from her birthday. She had these slender little Egyptian teacups, with matching square saucers.

He seemed strangely interested in her hallway, walking up and down as if to measure it. "Itty bitty," he said to her.

"Not when you live alone," she had answered, as she left the kitchen, and the thought that had come into her head was this: he's trying my little flat out for size, he's a seaman after all, a home for him is just a place to dock.

The hallway reeked of sweat. When Gemma saw the humans at the door, and therefore ready to go out, Gemma got busy and brought out her leash. The three of them stood there, in the hallway: Gemma with the leash, the sailor – leaning backwards into the coat-rack, and Lina Pavlovna herself, struggling with a strange feeling of disorder. It made her kick the wholly innocent Gemma; the dog whimpered and hid under the table, but it didn't make Lina Pavlovna feel any less horrid.

The sailor drank his tea hastily.

"Don't be in such a hurry," she gently admonished him. "Hold that mouthful of tea with the liqueur for a moment, and when you are gone it will one day come back to you as a lovely memory."

"If you say so," said the sailor. "But I'd rather just shack up with you right here."

What a crude phrase. She shuddered, but the meaning triumphed over the form.

"And whose orders can they be, to make you go?" she teased.

"I've got the day watch to relieve," he said. "Everyone tries to skive off early. There's no order in the fleet these days."

"We live in disordered times," she muttered in her desperation.

Unmistakably, he was looking to leave. She felt physically ill, thinking of her expectations of the night and the following morning, and all that she had dreamed up.

"How long will you be in town for?" she asked.

"We push off tonight," he said. "That's the service for you. It's so nice here with you, but I've got to scatter, I mean, run along. The nor'easter, the wind, you know…"

She didn't understand what that meant, but she understood something else. The sailor's face looked strange: here he was, still chewing a biscuit, but it was as though he had blinked out of existence already.

"Why don't I give you my address, just in case?"

"Oh, yes!" he said, and she ran to her bedroom to look for something to write it on.

The hot meat pie that was the sun had vanished. And the room looked different, as though abandoned.

"I'll write it on this calendar page," she said, returning with a calendar open to today. "So you don't forget."

He rose, and then he did the unimaginable – he kissed the page. "For all my days," he said, and placed it in his pocket.

He took his cap down from where it had hung on the hook – of all places – just above Lina Pavlovna's raincoat and when, cap in hand, he embraced her, it wasn't sweat she inhaled but the scent of a strong, virile male. She felt a stab of fury at the loss of her morning with the sailor, the loss of a man who would sleep the morning long.

"What is the name of your cruiser?" she asked dejectedly.

"Watch for the *Columbine*."

"A strange name for a ship…"

"Well, really it's *Columbus*. But, you know, a ship can have the nature of a woman. Walk me down to the embankment and I'll tell you all about cruisers with feminine wiles."

A joyful pang: it wasn't all over yet! She gave Gemma, who was getting in the way underfoot, a little kick away from the door, and hurried down with him.

"All natural objects are either male or female," he said.

"I know. Everything has a grammatical gender."

"That's not what I mean. Take your armchair, up at home: at first it looks soft, feminine, but no, it's masculine – keeps trying to push you off. Your hallway is feminine, though. I could stay there forever."

On the embankment, he grasped her by the shoulders and, giving her a little shake, kissed her awkwardly on the lips and quickly ran off, without looking back.

She walked back up her street with an effort, puzzling over that ridiculous kiss – first the calendar page, then her – a kiss which didn't stir a thing inside her. "A waste of the liqueur," she was thinking. "What a waste. Now I'll have to run to the shop if anyone else comes over." Sure, she could keep an eye on *Columbine* the feminine cruiser. Which one would that be? Her thoughts ran on apathetically and didn't seem to join up. How strange, the way he had pressed up against the coat-rack. "I could stay here forever," he said. So stay, the devil take you, stay! Why can't people just get what they want? Why does everything in the world have to be pell-mell?

The words from 'The Lady with the Dog' surfaced again in her mind. That broad got lucky, no doubt about it. Maybe because she had a spitz, and not this ridiculous stumpy dachshund. But it wasn't all bad, not at all! He did kiss her, even though he was in a hurry. And told her the name of his ship. He hadn't given his surname, but she could find out the cruiser's routes, get a spitz of her own and go down portside. And he, so big and handsome, would doubtless come ashore to her, and she would whisper in his ear: "Come then, I've got some very good vodka laid in, the special birch-filtered kind."

Lost in her daydream, she was surprised to hear barking from behind her own door. It was Gemma, raging against solitude. "I wonder what time it is," she thought, "I seem to have lost track." But the kitchen clock had stopped and brazenly showed yesterday's time. "I must have lost my mind completely. Forgot to wind it, and now it'll go haywire. It'll show whatever time it pleases now."

She went to the dresser, where her little gold watch – self-winding – lay in a crystal-glass ashtray on the top. But the watch wasn't there. She always put it in the same place, and might well have laid it just beside the ashtray, without looking. But there was nothing on the top of the dresser. The beautiful little toy longboat, chiselled from colourful semi-precious Urals stones, was missing too. Her first panicked thought was to run to the *Columbine*, but immediately knew that neither it nor the *Columbus* would be there, no more than her watch and toy longboat were here.

She went to clear away the teacups. Of course the silver spoons, brought out only for special occasions, were also gone. Stumblingly, clutching at the walls, she made her way to the coat-rack. Her dummy coat – the ancient ragged jacket that always hung under her raincoat – was where Lina Pavlovna kept the cash, in an old mitten tucked into a pocket. The mitten was gone. How heavily he had leant on the coat-rack, how he'd wanted to stay...

She crumpled to the floor, weeping, her face all but touching the door mat, and Gemma, that useless bitch who couldn't spot a thief, was licking her with a certain disdain. "Oh, God," thought Lina Pavlovna, "and it's only Thursday. At least I've got enough dog food for tomorrow. And I can have crackers... and hard cheese." The phrase had completed itself, unbidden. "And what I'm I going to do now with the stupidly expensive – unaffordable in current circumstances, really – hat and veil?"

No, it was a spitz in the story, and it should have been a spitz today. So don't go thinking you'll find him with just a stupid dachshund in tow. She sat there bawling her eyes out and didn't hear the dachshund quietly howling along.

Translated by Ilona Chavasse

The Death of an Official
Galina Scherbakova

He waited to see which way she would lie down. Would it be
her left side or her right? Would it be heavy breathing and the
sulks or would she tenderly tell him: "Goodnight, Senya"? He
knew that it was ridiculous, to feel so in thrall to your wife's
moods and gestures, the tone of her voice, But it had been that
kind of day.

That morning, his boss had overtaken him on the Leningrad
road into Moscow centre, barely missing a collision, and stuck
his tongue out as his car sped on. And when they crossed paths
in a corridor at work, the man had poked him in the stomach
and said: "Getting fat, Semyon Petrovich." He'd weighed
himself just a few hours before, he hadn't gained an ounce,
not through all his week of the 'Kremlin' diet that everyone at
the top was doing these days. The tongue and the poke in the
stomach, these were all bad signs. When they demoted a friend
of his to obsolescence a few years back, that too had started
with small things. "Your haircut's not quite right, Michalych,"
his boss had told him. You can't tell your hair to grow any
slower, can you, but there they all were the next day, crowding
the mirror in the gents, preening and prettifying themselves
like cheap whores. He had sniggered a bit, at the time, but two
weeks later Michalych was history.

And who did they bring in to replace him? You might have
expected a Tikohonov look-alike, young and handsome, like
the character he played in "We'll Make it to Monday"... Well,

186

tough shit! It was a broad, no one could stand to look at her, but everybody came to roll out the red carpet, and there was a queue for pulling her chair out for her. Turned out she had worked with Himself, in Germany, way back when. No one knew whether this had been confirmed, but it seemed plausible enough: the skinny broad spoke German like a *Kraut* and was a judoka to boot. So they all paid her court.

There was a great deal of that going on lately. Of what, you say? You know the kind of thing. Semyon Petrovich forbade himself to carry on thinking these kinds of thoughts through, much less verbalise them. With the technology available these days, any noise got picked up. Better not to piss too noisily at work, either. Better to dampen the pressure and do your business quietly, unobtrusively…

Now he was trying to pick up his wife's movements. He'd become that receiver gadget himself, he wasn't to have any peace, always listening, watching, receiving.

The next day there was another traffic jam on the road into the city centre. There was chatter that Himself hadn't managed to get through it yet. Most chauffeured passengers sat there with headphones in their ears. He had heard that this was the fashion now – listening to Tolstoy audiobooks. He himself hated anything stuck in his ears. It was a childhood thing, having cotton wool stuffed in his ear, or a scope. It would send him into a rage, and he would lash out violently at the doctor or his mother. This was problematic, since children often get earache.

With the car standing still, he listened to the crunching, hissing silence of the traffic jam. The drivers called out to each other cautiously, monosyllabic. It was a tricky place to get stuck. On their portside was the leader of another political party, a crude type. He was demolishing some apples noisily and throwing the cores out through the open window, right under the wheels of Semyon Petrovich's car.

"You oughtn't litter," Semyon Petrovich said, very civilly.

"You just shut your trap," said the other man, and rolled up his window.

There was a cramp in his chest. According to the hierarchy they were exactly equal, the one in the Duma, the other in government. So how had he dared? "Shut your trap." It was unbelievable. What a phrase to choose. He hadn't joked it off, like "very well, m'lord," for example. That was how one of their young courier lads always tipped his hat at his elders' corrections. "Very well, m'lord," he'd say, and it felt cheerful somehow, and right. Everything as it should be. Someone once replied to him that we're not lords, young man, but the lad just laughed: "Who are you then? I can say sir and master, but not m'lord? What's the bloody difference?" At the time he'd thought that would be the end of the boy, he'd get the boot. But no. There were no repercussions. In fact, a little later they promoted him. Semyon Petrovich wondered idly whether, as he ran about now in the top ranks, the boy still permitted himself to joke about in that way…

That bloody "shut your trap" tipped him into a foul mood. He didn't notice the car starting to move again. Finally, they arrived, but all that morning his heart was heavy. His wife had said to him repeatedly: "You've got to make yourself harder. If you can't tell them to eff off out loud, just do it in your head. And you'll start to feel better."

At the meeting he felt especially gloomy, and suddenly needed the toilet. But his long experience of interminable meetings stood him in good stead, and he wasn't worried on that score. He could wait. And just so, his nerves calmed and his bladder also.

Yet as soon as the break was announced, he dashed head-long from the room. He had been first to rise, even before the convenor had finished his sentence, but it didn't matter, in a moment everyone was heading for the door. He made it first to the toilet, and was the first to leave his cubicle, unburdened and almost happy. He was washing his hands as the chief of their entire bureau came alongside him to use the next sink over. Their eyes met in the mirror, and he thought he detected a trace of hardness and even blame in the chief's face. But why, what had he done? He looked himself up and down, everything was as usual. His suit, his tie... the whole – what did they call it now – dress code. He tried to catch the chief's eyes again, and again saw the same hardness and blame in those eyes. They left at the same time, and as he hung back to let the man pass, he asked, because he couldn't help himself:

"Something the matter?"

"It's rude to stare at people."

"Oh no, I didn't mean... excuse me. I seem to be a bit dazed and dizzified today." He had said it like a little joke, inviting the boss to laugh with him at the silly word.

"No such word in Russian," said the man, and walked abruptly away.

He didn't know why he followed after the man. He only wanted to explain... But something stopped him in the doorway. A strange and sudden noise that pushed at his ears from both sides. He had to cover his ears with his hands, and then, unsteady on his feet, he collapsed.

We mustn't forget this was the lavatory. People don't stick around, they come and go quickly. So the first ones to come after him, they had to walk right over him. And no one trod on his chest or his stomach, no, everyone was stepping over him carefully; he was still able to perceive that fact, and even thank his comrades wordlessly. But then the noises in his ears came together in the middle and sort of exploded, and he didn't see or hear anything any more. His soul, released, flew up unburdened by the words of gratitude, which remained, absurd and useless, stuck to the tip of his dead tongue.

Translated by Ilona Chavasse

What a Girl
Ludmila Petrushevskaya

For me now it's as if she were dead, maybe she really is dead, although in the past month in our building they haven't buried anyone. Our building's the usual — five stories, no elevator, four entrances, across from a building just like it and so on. If she were dead, everyone would know. So she must be living somehow or other.

Here look: stuck to this drawer with the blank book cards I have a picture, a snapshot. That's her, Raisa, Ravilya, accent on the last syllable, she's Tatar. You can't see anything in the snapshot, a face covered by hair, two legs and two arms: in the pose of Rodin's *Thinker*.

She always sits like that, even recently at my birthday party she was sitting like that. That was the first time I'd ever observed her with other people, until then we'd always seen each other one on one, or two on two — her and her Sevka and me and my Petrov.

It turned out she didn't know how to dance and so she just sat there, quiet as a mouse. My Petrov pulled her up to dance, but after that dance she went right home.

No, she can't dance, but she's a professional prostitute. Where did Sevka find her, what cesspool did he pull her out of? She'd just come out of prison and again begun going from man to man, but then he upped and married her. He told me all this himself with real emotion, but made me swear to God not to tell anyone else. He also told me about her father, how

191

from the age of five Raisa glued little pillboxes together, she and her mother did this for her father, her father got the job because of being an invalid. But then her mother died, had a heart attack in hospital, and her father started openly bringing women to their room. Terrible things went on. Raisa ran away from home and wound up in an empty apartment with some boys who kept her there for two or three months, until the police finally arrived. But that's all history, it doesn't concern anyone now, what matters is that Raisa's still at it.

Sevka goes to work and she stays home, she doesn't work anywhere. Sevka leaves her lunch – comes home and she hasn't even heated it up, hasn't even been in the kitchen. She lies on her back all day, smokes or pokes around the shops. Or cries. She'll start crying for no reason – and cry for four hours straight. And of course our neighbour comes running to me, pale as death: quick, you have to help Raechka, she's crying. So I rush over with validol and valerian. Although the same thing happens to me sometimes – and not for no good reason, not just because – and I just want to lie down and die. But what's going on inside me, what I have to bear – no one has any idea. I don't scream, don't thrash around on an unmade bed. Only when my Petrov tried to leave me the first time, when he and that Stanislava wanted to get married and were already looking to borrow money for the divorce and an apartment and they wanted to adopt my Sasha – that was the only time in my life I broke down. True, Raisa defended me then, like a bear protecting her cub, she went at Petrov with her fingernails.

This happens to my Petrov three or four times a year, this falling hopelessly in love, forever. Now I know. But in the beginning, the first time he walked out, I nearly threw myself out of our third-floor window. I was literally shaking with

impatience to end it all because the night before he'd told me
he was going to bring Stanislava by to meet Sasha. First thing
in the morning I took Sasha to my mother's on Nagornaya,
then went back and hung around all day waiting for them.
Then I climbed up onto the windowsill and started attaching
a piece of wire left over from when Petrov put up a clothes
line in the kitchen for Sasha's nappies. The wire was strong,
covered with vinyl. I attached the wire to a spike Petrov had
driven into the cement wall ages ago to reinforce the cornice.
We'd just been given our room, Sasha wasn't born yet, and
I remembered Petrov pounding the wall for nearly an hour.
I wound one end of the wire round that spike, but the wire
was smooth and kept slipping off. Finally, though, I fastened
the wire, then made a noose with the other end for my neck,
I somehow figured out what to tie where. And just at that
moment I heard a key in the lock. I forgot everything – I even
forgot about Sasha, the only thing I remembered was that they
wanted to adopt him, and because of that it was as if they'd
ruined him for me, as if I hadn't given birth and nursed him.
I was afraid Petrov and Stanislava were about to walk in the
door, I gave the window handle such a jerk the sticking plaster
cracked. We'd caulked the window for the winter.

In the room it was already dusk, out of the window I could
see the building opposite, empty, dark – no one had moved in
yet – with only a streetlight burning not far down below. Again
I tugged at the window, so hard the frame gave way. And just
then Raisa rushed into the room and grabbed me round the
legs. She's weak, and I'm strong and just then I was furious,
but she clung to my legs like a dog and kept saying: "Let's do
it together, let's do it together, wait for me." And I'm thinking
to myself, why are you butting in, what's so bad about your
life – I even felt sort of offended. My life, you could say, had

fallen apart, my husband had left me, left me with a child and wanted to take the child away – what did she have to complain about? But Raisa kept trying to swing her knee up onto the ledge of the open window, although to throw herself from our third floor into deep snow without a noose around her neck – that would have been ridiculous. I pushed her away with all my might and my hand hit her face – her face was wet, slippery, ice-cold. So then I jumped down from the window and shut it. The sticking plaster had wrinkled and there was no way to stretch it back into place, and besides my hands were trembling.

The only thing left in my mind after that incident was a coldness. I don't know, maybe Raisa had something to do with it, but I just realised that all those senseless acts and rages at the first stab of heartache – all that was not for me. Why should I compete with Raisa?

And as it turned out all I needed to do was use my head. I worked it so that Stanislava was soon a fairy tale. It wasn't hard to do because Petrov was stupid enough to let slip to me what she did and where she worked, plus she had an unusual name. Petrov had other women after her, I often didn't even know their names, but they were no cause for worry, much less hanging myself. Whenever Petrov raised the subject of divorce I just brushed it off. His tears had no effect on me, his telling me that he hated me. I'd just say with a smile: "Can't run away from yourself, lover boy. If you're schizophrenic, then go and see a doctor."

The truth is he was stuck with me: I was registered in his room and he knew I would never un-register. I had nowhere to go. To swap our smallish room for two even smaller ones was impossible. And another thing: when Sasha was born, Petrov's plant had promised him a two-room apartment. That's why I always knew he'd have his fun and then come back, because when the new building was finished and the question of tenants came up, he, alone, and what's more divorced, would get nothing. Whereas when we got the two-room apartment – then we could swap it, and get divorced. So every time Petrov stayed with me to wait for that two-room apartment. Or maybe that wasn't it and he came back to me for some other reason. Because I always felt that if Petrov ever really got the urge, he wouldn't think twice about the apartment, or anything else, he'd just walk out as if we'd never been together. When his latest affair was ending, he'd begin spending evenings at home, he'd watch me flying back and forth between the kitchen and our room, he'd help me with Sasha – he'd even pick him up from kindergarten and put him to bed when I had the evening shift. And finally, he'd show up with a bottle of semi-sweet champagne, knowing it's my favorite. I have to admit I always saw that moment coming and always prepared for it. He'd say with a sigh: "Have a drink with me?" – and I'd go and get the Czech wine glasses from the sideboard in the kitchen. It was always exciting, like a first date, except that we both knew how this one would end. Those zigzags in our life gave it spice. Petrov would whisper to me that I was the sexiest, the most loving, the most passionate.

Whereas Raisa, in that department, was like a brick wall. The guys we knew who'd been with her – you couldn't say they'd slept with her because it usually happened during the day when Sevka wasn't home, all you had to do was find her in her room alone, and you could easily get what you wanted – anyway the guys said it was boring with her and that she acted not so much as if it didn't matter, but as if it disgusted her. And she never wanted to talk to anyone afterwards, the way you usually do – people aren't just animals, after all, they're thinking beings, they want to know what makes the person next to them tick, who that person is. Petrov and I would sometimes talk the whole night, especially after his zigzags, we couldn't stop. He'd tell me about his women, compare them to me, and I couldn't get enough – I kept trying to get more and more details out of him. Together we'd make fun of Raisa, but not in a mean way. You see, all the guys we knew, literally all of them, even the ones who came to visit from Petrov's home town, they'd all been with Raisa. And they all told us about her.

Take Grant, for example. We wrote to him that if he got here and no one was home, we'd leave a key in the apartment next door with Raisa, and that she was almost always there. We'd been doing that for a long time – leaving a key with Raisa, it's easier that way. And we had her key. So as not to have to ring the bell every time and involve the neighbours. When we both got home from work, Grant was sitting on Sasha's sofa bed, red-faced, sad, leafing through a monograph by Sisley. Raisa's keys to our door were on Sasha's desk. Right away we knew what had happened and burst out laughing. I said: "So, did Raisa crack?" Grant looked at us, frightened, shocked. But then, when we'd explained everything, he sobered up and calmed down. He gave us all the details. He said that when she opened the door, he even asked her: "Why are you so scared of me? I don't bite." She sprang away into the corner. She was in just her housecoat, she always goes around like that at home. Grant also said that he had the impression she'd do anything because she's afraid of something, literally out of her mind with fear. And because of that he had this horrible feeling afterwards, as if he'd insulted her, although she didn't say anything and didn't resist.

We calmed him down and told him not to worry. That's how

she appears to everyone at first. She seems like a mousy little dark-haired girl, and of course she can't dance, and whenever we have guests she sits on Sasha's sofa bed without a peep, and you can't get her to dance unless you really try because she's afraid of crowds. And all the guys we know fall for this, it arouses their hunter's instinct, they all pull her out of her corner by the hand, and she's literally trembling all over. Then she goes home.

When I first got to know her she made me feel a sort of stinging pity, the kind you feel for a newborn animal, not a little animal, but one that's just been born, there's nothing cute about it, and it literally stings your heart. There's no love mixed in with this feeling, it's pure pity, the kind that takes your breath away.

It all began with her ringing our bell one night after three a.m., unaware that we were strangers, that it was the middle of the night. I opened the door, she was standing there in her housecoat, with wet cheeks, tears dripping from her chin, hands in her pockets, trembling all over – she asked me for a cigarette. I took her into the kitchen, turned on the light, and found an open pack of cigarettes in Petrov's coat pocket. We had a smoke, then I said: "Where's your Sevka?" Through puffy lips she said: "Away on business." We sat there for a long time – I made her some coffee – until she stopped trembling. Then I had this sense that Sasha in his sleep had thrown off his covers, I went into our room, pulled the covers up, went back into the kitchen – again Raisa was hunched up on her stool, crying. "What's wrong?" I said. "You must be missing your husband." She looked up at me and said: "I'm afraid of the atomic bomb." It wasn't death she was afraid of, it was the bomb, can you imagine? You could see she wasn't playacting, not at all, that's something she never did. She always did what she had to do, and she never pretended. That's what was strange about her – she had no resistance, I guess. Something in her was broken, some instinct for self-preservation. And you immediately felt that.

Before leaving – standing in the doorway – she began to cry again and went back to her place like that. I didn't try to stop her – it was already morning and I had to be at work by nine. And then, when I got to work, I told everyone about the girl next door, what a girl, the conscience of the world. I even began to feel proud of her.

We couldn't live a day without each other. Either she and Sevka would hang out in our room, or we'd go to them. I'd go to bum a cigarette – and she'd say: sit down, let's have a smoke. And two hours would go by. I'd tell her everything, just like I'm telling you now. That's the way I am: talking about myself makes me feel better. So we'd sit there for two hours discussing the world's problems – life, people. I'd sit there calmly, talking on and on. I'm a good housekeeper, I get everything done first thing, lunch is already made, and right after lunch I race off to the institute when I have the second shift. But she both doesn't work, and gets nothing done – as if she weren't even Sevka's wife. He goes to work, then to the store, then flies home like a madman, as if he had a baby screaming there. He walks in, puts everything away – although with Raisa, except for the overflowing ashtray, there was never any mess. She didn't dirty a dish, Sevka would leave her soup in the kettle, meat in the frying pan – and she wouldn't even check to see what kind of soup, wouldn't even stir it with a spoon.

Sevka took her to the doctor, got the day off work and just took her. The doctor said she was completely emaciated, practically dystrophic. Like someone living through the blockade. He prescribed aloe shots.

She bought a syringe – and now for fun she'd inject herself in the leg, above the knee. She had everything she needed – the gauze, the rubbing alcohol, the container for sterilised cotton. She boiled the needle herself. Where did she learn that? Then she'd sit down by the window and say: "Turn around" – and you'd hear a hissing sound, a sort of wheeze. I literally shuddered inwardly, I looked at Sevka, he'd be white as a sheet, leaning against the lintel. And she'd say, "All over, you idiots," – but she hadn't taken the needle out yet and was still watching the last drops run out of the syringe.

So that's how we became friends. I can't think how many times she came to blows with my Petrov because of me. She didn't know how to swear properly, so she'd only ever say: "You're a real bitch, got it?" I guess that's how they swore in prison.

Petrov recently took up with a new girl, she works at our institute, in Antonova's lab. You know her: she's that fat, flaccid waste of space. My Petrov keeps coming by for me at work, even when he knows I'm on the second shift and can't go home. Still he says: "You going home?" I say, no. "Then I won't wait for you" – and he makes a beeline for her in the lab. Meanwhile she, strangely enough, has started coming by the reference room to see me. And suddenly Petrov appears. We three chat for a bit, and before I know it he's invited her to our place. He likes having people over, can't live without parties. If we have an empty evening, he sits around moping, then suddenly gets up and goes out.

Well the time was coming when that emptiness would have to be filled up with something. I could just feel it in my bones. I'd look around me and notice all the different girls I knew and wonder: this one or that one? At the time we were always having people over. I'd practically moved Sasha to Mama's on Nagornaya, even though she already had her granddaughter there. We had guests every evening – it was hectic, Petrov and I were living like innkeepers, groups of friends would show up with guitars and bring wine. I'd make my famous cookie roll with chopped nuts in cellophane and the fried onions with egg yolk and black-bread croutons. But I had the feeling that it was all a complete waste of time, that everything was going to pieces, any minute now it would all blow up, because in spite of the songs and the guitar and the dancing, in spite of the tape-player and the good-looking guys and girls, those evenings of ours were forced, boring.

I'd look at those very young girls who'd been ripening, whole bunches of them, while I gave birth to Sasha, brought him up, went to the store, fed Petrov and washed all his clothes, while we bought the tape-player and the small bed and desk for Sasha now he was older. Those girls would go on the attack, whole battalions of them – pretty, with saucy haircuts, managing just fine on their meager stipends and wages, ready for anything, aggressive. But I knew enough not to be afraid of them. After all, I knew my Petrov. I looked at all those girls and I knew that he wanted Raisa, and not just for the hell of it, but forever.

But their relations, strangely enough, not only did not improve, they got even worse. She couldn't bear the sight of him and now mostly stayed away when he was home. She couldn't forgive him for my being ready to collapse from the uncertainty – I'd told her everything, except my main suspicion.

So then he went and invited that fat, flaccid Nadezhda from the third lab to come over. He has this strange habit: he always brings the new girl over to our place.

I can't understand what makes him do it. Sometimes I think he does it for me, to hurt me, to make me suffer that much more and make his zigzag that much sweeter for him. But other times I think that I have nothing to do with it, that Petrov brings the latest girl over for his own peace of mind, so that it's all above-board, without deceit, and so that the girl knows exactly what she's getting herself into, what she's up against – because after that Petrov always seems to stand back, he steers clear of the dead space separating me and this other woman so that we'll fight with each other, and not with him. Or maybe Petrov isn't capable of such subtle psychology and it's just that in the beginning, before things have progressed to the point of going to bed together, he tries to lure that other girl with the ambiguous and ticklish role of a married couple's girlfriend. Petrov, after all, isn't much to look at, and what all these women see in him, I don't know.

Anyway, in the midst of all the bedlam at our place there appeared that girl Nadezhda. I even had the feeling that Petrov wasn't very interested in her, that she was only a pale imitation of me in bed and that this time his zigzag wouldn't last long. She was so very meek and undemanding. There was nothing in her of the wild game you have to be afraid of frightening away. She was like the livestock you can herd with a stick. So I felt sorry for her. We even got to be somewhat friendly. We'd leave the institute together when I had the first shift. Little by little I realised that she didn't understand anything about life, didn't know anything about anything – about good underwear, about books, about food. She just blindly felt – with all of her skin – kindness and warmth, and then, without changing expression or saying a word, she went toward that warmth. At our institute she'd racked up several affairs that didn't go anywhere and even one pregnancy, as a result of which the baby was born dead. I remembered that event and remembered that the older women in our office said Nadezhda was better off that way.

Our three-way friendship lasted a fairly long time and would have lasted longer, if not for one incident. Leaving our room to get the coffeepot in the kitchen, I glanced at myself in the hall mirror. The mirror reflected part of the room and the table at which Petrov and Nadezhda were sitting. I saw Petrov cautiously, like a child, stroke Nadezhda's chin with his curved palm, which she then took and placed on her breast.

I controlled myself, but one thing really got me: how could I have missed that? Why was I always thinking about Raisa when the real danger – here she was, right under my nose and, scariest of all, there was nothing special about her. I mean Raisa was "the conscience of the world, what a girl", whereas Nadezhda was a waste of space.

Petrov went to see Nadezhda out and came back at one in the morning, drained and utterly exhausted, destroyed. I didn't touch him, didn't say anything because I knew that in that condition Petrov only wanted one thing: to sleep. If I'd said something and kicked him out, he would have slept in the kitchen, in the stairwell, on the window ledge. He might have gone to Nadezhda's and stayed there. For some reason, he'd come home. So there was still hope. This wasn't the final stage. It was just the beginning of a new zigzag, which was nothing but Petrov's protest against the monotony of married life. Nothing else made Petrov rush around like that. It's just that one fine day he'd become bored. Sometimes he'd get hold of these ridiculously badly retyped lectures and medical tips – pure pornography, basically. We'd read this stuff aloud to Sevka and Raisa, though I have to say it made no impression on them. They'd listen politely, but indifferently, as if we'd suddenly decided to read them tips for sufferers from atherosclerosis. Although those lectures made Petrov and me laugh till we were red in the face. For us that would be the beginning of a zigzag, but a brief one, devoid of the total heartfelt conciliation that occurred on those evenings when Petrov would return to the bosom of the family.

So anyway, figuring that this time too Petrov would come back of his own accord, I ignored everything – his coming home late, his complete neglect of Sasha and not teaching him to read any more. But a little while later a neighbour in the apartment told me that all that week, when I was working the evening shift, Petrov had been coming in with some plump girl and showing her out just before I got home. That week Sasha wasn't there either – Mama picked him up every afternoon from kindergarten and took him back to Nagornaya, so our room was free.

I immediately called Mama and asked her, just this once, to sit with Sasha that evening at our place, to put him to bed and wait till I got home. Mama didn't want to because she had so much to do on Nagornaya, my older brother had literally dumped his child, Ninochka, on her. But I talked her into helping me – my brother could get by this one evening without her. I don't remember what awful things I said about my brother so as to win Mama over and make her come to me. She didn't know anything about Petrov's zigzags, and if she'd found out, right away she'd have come between us. That's why I never said anything, and why she got on fairly well with Petrov.

Just as I knew he would, Petrov brought Nadezhda over again that evening, and they ran smack into Mama. There was a scene of some sort between Mama and Nadezhda. Because, as I said, the war was not between me and Petrov, but between me and Nadezhda. I imagined that Nadezhda would turn weak at the sight of Petrov's enraged mother-in-law and that at the sight of his crying child she'd back off.

And maybe she did back off. But not Petrov. He didn't come home that night, and it began to seem as if he never ever would. He came home a few times – for his razor, for socks and shirts, then for the tape-player. He looked unkempt, thinner and taller, and he suddenly reminded me of that sweet boy who'd once been madly in love with me.

I didn't say a word, without a sound I gave him the tape-player and everything else he wanted, whereas he behaved grudgingly, as if in his mind he'd been answering the questions I didn't ask. Still I said nothing, though by now it was clear that no amount of nobleness on my part would bring him back.

That's when I realised that I was losing everything, my whole world. Only Raisa was still with me on this side, while the whole world was on the other side. Frightened by the unexpected result of her interference, Mama was now angry at me for setting her up. And Sasha? I'm a sober-minded woman. I understand that a child's attachment and love are not directed at his parents as individuals. Any other combination of face, figure, hair colour, personality, intelligence, he would love just as much. He would love me if I was a murderer, a great violinist, a store assistant, a prostitute, a saint. But only until such time as he'd sucked his life out of me. And then, with no caring for me as a person, he'd leave. Thoughts of this impending betrayal depressed me every time I bent down in the semidarkness over his freshly washed face to hug him goodnight. Maybe I owed this feeling to Petrov who'd taught me to expect betrayal.

Mama didn't love me any more either. And anyway she'd

never loved me as a person, but only as her creation, her flesh and blood. Now, late in life, she was morbidly attached to Sasha and to her other grandchild, Ninochka. Petrov and I, my brother and his wife, were nothing to her – just relatives.

I went to Raisa and told her everything. I have experience, as you can see, in stories like this. I tell them to the girls at the institute, I even tell them to chance acquaintances, like the women you loll around with for three days in hospital after an abortion. But with Raisa it was different. She really understood that she was my only friend in the world. That I was talking about not a zigzag, but the loss of a place to live for Sasha and me, about the loss of my hope for the two-room apartment I wanted so desperately I'd even seen it in my dreams. I can't think how many times Petrov and I, during our nighttime conversations, furnished that apartment. Petrov wanted to decorate the kitchen wall himself, like Siqueiros, with an enormous fresco, he even wanted to decorate the white enamelled tray from the gas stove, he wanted to decorate the refrigerator. These were all dreams, although my Petrov draws quite well with pen and ink. He draws the portraits of famous jazzmen from pictures in magazines, puts them in thin black frames and hangs them on the wall. Petrov can play jazz piano. For a few years he performed at the Victory Club, until he began to feel too old for all those amateur shows, for the out-of-town tours to collective farms, for the mandatory accompanying of solo singing-class students. Petrov learned both percussion and a bit of contrabass. And a few times he sang (backed by his quartet: piano, guitar, contrabass, drummer) the English song *Shakohem* – I think that's how it's pronounced. But no one appreciated his simple, not raspy, not inflected voice, his impeccable English accent. He didn't sing the way he talked, there's something artificial about that too. He sang simply, loudly, woodenly, in a monotone, but there was such frankness about it, such manly sincerity and vulnerability. When he sang he was all tense, like a guitar string, and he quivered slightly in rhythm to the music. I only heard him once, when Sasha was two months old. I had no time for Petrov that evening, my milk was literally crushing my breasts, they were hard as wood, hard as cut glass. I was frantic with worry, I could feel that Sasha wanted to be fed, and Petrov's number, as always, was the last one on the programme. Finally he and the guys came out on stage, they pushed the piano to the centre. Petrov was carrying a small microphone, brand new. The drummer took a long time setting up, then they played *Chamberlain*, a soft little waltz, and then finally *Shakohem*.

Petrov sang, his tall skinny body quivering in time to the music, and I even listened for a bit, spellbound, but my breasts were bursting, I knew I had to run home to Sasha, that he was screaming to be fed. I had no time for Petrov, just as I have no time for him now, because Sasha has taken up everything in me, just as my surging milk took up both breasts. I still don't know how that made Petrov feel, my running out like that, and whether the audience clapped for him as hard as he deserved – I never asked him, and he never told me. I didn't explain anything, at the time we didn't talk much.

I don't know why I told Raisa all this. I cried in front of her, as if she alone could save me. I didn't know how to get Petrov back. Not only had the apartment – my dream – collapsed, now there was the terrible spectre of Sasha's growing up without a father, my worst fear, maybe that's why I always clung to Petrov. I'd be a single mother, Sasha would long for male guidance and leave me for the first guy to lure him away. He'd follow any pair of pants, hungry for a man's attention, he'd join a gang and go to prison.

I cried in front of Raisa and she sat there like a statue, in her pose on the edge of the daybed. At the word "prison" she didn't even flinch.

But by the next morning I'd dried my tears. It suddenly began to seem to me that this was just another one of Petrov's zigzags, because he didn't love Nadezhda and between us there'd been nothing bad, no quarrel, no discussion – it was only my mother who'd fallen out with him, and my mother wasn't me. When I went to work I even had the crazy thought of going to talk to Nadezhda. But then I let it go. You could get her to budge only with something good for her, only with concern for her and kindness, and what good did I have to offer her? Here she'd only just leaned her head against my Petrov – and I wanted her to kindly leave him? She wouldn't understand. But that wasn't the main thing – the main thing was to convince Petrov to at least make it look like he'd come back to us. He could go where he liked, if only Sasha saw him. But how to propose that to Petrov? He wouldn't do that of his own accord, or if I asked him.

So I went to Raisa and asked her to call Petrov on the phone. Well, she could say, you know, I haven't seen you in a long time, you should come by, we could talk – something like that, simple and undemanding, was my suggestion. She agreed. But she agreed with a somehow frightened look. Which, at the time, I didn't notice.

That evening I dropped by Raisa's. She was lying on the daybed and smoking. She told me that she'd talked to Petrov. That he'd be back tomorrow. That's all she said, and then suddenly, as usual, she began to cry. I brought her a glass of water from the kitchen and rushed off to get Sasha from kindergarten.

The next day Petrov returned with his briefcase and the

tape-player. In the briefcase two shirts and some socks were balled up in a newspaper. Our room was clean and cosy, we had breakfast the three of us. Sasha reached for Petrov's newspaper and began asking him which letter was which.

True, the end of this zigzag was not yet in sight. Petrov paid no attention to me and was rarely home. But this was still better than his complete absence.

Because of all I had to do I somehow didn't have time to drop in on Raisa. And I didn't feel any particular need to. Home had taken everything I had. At Petrov's plant the question of the apartment would soon be decided. I ran around registering for furnishings, standing in line.

By now Petrov had begun giving me questioning looks, he watched me with obvious satisfaction as I flew back and forth between the kitchen and our room, as I talked to Sasha. One evening before dinner he went out, without a word, and returned with a bottle of semi-sweet champagne.

He said:

"Have a drink with me?"

I ran to the kitchen for the Czech wine glasses.

We clinked glasses. And I said jokingly:

"To Raisa. To our kind genius."

Petrov grinned maliciously and said that the guys were right about her: she really was a brick wall.

It was only then I realised what had happened and felt sorry that Raisa had so betrayed me.

And she stopped existing for me, as if she were dead.

Translated by Joanne Turnbull

The Stone Guest
Olga Slavnikova

"Here we are, Anya. Our seats!" said a tall, hook-nosed man of about thirty-five as he slid the door to their sleeping compartment aside, allowing his companion to pass.

His companion, moving a dry blond lock off her face, slipped hesitantly into the dim space, which was stuffy and mysterious the way compartments always are before the train gets going. Before sitting on the berth, she stroked it with a slightly trembling palm and touched the little table before putting her small patent bag down. The young woman was definitely not behaving like an ordinary passenger accustomed to trains and life on a train. It was as if she were blind – or simply could not believe her eyes, which were translucent and moist, like melting ice. The man deftly took her robe, cosmetics bag, and fur-trimmed plush slippers – all of it new, without so much of a mote of dust from her former life – out of her suitcase, cleared away the luggage, and took her hands in his.

"Everything's fine, Anya, it's fine," the man began, warming her bloodless veins and bones.

"I don't feel so good, Vanya," the young woman said tonelessly. "I should be at the cemetery right now…"

Right then the train jerked, and out of the window, which was framed by brocade curtains, the train station columns sailed by like giant legs of a plaster cast. The passenger's pointed face reflected panic, and her eyes darted from the window to the slightly ajar compartment door, where a watery mirror also presented sooty station buildings, concrete walls covered with faded graffiti, and ledges of apartment buildings sailing away. The man gave his companion a quick hug.

"Shh, shh… Everything's fine… We're married, we're on our honeymoon," he intoned, stroking her dry, messy hair. "Forget about the cemetery."

The cemetery in question was an artifact of the 1990s famous throughout the land – the so-called Lane of Gangster Glory, which was still grandiose, albeit a little dilapidated. Here lay the heroes of the crime wars, the masters of that memorable decade when Mercs and BMWs rolled through the streets, fit to bursting with pop-music-giant-boom-boxes on wheels until gun barrels poked out lowered windows to turn enemy gang muscle into fresh corpses. In those days, every last engineer and schoolteacher in that glorious town knew the names Hog, Vovan Ferz, and Sasha the chinaman. Now those bosses had been laid to rest in their posthumous estates, surrounded by classical colonnades decorated with occasional scraps of spider webs covered with leaves from the year before last and tremulous rain tears.

The main attraction at the Lane of Gangster Glory were the statues. At one time, the press loved making snide remarks about the broad swathes of gold religiously gilded onto the stone necks and the cellphones and Merc keychains in the heavy stone hands. The wave of newspaper articles passed, but the cellphones and gold chains remained. The rounded stone faces with their shiny snub noses had something in common, almost innocent in their expression; there was something earnest in the objects of well-being the statues displayed ("I have a pan," "I have an apple," from beginner English lessons). Only one

210

of the stone dead seemed like a grown man.

At one time he had enjoyed great authority, witness his moniker: the Commodore. The sculptor who had sculpted the Commodore twelve years before had previously specialised in granite, bronze, and plaster Lenins, the demand for which never abated but only grew – just as if the country saw a new small town or factory pop up literally every month which needed its own Lenin at its main entrance or at the district committee. Due to this creative experience, the author gave the Commodore a characteristic Lenin-like stride that aimed from the pedestal into the future; the sculpture's right arm, thrown up to indicate to the workers the path to communism, seemed to stop halfway there because the cellphone held tight in his hand (a shovel-shaped Siemens) suddenly seemed to ring. In the fellas' shared opinion, the sculpture's resemblance to the original, was striking, despite the whiff of Lenin. The sculptor had managed to convey the slant of his heavy brow, his sagging cheeks, and most of all, the predatory, wolfish connection between the large bared teeth and the pointy ears pressed to the skull. The statue had a secret known only to the closest brotherhood: under the stone jacket, elegantly detailed and covered by a polished flap, there was a Glock, executed, as was the Commodore himself, twice life-size. Naturally, the originals of the gun, cellphone, and Merc keys had been laid to rest with the Commodore in his palatial oaken coffin.

Unlike the majority of gangster grave sites, the Commodore's memorial looked tended: no precipitation had splashed the sculpture, and none of the cemetery visitors still among the living left trash on the iron bench directly under the Commodore's one-ton gaze, where no matter the season, you could see a stooped blonde with an irregular face that looked like make-up applied to a blank space. The blonde appeared before the statue's eyes, which were drilled deep in the granite, regularly, once a day.

Anya hadn't been the Commodore's official and legal wife, although she'd lived with him for two years and eight months. The Commodore had gone to the same school as Anya and had graduated by the skin of his teeth when Anya, a top student and good girl, was just going into fourth grade. Crashing in on Anya's graduation day with a gym bag full of booze and a bouquet of blood-red roses for his favourite teacher, he saw her, slender as a dragonfly, wearing a stiff, iridescent dress sewn from a nylon curtain. Saw her and took her for his own.

At first Anya was tickled pink to be moving from her parents' soot-encrusted prefab building to a spacious apartment downtown with a view of the Main Post Office. Anya's cup was full. The incredible tall refrigerator groaned from an abundance of delicacies, and Anya had practically the first mink coat in the city – Italian, exquisite, and as bushy as a Christmas tree. But she didn't have a rouble of her own. Anya would filch small amounts from the Commodore's pockets when, after his labours and revelries, he would come over, smelling terrible, like an overheated truck, and fall crosswise on the bed, smearing his flat cheek against the silk pillow. Anya was advised not to leave the apartment to go into the city. There was always a husky, big-arsed guard sitting on a low, almost kiddie stool in the front hall: Sasha, or else Gosha, or else Lyosha. She'd been forbidden to feed them, like animals in a zoo. But Anya couldn't leave. She guessed that the Commodore simply couldn't imagine her free of him and alive at the same time.

Fate had other ideas, though. One fine April day, the Commodore, yawning and sneezing in the nice sun, left his office and got in his Merc, which took a hesitant hop and burst into flames.

The Commodore was buried in a closed coffin. The main avenue – called Lenin Avenue, naturally – was shut down for the funeral cortège. An open truck drove slowly ahead of the hearse so that people could sit there and throw handfuls of white roses under the wheels of the Commodore's final transport. After the doleful gangster parade crawled past, all this luxury was left in the thoroughfare trampled, like sodden dollars, which is basically what they were. Gawkers lined the avenue like a dark forest, mysterious and foreboding. Anya sat in the hearse beside the coffin, staring senselessly at the bronze corner ornament. At the cemetery, the gusty wind that lashed the earnest priest's piebald beard seemed to Anya like a gust of freedom.

But it wasn't.

The morning after the funeral, a lawyer came to see Anya, who had overslept, having spent the night in the apartment without a guard for the first time. He looked like the chicken and the egg: narrow-shouldered, with broad womanish hips and a totally bald, egg-shaped head to which glasses were attached to imply eyes. Laying out his papers, the lawyer told the widow the deceased's final wishes. It turned out that Anya, who was not legally married to the Commodore, could lay no claim to any inheritance by law. Fortunately, though, the Commodore had left a will, according to which Anya was to get this apartment with all its furnishings, the 1991 Audi, and a monthly allowance of five hundred U.S. dollars. The only condition was that the widow had to visit the Commodore's grave every day.

"Our law firm and I personally have been assigned to oversee the fulfilment of this condition," the little lawyer explained. "Note, esteemed Anna Valerievna, if you miss

213

even one visit, highly undesirable consequences will ensue immediately. That is, the following day, I will have to put you out on the street. And no more money, naturally. Today counts, so get ready and we'll go to the cemetery."

So began the custom. That day, after standing modestly behind the thoroughly chilled Anya in front of the mound of icy wreathes, which rang like Aeolian harps in the chill wind, the lawyer handed her her first thick envelope of dollars. All spring, summer, and early fall, either the little lawyer or else his assistant, a mournful sort with long, limp hair and round, soap-white ears that poked through his hair, would accompany Anya to the Commodore's resting place. Together they observed the memorial's progress, as the grave got dressed in stone, so that while it was being worked on it looked like an old rain-drenched campfire site. Finally, the moment arrived and Anya saw her stone husband. The granite Commodore looked at her out from under his bulging forehead, and the chilled Anya imagined a glassy, sinister, utterly immortal life hidden in the deeply set pupils.

"Well, he can look after you himself now," the little lawyer announced with relief.

"What do you mean look after?" That scared Anya. "Does he have a video camera in him or something?"

The lawyer shrugged his sloping little shoulders so that he looked like a squeezed tube of toothpaste.

"The technology isn't on site," he said vaguely. "And remember, Anna Valerievna, all it takes is one lapse. We'll know immediately."

At first, Anya thought the Commodore's will would give her a salutary respite until she could arrange her life differently somehow. But it turned out that finding a good job with a decent salary was totally unrealistic without friends or connections.

What was she supposed to do with herself? It would take half her life to buy an apartment. And moving back with her parents was out of the question. Her sister was still there and she'd given birth to twins. You'd think Anya could simply live as she liked and not work – but she had no vacations from her daily cemetery duties. Every time summer came she had a passionate desire to go to the sea. At night, she dreamed of the sea – blue-green, smoky, hazy in the half-ring of airy mountains. But Anya could only see it on television, mainly in ads for shampoo and Bounty chocolates, which she devoured, throwing the dirty wrappers on the leather sofa.

The leash the Commodore kept her on was three hundred kilometres long. That was the distance Anya, a fearful and inept driver, could go from home without risking being late for her date with the statue. Within that three-hundred-kilometre radius, besides the regional capital itself, with its factory suburbs sprawling like blouse sleeves, there were two small towns: Kamensk and Talda. Never in a normal life would Anya have taken an excursion to a hole like that, but now she went every week and knew the sights by heart: two nearly identical Palaces of Culture, the fanciful Kamensk Drama Theatre, which looked like it was made of gingerbread, and the Talda Trinity Cathedral, which looked like a Russian tile stove refashioned for religious services. Krasnokurinsk, a city of half a million that spread the specific acrid smell of ferrous metallurgy, was beyond her reach. Sometimes, in desperate intoxication, Anya would race down the highway toward Krasnokurinsk's orange smoke, which flowed like Fanta from the smelters' smokestacks, but the approaching point of no return made her heart pound as if it were about to burst, and Anya would turn around, sobbing.

Thus, Anya's world became as small and flat as a pizza, with three towns, one sawmill town, and one small lake full of scum and fry, where at the height of the heat Anya would swim with the local snot-nose little boys. Now she dreamed of the sea as green aspic with a solid mass of seaweed swaying inside, wheezing from the stirring of the wave. Anya never did figure out where the video camera was in the monument. But the sense of being watched in front of the granite Commodore was so tangible that for a while Anya would sit on the iron bench in an unnatural pose, as if at a photo studio. Even later, when she'd become accustomed and embittered, the feeling still wouldn't go away. The statue seemed to generate a field – the deceased's field of vision, which covered the bench and about five metres of the dark red jasper slabs that constituted the path.

If there was a video camera on, then the people so authorised in the lawyer's firm were watching an interesting film. They saw Anya, eyes cast down, standing in front of the statue for exactly a minute and leaving without looking up; they saw a weeping face, puffy and contorted.They saw her twisted faces, her tongue poking out, and her bony fist threatening the statue. The lawyers watched a dreary Anya wearing a shapeless, full-length smock, they watched her wearing a hiked-up mini skirt and torn fishnet stockings smacking her own protruding arse and her dirty smeared mouth pooched out in a kiss. For a while, the gangster's widow pulled out all the stops. Their industrial town saw the opening of nightclubs, concrete structures entwined with flashing lights as glaring as a welding iron. There, Anya, wearing a cheap dress, sipped cocktails and picked up humanoids who bore a fatal resemblance to the guards Sasha, Gosha, and Lyosha – who sometimes even paid her fifty dollars a night. In the morning, discovering a stranger's white body of somewhat porcine outlines beside her, Anya's aching head would realise that there was no happiness and never would be. She managed to stop herself in time. If she was to fulfil the Commodore's terms, she couldn't end up in some clinic, to say nothing of a jail cell.

Now Anya truly felt like the Commodore's wife – much more so than before, when the Commodore was flesh and blood and not stone. Sometimes she would suddenly make the desperate decision not to go to the cemetery. Just not go and that was it. Crying and muttering, she would stuff her things into a suitcase, to go away somewhere, anywhere – to the train station, to a street bench, into that measureless expanse of despair and insult created by the imagination of squabbling lovers. Then she'd come to her senses, throw the jumbled cheap garments on the floor, grab a dirty taxi on the street and get there in the nick of time – at eleven thirty, eleven forty-five, eleven fifty-five.

The Commodore, in turn, started calling her. More and more often, a familiar number would show up on Anya's cellphone: his number, listed in her contacts as "Husband." Anya tried to convince herself – aghast at the cellphone itching in her minty palm – that more than likely they'd put the Commodore's phone in his coffin without its SIM card, and now either the lawyers or the gangsters were trying to scare her, having put the SIM card in another device. But when she opened the phone and shouted "Hello!" the response was a vast and sinister silence, as if she'd put her ear to a hole that led to oblivion. The silence said "Aaaaaah" – voicelessly, only with an infinitely deep throat prepared to swallow human reason.

Anya's final rebellion occurred in the ninth year of her enslaved widowhood. Having saved some money, painstakingly checked flights, paid a tour agency for a hotel where she had no intention of spending the night, she flew to Paris. The airplane was like a dream. Diving in and out of a humming drowsiness, Anya seemed to fall out of the Boeing and then with a heavy, drunken effort find herself inside it again. At Charles de Gaulle, whose vast enclosed spaces amazed her, Anya felt like a fly crawling across a ceiling. A small blue taxi with an indicator on its humped roof took her to the Louvre. Anya had approximately five hours for absolutely everything. Too warmly dressed for a foreign February, Anya dragged her feet in their fur-lined boots along the endless palace façade and couldn't believe that this pallid water, which seemed to disappear along with the reflections and ripples, in the gleam of the naked sun, was the Seine. The statues here were bright white, every last one of them blind. Anya was very tired, but to sit down she had to order something. At the many cafés, people were sitting at little tables that had been brought out on the sidewalks. Lots of people: elderly, big-nosed gentlemen with newspapers; old ladies in cheerful little scarves; androgynous youth who had tossed their backpacks into a pile. Looking at them, looking at the crowd, Anya felt alien to them all – much more alien than if she'd stayed home, than if she'd died.

She nearly overstayed the time when she had to go to the airport. En route to Charles de Gaulle, the taxi got stuck in a traffic jam. What Anya suffered, her hands clenched in her lap and dry, fearful eyes looking straight ahead – God forbid anyone should have to go through that. She made her flight in the nick of time. There was a snowstorm at home. The drifts smoked and the dark pines at the cemetery swayed in the snowy haze. It looked like milk was flowing over the stone Commodore, and Anya thought the statue might step off the pedestal and smash to bits at any moment.

Now life relentlessly forsook the gangster widow. The

monthly five hundred dollars, which at one time was quite decent money, now barely covered the basics. Her old Audi, junk now, had stopped running, and Anya didn't have the funds for expensive and pointless repairs. Now even Kamensk and Talda were a vague dream. The car rusted outside Anya's windows, and trampled burdock grew under its wheels, poking through the old asphalt. More or less the same thing happened to Anya herself. So it was until one day, sitting on the bench in front of the sun-dappled statue, she noticed out of the corner of her eye a tall man behind a lilac bush taking her picture with his top-of-the-range camera.

Ivan Vetrov, also known as Juan Ignacio de Huerte, was the descendant of Spanish Communists who fled Franco for the Soviet Union. His passport showed his Russian surname, which they'd acquired just in case, when anti-Fascists started being quietly imprisoned, too – especially those in whom noble blood flowed too thick and bright, temptingly sweet for Lubyanka's specialists. Despite his background, Vetrov wasn't particularly good-looking – too swarthy and bony. He had a jutting hooked nose and hungry deep dimples, as if the shortage of building materials experienced by his father and mother in their Soviet orphanage had been stamped on his DNA. Not that this bothered Vetrov. His camera was his real face, his vision, his way of thinking. Ivan Vetrov was quite a famous art photographer, a master of the female portrait. His works brought out what the woman who served as his model could never have seen in the mirror. A mirage almost, dominated by one actual feature – a broken brow, a recalcitrant lock of hair – an unexpected and untouched image, as if the woman had never been photographed for her passport. Fluttering around his model, across the floor, along the walls, practically across the ceiling, Vetrov captured with incredibly precise clicks of his camera the precious moments of truth ordinarily wiped away by snatches of ordinary time. His photo sessions were like a religious ritual, like a spider's dance around a trapped fly. The woman, feeling drawn into an intimate process and feeling recognised in this process, experienced a desire to say more and more about herself. Fairly often, this ended in bed.

Ivan Vetrov's fame as an art photographer grew, and he had exhibitions in Paris, Boston, and New York, but Don Juan's main talent was his understanding of female nature. He knew simple things, for example: any woman almost always feels bad; any woman hides something from whoever she's talking to. Above and beyond beauty – or rather, what is accepted as beauty – Don Juan appreciated in women their gift of desiring, whether a man, a new car, a trip to a resort, it didn't matter. He saw that men, despite their ambition, were much more indifferent to life. Women desired Don Juan – and he saw no reason to deny them. Passions seethed around him. Don Juan would have been glad to choose one out of them all – but he couldn't find a reason to pick one over another. He took life and fate too seriously, this degenerate cavalier with the creaking joints and hair that had early turned the colour of cold coals. He really did need a reason much loftier and weightier than youth and beauty. His lovers included a failed fifty-five-year-old actress who wore heavy sapphire earrings the colour of her faded eyes in her stretched out earlobes and who read cards for money. She'd taught him that a woman who has known despair is priceless. Don Juan's heart was especially touched by her, but he couldn't get over the age gap. He was waiting for fate to give him a sign, suspecting that Don Juan of the old Spanish legend, who had served as a model for Pushkin and Byron, had in fact been not the hunter but the prey.

The detached widow Vetrov espied when he went to shoot the Alley of Gangster Glory for his own increasingly popular blog drove his loyal Nikon mad – as if an entire flock of birds were beating inside his camera, ready to fly out. Those golden instants of truth that Vetrov picked out from the various, sometimes unimaginable poses swarmed around the downcast figure like a swarm of midges. Don Juan realised that by jumping out of the bushes with his camera dangling from his neck he basically looked like a madman. Ignoring her distraught murmuring, not even introducing himself properly, he dragged her away from the cemetery to his studio. Even at first glance, this abashed woman, who had put her black bag, almost a knapsack, right on the trampled floor by the front door, represented an entire photo exhibit – and her potential was inexhaustible. Her dominant feature was her eyes – something that happens much more rarely than the mascara manufacturers think. After he'd shot an entire treasure on film and digitally, dreaming of being left alone at last with his files, Vetrov lightly let his exhausted model go home or wherever she planned to go at this time of night. The files were such, though, that Don Juan quickly realised this woman had actually not left and never would. Frightened that she had given him the wrong phone number in order to be rid of him, Don Juan started calling her at four in the morning.

He took her by storm, by some insane flamenco that carried them off not to bed but to his fat old leather sofa, which wheezed under them asthmatically. Afterward, lying alongside her damp body, which was skinny and glassy, like some marvellous insect, Don Juan guessed that the fortress had not been taken at all, that a *fata morgana* loomed on the horizon as before, and he would have to take her cautiously, with a slow, studious caress that, God willing, would last an entire lifetime. At first, Don Juan was worried that he would have to destroy a woman's great grief. Out of the corner of his eye he noted the dates on the statue's pedestal and was amazed at the length of her mourning over such a brute. Then he heard Anya's real story, and his heart eased. Vetrov knew quite a few tragedies that had occurred to good and weak people, whom the changes of the 1990s had deleted live from the list of the living. Of them, Anya's tragedy was the most womanly and brought out the greatest strengths of Don Juan's exceptional nature. This was the very reason, the grounds for choosing you couldn't dispute.

Don Juan told Anya her problems were over. He had inherited his apartment and he made money. He moved Anya in, allowing her to pack in her black bag only her I.D. and documents and a few pieces of clothing to be going on with.

His future wife's name aroused a romantic agitation in Don Juan and seemed to confirm his identity. He shuddered, though, when he heard the moniker the granite deceased went by, whose full name, etched on the pedestal, was perfectly ordinary and said nothing about its owner. Naturally, Don Juan had no intention of inviting that fat-legged statue with a face like an ice-coated tuber to his place. Nevertheless, he understood that circumstances were such, and the plot had been launched, and the only question was when to expect the Commodore's visit. The thought of this visit gave Don Juan the willies, compelling him to hurry the wedding along as much as possible. The former actress with the purplish wrinkles, her earrings shaking, wept dry-eyed and gave him her blessing.

Anya's behaviour before the wedding would have seemed odd to anyone – anyone except Don Juan. Under various clumsy pretexts, Anya would disappear every day for a couple of hours, or three – and Don Juan knew full well where she was rushing off to and why. He understood what a woman went through leaving one man for another. During this dangerous period, there is always a shaky renaissance of old feelings – a burst of memory, the pain and guilt that the former man, if he proves smart, can exploit. In this sense, Don Juan had nothing to worry about. His Anya was running to see the Commodore in the cemetery. She went there daily, as she'd grown used to doing all those years. Even the morning before they planned to marry at the registry office, she slipped quietly out of bed, dropped a skillet in the kitchen, sending it dancing with a dull crash, and disappeared – for a long time. The stylist invited to their home barely had time to put up her tousled curls in which cemetery lilac blooms had gotten caught, like dead flies. Don Juan wasn't angry. He had a plan. After the registry and church, there would be the inevitable restaurant and the next day a train to Moscow and from there a plane to Spain, Costa Dorada, the sea.

Don Juan had chosen the train for the first leg because he was afraid too abrupt a separation from the patch of earth that was Anya's sole reality might lead to a severe shock. He was hoping that the landscape she would see out of the train window, the calm succession of utterly ordinary houses, fields, and woods, would help Anya accustom herself to being outside the circle drawn by the Commodore's evil will. An hour after the train set out it became clear that Don Juan had been wrong. Anya was running a high fever, her teeth were chattering, and she was grimacing, shivering under two blankets. Don Juan was about to try to make cautious, gentle love to her, but Anya was so sensitive, was shivering so, she was like a chick plucked live. Don Juan tried to feed her, made her go to the dining car, but

223

Anya nearly fainted on the clattering platforms between cars, and in the dining car she broke a plate and burst into tears. Don Juan tried to distract her, entertain her – but as evening drew nigh, and the compartment's yellow lamp was reflected in the window, on a backdrop of black pines and the sunset, even he surrendered to a sense of dread. Something told Don Juan that the Commodore would appear today. Having no other weapon, Don Juan kept at hand his unsheathed camera, all set to shoot.

They'd nearly fallen asleep when they heard the sound. It was like a giant blacksmith's hammer banging, coming closer and closer – across the floor of the train, a train racing in horror – and breaking through the floor of the fragile box of a train car all the way to the couchette. Anya sat up abruptly in the couchette, the way the dead sit up in their coffins in films. Meeting her translucent, electric gaze, Don Juan tossed her her robe and jumped into his jeans. Right then the compartment door blazed up unbearably in the mirror and was flung back.

The stone Commodore was standing in the corridor, visible up to his shoulders. Behind him, the darkness rustled like a long black pelt. For a second the statue floated, as if soused with water, and the top of his granite head appeared, white with pigeon droppings, and the Commodore stepped into the compartment so that the tea-glasses tinkled like an old steel alarm clock.

"Hey, hi there," the loud, laboured voice boomed as if from a cave.

Don Juan scrambled onto the treacherously soft berth, trying to see how Anya was doing behind the stone chump. His head came barely to the Commodore's dusty, rough shoulder.

"What do you want? I didn't invite you!" he shouted, throwing his head back and looking into the deep-drilled eyes, where there was definitely something optical gleaming. Maybe he was dizzy, or maybe it was something else, but it seemed to Don Juan that the Commodore was wearing strong glasses.

"He says he didn't invite me! I don't remember asking you," the Commodore droned, his pocked granite mouth smirking.

The statue's fluid mimicry was reminiscent of the slow, breathless bubbling of thick porridge; the grains of granite stirred like grayish groats. Don Juan picked up his Nikon with shaking hands and clicked. The stone mobile phone immediately flew at him like a meteorite, and from out of nowhere the statue now had a huge granite gun, held in front of his smooth left cheek. The bottomless black hole stared at the bridge of Don Juan's nose, and he thought the stone weapon just might fire as well as a real one.

"Hey, haven't you ever had a barrel pointed at you? Are you just going to stand there, you half-assed jerk?" the Commodore said loudly, bringing his stone gun closer to Don Juan. "Okay, this isn't about you, it's about my Anya. Why don't you go to toilet. You have my permission."

"Anya's my wife now. And I'm not going anywhere! Don't touch her!" Don Juan shouted in a strained voice, feeling the locks of his hair stir on the back of his neck, right where the little stone nucleolus would exit, splattering his brains.

"Is that so? All right then. I respect that." The Commodore frowned and stuck his stone cannon into his side, where it buried itself, creating a fat bulge in the granite. "Anya... I mean... Hi, see... "

At that moment the Commodore moved slightly to one side, and Don Juan saw Anya sitting on the bed, squeezing her rumpled robe to her chest and smiling with a pitiful, screwed up face covered in fine wrinkles.

"Vasya?... Is it really you?" she said barely audibly.

"Well," the Commodore confirmed. "You little fool, hey,

don't crawl under the blanket, I'm taking your picture, get it? No? Come on, hop out and sit up straight!"

"What camera, you cartoon hero?" Don Juan hollered, jumping up, nearly dropping his heart on the floor, rushing under the stone elbow toward Anya. "Why'd you show up? To drive her to her grave?"

"Listen, Anya, this new guy of yours is so dumb. He's read Pushkin, but he has no idea how life works," the Commodore rumbled, and the booming stone voice was cut through with the same imperious nasality the boss probably had when he was alive. "I'm explaining: a camera. Right here." The Commodore ran his implausibly fluid arm in front of his eyes, where some kind of optical device was shining, as was now quite obvious. "My head opens up, like a bar. See? I thought it up myself and paid through the nose for it. Anya, I wanted things to be handsome. The widow at the grave every day and all that. And you got a handsome life for that, too: money, an apartment, a ride, hey, whatever else a woman needs. Who knew it would come to this? Damn inflation. It's a scandal! Pretty soon five hundred bucks won't be enough to feed a cat. And then there's this cockroach of yours, this so-called husband, he wanted to take me down a peg, telling you you didn't need all that, you'd have enough of your own. He thinks I've come for him. Ha! As if I needed him. On top of everything else, they made me look like Lenin's brother. If I'd known, I'd have had some other genius carve my statue. There's lots of those Lenins, all as empty as bottles. But they've given me the main one, the real one… He's what makes you want something red, makes you want blood, or at least flags, if worse comes to worst. It's because of him, that bastard, that I'm so dangerous. Explain to your cockroach he'd better not get fresh 'cause I could get pretty riled. No cop's going to take away my barrel now."

226

"You might think you'd never spilled any blood. A real angel!" Don Juan parried maliciously, squeezing Anya's icy hand.

"I did, but by the rules. No right-thinking person could say the Commodore's a bum. But that's not worth a rat's ass to me now." The Commodore's nasal voice suddenly fell. "My conscience has woken up, that's what. The minute I calmed down, see, it popped up. While I was alive, I didn't have time to think about things. But since my life, it gives me the shakes, just like a hangover. That Lenin is like raw vodka, too... So Anya, don't hold it against me. If I could have, I'd have rewritten my will, but now I have no rights. I'm dead. That joke of a lawyer, when he takes the camera out he could at least wipe the shit off my head. He's just chomping at the bit to take the apartment away from you. What does the will say? That you have to visit my memorial once a day. But I am the memorial. Fine. You go off with your cockroach, that's your business. I'll come, too. I'm not proud now. The lawyer will take the camera, look at the film, and there you'll be right on schedule, date and time, there it is. Those five hundred bucks will come in handy."

"You mean you're going to come to us every day with your special effects?" Don Juan exclaimed, feeling horror, genuine horror, crushing down, like a heel, on his gasping heart.

"Well" – the Commodore suddenly squinted very recognisably somehow, and Don Juan imagined the wedge-shaped beard jutting out from the granite jaw like the ashtray in a car door. "Can you stop me, comrade?"

With those words, the Commodore extended his right arm over his granite cellphone, and the stone phone gurgled and jumped up from the crushed blanket. Forgetting everything for a second, Don Juan went back to his Nikon: whatever landed

227

in the frame was going to go viral. He couldn't help himself. His numb index finger swished through the files. There was no Commodore whatsoever on the screen. The compartment was filled with patterns of murk, like streams of soot being drawn into a vent. Looking up, Don Juan saw the same stringy darkness flowing through the door. A heavy step swelled tentatively – one, and another, definitely the Commodore, flattening the train, descending as if it were an iron staircase.

The sepulchral thunder suddenly fell away, broken off by a hollow, plaintive sound. Suddenly, out of nowhere, the train's wheels started knocking, yellow lights floated by, a well-lit construction site passed, and a town stretched out. Anya sat there, her teeth chattering, blinking senselessly. Her robe was still crushed to her chest, as if it had frozen into trickles of ice.

Don Juan grabbed Anya, pressed her close, and pressed himself to her, feeling their shared blood racing quietly.

"Vanya... Do you really need me with a dowry like that?" Anya said in a weak voice.

"Yes, and never ask that question again," Don Juan said quietly. "All kinds of things happen in life. Life's a strange thing. There can be inexplicable phenomena. We'll live as long as we live. And we'll be happy anyway. And the Commodore – well, what about the Commodore? A lot of noise, thunder, and rocks got thrown around and that's essentially it. His conscience woke up. Let him run with it a little now."

Translated by Marian Schwartz

The Gift not made by Human Hand
Ludmila Ulitskaya

On Tuesday, after the second lesson, five select pupils left
Class 3B. All morning they had been feeling like birthday girls.
They were dressed differently: not in brown school uniform
dresses with black aprons, or even white aprons, but in Young
Pioneer uniforms, dark below, white above, albeit without the
red neckerchiefs. Silken, vitreous, rustling, those were hidden
away, as yet pristine, in school briefcases.

The girls were the best of the best, top of their class, their
behaviour exemplary, and had attained the necessary but not
sufficient age of nine years. There were other nine-year-olds
in Class 3B who, by reason of their imperfections, could never
aspire to join the Young Pioneers.

Accordingly, after the second lesson of the day, the five
girls from 3B plus five from 3A and five from 3C put on their
coats and overshoes and lined up in twos in front of the school
porch. To start with there was an extra girl, but then Lilia
Zhizhmorskaya felt so nervous she went to the lavatory and
was sick, and afterwards had such a headache she had to go
to the school nurse who told her to lie down on a cold couch.
That evened the numbers.

The parade was headed by Senior Pioneer Leader Nina
Khokhlova (very pretty, but boss-eyed), Lvova (chairperson
of the Troop Council, a very grown-up thirteen-year-old),
Kostikova (the drummer girl), and Barenboim (a girl who
had been attending the Young Bugler Circle at the Pioneers'

Club for a year but had yet to learn a tune and could only parp isolated notes).

Bringing up the rear of the parade were Klavdia Dracheva, wearing not her Curriculum Manager but her Party Organiser hat; a female representative of the Parents' Committee with two black and russet vixens sprawled lasciviously over her shoulders; and an aged Community Activist, evidently able to walk on water to judge by the irreproachable black gleam of his boots despite the swirls of clinging mud.

Senior Pioneer Leader Khokhlova signalled the off, simultaneously bobbing the pom-pom on her hat and two great tassels on the furled troop flag. Drummer Girl Kostikova rattled out, "The aged drummer, aged drummer, aged drummer soundly slept." Barenboim puffed out her cheeks, produced an out-of-tune bugle blast, and they all moved off along an only slightly circuitous route, through Miussky and Mayakovsky Squares and down Gorky Street to the Museum of the Revolution. Many similar columns from boys' and girls' schools were converging because this was an operation on a municipal, indeed republican, indeed union-wide scale.

Looking more like wolves, muscular lions with rickety legs, which since time immemorial had been accustomed to survey a more select class of person, looked down from their portals with melancholy as the ranks of the best of the best, who seemed surprisingly young, marched past.

"What a lot of boys," Alyona Pshenichnikova remarked disapprovingly to her friend Masha Chelysheva.

"They're not rough boys," Masha noted.

In their warm coats, with the ribbons of their snug fur hats tied under their chins, the boys really did not look rough.

"But still, there are more girls," Alyona insisted, making a point whose importance she was not altogether clear about.

230

They were led into the Museum and, as one, had their breath taken away by the imperial revolutionary magnificence of polished marble, burnished bronze, and velvet, silk and satin banners of every hue of hellfire.

They were conducted to the cloakroom and, in formation, took off their winter clothing. Galoshes, sashes, mittens – too much to cope with. They were confused and had not enough hands because one was holding a package with their pioneer neckerchief which they couldn't put down anywhere. Only fat Sonya Preobrazhenskaya slipped the precious bundle into a breast pocket she found on her white blouse.

Senior Pioneer Leader Khokhlova, her face in red blotches and clutching the heavy staff of their Troop's banner at arm's length, led them up a wide staircase. The carpet, held in place on each step by a brass rod, was as yielding and springy as moss in a dried up marsh.

At the rear of their column was the representative mother, who had shed an insignificant coat she had been wearing under the luxuriating foxes, her chin sinking deep into their fur. Beside her walked the ancient Community Activist in his immaculate boots, his bald spot outshining his gleaming boot tops.

"Alyona," Svetlana Bagaturiya whispered into Alyona's neck, "Alyona! I've forgotten it all, I swear by my mother."

"What?" the self-possessed Alyona asked in surprise.

"The Solemn Promise," Svetlana whispered. "'I, a Young Pioneer of the Union of Soviet Socialist Republics, in the presence of my comrades…' I've forgotten what comes after that."

"…do solemnly swear to love my motherland with all my heart," Alyona prompted her loftily.

"Oh, I do remember it, thank God, I do remember it, Alyona," Svetlana said with relief. "I thought I had forgotten it!"

More and more of them came in but nobody got flummoxed or ended up in the wrong place. All stood neatly in the places allotted to their schools and classes, and the whole long hall was lined from end to end with display cases of presents to Comrade Stalin. There were gifts of gold, silver, marble, crystal, mother-of-pearl, jade, leather, and ivory, fashioned from everything that was lightest or heaviest, softest or hardest.

An Indian had written greetings on a grain of rice and some other time, only not today, you would be able to look through a magnifying glass and see wavy lettering which looked like fly droppings. A Chinaman had carved 109 balls, one inside the other, and again you needed a magnifying glass to see, through gaps in the minute tracery, the very smallest, innermost ball, smaller than a pea.

An Uzbek woman had spent her life weaving a carpet out of her own hair. One end was coal-black and the other a blueish white. The middle was greying, mottled, and rather sad.

"I expect she's bald now," Preobrazhenskaya whispered.

"It wouldn't matter. Uzbek women wear a hijab," Alyona observed with a heartless shrug.

"It was only before the Revolution they went around like that, when they were backward," Masha Chelysheva interjected.

"A backward woman wouldn't weave a carpet as a present for Comrade Stalin," Preobrazhenskaya defended the venerable old lady.

"Perhaps she didn't weave all her hair into the carpet. Perhaps she left some," Bagaturiya speculated positively, touching her own long, full pigtails tied above her ears with ribbons.

"Wait a minute!" Masha suddenly gasped. "Take a look at this."

It was not much to look at. In a display case a square rag was embroidered with a portrait of Comrade Stalin, not particularly pretty, sewn in cross stitch. It did not even look much like him, although there was no mistaking who it was supposed to be.

"Well?" Preobrazhenskaya responded. "What's so special about that?"

"Yes, what is it?" Alyona enquired, concerned.

"Read what it says!" Masha jabbed a finger at the inscription. "This portrait of Comrade Stalin was embroidered, using her feet, by T. Kolyvanova who has no arms."

"It's Tanya Kolyvanova!" Sonya whispered, swooning with delight.

"Are you crazy? Kolyvanova doesn't have no arms, and with the two she has she could never embroider like that, let alone with her feet!" Alyona brought them back down to earth.

"But it says here 'T. Kolyvanova'!" Sonya persisted, hoping for a miracle. "Perhaps she's got a sister with no arms."

"No, her sister is in Year 7. She's called Lidia and does have arms," Alyona recalled regretfully. She frowned, shook her little head with its complicated rings of braided hair and added, "But we can always ask."

At this point, the whole body of children were on the move again, proceeding in orderly ranks to another hall. On one side stood the drummers, to the other the buglers, and in the middle the standard-bearers with flags unfurled. A Pioneer Leader, presumably the absolutely most senior, loudly commanded,

"Dress ranks on the banner! Atten-shun! The mother of Zoya Kosmodemyanskaya and Shura will speak."

They all got in line, stood up straight, and a small elderly woman in a dark blue suit stepped forward to tell them that Zoya Kosmodemyanskaya was a Young Pioneer who set fire to a stable block of the German invaders and was killed by the Nazis.

Alyona Pshenichnikova cried, although she had heard all this long before. At that moment all of them wanted to set fire to a Nazi stable block and even, perhaps, die for their motherland.

Then the old Community Activist told them about the very first Young Pioneers' Gathering at the Dynamo Football Stadium, when Mayakovsky recited his poem, "We will rise with rifles new. We'll put bunting on the bayonets," and all the Young Pioneers taking part in that Gathering were allowed to travel free on the trams for the rest of the day, even though tickets usually cost four, eight, or eleven kopeks.

Then all of them recited the Young Pioneer's Solemn Promise and had their neckerchiefs tied for them, except fat Sonya Preobrazhenskaya who had somehow managed to lose the one she had put in her breast pocket. She burst into tears, but Senior Pioneer Leader Khokhlova took her own neckerchief off and tied it round the weeping Sonya's neck and she stopped crying.

They sang "Campfires ablaze in the dark of the night!" and left the hall in regimented columns, quite different people, proud and ready to perform great deeds.

The next morning all the girls who were now Young Pioneers came to school a little earlier than usual. Their red neckerchiefs lit up Class 3B. Fat Sonya re-tied hers during every break between lessons. Gaika Oganesyan, who was very naughty, put an ink mark on the red corner peeping out from the collar of Alyona Pshenichnikova who sat in the desk in front of her. Alyona sobbed all through the lunch break, but just before it was over Masha Chelysheva came across and whispered in

234

her ear, "Why don't we ask Kolyvanova about the girl with no arms?"

Alyona cheered up and they went over to Tanya Kolyvanova who was sitting in the back row tearing pink blotting paper into tiny pieces. They asked her, without any great expectations but just in case, whether she knew a girl called T. Kolyvanova who had no arms.

Kolyvanova looked very sheepish and said, "She isn't a girl, she's a grown-up."

"Is she your sister?!" the newly enrolled Young Pioneers yelled in unison.

"No, she's just a relative. We call her Auntie Tomka," Kolyvanova replied, looking down at the desk and plainly not specially proud of her famous aunt.

"Can she sew with her feet?" Alyona asked Kolyvanova sternly.

"Yes, she does everything with her feet, eating, drinking, fighting," Kolyvanova said artlessly, but just then the bell rang and they had to stop.

All through the fourth lesson Alyona and Masha were on tenterhooks, sending notes to each other and the other members of their Organisation, and when the lesson ended they surrounded Kolyvanova to continue the interrogation. She confessed straightaway that her aunt could sew with her feet and really had embroidered the gift for Comrade Stalin, only it was all a long time ago. She hadn't been a heroine in the war, and her arms had not been shot off by the Germans, she had just been born like that. She lived out at Mariina Roshcha and you had to take a tram to get there.

"Fine. You are free to go," Alyona dismissed her.

Kolyvanova was only too happy to slip away, and the full complement of the class's Young Pioneer Organisation settled

235

down to its first meeting.

The main item on the agenda was obvious and somehow just decided itself: election of the chairperson of the Patrol Committee. Sonya took great satisfaction in writing in a notebook: "Minutes". They voted. "Unanimous", Sonya wrote, and added on the next line: "Alyona Pshenichnikova".

Alyona, in the fullness of power now bestowed upon her, took the bull by the horns:

"I move that we invite that girl with no arms, I mean that lady, Tomka Kolyvanova, to a meeting of our Patrol to tell us about sewing the gift for Comrade Stalin."

"I think I really preferred… there was a little golden table with chairs round it and a samovar on it with little cups, and it even had a little tap, and everything was really, really tiny…" Svetlana Bagaturiya murmured dreamily.

"You appear not to understand," Alyona said reproachfully, "that anyone can make a little table and samovar, but you try sewing with your toes…!"

Svetlana was abashed. She had allowed her head to be turned by a miniature samovar when there was a heroine living nearby. She knitted her generous eyebrows and blushed. In fact, she was well respected in the class for her top marks and because she was more or less a Georgian like Comrade Stalin, lived in an apartment block belonging to the Communist University where her father was studying, and had even been called Svetlana in honour of Comrade Stalin's daughter.

"Right then," Alyona summed up. "As Young Pioneers we shall instruct Kolyvanova to bring her Aunt Tomka to our meeting."

Sonya rummaged around with her chubby little hand in her briefcase and brought out an apple. She took a bite and passed it to Masha. Masha took a bite too, but the apple was sour and she was feeling an unfocussed sense of dissatisfaction. The long ends of the red neckerchief lay clean and bright on her blouse, and yet something was missing.

"Perhaps we should invite my grandfather to a meeting," she proposed modestly. Her grandfather was a real admiral, as everybody knew.

"Excellent idea, Masha!" Alyona responded. "Make a note, Sonya: Admiral Chelyshev also to be invited to a Patrol meeting."

That "also" struck Masha as demeaning, but at this point the door opened and in came the cleaners with mop and bucket and it was resolved to close the meeting.

The diffident Kolyvanova suddenly dug her heels in and refused point blank, even though she could give no coherent explanation of why she didn't want to bring her armless aunt to a Patrol meeting. She continued to resist until Sonya said, "Tanya, why don't you ask your sister Lidia to ask her."

Tanya was taken aback. How could Sonya Preobrazhenskaya possibly know Lidia was forever running off to see her aunt? She agreed, nevertheless, to ask her.

Lidia couldn't for the life of her imagine what a bunch of third years could want with her crippled aunt, and when she was told she guffawed, "Oh, that's really wild!"

The following Sunday she took her five-year-old brother Kolya and went to visit her.

All the Kolyvanovs lived in less than ideal circumstances in huts and hostels, and only Tomka lived like a proper human being, with a room to herself in a brick-built house with running water.

She was pleased to see her niece. Lidia always made herself useful when she came, and would do the laundry and cook a meal, although not purely out of the goodness of her heart. Tomka was not short of a penny, especially in the summer, and would give her a three-or-five-rouble note.

Their age difference was not great, barely ten years, and they were more just like friends.

"Aunt Tomka, a bunch of Young Pioneers in Tanya's class want you to go to their meeting," Lidia informed her.

"What would I want to do that for? Having to travel! If they need something they can come here. What is it anyway?" she asked puzzled.

"They want you to tell them about embroidering that cushion thing," Lidia explained.

"Well, they've got fancy ideas, expecting me to tell them this and show them that. If they come here I'll show them more than they're expecting!" She was sitting on a mattress, scratching her nose with her knee. "Only it'll cost them. If they bring me a bottle of red I'll show and tell them anything they want."

"Come off it, Tomka, how could they do that?" Lidia had already undressed Kolya and was busy in the corner of the room sorting out a dirty nappy.

"Well, they'd better bring a tenner at least, no, fifteen roubles! We'll find a use for it, eh, Lidia?" She laughed, showing little white teeth.

She had a small, quite pretty face with a snub nose, only her chin was too long. She had a full head of naturally wavy hair which seemed it ought to belong to a different person.

"Idiots. Whatever next!" She shook her head but was secretly pleased that a whole delegation was coming to see how she managed with her feet. She had a penchant for showing off and surprising people. In summer she would sit on her ground floor windowsill looking out to the street, shove a needle between her big and second toes, and do her embroidery. People going by would be amazed, and the kind-hearted would put money in her white dish.

Tomka would nod and say, "Thank you kindly, my dear." They usually were old dears.

"Will you come with them, Liddy? Come and keep me company," she urged her niece.

"Of course," Lidia promised.

**

It was resolved that they would visit T. Kolyvanova at home. Masha had nine roubles, and the others skimped on lunch for two days. For almost a week their secret plan kept the Young Pioneers puffed up like balloons. For some reason they were convinced that young people who did not belong to the All-Union Leninist Movement of Young Pioneers must on no account know anything of the seriously mysterious life they were leading.

Gaika Oganesyan was almost sick with curiosity, and Lilia Zhizhmorskaya was darker than a thundercloud because she was sure they were plotting something against her.

Tanya Kolyvanova was strictly warned that if she let the cat out of the bag she would find herself in court. The idea of taking her to court occurred not to stern Alyona but to frivolous Sonya Preobrazhenskaya. Masha, who was the enterprise's principal funder and had thereby regained her status after the slight to her grandfather, cheered up considerably.

The expedition, arranged for the Wednesday one week after the Enrolment Ceremony, almost fell through. On Tuesday the Senior Pioneer Leader came to their class and told them not to worry, an excellent Leader had been appointed for them from

Class 6A, a girl called Liza Tsypkina. Unfortunately she was ill but would come to see them as soon as she was well again, perhaps as soon as tomorrow, when she would help them get their work as Young Pioneers off the ground.

"So don't get demoralised in the meantime," she advised.

"We are not getting demoralised, we have already elected a chairperson," Svetlana Bagaturiya confidently informed her.

"Oh, well done!" Nina Khokhlova congratulated them, made a note in her little book, and departed.

The girls exchanged glances, agreeing without any need for words that they could do without this Tsypkina to lead them.

The next morning they warned their families they would be late back from school because of a Young Pioneer event. They hid in the toilets during all the breaks, just in case Liza Tsypkina had recovered and might take it into her head to start leading them today.

After school, with the full Patrol present, and augmented by non-Party member Kolyvanova, they hid behind the coal shed at the back of the school to wait for Lidia who, being older, had five lessons a day.

When she arrived they proceeded to the tram stop. Masha Chelysheva vigilantly kept look-out, as they had a feeling they were being followed.

Over the past week it had got much colder and a covering of snow had fallen, but the right tram arrived before they got chilled through. There were not many people in it, so they were even able to sit on the yellow wooden benches.

The Kolyvanova sisters felt no delight or excitement about the excursion. Svetlana Bagaturiya, even though she was from another town, was also allowed to travel around freely and even went on shopping errands to Petrovsky Arcade in central Moscow on her own. Alyona, Masha and Sonya, however, had never been in a tram on their own before, without adults, and bought their own tickets and unbuttoned the collars of their fur overcoats so everybody could see their red neckerchiefs, which indisputably proclaimed their self-reliance.

Mariina Roshcha was far from the centre of Moscow and, despite its name, was a grove devoid of trees, overgrown by blackened weeds, and otherwise covered in shacks, dovecotes and huts, and enmeshed in stout clothes-lines from which frozen washing swung like plywood.

Alyona's self-confidence suddenly deserted her. She had never seen such a desolate place and just wanted to go home, to her trim house in Arsenal Lane, so near that palace where the lions with their frosted mains and skinny backsides sat above the gates.

"Everybody out," Lidia said, and the subdued girls clustered round the exit. The tram clattered lengthily to a halt and they had no option but to jump down from the high step.

Next to the tram stop were two two-storey brick buildings. The rest of the houses were ramshackle wooden affairs, and some way off they could see a number of real peasant log cabins that enjoyed the amenity of a well. There was no one to be seen other than a solitary, stooping old lady wearing felt boots and a large headscarf scuttling from one building to the other. Suddenly a cock crowed and another immediately responded.

"This way," Lidia said, pointing rather proudly to one of the brick buildings.

She opened the main door and they entered a dark corridor. A light bulb was shining only on the upper floor and they could hardly see.

"That way, that way," Lidia pointed, and they all stopped at a second door beyond which was another corridor with a bend.

"Here," Lidia said, banging her fist on a door and opening

it without waiting for a reply.

The room was small, long, and dimly lit. A trestle bed stood by the window and had what looked like a big girl lying on it, with a heavy blanket covering her lower body. She sat up and lowered large legs to the floor. Her dress appeared to have wing sleeves, but there were no arms beneath them. When she walked round the room she was seen to be small and skinny, and waddled unsteadily like a duckling. Her legs were set slightly too far back and her feet were abnormally broad, her toes large, fat, and splayed out.

"Ooh!" Svetlana Bagaturiya exclaimed.

"Oh!" exclaimed Sonya Preobrazhenskaya.

The others said nothing, and the woman without arms said, "Well, come in then, now you're here. What are you all milling around in the doorway for?"

Alyona, instead of delivering the long sentence she had practised for declaring the meeting open, said meekly, "How do you do, Aunt Tomka."

For some reason at that moment she felt more ashamed than she was ever to feel again.

"Go and put the kettle on, Lidia," Tomka ordered her elder niece, adding proudly, "We have a tap right in the kitchen. No need to go outside to the pump."

"We used to have a pump too," Svetlana said with her wonderful Georgian accent.

"Where are you from, black girl? Armenia, or are you a gypsy?" The woman without arms asked amiably enough.

"She is Georgian," Alyona replied pointedly.

"Oh, well, that's different," Tomka said approvingly. "Right then," she continued briskly, as if trying to prevent this fine Georgian thread from leading too soon to the important topic which had brought them here. "What have you got for me? Give it here." She pressed her long chin down on to her chest and they noticed she had a little bag hanging there, made of the same green calico as her dress.

Acutely conscious that something in life was not as it should be, Alyona unfastened the catch on her briefcase, pulled out a pile of crumpled banknotes and, so flushed that sweat stood out on her nose, pushed them into the bag round the woman's neck.

"There," she murmured. "Please take this, thank you."

"Well, take a good look, take a good look now you're here." Tomka indicated a wall with her chin. It was festooned with embroidery and hung with pictures of cats, dogs, and cockerels.

"Did you do the paintings too?" Masha asked in amazement. Tomka nodded.

"With your feet?" Bagaturiya enquired rather foolishly.

"Depends what I feel like," Tomka laughed, showing a long, pointed tongue through her little teeth. "Sometimes I use my feet and sometimes my mouth."

She bent her head down to the table, wriggled her chin about, and looked up. A paintbrush was stuck in the middle of her smiling mouth. She quickly slid it from one side to the other, then sat on the bed, raised her foot, twisting her knee joint in a bizarre manner, and the paintbrush was clenched between her toes.

"I can use my right or my left foot, makes no difference." She adroitly transferred the paintbrush from one foot to the other, sticking out her tongue and performing a complicated gymnastic move with it.

The girls exchanged glances.

"Can you even paint a portrait of Comrade Stalin with your foot?" Alyona persevered, trying to channel the conversation in the right direction.

243

"Of course I can, but I prefer painting cats and cockerels," Tomka said tantalisingly.

"Oh, that grey cat there is so sweet. She's just like our one," Svetlana Bagaturiya said, pointing admiringly to the portrait of a cat with irregular horizontal stripes. "We had to leave Duchess in Sukhumi with my grandmother. I really miss her!"

"I like the cockerels most… that one with all the different colours," the younger Kolyvanova piped up quite unexpectedly.

"You never told me that before, Tanya," the artist exclaimed.

"But tell us about the gift for Comrade Stalin," Alyona Pshenichnikova purposefully steered the conversation in the required direction.

"Oh, you and that gift," Tomka said, suddenly almost peevish.

At this point Lidia came back in and announced, "Tomka, the stove's gone out. We're out of paraffin."

"Well, if there's none we'll do without," Tomka said, airily waving the paintbrush clutched in her toes. "Come here. Closer."

Tomka whispered something secret in Lidia's ear. She nodded, took the little bag from round Tomka's neck, and went over to the door to put on her outdoor clothes.

Settling herself comfortably, more or less crosslegged, and gesticulating with the paintbrush, Tomka began her story.

"All right then, the gift…" She gave a sly, girlish laugh. "My efforts were not wasted. It took me a long time to embroider it, a couple of months, maybe four. My neighbour Vasilisa put it in the post. I told her to make sure she paid the postage for a reply too." She laughed again, but then looked more serious. "To tell the truth I wasn't really expecting a reply, but I got one. It was on a big sheet of paper with an official stamp at the top and another at the bottom, thanking me directly from his

244

Secretariat. There it was: "The Kremlin, Moscow." Right, I thought, dear Comrade Stalin, here's where you do your stuff."

The girls exchanged glances again, and Alyona looked across anxiously at Masha.

"At that time we were living in the Nakhalov huts. One wall was solid ice and if they heated the place properly the water would drip down, and there were six of us living in a room like that: our mother, who was just a yokel; my sister Marusya, who was a drunken deadbeat, a complete asshole; and her snot-nosed little bastards..." Tomka looked sternly at the spotlessly clean girls, who were rivetted to the spot. "They hadn't an ounce of sense between them. They were incapable of looking after themselves, let alone me with no arms. Anyone God has given no brains to is in big trouble, say I. Anyway I took that paper in my teeth and went to the Housing Department."

Svetlana Bagaturiya had propped her chin on her fist and was so engrossed, she was gaping. Sonya was wide-eyed, while Masha Chelysheva, reluctant to breathe in the bad air, was even more embarrassed to breathe it back out.

"When I get there there's a queue for the office, and bold as brass I kick the door open and go right in. When they see me, they can't believe it." She sniggered with self-satisfaction. "Anyway, I plonk that paper down on the biggest table I can see," she belched robustly, "and I says to them, 'Well, what do you think of that, then, here's the great Comrade Stalin, the father of all the peoples, knows my name, and he's writing to me, humble as I am, to thank me for working hard for him with my feet, and the place I'm living in is so small there isn't room for a pisspot. What kind of hard work have you got to show? How many times have we come in here begging and begging. Well, now I'm going to go and complain to Comrade Stalin himself.' You get the picture, then, do you, Young Pioneers? This pad I'm living in now I near enough got from Comrade Stalin himself personally!"

She twisted her mouth and wrinkled her nose in a grimace. "You don't see it, do you, you sad little wet knickers. Well go on, put your coats on and just piss off!" she added with unexpected vehemence. She jumped off her mattress and started singing in a loud, reedy voice, hammering her bare heels on the floor and swivelling her hips, "Cu-cumbers, red tom-atoes..."

The girls retreated to the door, hastily tucked their fur coats under their arms and spilled out into the corridor. From behind the door they could hear Tomka shouting, "Tanya! Tanya! Where do you think you're going?"

But Tanya Kolyvanova pulled on her coat in solidarity. Bumping into each other, they ran down the bending corridor and, all squeezing through the outside door at the same time, poured into the street.

It was already completely dark. There was a smell of snow and smoke, and the quiet stars of the countryside twinkled in the blackness of the heavens. They ran to the tram stop and clustered round the metal sign. Sonya and Svetlana were unaffected but Masha was wheezing, suffering the first asthma attack of her life, of which there were to be many more. Alyona had tears streaming from her thick eyelashes which were sticking together in the frost.

She was unbelievably upset but could not have said why.

"What a vile, repulsive cheat," she thought. "And she doesn't love Comrade Stalin."

"I'm going to be in trouble when I get back home," Sonya said, taking it all in her stride.

Two women in rustic half-length fur coats came to the stop

and stood there. It was a longer wait this time, but eventually in the distance they heard the wonderfully welcome ringing of the tram bell as, with its one clear eye, it came into sight round the bend in the road. They were already climbing in when Lidia appeared, having run her errand for Tomka and in a rush to catch up her sister.

Tomka, meanwhile, with a bottle of wine in her neck knapsack, not bothering to put on her ankle boots, went up to the second floor and hammered with her bare heel on the brown door. Getting no reply, she turned round, took a step backwards, nimbly pushed her foot into the door handle and, staggering, opened the door.

It was dark inside but that didn't worry her.

"Yegorych!" she yelled from the doorway, but nobody replied. She moved deeper into the room. A mattress was lying in the corner and Yegorych was lying on it. She knelt down. "Yegorych, feel what I've brought. Take it, will you? Come on, then!" she urged him.

Yegorych, still half asleep, raised his dishevelled head from the big greasy pillow, stretched out a gnarled fist to Tomka's knapsack and said in a sleepy, good-natured voice, "You always want it. What's that you've brought me?"

He was her pal and she had brought him a gift. She could drink a little herself, but didn't really like getting drunk. Any more than she really liked Comrade Stalin, as a tearstained Alyona Pshenichnikova had ascertained.

Translated by Arch Tait

Philemon and Baucis
Irina Muravyova

I

In a dacha outside the city lived Philemon and Baucis. In the mornings the sun came filtering in through heavy curtains, to scatter in hot patches of light over Philemon's bulldog chin, sagging open as he slept, and the pleated folds of his neck; then, slipping away towards the other bed on the left, it found Baucis's gnarled, skinny hand stretched out on the silk eiderdown and lit up her fingernails, veins and brown age spots, before creeping on up towards her open mouth with its fringe of black hairs, where, losing all interest in the sleeping couple, it gave a sardonic grin, faded and left the room. Next a grunting sound would be heard. She was always the first to wake up: wiping away a dribble of saliva with the palm of her hand, she would take an anxious look at the snoring Philemon to make sure he was still alive before hurriedly thrusting her swollen feet into a pair of worn slippers and setting about the business of living.

She scurried about at her tasks with a sense of urgency, for by the time Philemon was awake she would have to prepare breakfast, fetch water and clean the veranda (dirt was something she could not abide). There had been a heavy downpour overnight, the clay paths were treacherous, and, anxious not to fall, she stepped warily in the rubber galoshes she had slipped on her bare feet, leaning to her right, where in a tall enamelled pail icy, limpid water slopped back and forth from her awkward movements.

"Zhenya!" eventually came the quavering tones of Philemon's voice. "What time is it?" "Ten o'clock already, Vanya," she replied, half-opening the door from the veranda. "Time to get up. Is your headache better?" "Better just check," he said, clearing his throat. "God helps those who help themselves," she clucked soothingly, perching on the edge of his bed to fit the black rubber sleeve of the blood-pressure gauge round his arm. Then they both held their breath. "Well, that's all right, then," came her sigh of relief. "You're doing just fine: a hundred and forty over eighty. Now come and have your breakfast – they'll be bringing Alyona soon."

Three years previously their younger daughter Tatyana had given birth to a large pallid baby. Tatyana was unmarried. She had turned out so like her father, with the same bulldog looks, that for a long time no man had shown the slightest interest in her. But eventually she had come back pregnant from an organised group tour to Hungary and Czechoslovakia.

"He'd damn well better marry her, the swine!" thundered Philemon. "Otherwise I'll have his guts for garters – have him kicked out of the KGB, the son-of-a-bitch! His feet won't touch the ground... Think they can run rings round us, his sort!"

But time passed, and Tatyana remained unmarried. The later stages of pregnancy found her pounding away on her typewriter at nights and disappearing into the library for hours on end; and a month before the baby was due she was awarded her master's degree and landed a senior teaching post at the polytechnic. Presumably this gave the KGB officer with the small premature bald patch and fastidious expression pause for thought, for although he did not marry her, neither did he exactly go out of his way to avoid her. Tentative talk of a three-room flat in a housing co-operative would sometimes fall from his impassive lips; and two days after the birth of their child he turned up at the maternity unit bearing some greasy-looking defrosted strawberries in a plastic bag.

They called their little girl Alyona. The older she grew, the less her fairy-tale name seemed to suit her. Tatyana, unbalanced by her maternal instincts, force-fed poor Alyona like a guinea-pig in some bizarre experiment. At the age of three she looked like a six-year-old, and they had to buy her clothes in the young schoolchildren's section of the children's department store. To an accompaniment of songs, exhortations, toys, books and rattles they would seat this pasty-faced creature at the table, decked out in enormous ribbons and snugly wrapped in a towel, then cram into her reluctant mouth caviar on rolls, morsels of calves' liver, and blackcurrants mashed up with sugar, all washed down with thick carrot juice. Swathed in towels, Alyona would attempt to resist, giving voice to deep-throated howls and kicking out at the high chair with her thick-set legs. "Watch the little birdie flying there," Tatyana would appeal to her. "And now let's catch him – yum!" Choking, Alyona would bring up everything she had eaten; and straightaway they would wash her, dress her in clean clothes, spread new caviar on new rolls, pulp knobbly fresh carrots in the screeching electric juicer.

"Get up now, Vanya," said Baucis on days when their granddaughter was expected. "They're bringing Alyona today."

"Are they?" exclaimed Philemon, agreeably startled. "So we'd better get down to the market, eh Zhenya?"

"Yes, let's go before it gets too hot. Or you stay at home, and I'll go on my own."

"No, I'll come with you, there's no need to go on your own," he quavered. "Uh-huh-huh…"

She made sure he remembered to take all his medicines, then crawled under the bed and spent some time rummaging around in search of his ankle boots. They set off for the market together, she, like him, greeting acquaintances with much ceremony, commenting with approval on the weather, asking after people's health, cooing over babies in prams, and even chuckling like him: "Uh-huh-huh, huh-huh…"

Sometimes Philemon flew into fits of rage. She was afraid of these, any one of which could easily end in a stroke. Some boys from the other dachas might be sitting on somebody's fence and breaking branches off a rowan tree. His face flushed purple, his stick with its heavy bronze handle held in the air, Philemon would rush at the fence, wheezing: "I'll have you lot! Ruddy hooligans! I'll do for you, you scum!" Then, grasping his elbows from behind, she would urge him, "Come on, Vanya, don't bother yourself with them! Va-anya!" Panting heavily, with whistling indrawn breaths, Philemon continued on his way to the station, gradually calming down as he went. "What a rabble! What a bloody shower! I'd have the lot of 'em shot out of hand!" And again she sought to placate him: "Of course, of course… Why sully your hands with them… You should think of yourself more." "There's no discipline, Zhenya!" Philemon lamented, still a pale shade of purple from his recent outburst. "That's why you get that sort of behaviour – discipline's all gone to pot everywhere. People have got out of hand…" "Shush, Vanya," she hissed, instantly assuming a false, lopsided smile. "Well, look who it is! It must be ages…" "Uh-huh-huh," Philemon chuckled, softening now, as he clownishly squirmed with incoherent delight at the sight of one of their dacha acquaintances with a shopping trolley. "Well, well, look who's beaten us to it! Bet you haven't even left any blackcurrants for us at the market, eh? Uh-huh-huh…"

After lunch an official car would draw up outside the fence of their dacha. Alyona was delivered to her grandparents courtesy of Tatyana's boyfriend. Tatyana – thin, with brittle bright-blond hair and thickset jaw – emerged from the car, staggering under the weight of her sleeping daughter, while they came running helter-skelter down the veranda steps towards her. "Here's our little girlie and her mummy," cooed Philemon. "Here they are, then. Who's brought granddad's little girlie to see him?" After she had eaten, Tatyana, feeling tired, picked berries in a low-cut summer frock or lay swinging in a hammock with the newspaper, while they filled a plastic bathtub with water, carried it out into the sunshine and between them, their hunched shoulders colliding, bathed pot-bellied, overfed little Alyona, who lay splashing soapy water over the sides with her chubby hands. In the evening Tatyana pencilled in her eyebrows, slapped on a thick layer of pink lipstick and rushed off to catch the train back into town, while they stayed with Alyona. Then Philemon read fairy-tales to her nearly nodding off himself as he monotonously rocked her cot. Usually Alyona would start hiccuping noisily. "Oh dearie me," Philemon would fret. "Bring us some juice, Zhenya – nice raspberry juice for our little girlie…"

When she had had enough raspberry juice and the hiccups had subsided, Alyona went off to sleep. Now Philemon opened his newspaper while she finished washing the dishes with her gnarled, flattened fingers. Thoughts came crowding into her head as she fought against fatigue: tomorrow she'd have to go to the market again (they'd forgotten to buy rhubarb, and Philemon's digestion was playing up!), wash out all Alyona's tee-shirts, and give the upstairs room a good clean, because on Friday Tatyana might not come on her own, but bring that elusive boyfriend of hers. Then they'd have to do their utmost to give them a taste of happy family life, with a slap-up meal, and their baby girl all spick-and-span and hiccuping from all the goodies they'd fed her, so as to give that indecisive fellow with the premature bald patch and impassive lips the firm impression that this was his home, his dacha, his wife and daughter.

"Damn me," Philemon wheezed, shaking his grizzled, trembling fist at something in the newspaper. "Damn me, there'd have been none of this in the Boss's day! They'd have bloody well had the whole damn pack of 'em shot out of hand!" He raised his bleary eyes to the small portrait framed in funereal black. With its large nose and black moustache, buttressed from beneath by the stiff collar of a military-style jacket, the face peered back at Philemon through narrowed lids with an affectionate, crafty expression. "Uh-huh-huh," Philemon sighed, feeling calmer now. "Uh-huh-huh…" He lowered his voice. "Zhenya, I think I should report that Jew: he gets hold of foreign newspapers to read. And that's just for starters, 'cos even worse, he listens in to Western radio. You can hear everything from their veranda. If they think they can put one past me… We should report them…" She was holding her fingers apart as she dried them with a clean towel. "Think of yourself, Vanya!" she said. "You've done your bit. Anyway, where could you report them to these days?"

Deep down she felt that at the time Philemon had done the wrong thing in zealously upholding the ideals of his Communist youth. Now in their old age, thanks to this fanatical obstinacy of his, they had no chauffeured official car to call their own, no daily domestic help, no dacha in the government countryside resort. They did, it was true, have a one-bedroom flat, a good pension, exclusive hospital treatment and special food parcels twice a month. Yet there were others – much smaller fry than Philemon, without long years of high-ranking service in the Uzbekistan Central Committee to their credit – who had more than them! And she looked with compassion at her honourable, uncompromising old man, sitting engrossed in his newspaper beneath that large-nosed, much lamented face, and thought that of course he was right again: they ought to report such goings-on. Yet with things as they stood nowadays you didn't know where to start. Who would you report them to? You could end up a laughing stock.

"Come to bed, Vanya," she urged. "Alyona might wake up in the night, and then we'll be worn out in the morning. We'll have to go to the market first thing, I haven't got anything for dinner yet... You can stay in the playground with her while I do the shopping..." Grunting, they lowered themselves into their beds with the identical silk eiderdowns. It never took Philemon more than a moment or so to start whistling through his fierce-looking pug nose. She would get up to straighten the pillow under Alyona's head, check the gas was switched off in the kitchen and the front door locked, then go back to bed. The moon, filtering through a crack in the curtains, licked at her sideways-drooping cheek with its tuft of long black hairs. Cool, jasmine-scented air came wafting in from the garden. A nightingale that had bided its time burst into song somewhere between heaven and earth; and to the sound of its untiring voice she would fall asleep.

One night she was woken by a high-pitched yammering sound. She opened her still unseeing eyes with a shock and sat bolt upright in bed. "I'w do-ooh for ya! A-a-ah! Do-o-ooh for ya! Sh-shoo!" Philemon was squealing in a high, quavering voice, making odd tearing movements with his frail white fingers. "I'w do-ooh for the sss-cum!" "Vanya!" she screamed and ran over to him. His face was bright purple, his eyes shut tight. "Vanya!" she moaned and, without thinking what she was doing, shook him by the shoulder. Philemon, purple-faced, opened his bulldog mouth, and at once his short fleshy tongue lolled out as if torn off at the root. She thrust her bare feet into a pair of rubber galoshes, tore outside as she was, bareheaded and in her flannelette nightdress, and ran gasping for breath down the pitch-black road towards the security guard's hut, which had the only telephone for the whole dacha settlement. An hour later, wheezing sibilantly and with a white sheet draped over his short body, Philemon was being loaded into an ambulance by two medical orderlies, while she, hugging her capacious sagging bosom in the flannelette nightdress, explained to them that she couldn't accompany her husband to the hospital as there was no one else to stay with their granddaughter. Going back into the bedroom, which was filled with black silvery darkness, its window open to the thickets of jasmine outside, she sat on the untidy bed from which they had just carried the purple-faced old man, and began to weep in a quiet, subdued fashion. Her tears were somehow unpremeditated, almost mechanical. Poor Vanya. Please God, don't let him die. A lifetime together. The phrases were imprinted ready-made inside her head, as if someone had written them there in bold type: Don't let him die. Poor Vanya. A lifetime together. Alyona woke up and started howling in a deep voice. She struggled to pick the child up. "Stop crying now. Granddad's not very well. Poor Granddad." Alyona gave a resounding hiccup and went quiet. In the morning Tatyana came by taxi and stayed with Alyona while she hurried off to the Kremlin hospital. Philemon lay limply in bed, looking somewhat paler now, enmeshed in a network of tubes; he recognised her and struggled to move his short arm with its covering of grey hairs. She sat with him for half an hour, straightening his sheet and rubbing a warm damp towel over the bulldog face with its sparse growth of spiky bristles, then, her heart thumping, shuffled out into the corridor to waylay the doctor attending him. He reassured her that Philemon's case was not hopeless: he'd not suffered a major stroke as such, and there was every reason to hope for a recovery. It was as if a weight had been lifted from her shoulders. She stayed in the city throughout that hot July, every day making her way by trolleybus to the market and then on to the hospital, every night cooking diet soups or grating chicken liver for him, distrustful even of the Kremlin hospital and muttering to herself that you couldn't beat good home cooking. Once as she was sitting by his bedside she dozed off suddenly, and her gaunt head with the grey-dappled hair in a bun at the back nodded forwards. She dreamed she was sitting on some sort of wooden bunk, combing her hair, in a sweltering dormitory hut full of naked women. So bizarre and frightening was the dream that she woke up moaning gently in her frail elderly voice. In front of her, ruddy-cheeked and wearing his own red pyjamas, lay Philemon, using his stubby, hirsute fingers to tuck in with obvious relish to some strawberries she had brought him. Still half-asleep, she thought he had cut himself and had blood all over his fingers, and this gave her a nasty shock. But Philemon, now almost fully recovered, suddenly winked at her with his right eye, recently operated on for a cataract, and said: "D'you remember how I proposed to you, eh?" With a toss of her head she burst out laughing, holding her hand in front of her mouth with its fringe of black hairs. "Well, who'd remember that?" she responded, still laughing. "How many years ago was it? Nearly fifty! My, you've got your faculties back, and no mistake!" "You can say that again," said Philemon, licking sweet strawberry blood from his thumb. "Uh-huh-huh... I'm gonna marry that dark-haired lass, I said to meself – and marry her I did! D'you remember, Zhenya?" She shook silently with tingling, blissful laughter. "Marry her I did? You old rascal, you! Just about on the mend again, and talking like that! Lie still now! Shall I grate an apple for you? I brought the grater with me rather than do it at home so it'll be nice and fresh." Philemon was not listening. "Aye…" he continued. "Marry her I did! With all the trimmings. And then I took that dark-haired lass with me, over the hills and far away. Uh-huh-huh…" She took the grater out of her bag and was about to start grating the apple for him when suddenly her head nodded forwards and she fell asleep again. And again she was surrounded by the naked women in the sweltering barracks.

More than a year went by. The dacha season was nearing its end, although the days continued hot and sunny. One Sunday morning she rose very early, heated up a pail of water and then for some reason carried it out into the dense tangle of nettles behind the shed. "I'll wash here," she said to herself, completely forgetting that she had her own little bathhouse, painted bright blue. Philemon had taken a steam bath in there the day before. With a bundle of birch twigs she had thrashed his hunched red back with its peppering of large pitch-black moles while he stood holding his shaggy, grey-haired stomach in with his hands, issuing orders: "Pile on the heat, Zhenya! More steam!" "What do you want with more steam, Vanya," she reasoned with him as she stood there barefoot, her satin housecoat half-undone, wiping the streaming beads of sweat from her face with one forearm. "You think about your blood pressure, never mind more steam!" "Oh-ho-ho!" roared Philemon, his stocky frame bloated with blood, and then let his stomach out again. "Nothing wrong with my blood pressure. Steam baths can't

257

do us Russians anything but good!" He leaned forwards with his elbows on the bench and his back to her, so that she could beat him some more with the birch twigs and rinse off the remaining soapsuds. She suddenly felt sick at the sight of his hunched red back with its large pitch-black moles, his splayed bandy legs with their sparse covering of slicked-down hairs, the frothy wisps of lather on his buttocks... "I feel as if I can't breathe in here, Vanya," she mumbled. "Dry yourself off now, and let's go and have our tea. It's time to get Alyona ready for bed..." "Can't breathe?" said Philemon, suddenly cowed. "How come you can't breathe? Let's get out then..." They had their tea on the veranda: she, Philemon, Tatyana and Alyona. In the garden apples fell from the branches, plummeting to the ground with a gentle hiss. Each falling apple made her jump. The low-hanging pink lampshade left behind by the dacha's previous owners cast a circle of light on the table, inside which shone glistening-wet beads of caviar, white aerated bread, and a golden-crusted apple pie, slightly burnt at the edges, which had been cut into generous slices. Tatyana's voice sounded like a duck quacking as she cajoled Alyona to drink up all her cream. The child was choking on her glass and blowing bubbles of cream. "Oh, oh, oh!" quacked Tatyana, manoeuvring her bare bony arm to wipe Alyona's chin. "Watch out, Grandma might come and gobble up our cream – yum! Some nasty little girl we don't know might gobble it up – yum!" Alyona started breathing heavily, like a frog, and brought up some vomit on her lace-trimmed bib. "Oh dear, oh dear!" quavered Philemon. "Poor little thing... Give us a cloth, Zhenya, she's been sick again..." She started running into the kitchen to get a cloth, but was suddenly transfixed with terror: even as she watched, a puffed-up creature with purple quivering cheeks was clambering on to another smaller creature with bulging eyes and an enormous green ribbon on its head which gave it the appearance of a frog. Flapping about between these two was a bare, bony fish with ribs sticking out this way and that and brittle hair standing on end. The fish was quacking stridently, opening wide its narrow, naked mouth to reveal broken fragments of white bone inside. She leaned against the door frame and screwed up her eyes. Her head had started ringing, slowly and solemnly like the tolling of an Easter bell. "Give us a cloth, Zhenya." The familiar voice had a menacing edge to it. "A cloth, give us a cloth. What's up?" She opened her eyes. Sitting looking at her in the circle of light from the lampshade were Philemon, red and wrinkled from his steam bath, the anaemic-looking Tatyana with her bare collar-bones, and Alyona, huge and woebegone, gorged on a diet of sugar and fat, with pink and white vomit on her lace-trimmed bib. Suddenly remembering what she was supposed to do, she found a cloth and, trembling unaccountably with fear, handed it to Philemon. Their hands touched briefly. She imagined he was about to strike her – about to slash her wrists with something sharp and sweaty held in his hand. Hastily she backed away, smiling submissively. Tatyana picked up Alyona and ran into the kitchen to clean her up. Philemon handed the cloth back to her now it was no longer needed. "Uh-huh-huh," he muttered, threatening her quite openly now with a small sharp knife. "Uh-huh-huh, Zhenya…"

That night she hardly slept. She kept getting up and going to the window to look at the slithery, overripe moon, struggling to stay up in the sky. She was too scared even to steal a glance at where Philemon lay snoring noisily. She felt that in spite of the loud snoring his green eyes were open wide in the dark, following her every move. Underneath her eiderdown she felt a little easier: it provided her with a defence, a coat of armour.

Yet no sooner had she wrapped herself in it than her eyelids began to droop. No, she mustn't sleep: Philemon was just waiting for her to drop off. To do what? She really had no idea. Perhaps (she began to imagine) he wouldn't kill her at all, but on the contrary climb into her bed for a kiss and cuddle ("I said I'd marry her, and marry her I did," she remembered), and then she'd have to lie still beneath the weight of his large hairy stomach. Or she imagined him sending her outside to stand watch over the house in place of a guard dog (she was troubled by a vague memory of something to do with a guard dog, but couldn't quite work out what it was). Or – and this was the most frightening of all – she could almost feel the touch of that small sharp knife of his with the hairs sticking to it…

As it grew light she threw on her dressing gown and began moving silently about the house. She went into their granddaughter's room. Instead of Alyona there was a dead, swollen doll lying in the cot, pretending to be asleep. The doll didn't want to turn back into a human being, didn't want to grow, because it knew it had only a life of misfortune and ridicule to look forward to. She was shocked and felt sorry for the doll, and stroked its head with a hand dappled brown with age spots. Next she crept stealthily up the creaking stairs, stopping outside the room where Tatyana was sleeping with that fastidious, stubborn man of hers, who had come by train the previous evening. First she heard a hoarse wheezing, followed by gurgling from a woman's throat, a liquid flow that sounded like: "arl-narl-arl-narl…" She realised that Tatyana's boyfriend must be strangling her, had perhaps already killed her; yet she was too terrified to intervene and decided to stand and listen a little longer. "Arl-narl-arl," came the mumbling. She couldn't understand a word, although Tatyana was speaking quite loud. By contrast the boyfriend's quiet responses were not only easy to make out, but for some reason lodged in her memory at once. "One can in principle achieve physical gratification with any woman," he said, articulating precisely, his teeth clashing together as he took a bite of something. "Any woman, I would say, in principle. But whether one can settle down to family life with any woman is a very, very big question indeed. A question of principle, I should say." Again he took a bite of something, and a loud quacking came from Tatyana in response. "It's not my intention in principle to avoid the issue," he continued. "The time we've been together speaks for itself. And if I can be assured that my household will be run entirely in accordance with the principles laid down by me, I shall be prepared to start considering my decision as early as tomorrow." He must have started strangling Tatyana some more, for again she uttered a hoarse gasp. "We can in principle get married, provided such a step doesn't bring disorder and indiscipline into my life," he said. A stream of: "arl-narl-arl" poured from Tatyana's throat, then her boyfriend said, "Agreed," and they both fell silent. Unable to hold back any longer, she opened the door a crack and peeped in. The long strand of hair which Tatyana's boy-friend combed over his head by day to cover his bald patch now hung down to one side as he lay on her anaemic body, gently strangling her and at the same time moving rhythmically up and down. They had not noticed her intrusion and, pale blue in the light of early dawn, continued their conversation. All this aroused in her mixed feelings of fear and disgust; although deep down she recalled that at one time she herself had wished for Tatyana and this man to lie together like that at nights in the room she had scrubbed clean specially. Trying not to make too much noise breathing, she went downstairs, crawled under her eiderdown and fell fast asleep. Very soon she was awake again; jumping feverishly out of bed, she heated up a pail of water in the kitchen and went out into the dense tangle of nettles behind the shed. "I'll wash here," she said to herself and began hastily to undress. Removing every last stitch of clothing, she let her thinning grey-dappled hair down over her shoulders and began carefully pouring water over herself from a dark blue pitcher. The water was too cold, and her skin turned to goose-pimples all over. Then she took a bar of household soap and quickly and energetically lathered herself all over, before once again scooping water from the pail. "Zhenya!" she heard Philemon's quavering voice call from somewhere close by. "Zhenya! Where have you got to?" Terrified, she squatted down and pressed her head against her trembling knees. She was hidden from him by burdocks and nettles. The ground shook with approaching footsteps: Philemon was using his stick with the heavy bronze handle to poke through the grass in search of his Baucis. She crouched bow-legged on the ground, covered in a bluish-grey film of household soap, her teeth chattering with fear. She realised that he was level with the back of the shed and would catch sight of her any moment. "Lord save and protect me!" she whispered to herself and crawled straight into the nettles, oblivious to their stinging. Squat and purple-faced, Philemon stood five paces from her, wearing his white sun hat and white nightshirt, with slippers on his bare feet. His bleary, ailing eyes could not see her. "Zhenya!" he mumbled anxiously. "Where on earth has she got to?" Then, taking the key from the wall, he set about unlocking the shed. She remembered that it was not really a shed at all, but a prison-camp barrack made up to look like one to stop neighbours from the other dachas asking awkward questions, and that in fact they had just arrived in Uzbekistan from Moscow for Philemon to take up his new post as commandant of the women's camp. She remembered being left behind with Larisa, who had just been born, her milk drying up during the journey to their new home, and having to heat water up in a big cast-iron tub to bath Larisa and wash herself. The house they were supposed to live in had not been finished yet, so for the time being they moved into a small dacha, leaving all their suitcases piled up in one corner. Having already seen to it that the man responsible for their reception and accommodation was hauled over the coals in appropriate fashion, Philemon told her she'd have to make do for a few more days. They had arrived the day before, she worn down by the wailing of her hungry daughter and one of the migraines which would suddenly overtake her and then drag on for weeks on end. They were met at the station and taken to the house of a fat Uzbek who looked for all the world as if his layers of fat had been trussed round and round with invisible threads. Here they were invited to sit on feather mattresses laid out on the floor and were served rich pilaff, wine and hot tea, while the Uzbek smiled a smile like a recumbent moon, the medals on his chest jingling urgently. "Aye," Philemon said to her, stretching his bulldog jaw in a yawn as he got into bed. "Aye... I'll sort this lot out. Think they can run rings round us..."

He stood there a little longer, poking about with his stick. Then he took off his sun hat and wiped his eyes with it. She had never seen him cry before. "Zhenya," he sobbed, "where are you? Don't frighten me like this." His chin started quivering slightly. She just knew he was putting on an act to make her come out of the nettles. "Oh no, you can forget that," she muttered to herself. "You can just stew for a bit longer..." Philemon turned round and, sobbing, went back to the house to wake up Tatyana and her boyfriend. Meanwhile, keeping her head down, she crawled to a section of the fence with a

263

large hole covered with sheets of plywood. Here she made her
break for freedom into the forest of fir trees which began just
the other side of the fence.

"No one's going to escape from my camp!" said Philemon,
bringing his hairy hand down hard on the table. "There are
no forests here, nowhere to hide! You'd better be sure they're
back here again by tomorrow!" She nodded approvingly as she
washed the dishes. Philemon was tearing strips off a pimply
man in uniform standing in front of him while, scalding his
mouth, he ate the borscht she had prepared. Good, thick,
blood-red borscht it was, with specks of yellow fat swimming
in it. The man in uniform stared at the plate with a sullen,
hounded look in his eyes. "Got that?" wheezed Philemon,
knocking back a glassful and taking a deep breath as if
surfacing from the bottom of a river. "That's all, you can go."
She dried her hands on a clean towel and sat down next to
him. "Who's escaped then, Vanya?" "Two of those bitches.
One Jewish, the other Russian. Yesterday, it was. We'll catch
'em again, and then, you see, I'll give 'em what's what! They
won't forget me in a hurry!" His clear blue, bulging eyes had
turned bloodshot. "No sirree!" The baby started crying in the
next room. She went in, then came back again. "Have you seen
our little toothy-woothy?" she crooned. "Lala's second tooth
is coming through!" "Hm… Damn me!" Philemon grunted
approvingly, patting her on the arm. "A tooth, eh? Let's take
a look…" They stood over the cot, admiring the little squirrel
tooth in the infant's mouth. "Damn me," Philemon repeated,
and then frowned. "You know, one of those sluts that got
away is pregnant. Six months gone, so they tell me." "No!"
she gasped in disbelief. "She couldn't even care less about her
baby, then? Risking her own life like that, and never mind the

baby – what sort of a mother is that?" "Come on, Zhenya, let's go for a spin," yawned Philemon. "Wrap our little girl up well. We'll get a breath of fresh air." He sat in front next to the driver, she in the back. The whole steppe was ablaze with dark-red poppies. "Damn me," he said, turning round to her with a grin across the width of his jaw. "Remember in the royal box at the Bolshoi? Looks the same sort of colour…" That night he heaved his hirsute, well-fed belly on top of her. Compliantly, anxious that he might no longer find her attractive, she panted with feigned pleasure. "My dark-haired little beauty," he grunted as he was dropping off to sleep a few minutes later. "Damn me… I'll kill those bitches, you mark my words. Hang 'em from the nearest tree. Think they can run rings round us…"

It was getting on for midday by the time they found her and brought her home. She came out of the forest without protest, her naked body covered in crimson nettle stings, her large work-flattened hands hanging inertly at her sides. Tatyana's boy-friend and a freckle-faced policeman stood either side of her, guiding her uncertainly towards the garden gate. With a frown on his face, the policeman moved awkwardly as he tried somehow to shield her from view, although as luck would have it the only person in the lane at that moment was Tatyana, leaning pallidly against the fence. At the sight of her mother she began shaking as if in a fever, and started to take her jacket off. "Right, then," said the policeman, frowning and looking away from Tatyana. "It seems fairly clear to me that what's needed here is medical assistance. A mental home, or something of that sort. There's nothing we can do to help." "Oh, Mummy," breathed Tatyana, her lips quivering uncontrollably. "Why, why?" "It's a waste of time, in principle, asking pointless questions," said her boy-friend, articulating precisely. He bridled with anger. "We have to get her inside the house." She heard what he had said and tossed her head. "I'll go by myself," she mumbled. "It's time for lunch, I'll go myself..." She climbed the veranda steps, supported by Tatyana, and saw in the doorway the portly, panic-stricken figure of Philemon. At the sight of his naked, dishevelled Baucis, her whole body a mass of red blotches, he began to back away from her, cringing and covering his face with his hairy hands. Baucis was choked with fear, and would have fallen if Tatyana and her boy-friend had not caught her in time. "Dad!" Tatyana screamed hysterically. "Get her something to put on! Anything! She can't walk around like this!" "Yes, of course, of course," said Philemon. Still cringing and backing away, he cast around for a garment of some sort. "What on earth's the matter with her?" He grabbed an old raincoat from the coat rack and handed it gingerly to his daughter, afraid of touching the old woman's naked body. Tatyana's hands were shaking as she slipped the raincoat over her mother. "What are we going to do?" she asked tearfully. "She'll have to be taken away," said Philemon, trembling fearfully. "What else can we do? She needs proper medical attention. The doctors know best... Proper medical attention... Otherwise, who knows... She's not well, is our grandma... Bad business all round..." Suddenly Baucis fell to her knees in front of Tatyana before the boy-friend could catch her. "I'll be your servant," she pleaded, "I'll wash your feet. Don't send me away." "Oh, Mummy!" Tatyana sobbed uncontrollably. "Oh, my God! Come inside and lie down, have a sleep. Oh, Mummy!" Her teeth chattering, she went inside and lay down in bed without taking the raincoat off. "All right, I'll have a sleep," she mumbled. "What a to-do... Have a sleep..."

Philemon was crying and wiping the tears from his quivering bulldog cheeks with his grey-haired fists. "At least take me back to town, then," he begged Tatyana. "Or you, Boris, give me a lift into Moscow, there's a good chap. I can't stay in the same house as a mental case. Just looking at her could send my blood pressure shooting up." Tatyana had regained her composure. "We mustn't rush into anything, Dad," she said reasonably. "Let's keep an eye on her for a couple of days. I'll be here anyway, and Boris is staying today and tomorrow. I feel sorry for her. It could just be some age-related condition that'll go away again." "That is in principle quite feasible," her boy-friend confirmed. "I heard of a colleague in our department who experienced a similar episode with his aunt which in principle had no lasting effects..."

II

"Perhaps I could stay at home, Vanya?" she whispered in her sleep. "The children are poorly, and I don't feel..." "No, you can't," replied Philemon. "You have to be at the concert. All the top brass'll be there. And don't you dare show me up." They sat in the front row of the packed hall. On the stage, which was decked out with flags and flowers, stood three rows of women in white hospital robes. She remembered as she slept how proud Philemon had been of this idea, which he had thought up himself: a week before the concert sixty new hospital gowns had been delivered to the camp. Now these dead women in their clean white burial linen, flinging open mouths full of rotting teeth, sang at full pitch: "...our tanks are swift as lightning..." Philemon wrinkled his brow with pleasure, although the lower half of his face retained its usual fierce expression. Their song finished, on the word of command the dead women executed a left turn and shuffled off stage

267

in their felt hospital slippers. The audience applauded. Then three women who had not taken part in the singing appeared on stage, dressed in the same white gowns and with large wreaths of poppies on their heads, which made it look as if flames were leaping from their hair. They presented the visiting V.I.P. with an enormous embroidered cushion which had, worked in red silk in the middle of it, the promise: "Through honest toil on behalf of the Motherland we shall earn the forgiveness of Party and People!" In her dream she could not make out the figure that had accompanied Philemon up the steps. She had only a sense of the word "V.I.P." itself, and gradually she began to feel that Philemon's hairy fingers were supporting something rough-textured and dark in creaking boots, something that had neither body nor face. As the V.I.P. extended a hand of sorts to accept the gift of the cushion, one of the dead women with red fire in their hair spat in his face. "Bastard!" she screamed as they hurriedly dragged her away, hitting her as they went, "Bastard!" They stopped the dead woman's mouth, yet still she managed to call out through blood and sputum: "Go to hell, the lot of you! Bastards!"

Philemon was a fearsome sight as he sat next to her in the front row, waiting for the concert to end. Stony-faced and unmoving, no longer applauding, no longer wrinkling his brow, he sat quietly grinding his teeth. Eventually he turned his unseeing eyes on her. "You can go home on your own. You won't be needed at the supper." "What about you?" she asked, snuggling into the raincoat Tatyana had draped over her naked, nettle-stung body. "Me?" Philemon retorted, clenching his knotted, black-haired fist. "I've got things to see to."

There was a pleasant, appetising smell of pilaff, wine and fresh bread in the house. The old Uzbek woman, one of the locals, bowed and told her in a whisper that the children had gone to sleep a long time ago. She slipped off the irksome raincoat and let it fall to the carpet, then stretched out on the bed and closed her eyes. Philemon came back in the middle of the night. An acrid, suffocating smell of sweat hung about him. "Well?" she asked, sitting up on the feather mattress. "Have they found Alyona?" "I'm having her shot," Philemon replied, his heavy jaw gaping in a yawn. "Sabotage on behalf of foreign intelligence. Enemy operation carried out on camp territory. Think they can run rings round us..." He stood his shiny new boots against the wall and scratched his stomach beneath his shirt. "They won't forget me in a hurry, no sirree..."

"You let me know just as soon as she wakes up," Philemon mumbled faint-heartedly, hiding behind the large blue teapot with the red flower pattern. "I can't even bear looking at her... Not until we've made sure... No way... It's not like a normal illness... Can't even live out my last years in peace... What sort of life is that?"

Tatyana went in and bent over her. Tatyana was wearing a white hospital gown. The poppies in her hair had long since withered and turned black. As she leaned forwards a smell of pilaff and fresh bread wafted across from her body. "Mummy, are you feeling better?" said Tatyana. "Where's Alyona, then?" she asked with sudden guile, remembering the name of that little woman with the ribbon in her hair. "It's time for her afternoon tea. Tell them to pick some berries for her." The word "berries" made her feel slightly queasy, but she overcame this without letting on to Tatyana. "Tell them to pick some berries, otherwise I'm going to put in a complaint against the lot of you. And I know where I can go to do it, too, thank God – it's not as though we're living in the desert here. You're starving that child to death..." With an anxious sigh Tatyana went back out on the veranda. Philemon and her boy-friend looked at her. "She's a bit better," Tatyana said doubtfully. "She's had a sleep and seems a bit more like her old self." "It all takes time," her boy-friend concurred. "Of course, we won't leave you on your own with someone who's mentally deranged. Although it'll mean putting ourselves out quite a bit, in principle…"

She woke in the night and realised that this was the last night before their wedding. Tomorrow they were going to be married. He'd got a strong pair of hands on him: like iron, they were. When he'd grabbed her breasts a few days ago the pain had taken her breath away. Well, he was a man, wasn't he? They were all the same. At least she'd feel secure with him – he'd look after her properly. The pain you could put up with. His mother and sister lived out in the sticks somewhere, but he'd made his own way in the world, got himself educated. Salt of the earth, his kind were – the backbone of Soviet power. Everything they'd struggled to achieve depended on people like him. Anyway, you couldn't just pull away from him when he had hold of your breast, could you? She laughed out loud in the darkness. For a while she sat there thinking, then suddenly knew what she had to do. First thing tomorrow he'd have his yoghourt. He always had his yoghourt with blackcurrants, every morning. That was before breakfast. Then they'd have their breakfast together. Feeding Alyona would be a joint effort, both of them sharing titbits with her and telling her nursery rhymes and fairy-tales until they were blue in the face.

Best to put it in his yoghourt, she thought. I'll do it now; nobody'll guess. And then there'll be no wedding. It'll all be over by the time Tatyana and Alyona wake up. I'll have the breakfast ready on the table and tell them he's gone. Gone where? How should I know, just gone, that's all. My breast still hurts now. Just shows how rough he can be. That's not to say we haven't had a good life together – nobody could wish for better. All the same, I've got to do it. I'm afraid of him: that's why, that's the main reason. He'll come and grab hold of me again, strip me naked in the night and roll on top of me. And then it'll be morning sickness and having babies all over again. That's what I'm afraid of.

Trying not to let the door creak, she went out on the veranda, which was bathed in gentle light from the overripe moon. She picked up a thin glass dish for serving jam, then a hammer from the porch and went out on to the steps. There she smashed the dish with the hammer. Nobody had heard. He was asleep. Good. Surreptitiously she set about pounding the dish with the hammer, trying to grind up the broken splinters of glass. This was a method favoured by the Uzbeks. It was clean and simple. Once you started bleeding from the stomach you'd had it. She scooped up the pieces of ground glass and returned to the veranda with them held tight in her fist. Opening the door of their generously stocked refrigerator, she scattered the tiny fragments in the butter dish and replaced the lid. Then she wiped her hands, changing the towel by the washbasin while she was at it (Tatyana and her slovenly ways again!) and went back into the room. He was not there: his bed, neatly made beneath its silk cover, dimly registered empty. She snuggled down under the eiderdown and went to sleep.

"He's such a wonderful father!" she trilled to her mother as she unwrapped the presents. Her mother's eyes shone greedily, and her hands were shaking; in her whole manner there was something cowed, craven and insincere. As a child she had always been sick with fear of her mother, and since reaching adulthood had never once sought her advice or confided in her.

"He'll do anything for the children, anything! Tatyana wants to take up ballet, and any other father would have told her to forget it – you know the sort of thing: 'You a ballerina? You can drop those fancy ideas!' But not him! He said: 'Fine, if that's what you want, we'll get you into the Bolshoi ballet school, and you can dance to your heart's content.' He'd do anything for them!" Her mother's hands trembled as she snatched a length of grey gaberdine. "Is this for me, too?" she asked, flashing the same false lopsided smile her daughter assumed whenever she wanted to make a pleasing remark to someone. "It's all for you, all from him! 'We've got to do her proud,' he said. He chose it all himself: shoes, winter clothes, everything! 'For Nina Timofeyevna, with regards from her devoted son-in-law,' – those were his actual words. Ha, ha! You see what sort of a man he is?" "Of course, Zhenya, of course," her mother replied with a toss of her mobile head. "We know what sort of posting you were on... Very demanding work, I should imagine. They won't take just anyone for that, only people of the highest calibre, people of spotless character. Oh yes, we know about that. But what's the climate like there, the weather?" "Very hot, Mummy. Almost too hot in summer. But we had this marvellous house there, with two verandas, and our own orchard. And in spring it's so beautiful, it really hits you in the face. Poppies everywhere – all the desert and the hills ablaze with them. Just incredible. I stayed at home with the children. We had a nanny, a woman came every other day to do the cleaning, and another one came to cook for us, all local people. We used to drive into town for concerts or the theatre – we had our own chauffeur-driven car. I tell you, we had everything." There was an envious whistle from her mother's thin pimply throat. "Well I never! You know, people used to ask me, 'How's your daughter coping in a place like that after living in Moscow?' I'd say, 'Great, everything's fine,' but on the inside I'd be worried sick about you myself. After all, you were there on your own with two children, and I suppose Vanya was tied up with his work all day." "He was, all day. After all, we were dealing with criminals, and you had no time to think about yourself. Awful types, they were, enemies of the people. But Vanya was always humane – never treated them unfairly, always went by the book. After all, they were human beings too, and they'd been sent to us to be reformed. We hoped the voice of conscience might be awakened in them. We did what we could."

Small and waxen-looking, Philemon knocked at the door of Tatyana's bedroom. She came to the door in a frilly nylon nightdress, still half asleep. "What are you doing up, Dad? You're driving me round the bend, the pair of you!" "I know, I know," he mumbled. "But I really would like to get back to town. I haven't been able to sleep a wink, I'm so scared. I've never had anything to do with mentally abnormal people before, never in my whole life. Gangsters and criminals, yes, but at least they were sane. Only here I haven't been able to sleep a wink." "My God!" Tatyana exploded. "If only you could hear yourself! It's not as if we're talking about some stranger here, is it? Think of all the years you've been together!" "Who's interested in that now?" Philemon quavered, shifting from one foot to the other in his large tan-coloured slippers. "All right, we've been together, been through all sorts – but why should I be expected to sacrifice what's left of my life now for the sake of her illness? I didn't shed my blood for that, I can tell you... Always up there in the thick of it. Yes, we stayed together all these years – God only knows how..." Tatyana was aghast. "Have you started raving now, or what? Dad! Don't you at least feel sorry for her? Just take a look at her!" "I do, of course I do, I do feel sorry," Philemon rattled off in one breath. "Nobody's ever felt sorry for me, though, never in my whole life. I've always been there for others – for you and the family. Surely now I'm entitled to take things easy a bit. She could be planning to cut my throat – who knows what a crazy person might take it into their head to do?" Tatyana recoiled in disbelief. "Cut your throat? You've only to touch her and she'd fall over!" "Yes, cut my throat," Philemon mumbled, blowing hot breath into her face from his bulldog mouth. "I had a dream that she was going to do just that. You can never tell what's going on inside someone else's head. It's a nightmare! Take me back to town, away from here!" "Stop pestering me!" Tatyana hissed. "Waking me up in the middle of the night like that!" And she slammed the door in his face. Her boy-friend raised his head from the pillows, the long strand of hair hanging down from his bald patch. "This is a madhouse, if you think about it! And if you lot think I can cope with this on top of my work load… I'm sorry, I shall be forced to take appropriate action…"

She heard them moving about somewhere, going up and down the stairs, whispering. Excellent: now they'd be afraid of her. What sort of a deal was that anyway, loading all the work on to one person? Fetching water, looking after the children… And then in the evening she had to go to the Bolshoi. Comrade Stalin himself was to be there, and they were all going to sit in the royal box. But just before the ballet, would you believe it, Philemon found he had a sty. He literally howled with rage. "Vanya," she told him, "Vanya, it's not a crime! It could happen to anyone." He very nearly let fly at her with his fists. "What the bloody hell do you know about it! I can't let Comrade Stalin see me looking like this!" They smeared some egg white over the sty and powdered it so it wouldn't show.

Even so his eye stood out like a car headlight. She didn't like jewellery, but he told her to wear a necklace, and she didn't argue. Let him have it his way. A white necklace to go with her crimson dress. Where had he got it from? He didn't say. There was a strange smell to the necklace. The smell of someone's body, or of some sort of wood, she couldn't tell which.

"How come you've got a moustache?" Philemon shouted at her in a sudden rage. "What are you, a man or a woman?" She looked in the mirror: he was right, she had a moustache. Two hairs here, another one there... How had they grown? She hadn't noticed. She plucked them out with a pair of tweezers. When Comrade Stalin came into the box they all stood up. Philemon's eye with the powdered sty filled with tears, and his chin trembled. Men can have feelings too, you know. What could you say against him? He was a caring father and husband... "Caring" was putting it mildly, in fact: although he wasn't one to spoil the children, he put everything back into the house and family, and he'd never as much as looked at another woman.

"Don't expect me back tonight," said Philemon. "I've got to go on a tour of inspection round the camps. There've been reports of trouble there – breaches of discipline." And off he went. The house felt comfortable and clean and smelled of bread and wine. That night it was stiflingly hot, and she threw everything off, even the sheet. She felt at peace, free to be herself. No fingers groping at her body, no one snoring against her neck. He came back three days later in a buoyant mood, although his face looked tired and haggard. After his meal he fell into bed without even touching her.

The following day he disappeared without trace again. It was the same story the day after that. Each time he came back looking haggard, in a buoyant, truculent mood, and treated her and the children as if they weren't there. When she washed one of his shirts, she found it covered in hairs. It was a woman's hair: fair, like gossamer. She said nothing, just pretended that was how it had to be. He was a man: they were all the same. At least this was the first time he'd gone astray. Otherwise it was all work and family. Let him think he was cock of the walk, he'd be sweeter-tempered for it. Although, of course, her heart ached unbearably. She took it in her hands, squeezed it and wrung it out, twisting it like a rag; not a tear fell. Let him. He wouldn't leave her. There was Larisa, Tatyana. Would he chuck them all over for some prison-camp floosie? She never did find out whose hair it was. For a couple of months he kept coming home late and never touched her. Well, she didn't mind that, it gave her body a rest. Eventually he half-heartedly heaved himself on to her again without so much as a word. Gradually things got back to normal, just like before. There was no point trying to change men, was there?

We'll go to the market, she thought, we'll buy some rhubarb for Alyona, some rhubarb for you and some for me. What does Alyona want with rhubarb? Why, what do you mean? She may be just a child now, but when she grows up she'll have her share of tummy trouble too. We can put the rhubarb by until it's needed. Such a big lass she's turned out – there'll be boys chasing after her before we know it. Uh-huh-huh... I can't make that Boris out. If he marries Tatyana, well and good, but it'll be even better if he doesn't. That's just between you and me, though. I feel really sorry for Tatyana. She only makes out she's so hard. Actually she's got a weak heart. She had a late delivery and lost a lot of blood, so they gave her a Caesarean. And she's scared of that Boris, dead scared. He can go for weeks on end without even ringing her. Tied up in his work, he is. Of course, in his job you can't really relax or let your hair down much. Even so, he could think about his child, you can't leave it all to one person. It's only now that Philemon's come over all considerate like that: "Zhenya, Zhenya, let's hire a maid, why do it all yourself?" In the old days he'd rant and rave: "Get off your backside! What d'you think you are, a lady of leisure? We wiped all their sort out years ago!" She never said anything, never answered back. After all, people said that Buldayev had hanged his wife with his own hands – got fed up with her and hanged her, just like that. He was such a big shot that no one dared speak up. They put it out as suicide caused by a brain disorder, said she just couldn't cope with things any more. Maybe that's how it was. Even so there were all sorts of rumours going round. Philemon had once yelled at her in a rage, too: "I'll strangle you with my bare hands!" Of course, she'd just laughed... He was a man, wasn't he. They were all the same, all had to be cock of the walk.

"But you were going to stay today," Tatyana pleaded with him. "You've got some days off, haven't you..." Noisily her boy-friend sucked coffee into his long thin throat. "I can't manage today. In principle, I've got a full schedule all this week. But if there's any problem... I'll await further developments... Of course, if there's any problem... I'll send a car." "I'm sorry things have turned out like this, Boris darling," said Tatyana with a quiver of her father's bulldog chin. "They're old people..." "Yes," he agreed, "it's a nasty business, is old age. If only they could come up with some drug or other... It'd make things a lot easier, in principle. Where is she, in the living room?" "She's still asleep," Tatyana sighed. "I decided not to go in just yet. Dad's sleeping too: he took a sedative." "Why couldn't he sleep last night?" muttered her boy-friend, sucking in more coffee. "Was he scared, or what?" "Don't even ask!" Tatyana replied gloomily. Red streaky blotches began to spread over her pallid skin. "When I think of the mess they've got themselves into! And just think how they used to be: utterly devoted, in perfect harmony, always trying to please one another, never an unkind word." "Yes," her boy-friend agreed again. "If only everyone could live like that. What you might call the perfect couple."

At this point she shuffled out of the bedroom, taking short little steps and cringing, a fawning smile on her face. Instead of the raincoat she was now wearing a dress with a white collar which she kept for special occasions. Why on earth had they brought a dress like that to the dacha? They couldn't have been thinking. Anyway, it had come in useful now. She had not got round to combing her hair, which hung loose and grey-dappled over her shoulders, but she had managed to put her shoes on. "Mummy!" Tatyana wailed. "Why are you saying 'Mummy' like that?" she smiled, concealing her fear. "I've been your Mummy for forty years now! Ha, ha! I had a nice little sleep, and then I thought it's about time I got on with my work. Otherwise you could sleep your whole life away. Have you cooked today's dinner yet?" Tatyana and her boy-friend exchanged glances. Taking her time, she sat at the table and poured herself a cup of tea with shaking hands. They mustn't realise how scared she was, that was the main thing. Really she ought to ask if he was still alive. She smiled even more fulsomely: "Don't say you're planning to desert us, Boris? What a shame... Such lovely weather... You could have gone down to the river for a spot of fishing." The word "river" made her feel queasy too. It was the water: they'd throw the body in there at night, under cover of darkness, and what proof would there be then? She took a sip of tea and frowned: it tasted like dishwater. She'd have to make some stewed fruit.

Plenty of rhubarb, with blackcurrants and nettles. Nice and tart, and thick enough for a spoon to stand up in. Otherwise, what with Tatyana being such a bad cook, he might not marry her. Tatyana's boy-friend gave an indecisive cough. "Well, as far as I can see, in principle, there's no fundamental danger any more. I can leave you here without any qualms." Hastily adjusting his wayward strand of hair and licking off a grain of caviar which had stuck to his lip, he snatched up his briefcase and was out of the garden gate and gone before they knew it. "I'll go and pick some mushrooms in the forest for Alyona," she lied. "Or wild strawberries. I've always said, Tanya, haven't I, there's nothing to beat our wild strawberries straight from the forest. The taste, the aroma – there's nothing else to compare. And packed with vitamins." Tatyana just managed to contain herself. "Don't go, Mummy," she said. "Look, you're all shaky, and anyway, you're not quite... Listen to me, don't go!" I ought to ask her, she thought, ask if he's still alive. Otherwise what's the point of hiding? Perhaps they've even buried him already? If so, I'll take this dress off, and the shoes, and we'll cook the dinner. But what if he's alive? No, I don't want to risk it. It's only when you're young you get a thrill from taking risks. But at our time of life, uh-huh-huh... She pushed her cup aside. "Don't be silly, Tanya," she said reasonably. "I brought you and Larisa up, I've nursed Alyona for you – what makes you suddenly think I'm soft in the head? Can't I go for a walk in the forest?" And off she went, down the steps of the veranda, numb with terror because she had to turn her back on the locked door to his bedroom. Passing a blackcurrant bush, she flicked a maggot off one of the branches (they'd eaten all the berries, there was nothing left to give Alyona!) At the gate she turned round; he was standing in the doorway, looking at her. His mouth open, his eyes bleary (they'd forgotten his drops!), he stood there barefoot in his white nightshirt. She wondered whether he'd come running after her or not. How could he, though? His legs were all knotted and stiff; she'd have no problem getting away. So why not have a bit of fun now, she thought: I'll wave to him and call out, "Hello Vanya! Good morning to you!" She waved to him, her fingers trembling. "Where's she off to?" Philemon croaked hoarsely, clutching hold of Tatyana's shoulder. "Where's she going?" "For a walk," Tatyana said quietly. "She wants to pick some berries. She's feeling better." "Tanya, please," Philemon snivelled, "you're the only person I can turn to. Get me away from here, there's a good girl!" "I've told you, she's feeling better! She's gone for a walk. Now come and have your breakfast."

Two hours later Tatyana and two sympathetic women from neighbouring dachas set out to look for her. They searched the whole forest but saw no sign of her. Tatyana ran to the police station, and it was the same story all over again. She was found among some aspen trees and led home, clasping her hands to her heart and protesting her innocence: "What's all the fuss about? My God, can't I even go for a walk? The doctor told me to get plenty of fresh forest air." The other women just shrugged their shoulders and said,

"Look at her, Tanya: perhaps there is nothing wrong with her after all? She's probably just tired of slaving away in the kitchen all day and wants a bit of a rest." "What are you getting so worked up about? That's exactly what I've been saying!" she laughed. "Not even allowed to get a breath of fresh air! All my life I've been at their beck and call. At least now in my old age you'd think I'd be entitled to do what I want. I am entitled to go for a walk, am I?" Tatyana's pupils were contracting and dilating in turn as she looked at her mother.

"Are you having me on, or what? What's wrong with you?" "Can't you understand plain language?" she snapped back, waving her arms. "There's nothing wrong with me! I'm tired of slaving away in the kitchen, and anyone would tell you the same! Just let me get a bit of fresh air!" Tatyana broke down in tears. "Mummy, don't do this to me! My head's spinning! Are you all right again or not?"

Good job she's thick, she won't cotton on. Let her think I want to go for a walk. Always a bit short in the brains department, she was. Oh, bright enough at book-learning, but worse than a child when it comes to real life. Shouldn't be too hard pulling the wool over her eyes. All I need is for her to leave, so I'm left on my own with him. I'll bury him myself, too. If you want a job done properly, you've got to do it yourself, and that's a fact. It's kill or be killed. They wouldn't let me escape, so it's the only way. Not that I'm not scared, of course. Still, it'll be the very last time. Just this little bit more fear, and then I'll be free.

"No way!" Philemon chortled. "Trying to shack me up with your niece! You should see my woman: phoarr, real stunner, she is! I've been on cloud nine ever since we got married. Total respect, she's got: she'll wash my feet if I tell her to. No, you'll have to go a long way to find a woman like mine. She'll be here in a week or so, then we'll invite you over and you can see for yourself. I tell you, she's a right scorcher!" "What's her name?" asked the man in the military-style jacket worn unbuttoned at the chest as he filled their glasses with cold transparent vodka. "Tell me your woman's name, and we'll drink a toast to her." "Zhenya!" Philemon croaked tenderly. "Dark-haired lass, she is, like a little cat, but well-built with it." "Well, you've certainly got it bad," said the other with a sardonic grin. "Never known you to go all soft like that…" "What d'you mean, soft?" said Philemon with a look of surprise, emptying his glass in one. "Soft, you say… We can't afford to be soft in our line of work. I've seen enough women in my time, as you well know. Spent five years looking at 'em as commandant. Saw 'em naked and all sorts. They were obliged to wash in my presence if I demanded it, yes sirree! All part of the discipline! After all, I was supposed to be like a doctor – curing the bitches, rehabilitating them." "Well, and…" asked his friend with a sly look. "Did they – as part of the discipline?" "What do you think? Of course they did! Washed and dried themselves without so much as a squeak." "You're going to miss that job!" "Oh no, I've had enough of it now," Philemon frowned. "There's more important things to do in the world. When the Party commands, it's my duty to go without question. As for Zhenya, she'll go with me like a mare with her master. I'll take her by the reins, and she'll come trotting along behind. Yes sirree…"

I won't be able to manage him on my own, there's no way I will. What a mess. You see, that's just an act he's putting on all the time – pretending to be old and ill like that. He's not old at all. If he didn't die then, he never will. He'll just go on tormenting me. He'll make me wash his feet. I'll bath Alyona first, then wash his feet in the same water (no point heating up a new lot, is there?) That glass didn't work after all – I couldn't have ground up enough. Too late now, though – they've hidden the hammer, and the glass dishes too. It's time I was off. People used to live in the forests, good Lord they did – whole families, with children! I'll get settled in first, and then Alyona and Tatyana can move in with me. My little daughters, that I brought into the world and raised. As soon as I'm settled in I'll get them away from him, otherwise he's bound to put them in that prison-camp hut. "Get working!" he'll say. "Think you can run rings round me, do you... There'll be no theatre for you, none of that ballet stuff."

Quietly she pulled on her dress, then removed the pillowcase from her pillow and slipped into it a pair of rubber galoshes, a loaf of bread and a piece of soap in its holder. That should do, she thought, it's only to tide me over for now. Folk'll help me out when I get there. Of course, there are no forests here, but there'll be poppies growing thicker than any forest. I'll hide in among them and decide what to do then. The Uzbeks like us. The way they lived here before Soviet power – like the Stone Age, it was! She walked down the steps, steadying herself on the handrail. Moonlight crept over her face. The sky was turning grey in anticipation of dawn. Suddenly she decided she wanted to give Alyona a kiss. She set the pillowcase down on the steps and without a sound went back into the living room. Alyona was nowhere to be seen. She tried to remember which room she might be sleeping in and became confused. He was in the room off this one, Tatyana was upstairs. So where was Alyona? She couldn't be with him, could she? Oh God, oh God! She started crossing herself, making little signs of the cross on her chest with unpractised fingers. That was just an act he was putting on, for heaven's sake! How come Tatyana didn't realise? She stood in the darkness, shifting from one foot to the other. Well, it would have to wait for another time. Now it was goodbye.

Translated by John Dewey

Landscape of Loneliness: Three Voices
Svetlana Alexievich

When he said: "I love you," but didn't yet love me, didn't realise how deeply he'd fall in love, I said: "What does that mean? That word?" He hesitated and looked at me with such interest. I guess it was time and he decided he had to say it. Typical story. Classic. But for me love's a strange word... A short word... Too small to contain everything that was going on in me, everything that I felt. Then he left. We'd meet again, of course, the next day, but even before the door closed I began to die, I began to die a physical death, my whole body ached. Love's not a glorious feeling, not at all glorious, or not only glorious... You find yourself in a different dimension... life is shrouded, veiled, you can't see anyone, can't throw yourself into anything, you're in a cocoon, a cocoon of insane suffering which grinds up everything that happened yesterday, the day before yesterday, that may happen tomorrow, everything that happened to him before you, without you. You stop caring about the world; all you do is this work, this work of love. I dreamed about how happy I'd be when it ended. How happy I'd be! At the same time, I was afraid it would end. You can't live at that temperature. Delirious. In a dream. I'd suffered before him, ranted and raved, been jealous, I'd had a lot of men, I'm no prude, but what he gave me, no one had... He was the only one... We were soul mates, each other's whole world. No one gave me that experience of self-sacrifice, I suppose... He didn't even give me a child... Even... A

284

child? No, he didn't... And I'm a good mother... (Searches for words). Love throws you into the very depths of yourself, you dig and you dig, sometimes you like what you see, other times you're frightened. Love blinds you and makes a fool of you, but it also gives you greater knowledge. This woman said hello to him, and right away I knew she was his first love, they chatted about this and that, very social and what you'd expect. But I knew it... Knew she was the one... She didn't look at me, didn't even glance in my direction, there was no curious stare: who are you with, how are things? There wasn't anything except some sweet gestures. But I sensed something. They huddled together, together in the middle of a big crowd, a human torrent, as if there were a bridge between them. Like an animal I sensed something... Maybe because, before, when we happened to drive along that street, past those particular buildings, he always had this look on his face, this way of looking at those shabby, perfectly ordinary entrances... Something like that, that science can neither prove nor refute, that we can't understand, can't understand. (Again searches for words). I don't know... I don't know...

We were on the metro, we worked together, we taught at the same institute and went home the same way. We were colleagues. We didn't know yet, I didn't know, but it had already begun... It had already begun... We were on the metro... And suddenly he said gaily:

"Are you seeing anyone?"

"Yes."

"Like him?"

"Not really."

"How about you?"

"Yes."

"Like her?"

"No, not really."

And that was all. We went into a store together, he pulled an antediluvian string bag – by then they seemed funny – out of his pocket and bought some pasta, cheap sausage, sugar, and I don't know what else, a classic selection of Soviet products. Lump sugar… Cabbage pies in a greasy paper bag… (Laughs). I was married at the time, my husband was a big boss, we didn't live that way, I lived a completely different life. Once a week my husband brought home a special order (the orders were doled out at work) of hard-to-come-by delicacies: smoked sturgeon, salmon, caviar… We had a car… "Help yourself, the pies are still hot," he ate them on the run. (Laughs again). I was a long time coming to him, it was a difficult journey… A difficult journey… His sheepskin coat had been clumsily sewn up in the back, right side out, with the thread showing. "His wife must have died and now he's bringing up their child alone," I felt sorry for him. He was gloomy. Not good-looking. Always sucking heart pills. I felt sorry for him. "Oh, how Russia ruins you," a Russian woman I met on a train once confided. She lived in the West, had for a long time. "In Russia, women don't fall in love with beauty, it's not beauty they're looking for and not the body they love, it's the spirit. Suffering. That's ours." She sounded wistful…

We bumped into each other again on the metro. He was reading the paper. I didn't say anything.

"Do you have a secret?"

"Yes," the question so surprised me that I answered it seriously.

"Have you told anyone?"

I felt numb: My God, here we go… My God! That's how these things begin… It turned out he was married. Two children. And I was married…

"Tell me about yourself."

"No, you tell me about yourself. You seem to know everything about me already."

"No, I can't do that."

"Why?"

"Because first I'd have to fall out of love with you."

We were going somewhere in the car, I was driving and after that remark I swerved into the opposite lane. My mind was paralysed by the thought: he loves me. People kept flashing their lights, I was coming right at them, head-on. Who knows where love comes from? Who sends it?

I was the one who suggested it:

"Let's play?"

"Play what?"

"That I'm driving along, see you hitchhiking, and stop."

So we started playing. We played and played, played all the way to my apartment, played in the elevator. In the hall. He even made fun of me: "Not much of a library. Schoolteacher level." But I was playing myself, a pretty woman, the wife of a big boss. A lioness. A flirt. I was playing... And at some point he said:

"Stop!"

"What's wrong?"

"Now I know what you're like with other people."

He couldn't leave his wife for six months. She wouldn't let him go. She swore at him. Pleaded with him. For six months. But I'd decided I had to leave my husband even if I wound up alone. I sat in the kitchen and sobbed. In the process of leaving I'd discovered that I lived with a very good person. He behaved wonderfully throughout. Just wonderfully. I felt ashamed. For a long time he pretended not to notice anything, he acted as if nothing had happened, but at some point he couldn't stand it anymore and posed the question. I had to tell him. He was sorry he'd asked, he threw up... His eyes said: "Don't answer! Don't answer!" I could see in them his horror at what he was about to hear. He began fussing with the kettle: "Let's have some tea." We sat down and we had a good talk. But I answered all his questions, I confessed. He said: "Even so don't go." I told him again... "Don't go." That night I packed my things... (through tears and laughter). But there too... Now we were together... There too I sobbed every night in the kitchen for two weeks, until one morning I found a note: "If it's so hard, maybe you should go back." I dried my tears...

"I want to be a good wife. What would you like?"

"You know, no one has ever made me breakfast. I'd like you to call me to the breakfast table, that's all, I don't need anything else."

He got up every morning at six to prepare for his lectures. I felt downcast because I was a night person, I went to bed late and got up late. This was going to be hard, it was a hard clause. The next morning, I staggered into the kitchen, threw some curd cakes together, put them on the table, sat there for five minutes, and shuffled back to bed. I did that three times.

"Don't get up any more."

"You don't like my breakfasts?'

"I see what a huge effort they are, don't get up any more."

We had a child... I was forty-one, it was very difficult even physically, I realise now, though at the time I thought: Ah, it's nothing. But it wasn't nothing. Sleepless nights. Nappies. The baby got a staph infection. Which meant twice as many nappies and washing them a special way. I felt dizzy... There weren't any pampers yet... Just nappies and more nappies... I washed them, rinsed them, dried them... Then one day I went completely to pieces: the nappies by the stove had burned, the washing machine had overflowed and the bathroom was ankle-deep in water. I'd flooded it. The baby was screaming and I was mopping up the water with a cloth. It was winter. I sat down on the edge of the bath and burst into tears. I sat there and cried. Then he walked in... He looked at me in this cold way, like a stranger... I thought he'd come rushing in to help, I thought he'd feel sorry for me. I was going out of my mind. But he just said: "How quickly you 'cracked'." And turned around and walked out. It was like a slap in the face. I didn't even say anything back, I was so undone. Very hard... I was a long time coming to him, it was a difficult journey...

Later I understood... I understood him... He lived with his mother, who had spent ten years in the camps and never once cried and always sent jolly, humorous letters home. The letters still exist. In one she wrote: "Yesterday a very amusing thing happened. I had gone to see a flock of sheep during a blizzard. (A livestock specialist by profession, she was allowed out unescorted to treat sheep.) When I got back the guard dogs didn't recognise me – they could barely see me – so they attacked and we had a very funny tussle." She went on to describe how they'd rolled over the steppe gnawing each other. And ended: "But now I'm fine, I'm in the hospital, they have clean sheets here." They'd torn her flesh... Those guard dogs... He grew up among women like that... And here I was wailing because of a broken washing machine... His mother's friends had all come back from there. One woman had been so badly tortured she had a broken vertebra, but she always looked elegant and erect in her corset. Another woman... They'd taken her naked to be interrogated. Her interrogator had sensed her weak spot, he knew that by doing that he might break her. Her hair was gold, she was little, fragile. "They took you there naked?" "Yes, but that wasn't the funny part." She had been sentenced not for political crimes, but as a socially dangerous element (SDE). As a prostitute. In a dark alley, as that heavenly radiance was proceeding between two armed escorts, one of them, a backwoods boy, whispered: "You really an SDE?" "That's what they say." "Can't be." And he looked at her with rapture. It was a famous camp – the Aktiubinsk Camp for Wives of Traitors to the Motherland – a camp of beautiful women… They had lost everything in this life: husbands, relatives, their children had died of hunger in orphanages. That word – "cracked" – came from there. They arrested his mother and he was left with his grandmother. His grandmother "cracked". She beat him till he was black-and-blue, screamed at him. Her son had been arrested, her daughter and her daughter's husband. She had lost face. In his diary, he wrote: "Mama, a-a-a!"

His mother… She'd come to see us at the dacha, this was many years after the camps… She had her own room at the dacha. It was a big house. And I decided to clean it. I went in – there weren't any things lying about anywhere – and began to sweep. Under the couch I found a small bundle. Just then she appeared:

"My little knickknacks," that's what she always said: not my dresses or my shoes or my things, but my little knickknacks.

"Under the 'bed boards'?"

"I just can't get used to it."

And what do you think she did with her miserable little bundle? Did she unpack it? Hang it up somewhere? You'll never guess… She stuffed it under the mattress…

You could listen to her forever… I was such a long time coming to him…

Prison. Night. A suffocating cell. The door opens and in walks a woman wearing a fur coat and wafting French perfume.

I can't remember her name now, but she was a famous actress, she'd been arrested right after a concert. They all surrounded her and began stroking her fur coat. Smelling it. It smelled of freedom and their former female life. They were all beautiful women... Commissars always married beautiful women, with long legs and a good education, preferably from the formerly privileged classes, the ones who were left, who'd escaped notice. In Persian thread stockings. It was Nabokov who noted that the scratches life leaves on women heal, whereas men are like glass.

How much I remember, how much it turns out I remember... I was such a long time coming to him...

Nighttime... In the barracks... A young girl with long wavy hair... From an old noble family... She would sit for hours brushing her hair and remembering her mother. One morning they woke up and she was bald. She'd pulled out all her hair, no one had a knife, of course, or scissors, she'd used her hands. They thought she'd gone crazy. What have you done to yourself? They were trying to recruit her, she said, they'd promised to let her go free on condition she become an informer. The barracks wept, but she was smiling: "I was afraid I'd falter and they'd let me go, but now there's nothing they can do, I'm bald. That's it, I'm here to stay."

He grew up among women like that... And I was supposed to become like them... Like his mother... And I did...

***

"Who can explain fate? No one. People are mostly unhappy, but they want to be happy. It's a difficult question... I can't learn anything from other people; I can only dig around in myself. Life isn't very beautiful; it's we who make it that way in our minds. Maybe that's it, um-hum... I want to find a book about love that describes someone like me, a woman like me, not the usual heroes and princesses. I'm surrounded by ordinary life. Dislike is everywhere, all over the place: dislike for one's husband or wife, dislike for one's work, dislike for one's family. It's good I like to fantasise... My fantasies are everything to me... Tell me about a woman like me: an eight-hour workday, small apartment, small salary and vacation once a year. And I used to be very beautiful... Very beautiful when I was young...

What's my life like? I get up at six and make breakfast. Then I take the children to kindergarten. Drop them off and go to work. It takes me an hour (with two changes). By nine I'm at work. In my office. Forms, forms, forms... Money for goods, goods for money... I'm an economist at a large factory. After work I shop for food. First one store, then another... Loaded down I run for the bus. It's the end of the workday. Rush hour. People are angry, tense. I pick the kids up from kindergarten. Get home and figure dinner out. I'm an appliance, a machine, not a woman. After dinner my husband reads the paper, the kids watch TV, I wash the dishes, do the laundry, iron. Until midnight. Then I go to bed and set the alarm for six again... First I took the kids to kindergarten, then they walked to school, now they're in college. I had a first husband, now I have a second, but I still get up at six, still rush back and forth to work and from one chore to the next: cooking, vacuuming, shopping, washing, mending. Maybe that's it... The hardest thing to understand is our life. The hardest thing... The constant whirl... Round and round... Where's the joy? (Smiles for the first time). Here's an example... My younger son was five, wait, let me think, no, that's right, he was five. I was doing something in the kitchen, I heard him snuffling

292

behind me. I didn't turn round, I let him sneak up on me. He pulled a stool over, climbed up onto it and hugged me from behind, around the shoulders. He hugged me hard. And I felt such a masculine tenderness...

I'm surprised... I'm astonished... More than anything I'm astonished by how short life is. People say: "When I was young", but I was young only recently, I was still young yesterday. For some reason it took me a long time to get pregnant the second time. The first time it was a snap. But the second time, I just couldn't. For three years. One day I went into a church. I stood by the Virgin and it was as if she spoke to me:

"What do you want?"

"A son."

Maybe that's it... (Musing). No matter how far we are from the stars... No matter... They're there, watching us, looking after us, I went to bed again that night and thought, I can't remember what I thought. I'll be honest: I've always wanted to write letters to people, or rather to a certain person, I've always dreamed of meeting a person like that, even if we couldn't live together, I could write to him. Sometimes he would answer. Fantasies... Fantasies are everything... I'm sorry, I suppose, sorry that we're all lonely. (Pauses). Although no, I realise now... Women are never lonely, men are lonely. I feel sorry for them. Always. Even though they've let me down and haven't lived up to my hopes, I still feel sorry for them. I don't love them so much as I feel sorry for them. That's the main thing, the biggest confession I have to make. About my life. And actually, if I think about it, I've never known where my life is, unless it's with the children. Which is why I just cover my face with my hands and forge ahead...

My father was in the military. A veterinary doctor. We

moved all over the Urals with him. Our gypsy life drove my mother to tears, as soon as we'd gotten used to one place, we'd be sent to another. When Solzhenitsyn's *Gulag Archipelago* first came out here, everyone was talking about it. I bought a copy and gave it to my brother. A few days later he asked me:

"Have you read it?"

"Not yet."

"Read it. It's about everything you and I saw as children."

I began reading… The first things to enter my mind were not pictures, but sounds. And the barking of dogs… Some kind of weeping… not human weeping, but the weeping of a violin… My brother and I, we'd run out of the house, sit on a tree stump and listen. We lived on a mountain. Surrounded by the taiga. In a military settlement: a few houses for officers, a commissary in the centre, and soldiers' barracks. Down below was a prison compound. A camp. In the evening someone there played the violin. Papa said: "A music professor from Moscow." The first real music of my life. We didn't have a radio, or a gramophone and records, I'd never heard music like that before. As if someone were playing not down below, but up above… In the sky… And the barking of dogs… The camp was guarded by fierce Alsatians. And there were watchtowers…

We had a good view from up above, it was interesting.

"Look what a big bird house," my brother pointed out.

"Where?"

"Over there. A man's sitting in it with a rifle."

Mama found us and led us away…

Papa treated sick horses. The winters in the Urals were bitterly cold. Men streamed into the taiga. In endless columns… gray… black… They were going to work. The work was backbreaking. In the taiga they made trestles out of logs, then pushed timber-loaded trolleys on metal wheels along that wooden road to the main road. There the horses helped, they pulled the heavy loads to the station stop. Papa always said: "I'm sorry for the horses. Car engines will stall in the cold, but these are animals." Men in the columns collapsed. The Alsatians got them up, forced them to stand up... Black Alsatians, black men... Some of them would strip naked, their bodies exuding steam... That was how they protested when they no longer had the strength to work... Or else they wanted to die without anything on... without those black clothes... I don't know... And I still don't understand... One man put his hand down on a stump... And chopped it off... They picked up the hand, tied it to his back and made him walk the whole way to the hospital. Six miles from our settlement... Papa told us about it...

Once we saw an Alsatian tearing a man to pieces... A man who'd collapsed... "Wolf! Wolf!" I screamed. "People, help! Help!!"

Mama found us and led us away...

When Stalin died, everyone was afraid. A neighbour came and told Mama. Mama began to cry. But one officer... he was so happy he started dancing... He laughed and danced by the commissary... They locked him up in the guardhouse... (Pauses). I was a little girl... but I remember this clearly... Two men walked out of the compound carrying something. One was young, the other old. They stopped. My brother and I were playing nearby and I had two lumps of sugar in my pocket. I jumped up and ran to them! I gave them to the young man. He smiled. The old man began to cry.

Mama found us and led us away...

Maybe that's it, um-hum... From then on... from then on whenever I saw a lot of men, at a train station or a stadium, I always thought of that... Even now... I think of that... Decades later... (Happy or sad, you can't tell). I didn't pick a very good husband either. I didn't fall in love with him, I felt sorry for him... We met at some dances; he was five years older. I'd just started university, he'd already finished. He would walk me home and then stand around, he wouldn't go away. I'd look out the window and he'd be standing there in the dark, when I turned out the light he'd still be there. He froze his ears off that winter. I wasn't planning to marry anyone yet, certainly not him, but he said: "Without you I'll become a drunk. I'll fall apart." And, actually, as soon as we became friends he stopped drinking, stopped smoking. His sisters – there were four of them, he was the only boy in the family – couldn't get over it: "He loves you, he's become a different person. Completely changed." I thought so, too. That spring, on my birthday, he arrived with two buckets of flowers, he'd carried them around the city that way: a bucket of bird cherry in one hand, a bucket of lilacs in the other. "You're crazy!" I couldn't stop laughing. "Marry me. I'll fall apart without you." Mama tried to talk me out of it: "That's how he is now, but one day it'll start all over again. He'll go back to drinking. And you'll feel sorry for him." My mother knew me through and through. But we got married... Maybe that's it, um-hum... I was fond of him, cooked him delicious meals. The house was always neat. I baked the pies he liked. I thought: that's what love is. A clean house and hot pies. I wanted a daughter first... The doctors made me happy: "You're going to have a girl." I moved into my belly... (Laughs). My soul moved into my belly. Mama's advice: "When you've had your baby, ask them to bring it to you right away and make sure you kiss it. You may not want to, but you must." If you kiss it you'll love it. They brought me my daughter and I kissed her on the cheek. One child... Then another... A boy... My heart was full... I thought: and this is love... But he began to drink. A lot. Life was hard enough and now he wasn't bringing any money home. We lived in Perm, a big industrial city. When we were first sent there after university, it was considered well supplied with consumer goods, but gradually everything disappeared. Food, things. You'd walk into a store and there wouldn't even be any cans, no canned vegetables, no canned fish, nothing but three-quart jars of birch juice. As soon as any meat turned up, there was a huge line, if someone started to complain – that they'd been given a bad piece or that the meat was old and refrozen – they were kicked out of the line. Take it, or get out of here! Everyone was angry. I guess I'm strong... A good friend of mine couldn't take it: "Life is hopeless. My husband drinks." I remember the moment... I'm strong... He got down on his knees: "I'll fall apart without you." I didn't believe him... not any more. I decided to get divorced... He didn't fall apart, he found another woman who took him as he was. Here any man is in demand... Like after the war... Still... But two years after we'd divorced we were still living together in the same apartment, two small rooms – we couldn't swap them for anything. On days off he'd buy himself a carpetbag full of wine, cheap apple wine, and stretch out on the couch. Come evening I couldn't help saying: "Go eat something. You'll die of hunger." I felt sorry for him... That was my whole first marriage... My whole love... (Laughs).

I was left with two children: a daughter who had just started primary school and a son in kindergarten. Somehow I didn't complain, I was used to it. Whether or not I had a man in my life, the children were always my responsibility. Every year I took them to the sea, to Sochi. I never bought myself new clothes, I economised wherever I could, I wanted my children to grow up healthy. I scrimped all year to pay for our vacation.

If I took them to the sea, they didn't get sick, if I didn't, they'd be home with colds all winter. And that was that. I met my second husband in Sochi; we're still together. Whether it's love or not is hard to say... I know that the woman has to feel sorry for the man... Or maybe it's just the men I meet? (Laughs). The only strong men I see are in movies... On posters... In the ad for Marlboro cigarettes on TV... (Laughs).

We were lying on the beach. I felt wonderful: the sea, the sun. The children were in heaven. Bronzed, beautiful, my son looked like a little black boy, that's the kind of skin he has, it loves the sun. One day, a second day... A week... Some guy was following us around, if we went on an excursion, he'd go too, if we went into the dining room, he'd sit opposite us. Every morning we'd look for a new place to try to lose him, but he'd pick us out of the crowd. He always found us. Maybe that's it, um-hum... How can you escape fate? You can't... My son cut his foot on a sharp stone and we stayed home for a few days, didn't go to the beach. We read stories. One evening the landlady of the apartment where we were staying called to me: "Come quick! Come quick!" I went to the door and there he was.

"Good evening! I found you!!"

"What of it?"

"I was afraid you'd gone away. And I don't have your address.'

"What do you need my address for?"

"I'm going to write you letters..."

"..."

"What are you doing?"

"I'm reading the children a story."

"May I listen?"

"..."

No one ever courted me the way he did. Like in an American film. He took me to the most expensive restaurant. We danced a lot. It was raining. We were the only ones there. We danced by ourselves: "See, I reserved the whole restaurant for you." No one ever kissed my hands the way he did, every finger. Over and over again. He even kissed my footprints by the sea... In the sand... The first night we talked until morning... His young wife had died of cancer two years after they were married. His father, too, was in the military and had always been away working. His mother raised him. His mother had wanted a daughter and brought him up like one, he was her only child. He played with dolls until he was ten and he still likes to buy them as presents. But to look at him, he was so manly, so strong. And dashing. My soul began to sing, it never had before, though my soul is easily stirred. Just touch it! Touch it and it starts to ring and sing. But at the end of the vacation I came to my senses: "I have two children. No! No!" And that's how we left it... I went to Perm, he went to Chita. We were hundreds of miles apart. I thought I'd never see him again. It had been a wonderful dream... And now I'd woken up... And didn't remember the dream... I remembered something colourful, sunny, nothing real... Just a dream...

Six months went by... He called me every day... Courted me and courted me! Every day: "I love you." And I got used to it... I would just be thinking of him and the phone would ring. He also wrote to me. Every day. I have a suitcase full of his letters. Then he came to visit... I went to meet him... I forgot my gloves in the taxi. It was chilly out. October. He got off the train... Smiling for all he was worth... He took my hands and started warming them... Kissing them... That night he confessed: "I saw your hands and I was stunned. Everything inside me stopped." We passed a flower shop and

299

he bought me a bouquet of lilies. By the time we got home it was lunchtime. We sat down to eat. We laughed. Talked about last summer. Suddenly he stood up: "I feel so good here. So comfortable." And walked away.... As if someone were calling him... Then something absolutely incredible happened... He began to fall... Arms flailing in all directions... For a second I thought: what a joker, now he'll try to pull something! But he was already on the floor. "What happened? What's wrong with you?" "With me?" He only half heard me. Then he lost consciousness altogether... Now I was frightened: I didn't have a phone then. By the time I got down from the ninth floor, by the time I found a pay phone... A man I barely know comes to see me, and dies.... Dies in my arms... I didn't know where to run? What to do? I shook him by the shoulders and screamed:

"Wake up! Wake up!"

"What's the matter?" he opened his eyes.

"Were you joking?"

"I don't remember anything. I only remember coming here..." He got up and sat down on the couch.

"What's wrong with you?"

"That's it. I'm home."

He had lived alone for seven years. He was tired of loneliness. Of longing. Again we talked all night. Until dawn.

"What was that all about?" I asked him in the morning.

"I realised that I'd finally found you. And my heart stopped."

At first I was very afraid of hurting him, he's so... hmm... tender... so vulnerable... The first year he was always giving me flowers, even if it was just one. He confided in me: "I don't think I loved my wife this much. She was the first woman in my life. But this is real love." Every day some new thoughts... New

300

words… "Now I understand why some people kill themselves because of love. Hang themselves, shoot themselves or find some other way. I didn't understand before." Maybe that's it, um-hum… You can't remember everything… Just the bits that flash through your mind… As if you were flying along on an express train and couldn't distinguish anything out the window, except sometimes, like a child: "Mama, there's a car… there's a cow… there's a house…" He loves me, I believe him… We've lived together seven years. Do I love him? I'll have to think… Sometimes I do think… I don't know… I don't want to admit to myself that I'm used to him, that I feel sorry for him, but don't love him. I'm spinning the wheel of life… There should be a man in the house… That's life's law, nature's law… I'm spinning that wheel… I get up every morning at six – and stand over the stove. I go to work – everything's under control. I come home – and work one more shift. He loves me, I believe him… (Laughs). He still courts me… He is so touching sometimes… But he's never hammered a single nail, he doesn't know how, if the iron burns out, I'm the one who fixes it. (Laughs). Yesterday I repaired the telephone. My sister has a PhD, she's a feminist: "You have a slave's psychology." Yes, at home I'm a slave. Whatever my husband wants, I do it; whatever my son wants, I do it. My daughter… But at work I can stand up for myself; at work, men are afraid of me. I'll break their back. What can I do? I've grown a shell. Claws. I have a family to take care of. A home. But at home I'm a slave. That's right! I admit it. I'm an actress. Without that my house would collapse of its own weight. Maybe that's it, um-hum… I have to manage to act like a man in the outside world and like a woman at home. (Laughs). What can I do? My husband isn't a fighter. I've made my peace with that; it's not in his nature to fight. For him, life is a book. Dreams.

He loves to philosophise. He was better off before, when everything was equal and everyone the same. People didn't stick their necks out. They read a lot of books and sat around each other's kitchen tables discussing world problems. They collected stamps. But now everything's different; every day is a battle. You need to survive. To go on behaving the way we did before would, I think, be odd, absurd and dishonest. We're proud but poor. Our vacuum cleaner is twenty years old, barely turns over, the refrigerator is thirty years old. But I value my husband: he's an honest man, a good man, not an operator, not a dodger. I have a habit of taking the weak person under my wing. Sometimes when he's sad I ask him: "What are you thinking about?" "About death. Some day we'll be gone." It's typical of a man to think about death. I think about how to economise so we can buy a new car, remodel our little dacha. Where can I earn some extra money? How can I save it? My neighbour's husband, like mine, is a teacher. Both men teach history and are paid practically nothing. Well, at night he paints apartments and hangs wallpaper, before that he sold things at an open-air market. But my husband? Never… He couldn't bear to do that. He'd be ashamed. Besides he doesn't know how. He's taken a back seat. I'm the one who keeps our house together. I've made my peace with that because I feel sorry for him… And he can be so touching… So tender…

Maybe that's love? Also love… (Pauses). I've gone over everything I've said in my mind… But to be completely… and totally honest… I'm still waiting for something…. What am I waiting for?

**

He's walking along and… Sometimes, when I turn round, he's floating above the grass, his feet not touching the ground.

That's the only way I see him in my dreams... I, of course... Talking about it has the same effect on me... (Falls silent. Then fast and full of joy). It's all sounds, sounds... But the music is inside me, I put that record on and it all comes back again. All I have to do is close my eyes... I used to be afraid of death, until I realised that nothing disappears, nothing turns to dust, everything remains. Everything that ever happened to us. You can't begin anything again. From the beginning. Sometimes I think: you don't write symphonies, don't paint pictures, but that doesn't mean they don't exist, there's so much we can't even guess at, and that leaves us hope. My God, how lucky I am to have this. I revel in my thoughts, revel in my memories, revel in myself now that I've understood. It's an androgynous existence, how could I want another man? I can't get any higher. I get as far as myself, try to catch those bits and pieces... I'm in despair sometimes, but never for long. I go on and on. The way is there and I'm in no rush...

My first husband... That was a wonderful episode. He courted me for two years, then we married and lived together for another two years. I badly wanted to marry him because I needed all of him, I didn't want him to go anywhere. I remember it as a sickness... I don't even know why I so needed all of him. Why I couldn't bear to be separated from him, why I had to see him all the time and pick fights, and fuck, fuck, fuck, endlessly. He was the first man in my life. The first time was really so... um... just interesting: I didn't know what was going on. The next time, too... and, basically... a sort of technique... And it went on like that for six months... For him, though, really, it didn't have to be me, it could just as well have been someone else. But for some reason we got married... I was twenty-two. We were students at the same music college; we did everything together. I can't remember now how it happened, the moment escapes me, but I fell in love with the male body when it belonged to me... At that point I didn't even know... I sensed it as more significant than just one man, to me it was something cosmic... You break loose from the earth and spin away somewhere... Try to spin away... (Smiles suddenly). It was a wonderful episode. It could have gone on forever or been over in half an hour. So then... I left him. Left him of my own accord. He begged me to stay. For some reason I'd decided to leave. I was so tired of him... God, was I tired of him... I was already pregnant, already showing... What did I need him for? We'd fuck, then fight, then I'd cry, then we'd fuck again. If we'd had a child... I probably should have waited but I didn't know how to then. How to wait. To have patience. I walked out, closed the door behind me and suddenly felt so glad to be gone. Gone for good. I went to my mother's, she lived here, in Moscow. He came after me that night and was completely bewildered: I was pregnant, but always dissatisfied somehow, as if something were missing. But what? I turned the page... I was very happy to have had him, and very happy not to have him any more. My life has always been a treasure trove. Of beginnings and endings, beginnings and endings... I turned the page... (Again smiles).

Oh, giving birth to Anka was so beautiful, I liked it so much. First, my water broke: I'd been walking in the woods, for miles, and at some point, at mile X, my water broke. I didn't know what to do – did that mean I should go to the hospital right away? I waited till evening. It was bitterly cold. But I decided to go anyway. The doctor looked at me: "You'll be in labour for two days." I called my mother: "Bring me some chocolate. I'll be here for a while." Before morning rounds, the nurse said: "Listen, the head is already sticking out. Come with me." I could barely walk.... It was as if someone had stuck a ball up there... "Quick! Quick!" the nurse screamed. "Call the doctor." My stomach was so huge, it blocked everything, but then I saw the baby, it was coming out, that's when I began to shriek... Something started gurgling, quacking... The doctor said: "Here it comes. It's almost out," and showed it to me: "It's a girl." They weighed her: nearly nine pounds. "Listen, not one rip or tear. She took pity on you." Oh, when they brought her to me the next day... Her eyes, the irises were like saucers, dark, floating, that was all I saw...

So then... It was a whole new life. I liked the way I'd begun to look. It's just that... I was suddenly so much prettier... Anka fell right into place, I loved her very much, but somehow she wasn't absolutely connected with men in my mind. Someone had made her... Conceived her... But no! She'd come from the sky... She was always independent. When she began to talk, people would ask:

"Anechka, don't you have a papa?"

"No, I have a granny instead."

"Don't you have a dog?'

"No, I have a hamster instead."

We were like that, she and I... All my life I was afraid of not being me. Even at the dentist's, I'd ask them not to give me any painkiller. My feelings were my feelings, good or bad: Don't disconnect me from myself. We liked each other, Anka and I. And then we met him... Gleb...

If he hadn't been who he was, I would never have married again. I had everything: a child, work, freedom. Then he appeared... absurd, nearly blind, short of breath... To let a person with such a heavy burden – twelve years in Stalin's camps, he was just a boy, sixteen, when they took him – into our world... With the burden of that knowledge... of the difference... Our life together wasn't what I'd call freedom.

305

What was it? Why? Am I saying that I only felt sorry for him? No. It was also love. That's exactly what it was. (More to herself than to me). He's been dead seven years... And I'm even sorry that he never knew me the way I am now. Now I understand him more, I'm finally old enough for him, but he isn't here. So then... Even what I'm telling you... I'm again afraid... I'm afraid that I won't be me... It's terrifying sometimes... Like in the sea... In the sea I used to love to swim way far out until one time I became frightened – I'm alone, the water's deep, and I don't know what's down there...

(We drink some tea, talk about other things. Then, just as suddenly as they stopped, the memories start again).

Oh, those seaside romances... Short and sweet. A small model of life. You can begin them beautifully, and end them beautifully, the way you'd like to in real life but never manage to. That's why people like to go away. So then... I had two braids and a blue polka-dot dress I'd bought at Children's World the day before I left. The sea... I swam way far out, more than anything on earth I love to swim. Every morning I did exercises under a white acacia... A man came walking along, just a man, very ordinary looking, not young. He saw me and for some reason was glad. He stood there and stared.

"Would you like me to read you some poetry tonight?"

"Maybe, but now I'm going to swim way far out."

"I'll be waiting for you."

He was a bad reader of poetry; he kept adjusting his glasses. But he was touching... I understood... I understood what he was feeling... The gestures, the glasses, it was all nervousness. But I have absolutely no memory of what he read, or why it must have meant so much. Feelings are separate beings... Suffering, love, tenderness... They live unto themselves, we feel them, but don't see them. You suddenly become a part of someone else's life, without even realising it. Everything happens both with you and without you... At the same time... "I've been waiting for you," he said when he saw me next morning. He said it in such a way that I believed him, even though I wasn't at all ready. Just the opposite. But something was changing around me, I didn't know what or how. I felt calm because of what was about to happen to me, it wasn't yet love, but I just sensed... I had this feeling... That I'd suddenly been given a whole lot of something. One person had heard another. Had gotten through. I swam way far out... I swam back. He was waiting for me. Again he said: "We'll be fine together." And for some reason I again believed him... So then... He met me by the sea every day... Once we were drinking champagne: "It's pink champagne, but at the regular champagne price." I liked that phrase. (Laughs). Another time he was frying an egg: "It's a curious business about me and these eggs. I buy them by the dozen, fry them in pairs, and I always have one left over." Sweet things like that...

People would look at us and ask: "Is he your grandfather? Is he your father?" I was wearing a very short skirt... I was twenty-eight... It was only later he became handsome. With me. Why me? I was always in despair. I must serve him. There's no other way. Or better not get involved. A Russian woman is ready to suffer: what else can she do? We're used to our men, ungainly, unfortunate, my grandmother married a man like that, and so did my mother. We don't expect anything else, and that gets passed down. We're all ferocious dreamers...

"I was thinking of you?"

"What were you thinking?"

"That I'd like us to go for a walk somewhere. Way far away. Holding hands. I don't need anything except to feel you next to me. I feel such tenderness for you – I just want to look

307

at you and walk beside you."

We spent many happy hours together; we acted like complete children. Good people are always children. Helpless. You have to protect them.

"Maybe we could go away together to some island and lie on the sand."

That's my... How should it be? I don't know. With one person, it's one way. With another person, another way. But how should it be? Who can gauge? Where are the scales... That... All of Russian culture, everything we see and hear around us, is built on the fact that our best school is the school of misfortune, we grew up with it. So then... But we want good fortune... I would wake up in the night and think: What am I doing? So then... I couldn't stop worrying, and because of this tension I.... "The back of your head is always tense," he noticed. But how could I get it out of my mind.... What am I doing? Where am I falling? There's an abyss...

He scared me from the start... The breadbox... As soon as he saw it... He would begin methodically eating up all the bread. Any amount. Bread must not be left. It was your share. He would eat and eat; however much there was, he would always finish it. It took me a while to understand why...

They tortured him with a burning light... He was only a boy, for heaven's sake... Sixteen years old... They didn't let him sleep for days on end. Decades later he still couldn't bear bright light, even the bright summer sun. What I loved was the bright morning air, when the clouds were even higher, floating way high above you. But he could end up with a temperature... From the light...

In school they beat him and wrote on his back in chalk: "Son of an enemy of the people". The school director made them do it... Our fears as children... They stick out in us...

Come to the surface... They stay with you for good. Forever. I heard those fears in him...

Where am I going? Russian women love to adopt unhappy souls. My grandmother loved one and her parents married her off to another. I can't tell you how much she disliked him, how much she didn't want to marry him. My God! She had decided that at the wedding, when the priest turned to her and asked if she were going to marry him of her own free will, she would say no. But the priest was drunk and, instead of asking the question as he was supposed to, he said: "You be good to him, he froze his feet off in the war." So then she had to marry him. That's how Granny wound up with our grandfather – whom she never loved – for life. What a perfect refrain for our entire life: "You be good to him, he froze his feet off in the war"... My mother's husband was in the next war, he returned destroyed, spent. To live with a person like that, with what he brought back with him, was a lot of work, and it fell on a woman's shoulders. No one! No one has written anything, I've never read anything about how hard it was to live with the victors. With the men who returned from the war. Gleb put it exactly in one of his journals: in camp he realised that every other person in Russia had been in prison – for an arrested father, for an ear of wheat picked up on a collective farm field, for being late to work (ten minutes), for not informing, for an anecdote... Our men are martyrs, they've all suffered some trauma – either in the war or in camp. For many, the war ended with camp, whole echelons walked straight from the front to Siberia. Right after Victory Day. Echelons of victors. That's the way it is with us: we're always fighting someone. And the woman is always ministering... She thinks of the man as part hero and part child. She is his rescuer. To this day... The Soviet empire fell... Now we have victims of the collapse... Look at how many people have wound up on the sidelines, have been thrown off history's hurtling steam engine – the army has been cut, factories have been shut down... Engineers and doctors are selling stockings at open-air markets... Bananas... I love Dostoevsky, but he is all about prison compounds. The subject of the war is eternal in Russia, we simply cannot let it go... So then... (Stops). Let's take a short rest... I'll put the kettle back on... And then we can continue... I have to go the whole way from beginning to end. With my little cup of experience...

(Half an hour later our conversation resumes).

A year went by or maybe a little more... He was supposed to come and meet my family. I warned him that while my mother was easy to get along with, my daughter wasn't exactly... she was sort of... I couldn't guarantee how she'd behave with him. Oh, my Anka. (Laughs out loud). She put everything to her ear: toys, stones, spoons... Most children put things in their mouth, she put them to her ear – to hear the sound they made. I began teaching her music fairly early, but what a strange child, as soon as I put a record on, she would turn round and walk out. She didn't like anyone else's music, music by some silly composer: she was only interested in what sounded inside her. So then, Gleb arrived, very embarrassed, he'd had his hair cut too short, he didn't look particularly well. And he had some records with him. He started telling us something, about how he'd been walking along and happened to buy these records. Now Anka has a good ear... she doesn't hear words, she hears the intonations... She immediately took the records: "What brutiful records". That's how their love, too, began. Sometime later she disconcerted me: "How can I keep from calling him Papa?" He didn't try to please her, he was just interested. They loved each other. I was even jealous sometimes, it seemed to me they loved each other more than they loved me. Both of them. Both Gleb and Anka. I don't think that's the way it was really. I wasn't hurt, I had a different role... He would ask her: "Anka, do you stutter." "Not as well as I used to." It was never dull with the two of them. So: "How can I keep from calling him Papa." We were sitting in the park, Gleb had gone off to get cigarettes. When he came back: "What are you two girls talking about?" I winked at Anka – don't tell him, it was silly anyway. She said: "Then you tell." Well what could I do? I told him she was afraid she might call him Papa by mistake. He: "It's not a simple matter, of course, but if you really want to, call me Papa." "Only you watch out," my little miracle said in earnest, "I have one other papa, but I don't like him, and Mama doesn't love him." That's how it's always been with Anka and me. We burn bridges. On the way home Gleb was already Papa. Anka ran ahead and called: "Papa! Papa!" The next day in kindergarten she announced: "Papa's teaching me to read." "Who's your Papa?" "His name is Gleb." The day after that her best friend had this news from home: "Anka, you're lying, you don't have a papa. He's not your real papa." "No, the other one wasn't my real papa, this one is my real papa." There's no use arguing with Anka. Gleb became "Papa", but what about me? I still wasn't his wife...

I had my vacation. I went away again. Gleb ran down the platform, waving goodbye. But I began an affair almost immediately, on the train. There were two young engineers from Kharkov, also on their way to Sochi. My God! I was so young. The sea. The sun. We swam, we kissed, we danced. It was simple and easy for me, because the world was simple, cha-cha-cha and spin your partner, I was in my element. They loved me, worshipped me, carried me up a mountain on their arms... Young muscles, young laughter. An all-night bonfire... Then I had a dream. It went like this: the ceiling opened... And I saw the sky... Gleb... He and I were walking somewhere, along the shore, not over sea-polished pebbles, but over horribly sharp stones, thin and sharp as nails. I had shoes on, but he was barefoot. "Barefoot," he explained, "you hear more." "You don't hear more, it hurts more. Let's switch." "What do you mean? Then I won't be able to fly away." Then he rose up into the air, folded his arms like a dead person, and was carried away. Even now, if I see him in a dream, he's always flying. Only his arms for some reason are folded, like a dead person's, they don't look at all like wings...

God, I must be crazy, I shouldn't be telling you all this... I mostly have the sense that I've been happy in this life. Even after Gleb died. I went to the cemetery, and I remember thinking... He's somewhere here... Suddenly I felt so happy I wanted to scream. God... (To herself. Unintelligibly). I must be crazy... With death you're left one on one. But he died many times over, he'd been rehearsing death since he was sixteen... "Tomorrow I'll be dust and you won't find me." We're getting to the most important part... So then... In love I slowly began to live, very slowly... In slow sips...

My vacation ended and I went home. One of the engineers saw me all the way back to Moscow. I promised to tell Gleb everything... I went to see him... A magazine was lying on the table, he'd drawn all over it, the wallpaper in his study was covered with scribbles, even the newspapers he read... Everywhere there were just three letters: s... i... o... Big, little, printed, script. Followed by three dots... I asked him: "What does that mean?" He translated: Seems it's over? Question marks, too, were everywhere... Like the clefs... In sheet music... Well, we decided to separate. Now we'd have to explain somehow to Anka. We went to get her in the car, but before she could leave the house she always had to draw something! This time, though, she didn't have time. She sat in the car and sobbed. Gleb was used to her craziness; he considered it a talent. It was a real family scene: Anka crying, Gleb trying to explain something, and me in the middle... The way he kept looking at me... (Falls silent). I realised what a wildly lonely person he was. (Falls silent). Anka went on sobbing... A real family scene... Thank God, I didn't let him go... Thank God! We had to get married, but he was afraid. He'd already had two wives. Women betrayed him, were exhausted by him and you couldn't blame them... I didn't let him go... And I... He gave me a whole life...

He didn't like people to ask him questions... He hardly ever opened up, and if he did, then it was with a sort of bravado, so as to make the story funny and hide the starkness. That was his way. For instance, he never said "free", it was always "free-ish". "And now I'm free-ish." The mood didn't often take him... But when it did, he told such delicious stories... I could just feel the pleasure he'd come away with: how he'd gotten hold of some pieces of a rubber tyre and tied them to his felt boots, he and other inmates were being herded from one prison to another and he was so happy he had those tyres. Once they came by half a sack of potatoes and then, while they were working outside the compound, someone gave them a big piece of meat. That night in the boiler room, they made soup: "It was so good, you have no idea! So delicious!" When Gleb was freed, he received compensation for his father. They said: "We owe you for the house, the furniture..." His father was a famous man... They gave him a large sum... He bought himself a new suit, new shirt, new shoes. He bought a camera, went to the restaurant in the National Hotel and ordered the best things on the menu: expensive fish, caviar, cognac, and coffee with cake. At the end, when he'd eaten his fill, he asked someone to take a picture of him at this, the happiest moment of his life. "I went back to the apartment where I was living and it dawned on me that I didn't feel happy. In that suit, with that camera... Why didn't I feel happy? Then I remembered the tyres, the soup in the boiler room – that was happiness." We tried to understand... So then... Where does that happiness live? He wouldn't have given camp up for anything, wouldn't have traded it. From the age of sixteen until almost thirty, that was the only life he knew. When he tried to imagine his life without those years in camp, he became terrified. What would have happened then? Instead of camp? What wouldn't he have grasped? What wouldn't he have seen? Probably the very core that made him who he was. When I asked: "Who would you have been without camp?" he always said: "I would have been a fool driving around in a red racing car, the fanciest there was." Former inmates are rarely friends, something inhibits them. What? They can see the camps in each other's eyes, they're inhibited by the humiliations they suffered. Especially the men. Former inmates rarely came to see us, Gleb didn't seek them out...

They threw him in with common criminals... Just a boy... What happened to him there no one will ever know. A woman can talk about humiliations, a man can't. A woman finds it easier to talk about it because somewhere deep inside she's prepared for violence... That knowledge is in her... Even the sexual act... She begins life over again every month... Those cycles... Nature helps her...

Two third-degree dystrophies... He lay there on the bed boards covered with boils, drenched in pus... He should have died, but for some reason he didn't. When the guy lying next to him did die, Gleb turned the body over so that it faced the wall. And slept with it like that for three days. "That one

314

alive?" "Alive." That made two rations of bread. All sense of reality disappeared... All sense of his material being... And death no longer seemed strange. It didn't frighten him. It was winter. Out the window he could see corpses, neatly stacked... Mostly male...

He returned home on an upper bunk. The train took a week. He didn't come down during the day, he went to the toilet at night. He was afraid. Other passengers would offer him food and tell him their troubles. They would get him talking and then they'd find out that he'd been in camp.

He was a wildly lonely person... Wildly... Lonely...

Now he announced to anyone who would listen: "I have a family." He was constantly surprised by normal family life, he was somehow very proud of it. Only fear... fear gnawed and ate at him. He would wake up at night in a cold sweat: if he didn't finish his book, he wouldn't be able to feed us, and I would leave him... First fear, then shame because of that fear. "Gleb, if you want me to become a ballet dancer, I will. I could do anything for you." In camp he'd survived, but in ordinary life... the traffic cop who stopped him could give him a heart attack. "How did you manage to stay alive?" "I was very much loved as a child." The amount of love we receive saves us, it's what allows us to endure. I was a nurse... I was a nanny... An actress... So as to keep him from seeing himself the way he was, to keep him from seeing his own fear, otherwise he couldn't have loved himself. To keep him from finding out that I knew... Love is an essential ingredient, without it a person can't live, his blood coagulates, his heart stops. Oh, what resources I found in myself... Life is like running the hundred-yard dash... (Falls silent. Rocks ever so slightly in rhythm to her thoughts). Do you know what he asked me before he died? His only request: "Write on my gravestone that I was a happy

315

man. I managed to do so much: I survived, I loved, I wrote a book, I have a daughter. My God, what a happy man I am." If someone were to hear that or to read it... To look at him you would never have believed it... But Gleb was a happy man! He gave me so much... I changed... How tiny our life is... Eighty, a hundred, two hundred years would be too little for me. I see the look on my old mother's face in the garden, she doesn't want to part with all this. The way she looks at that garden! And in the evening... In the evening, how she peers into the darkness... Into nowhere... It's too bad, it's so too bad that he never knew me the way I am now... I understand him now... It's only now that I've come to understand him... So then... He was a little afraid of me, just a bit. He was afraid of my feminine essence, of a... Of a sort of vortex... He often said: "Remember that when I'm not feeling well, I want to be alone." But... I couldn't do that... I had to follow him around... (Finishes her thought in silence). You can't purify life before death, can't make it as pure as death, when a person becomes handsome and free, the way he really is. I suppose it's senseless to try and force one's way through to this essence in one's lifetime. To try and get closer to it.

When I learned he had cancer, I couldn't stop crying the whole night, and in the morning I rushed to the hospital. He was sitting on the windowsill, yellow and very happy. He was always happy when something in his life was about to change. First there was camp, then exile, then freedom, and now there would be something else... Death was just another change of scene...

"Are you afraid I'll die?"

"Yes."

"Well, first of all, I didn't promise you anything. And, second, it won't happen anytime soon."

"Really?"

As always, I believed him. I dried my tears and told myself that again I had to help him. I didn't cry any more... I came to his room every morning, and our life began. Before we had lived at home, now we lived at the hospital. We spent six months at the cancer centre...

I can't remember... We talked so much, more than ever before, for whole days on end, but I remember only crumbs... Bits and pieces...

He knew who had informed on him. A boy who was in an after-school group with him at the House of Pioneers. He wrote a letter. Either he wrote it himself, or they made him do it: Gleb had criticised comrade Stalin and defended his father, an enemy of the people. His interrogator showed him the letter... All his life Gleb was afraid... He was afraid that the informer would find out that he knew. He wanted to mention him in his book but then he heard that his wife had given birth to a retarded child, and he was afraid to – what if that was God's punishment. Former inmates have their own criteria... Their own attitudes... Gleb often ran into him on the street, he happened to live near us. They would say hello. Talk about politics, about the weather. After Gleb died, I told a mutual friend about his having informed on Gleb... She didn't believe me: "N.? That can't be, he always speaks so well of Gleb, about what old friends they were. He cried at the cemetery." I realised I shouldn't have... Shouldn't have... There's a line over which it's dangerous for a person to step. Forbidden. Everything that's been written about the camps has been written by victims. Their tormentors are silent. We don't know how to distinguish them from other people. So then... But Gleb didn't want to... He knew that for a person that knowledge was dangerous... For a person... For his soul...

He'd been used to dying since he was a boy... He wasn't afraid of a little thing like that... In camp, the criminals who headed up work brigades often sold other prisoners' bread rations, or lost them at cards; the ones left without any bread ate tar. Black tar. And died: the walls of their stomachs became stuck together. But Gleb just stopped eating, he only drank. One boy ran away... on purpose, so they'd shoot him... Over the snow, in the sun... They took aim... And shot... Merrily... As if they were out hunting... As if he were a duck... They shot him in the head, dragged him back to the compound with a rope and dumped him in front of the guard shack... Gleb hadn't had any fear in camp... But here he needed me...

"What's camp like?"

"It's a completely different life. And hard work."

I can hear... I can almost hear him saying that...

"Local elections in a nearby settlement. We were giving a concert at the polling station. I was the master of ceremonies. I stepped out on stage and said: Please give a warm welcome to our choir. Political prisoners, turncoats, prostitutes, and pickpockets all stood and sang a song about Stalin: 'And our song sails o'er the vast expanses to the peaks of the Kremlin'."

A nurse came in to give Gleb a shot: "Your behind is all red. There's no more room." "Of course my behind is red, don't I live in the Soviet Union?" We laughed a lot together, even at the end. Really a lot.

"Soviet Army Day. I'm on stage reading Mayakovsky's 'Poem about a Soviet Passport'. 'Read this. Envy me. I am a citizen of the Soviet Union.' Instead of a passport I have piece of black cardboard. I hold it up... And the whole camp garrison envies me... 'I am a citizen of the Soviet Union.' The prostitutes, former Soviet prisoners of war, pickpockets and Socialist Revolutionaries all envy me..."

No one will ever know how it really was or what people like that come away with. He was a wildly lonely person... I loved him...

I looked round as I was going out the door and he waved. When I came back a few hours later, he was delirious. He kept saying: "Wait a minute... wait a minute..." Then he stopped and just lay there unconscious. For three days. I got used to it. To his lying there and me living there. They put in an extra bed for me next to his. So then... The third day... By then they were having trouble giving him his intravenous shots... Blood clots... I had to tell the doctors to stop everything, he wouldn't feel any pain, wouldn't hear. And we were left completely alone... No monitors, no doctors, no more checks... I got into bed with him. It was cold. I burrowed under the blanket and fell asleep. When I woke up I didn't open my eyes: it seemed to me we were in our bed at home and the balcony door had blown open... Gleb wasn't awake yet... I still had my eyes closed.... Then I opened them and it all came back to me... I started tossing... I got up and put my hands over his face: "A-a-ah..." He heard me. The death throes had begun... and I... sat there holding his hand so that I heard the last beat of his heart. I sat there for a long time afterwards... Then I called the nurse, and she helped me put his shirt on, it was blue, his favourite colour. "May I sit here a while longer?" "Yes, of course, you aren't scared?" I didn't want to give him to anyone. He was my child... What was there to be frightened of? By morning he was handsome... The fear had gone out of his face, and the tension. That was who he was! That was who he really was! I'd never known him that way. He wasn't that way with me. (Cries. For the first time during our conversation).

I always shone with his reflected light... Though I was capable of things myself, I could create... It was always, of course, work. Always work. Even in bed... For him to be able to... first him and then me. "You're strong, you're kind, you're the best. You're wonderful." I've never known a strong man, a man who didn't make me feel like a nursemaid. A mother. An angel of mercy. I've always been lonely... I won't hide it... I admit it... I've had relationships since Gleb... Right now I have a friend, but he's also all in knots... Unhappy... Insecure... That's our life... Strange, incomprehensible... We grew up in one country with the ideas of Marx and Lenin, and now we live in a completely different country – after Gorbachev. On top of more ruins. On top of more rubble. The old values are gone, the new values still unclear. Even Gleb was braver, after Magadan... After camp... He had self-respect: Well, I survived! I endured it! I know all about it! He was proud. But this man has nothing but fear. He's fifty years old and he has to start a new life. Everything from scratch. And my role is still the same... I minister... minister... Always the same role...

Yet I was happy with Gleb. Yes, it was hard work, but I'm happy, I'm proud that I was able to do that work. Most of the time I have that sense, that happiness. All I have to do is close my eyes...

Translated by Joanne Turnbull

The Jewess's Farewell
Margaret Khemlin

World War III

In 1969, the entire USSR was preparing to mark the centenary of the birth of Vladimir Ilyich Lenin. Actually, there was a year to go before the anniversary, but there was a lot to fit in.

Basya Solomonovna Meyerovskaya had her own concerns about the impending anniversary. She was convinced that in 1970, on the morning of Lenin's birthday, 22 April, World War III would begin.

Seated at her small Singer sewing machine and fixing another dress for her plump little granddaughters, who could not get into any of the standard Soviet children's sizes, Basya Solomonovna sang to herself, "Meine saffering is known only to Gott."

She went out to the courtyard for a chat with her neighbours. They always listened closely because she was considered very clever.

"Well, of course, they are sure to time it for the centenary," Basya Solomonovna confided her suspicion. "Because they need it to be a surprise. Everybody will be having such a special holiday, the birthday of the Leader. In Moscow everyone will be celebrating, and that's when they will strike."

They meant the Americans. Obviously.

The neighbours wanted to know more: "Drop a bomb will they, or what?"

"Different things. Here a bomb, there not a bomb. Oh, weh

is mir…"

"Well, we've had our lives, but our grandchildren… Lordy, Lordy…"

After a few minutes for lamentation the conversation took a different turn. "How much sugar do you add to plums?"

Basya Solomonovna gave a detailed answer, then explained how to make a compress, how much vodka to use, and to be sure the paper was greaseproof if it was not to leak.

The neighbours agreed about the paper, but were less sure about the vodka. If they bought a bottle for a compress, you could be sure their husband or son would only drink it. Could she think of a way that didn't involve vodka?

Basya Solomonovna replied that you could perfectly well make a compress without vodka, and perhaps it would even be better to boil potatoes in their jackets and then, still in their jackets, mash them. The neighbours nodded: Basya Solomonovna had a good head on her shoulders.

After telling these things, Basya went back inside and again sat down at the sewing machine. Her daughter Vera came home. She was a physiotherapist. Her son-in-law Misha came home from work. He was a building site foreman, but teetotal because he was a Jew.

Laying the table, Basya Solomonovna started in on her topic: "Misha, what are people saying about the centenary?"

"Everything is fine, Basya Solomonovna. We are making preparations. One hundred and two per cent. We'll finish building the Central Cinema. In the provinces we'll finish off clubs. We've got time. I had this idea we should line the cinema ceiling with the cardboard bases of egg boxes, and paint them, of course. Blue, for instance. I passed the suggestion to my superiors and they've taken up the idea."

Basya was pleased. "You had the idea yourself? Good for

you, Misha. And will they give you a bonus?"

"I don't know."

Basya Solomonovna held the ladle above the soup tureen for a moment, carefully placed a brimming plate of borscht in front of her son-in-law and urged him, "Eat, Misha. Your work puts much strain on your nerves."

After that she poured soup for her daughter, then for her pudgy grandchildren. After that she poured half a plate for herself.

While they were drinking tea her granddaughters, concluding there were no cakes or desserts to follow, slipped away from the table and Basya returned to her primary concern. "Misha, the situation is serious. There's going to be war."

Misha, noisily stirring the sugar in his cup, gave Vera a meaningful look and she adroitly changed the subject. "Mother, Misha is tired. He'll go now and take a rest, read the newspaper. You can talk about it later..."

Basya Solomonovna pursed her lips. She had not been planning to discuss the global situation with her daughter, as Vera must well know. Fine, she would wait an hour or a bit more while Misha read the paper, and then be able to raise the issue. Misha, however, fell asleep over the newspaper, so the discussion did not take place.

Relatives arrived from Kiev: Basya's brother Ovram Pogrebinsky and his wife Lyusya. It was pointless talking to Ovram about such things because all he could talk about was football, but it was worth giving it a try with Lyusya. Lyusya had fought at the front and was a chain-smoker. She was a Don Cossack but looked more Jewish than Basya herself. She listened carefully and said, "Don't worry Abram with it because, as you know, Basya, he has diabetes."

Lyusya was never lost for a word, which according to

Basya was how she had won Ovram's heart when they met at the front. Ovram's wife and four children had been killed during the occupation and Lyusya had lost a child before the war, so they were in the same boat. She launched into an attack on the Americans.

"Well, just think, Basya, what they're getting up to in Vietnam. That's Vietnam, of course, the people there are illiterate, poor, don't know their own minds. But here?! And you say the villains are going to start a war against the USSR? You know, even if they drop an atom bomb on us, we have the bomb too! So then it will be the end of us and the end of them! That's something for them to think about, the slimy reptiles! The Ku-Klux-Klan bastards! We'll get them!" Lyusya added murderously.

Basya agreed. Yes, it would be the end of us, and of them too. Basya had no doubt that Lyusya would share her insights about World War III with the Kiev public. Her only regret was that Lyusya would not credit her as the source of the information. Lyusya was a good woman, but could be a little jealous of other people having ideas.

Some time later Misha's elder brother Vova, demobilised as a captain in 1949 and working since then in supplies at an arms factory, came from Kiev. His arrival was unexpected, because he and Misha only rarely saw each other. Anyway, Vova arrived in Chernigov without phoning them in advance, to see Misha. He asked him to come out for a walk. That was after lunch, at which not a word had been spoken.

Misha was away for forty minutes or so and, when he returned, said Vova had left without coming back to say goodbye in order not to miss the bus. All evening Misha was silent. There was a stillness in the house, like the hush before a storm. Finally, Misha invited Basya Solomonovna to accompany him through to the kitchen.

Misha: Basya Solomonovna, you know how much I respect you.

Basya Solomonovna: Yes, Misha, I always know that.

Misha: Basya Solomonovna, Vova tells me you have been spreading rumours that could land us all in hot water.

Basya Solomonovna: What rumours, Misha? *Weh is mir!* What has Vova been telling you?

Misha: Well, rumours, Basya Solomonovna, that in the year of Lenin's centenary the Americans are going to start a war and drop an atom bomb on us.

Basya Solomonovna: *Weh is mir*, Misha! I never said anything like that to Vova! I don't talk to him even when you are present, and when you are not it would never occur to me to say a word to him! Everything has been plain for you to see!

Misha: Basya Solomonovna, did you say that to Lyusya? About the war?

Basya Solomonovna: Well, yes, I suppose I did.

Misha: Basya Solomonovna, do you know Lyusya well?

Basya Solomonovna: I do, Misha, I know her well.

Misha: Then why on earth are you passing on such things to her? Vova says she has been telling everyone in Kiev it is a sure fact World War III is going to start and that she has that information from a totally reliable source. Vova works in a defence factory and his job means he has access to all sorts of military secrets. There's no stopping Lyusya, you understand that. Before we know it, she's quite likely to dash off a letter to you-know-who asking them to take the necessary measures to prepare for war. Vova could be in big trouble. They'll immediately think he's been blabbing military secrets to her. Basya Solomonovna, how could you be so irresponsible? And from Vova they'll make a connection to me. You know what they're like.

Basya Solomonovna felt numb. She was horrified. She burst into tears and, blowing her nose on the edge of a brown, post-war (World War II) jumper, wailed, "Misha, I'm sorry! But everyone's saying that…"

Misha was merciless: "Now everybody is saying that, Basya Solomonovna, but you said it first!"

Basya looked up proudly, and a transparent dewdrop appeared on the tip of her nose. "Yes! It was me. I did it, not Lyusya!" she thought to herself, and had to make an effort not to say it out loud.

The next day, Basya went to Kiev. She needed to talk to Lyusya. Lyusya swore she had not "deliberately" said a word to anyone about World War III. Only to Fridochka, Vova's wife. And, of course, who Fridochka might have passed it on to was anybody's guess. No, actually it was obvious. Fridochka would have trumpeted it to everyone she knew, including, of course, her uncle the dental surgeon, and his clients included, well…!

Basya and Lyusya wondered what to do. Ovram came into the room and the women told him about Fridochka and the way she had behaved. Ovram decided to go and see Fridochka's uncle, whom he had never met, and, disguised as an ordinary patient, to find out what he knew.

Fridochka's uncle worked at home and accepted patients only by personal recommendation. His Pogrebinsky relatives never went to him, and had never set eyes on him, because he charged very high fees. Lyusya immediately phoned Fridochka to ask for her uncle's address for "a senior comrade" who was a very good friend. Fridochka gave it to her.

Half an hour later the three of them – Ovram, Lyusya and Basya – were in the uncle's waiting room, Ovram clutching his cheek and groaning convincingly. He was allowed to go to the head of the queue. Five minutes later he came out of the surgery at speed and, grabbing the women by the arm, skipped out to the street with them.

He told them he only had to mention World War III for the uncle to start yelling, haul him out of the chair and call him a panic-monger. Vova had evidently already been to see him to explain the situation. This was beginning to look serious. If Vova had decided to talk to Fridochka's uncle about such a sensitive matter, then everybody really was in danger who knew about the start of World War III.

Ovram, Lyusya and Basya went home to compare notes. It turned out, as if things were not bad enough, that Lyusya had not, in fact, shared her thoughts only with Fridochka but also with her workmates at the shoe factory. Also with the queue at the dairy shop on Borshchagovka. Also in the butcher's shop on Podol – which had just had a delivery of good pork and she had to queue for ages and could hardly just stand there and say nothing! Also in the haberdashery shop on Kreshchatik. And on Bessarabka. Also at the hospital when she went to hand in Ovram's specimens. Also at the post office on Pechersk when she was paying in her rent, at the bus stop in Darnitsa, and in the metro only she could not remember which station.

And, of course, she had told Fridochka and Fridochka had told her uncle the dentist and Vova. But that was absolutely all.

Basya was distraught. Everyone in Kiev knew, so of course First Secretary Comrade Shelest himself would know all about it. As regards Chernigov, the regional party committee long ago knew everything because the mother-in-law of the committee's electrician lived in the same apartment building as Basya Solomonovna and had gone round to her for advice on reversing a garment and, naturally, talked with her about

World War III. And if they knew, so did Moscow: the Party bosses in Chernigov and Kiev were hardly likely to keep that sort of information to themselves.

The information, indeed, would have leaked also in the other direction. Given that the largest Worsted cloth factory in the whole of Europe was now operational in Chernigov and that there were two aviation units stationed there, it was a safe bet American spies were snooping about (to say nothing of how many there must be in Kiev). So in America itself they would surely have learned from their Chernigov and Kiev spies that Basya Solomonovna had guessed their plans for World War III.

But if everybody now knew everything, our people had been forewarned and would consequently be on the alert. The Americans, having lost the advantage of launching a surprise attack, would now never dare to take on the USSR. So Basya Solomonovna could really not see she had done anything wrong. The only thing she could be blamed for was getting under the feet of the competent Soviet agencies, who doubtless did not need her to tell them how to do their job.

As she said goodbye to Ovram and Lyusya, Basya Solomonovna said meekly, "I'll say it was all my fault." She made a resolution not to speak to anyone ever again, since things had turned out the way they had and her tongue had caused her relatives so much trouble. (Trouble, that is, in terms of their wretched, petty bourgeois mentality and obsession with private property.)

She went back to Chernigov and said nothing. She was silent for six months. "Yes" and "no" was as much as she said. She burned down like a candle.

Misha and Vera were worried about her, but what with work and their children, they had little enough time for that.

In early 1970 Basya Solomonovna passed away.

And on 22 April no one thanked her, albeit posthumously, for preventing World War III.

The Prayer

Everybody remembers of course how, when Saddam Hussein was being hunted in Iraq, a local peasant shot down a US military helicopter with an old Berdan rifle and was awarded a pile of cash by Saddam and a flock of sheep into the bargain.

There was a lot of fuss about it, but what was so surprising? After all, the man used a bullet, he had a firearm, he aimed and hit the target. Wow, congratulations!

Here, though, is a rather different case.

Samuil Yakovlevich Vikhnovich, a man living in Shvedsky Close in Moscow, had three sons, a daughter and a wife. His passport gave his "nationality" as Jewish, although he had never been detected engaging in anything Jewish, the more so because his wife was Russian. Vikhnovich worked in a sewing factory.

Then, suddenly, there was the war. His wife and daughter were evacuated and his sons went to the front line. Samuil went nowhere. In the first place, because he was the factory's manager, which was an important position, and Vikhnovich was a Party member. In the second place, he disapproved of his wife agreeing to be evacuated. "The two of us have lived our whole lives in the Close. You've no reason to be evacuated, because Moscow is not going to be surrendered. Our sons are volunteers at the front and you are not giving them your full confidence."

Vikhnovich was left to look after their home but, living in a large communal apartment, he was not alone. A couple of old ladies had also stayed, and a woman with no husband but a son, young Yura, who was ten. So there was someone to help Samuil with the household chores. They all ate together, in each other's room in turn. In the rooms, not in the kitchen: that was at Samuil's insistence, to keep things as they were before the war. The old ladies boiled potatoes and made soup. All the apartment's residents shared their food, and their sewing and mending and everybody's laundry too.

It happened, then, that of all the people in the apartment only Samuil had sons fighting in the war. The residents looked forward eagerly to their letters from the front. Samuil first read the letters alone in his room, then again in his room, only out loud for everyone. Then Yura read them, when Samuil was away at work and the old ladies were on their own.

Letters from his wife and daughter arrived more frequently, but Samuil did not show them to anybody because they had no ramifications for society.

When it was their apartment's turn, Samuil always went up for fire-watching duty himself (putting incendiaries in a bucket of water or throwing them off the roof). He did not let Yura's mum go up there, let alone the old ladies. They almost never left the building: only really when they volunteered to queue for bread, because they had experience at that dating from the Imperialist War.

And then one time when he was on duty, in the summer, on the night of 7 June 1942, Samuil went up to the roof and was looking at the sky which was as clear as clear could be. The stars were twinkling and the whole of Moscow was spread out before him if he looked down and into the distance (it was a six-storey building, very solid, built in 1879). It was dark, admittedly, what with the blackout, but you could still make out something.

He had been on duty for a couple of hours. Nothing.

Suddenly he heard the roar of an aircraft, right above his head. How the infernal machine had crept up on him is inexplicable, but there it was roaring directly overhead, even sort of nosediving. Samuil had a big sand scoop in his hand, a basket full of sand near him, buckets of water and a poker. He was psyched up, prepared to deal with incendiary bombs, but this was a dive-bomber.

It needs to be mentioned that Yura would often come up to the roof at night without permission. To watch, to help. Samuil would try to chase him away but it was a big roof and there was no getting rid of him. At the very moment the plane was showing off above Samuil Yakovlevich, Yura was jumping up and down next to him, sticking his tongue out at the German air ace.

There is no telling how long the plane circled above their heads. It circled over them and flew on. It was only then Samuil recovered his wits. He flung down the scoop with a crash, raised up his arms, clenched his fists and whispered, "God of Isaac, Abraham and Israel, bring down Thy wrath upon him, bring down Thy wrath upon him!"

At that very moment, out of a cloudless sky as they say, thunder boomed, lightning flashed and a fire blazed up. Yura clutched at Samuil's jacket, it was very frightening, and Samuil raged, waving his fists in the direction of the departing plane, 'Be you accursed! Be you accursed!' and more of that ilk.

Then the plane, which they could still see in the distance, burst into flames and hurtled towards the ground. Black trail of smoke, etc. Yura yelled and Samuil stood rooted to the spot. He pointed his hand in the direction of the ex-dive-bomber, "Look, Yura, we got him!"

In the morning Yura's mum came to see Samuil Yakovlevich and ask for a button to sew on to her son's trousers because for some reason they were forever getting lost. There was a custom among boys at the time of trading buttons at the flea market or, what was worse, cutting them off the clothes of people at Tishinka market who were not concentrating, and selling them at Palashi. And vice versa. What the boys made they spent on tobacco, so their profits went up in smoke.

Samuil Yakovlevich had already cut a great many buttons off his son's clothes and handed them over to Yura, although every time he warned that this was the last time, and knew perfectly well about Tishinka and Palashi.

In response to this latest request, he agreed but asked for Yura to come down to see him personally. The boy duly arrived, and started going on about how the buttons kept getting lost because his mum didn't use enough thread to sew them on properly. Samuil paid no attention and said, "Now, Yura, we need to have a serious talk. Have you told anyone about what happened up on the roof last night?"

Yura perked up immediately. "About how our side shot that plane down?"

Samuil quickly agreed. "Yes, our side…"

"Why? The whole city must've seen it, eh? Wasn't it great? But give me two buttons. So I have a spare. Please."

Samuil did so. He sat on his chair and pondered. Everything suggested it was actually he who had brought down the plane. Not by himself, of course. The plane was brought down by the God of the Jews, responding to his, Samuil Yakovlevich Vikhnovich's, request. Indeed demand. This was a fact, and a fact, moreover, that needed to be recorded without delay on some kind of scrolls. Samuil decided he should go to a synagogue.

The last time he was in a synagogue had been in 1900, in the little Jewish town of Chernobyl in Ukraine. He had gone in briefly to say goodbye to his father. Since then, however, never. The nearest synagogue was situated on Bolshaya Bronnaya, but for many years now had been functioning as a House of Folk Culture.

Samuil decided to go to the Choral Synagogue at Solyanka. That, he heard, was still performing as initially intended. As a well organised person, he planned everything carefully. By 7.00 am he would need to be at the factory, give instructions, conduct a meeting, phone the district Party committee about any new regulations, then at twelve noon he could quickly slip away for an hour.

Vikhnovich was welcomed at the synagogue. Three old gentlemen in small black caps and with beards were evidently authorised to deal with visitors. They asked him to cover his head with something, and recommended a handkerchief if he had nothing else. That, of course, was after they had asked him whether he was a Jew, whether he was circumcised, and what his father's and mother's names were.

Samuil Yakovlevich showed them his passport and got out his Party membership card. They inspected his documents. They all sat down in a small room which served as an office. There was an imposing black telephone and the desk was large. Samuil Yakovlevich told them his story. They asked for clarification.

"Which prayer did you recite?"

"Well, I just said, 'God of Abraham, Isaac and Israel'…"

"In which language?"

"In Russian, what else?"

"What are you saying! It is not supposed to be in Russian. And there is no such prayer. There is a prayer, 'God of Abraham, Isaac and Jacob…' Are you sure it was not that one?"

"Absolutely."

"And you really think it was you that brought down the plane?"

"Of course. Not on my own, of course. I asked God."

"And do you keep kosher?"

It went on and on.

Samuil Yakovlevich sat there, stumbling over his answers like a schoolboy. Every now and then the handkerchief fell off his head and the old men nodded and smiled. They talked among themselves in Yiddish, so their guest would not understand what they were making of it all. Samuil Yakovlevich lost patience.

"I can see you don't believe me. But I have a witness."

The old gentlemen were instantly alert.

"Who is the witness? A Jew?"

"No. A Russian, a boy. Yury."

"Well there, you see, you don't even have any witnesses."

Samuil lost his temper, and even started shouting, saying they were not Soviet people, they did not believe him, their thinking was narrow, but there was a war on and he had three sons at the front.

The old gentlemen waved their arms about and did their best to calm him. "Go home, Samuil Yakovlevich," they urged. "It's the times we live in. Everybody is suffering, everybody is working night and day. All sorts of things happen. People are on edge."

Samuil Yakovlevich said in parting, "I am a Jew. I prayed to the God of the Jews. I called on him to help and he answered my prayer. He – answered – me – personally. That is a fact! A fact! Don't you understand? But you keep asking what language I spoke, what prayer I used. I prayed to him with what I could remember. Who am I supposed to turn to now? The Orthodox Church? The Party district committee? The militia?"

The old gentlemen clucked disapprovingly. They expressed dismay. There was no need to go to the district committee or the militia. They themselves would gather some clever people, consult with them, and invite Samuil Yakovlevich along.

Samuil left them his address. He crumpled up his handkerchief and, still holding it in his hand, strode back all the way to the factory in Presnya, not even taking the tram.

He returned home late that night and did not turn on the light because of the blackout. He lay down on the sofa without undressing and stayed like that until morning, without closing his eyes. He fell asleep then, and woke up an hour later feeling reborn.

He went to the table, where a copy of yesterday's *Pravda* was lying unread. He took in the title of the leading article: "The Soviet rear is a mighty prop for the front." He felt even more elated and hurried off to work, because in this testing time of war it was out of the question to be late.

Now, a word about the amazing place where this all happened. There is no memorial plaque there. In 1976 a number of houses were demolished in Shvedsky Close, including that particular six-storey one. A new building was erected to house the Moscow Art Theatre. Incidentally, in that location, things did not go well for the theatre.

Gardner

On Sundays Iosif Matveyevich's son Arkadiy came to see him, and on Saturdays his grandson Alexey. Iosif Matveyevich did not like their wives, which is why they did not come. His own wife had died many years ago, and Iosif Matveyevich no longer grieved for her, but still missed her. To have his son and grandson at the same time was not possible because they did not get on with each other, and Iosif Matveyevich had given up trying to reconcile them.

Three years ago his grandson had had a daughter, Sasha, and of late Alexey would appear on Saturdays with his very independent little girl. While grandfather and grandson were having their tea, Sasha demanded to watch cartoons.

"Grandad hasn't got a video recorder," Alexey explained. Sasha nodded and again demanded a cartoon.

On his next visit Alexey brought a large box. "Grandad, here's a VCR! There's nothing to watch on TV. I've brought you some old films, 'Spring on Zarechnaya Street', 'Come, Mukhtar!' and some cartoons for Sasha."

Iosif Matveyevich was pleased, but expressed anxiety over whether he would be able to master the machine.

"You're an engineer, and it's only two buttons." Alexey quickly set everything up and loaded a cassette of cartoons. Iosif Matveyevich brought a dish with sweets and apples, put it on the coffee table by the sofa, and stroked the little girl's head, looked for a couple of seconds at the small animals running around on the screen and went to the kitchen, as usual, to drink tea with Alexey.

Ten minutes later there was an almighty crash, followed by Sasha shouting "Daddy! Grandad! Grandad! Daddy!" They rushed into the room. The dish was lying on the floor, broken in half, and sweet wrappers, sweets as yet untouched, and apples were scattered all over the floor.

"I didn't do it."

"It can't have done it by itself," Alexey said. "Have you cut yourself?"

"No. It did it by itself." Sasha sat there, her eyes fixed on the screen. Without looking away, she lifted her hands and turned the palms uppermost, showing that nothing had happened.

Alexey leaned over the porcelain fragments. "Well,

Grandad, shall we throw it out?"

Iosif Matveyevich took the two halves of the dish from his grandson and turned them this way and that. "You think everything should just be thrown away. I'll glue it together."

For as far back as Iosif Matveyevich could remember, he remembered that dish. It was 40 centimetres in diameter and made in the shape of a shallow basket. The wickerwork was so carefully crafted that you seemed to see air through the gaps between the finely woven cane. In the middle was a cream, folded napkin with a posy of wild flowers: forget-me-nots and bluebells. Both the flowers and the napkin seemed entirely real. The fringe of the napkin hung over one side of the basket-dish and every strand of the fringe was clearly delineated.

Iosif Matveyevich remembered trying as a child to take the napkin off the dish, and how it would not come. Later his son Arkadiy was caught out in the same way, and after him his grandson. And now Sasha.

Iosif Matveyevich turned the broken halves over, face down, brought them together, and it occurred to him he had never looked at the underside of the dish. It was only now, after putting on his spectacles, that he read the tiny letters in an oval surrounding a horse rider: "Gardner Factory, Moscow". Above the trademark was a double-headed eagle holding an orb and sceptre.

"The dish must be a hundred years old, if not more," Iosif Matveyevich calculated. "My mother said it was her dowry."

Iosif Matveyevich remembered, when he was a child, in the evenings the whole family would gather round a table in the garden, drinking tea, and red currants and gooseberries would be piled up in the dish. Or korzhiki, the special shortbread his grandmother baked.

He remembered their neighbour, a friend of his grandmother,

would tut-tut every time she saw the dish: "Fine style you live in, Feyga, to be soiling something of such quality during the week. It would grace the table on the Sabbath! How well the *challah* would look in it!"

His grandmother had laughed. "They've abolished the Sabbath, Dora dear!"

Iosif Matveyevich remembered the day he came home from the front, the only one in his family to do so. His father and two brothers had been killed: his father during the Dnieper crossing; his elder brother, Syoma, at Letki; his middle brother, Grisha, at Tomaszów.

He and his mother sat at the table alone. On it was that very dish, which she had kept safe throughout the evacuation, even when she had to sell her last dress for a piece of bread. She spoke to him of her relatives and neighbours who had been killed, or died, or were missing, and apologised she had nothing with which to cook him a good meal.

His demob rations Iosif Matveyevich had bartered in the train for a length of bizarre diaphanous fabric with sequins. "It's real gold! Your bride will thank you for it for a hundred years!" the vendor had cajoled him.

The people in the workshop set about gluing the dish back together and promised it would be as good as new. And indeed, the crack was barely noticeable. Iosif Matveyevich phoned Alexey and asked him to buy a holder so he could hang the dish on the wall.

Alexey brought a drill, inserted a wall plug, screwed in a wood screw and hung the dish up. "I've been all round town. There were no holders anywhere. I finally found one in a fancy goods shop. That dish should have been hung on the wall a long time ago."

In the night Iosif Matveyevich was wakened by a crash.

Half-asleep, for a long time he could not work out what had happened. He turned on the light, looked around the room – nothing. He went to the bathroom, everything there was fine. When he went into the kitchen he found the dish on the floor, smashed to smithereens. The screw had come out. Iosif Matveyevich scooped the debris up, put it in a towel, tied the towel in a knot and put it on the windowsill.

In the middle of the week Arkadiy made an unscheduled visit. He saw the marks on the wall and the empty wall plug. "What were you trying to hang up?" he asked.

"The dish with the napkin. Sasha broke it in half. I got it glued in a workshop. They did a good job."

"But now you've taken it down? Quite right. You shouldn't have cracked crockery in the house, even if it's been repaired."

"I didn't take it down. It fell down and smashed." Iosif Matveyevich tried to keep his voice steady.

"Father, are you upset? If you had asked me, I would have done it for you properly. Did Alexey hang it up? He's so useless." As usual Arkadiy got on to the subject of his son.

"No, Alexey did it well, all according to the instructions. No good crying over spilt milk."

"Pack it in, Father. You're probably imagining heaven knows what. You'll live for a hundred years yet," Arkadiy said quickly.

"Oh yes, I'll live another hundred years. It's not about me."

In the evening, Iosif Matveyevich untied the bundle of tiny fragments and spread them out on the kitchen table. He tried to put them together, but without great success. The patterning on the napkin was particularly damaged. The interweaving of the basketwork was all broken off and now, instead of tracery, there were uneven shards. Nevertheless, he found piecing the fragments together absorbing.

He worked on the fragments the next day and the day after, and the day after that, bringing together and again moving apart the different bits and pieces of porcelain, scrutinising their edges, turning them this way and that. He started eating breakfast, lunch and dinner in the living room, at the coffee table, so as not to disturb the pattern.

On Saturday Alexey arrived with Sasha. He nodded towards the table. "My father phoned and yelled at me. How am I to blame?"

The little girl threw up her hands in delight: "Oh, Grandad, are you doing a jigsaw puzzle?"

Iosif Matveyevich was baffled. "What's that, sunshine? What did you say?"

"You know, a jigsaw!" Sasha repeated.

Iosif Matveyevich looked at Alexey in bewilderment and he explained what a jigsaw was. "It's a picture cut into shapes to make it confusing, to puzzle you. Say, a dog's head, or a palace. What's most difficult is clouds in the sky. Sasha has lots but she's a bit too young for them yet. You need a longer attention span."

Sasha lunged at the fragments. "Let me have a go!"

"No, this one's only for grown-ups,' Alexey said, catching her arm. 'Grandad, put it away, could you, while she's here. She'll grab at it and cut herself. Or let me take it to the rubbish bins."

"I'll wedge the door with a cloth, very tightly so she can't open it. We can drink our tea in the other room and watch the cartoons together. All right, Sasha?"

As they were leaving, Alexey whispered to Iosif Matveyevich, "Don't be upset. It's not good to turn in on yourself too much. I'll bring another video cassette tomorrow, 'The Diamond Arm', or 'Striped Voyage'. Only phone me

340

when my father leaves so we don't bump into each other. Have you worked out how to use the video yet?"

"Yes, yes. I've watched all of it. Good films," Iosif Matveyevich said distractedly.

Sitting back at the table, assembling and disassembling the pieces for the hundredth time, he kept repeating, "Jigsaw-migsaw, puzzle-mazal."

The Leg

In 1975, old age pensioners Alexander Semyonovich and Klara Zakharovna were preparing to leave for Israel. A few years before, their son had emigrated with great difficulty. Protests by Western public opinion helped. Alexander Semyonovich and Klara Zakharovna were leaving under the article on "family reunification".

Their son told them on the phone not to think of bringing containers of belongings but only the bare essentials, to travel light to join him via Vienna.

All the time they were packing and filling in forms, their son's comrades, refuseniks who knew what to do and how, never left their side. They were, however, short of an answer when Alexander Semyonovich asked if he would be allowed to take his army awards and medals. He demanded immediate clarification, fell out with his refusenik guardians, and ordered them to stop interfering in his and Klara Zakharovna's personal affairs. Klara Zakharovna phoned each of the people her husband had insulted in turn, apologised, and begged them not to leave him and her without assistance.

Three weeks or so before they were due to depart, Alexander Semyonovich had a phone call from the factory where he had worked from 1930 to 1972, with a break during the war. He was informed that to mark the thirtieth anniversary of the

Great Victory of 1945 he, in recognition of his long service at the factory and as a war veteran, was being awarded a free holiday at a resort in Moscow province. He was to leave in two days' time and was entitled to fourteen days.

Alexander Semyonovich was taken aback, so did not tell them to keep their holiday because he was off to the Red Sea and the Dead Sea, and not for fourteen days but for the rest of his life. Instead he thanked them, and kept to himself his amazement that the factory was not apprised of his imminent emigration. He would take up the holiday offer.

"In the whole of my working life I've had nothing from the state apart from my salary, and how much aggravation they've given me, Klara, you know only too well. So as a matter of principle I shall take this holiday. What other preparations have we yet to make? We'll fit it all in."

Klara Zakharovna never argued with her husband, and was actually quite pleased he would be out of the way for these last days before their departure. He was very boisterous, and if some snag with their documentation meant his presence was needed, the holiday resort was only an hour away by train.

It needs to be mentioned that Alexander Semyonovich had been wounded in the war: he had lost his left leg, or more precisely, half of it from the knee down, and he wore an artificial leg. Although by law he was entitled not to work, he laboured on, false leg or not, at his same factory, "the Red Bookcase" as he called it.

The false leg, which Alexander Semyonovich went to great lengths not to notice and forbade others to, did him a major disservice. Nobody knows for sure what happened at the holiday home: whether the war veterans drank more than was wise during their celebration of Victory Day on 9 May, or whether it was something else, but Alexander Semyonovich was found on the floor by his bed with a head injury and with his false leg lying beside him. He had evidently stumbled while unfastening his leg that night, fallen, fractured his skull, and lost consciousness before he could call for help. He bled to death. The accident happened at night and nobody had gone in to check on him until the following morning.

Klara Zakharovna was terribly upset but there was nothing to be done about it. All her son's friends were constantly at her side and organised the funeral. They were going to put the false leg in the coffin, as Alexander Semyonovich had always had it with him in life, but Klara Zakharovna objected. He'll have both his legs in the world to come. What use would he have for one extra?

There was a week left before her departure. They signed off the apartment at the housing office, quickly sold or gave away the furniture to relatives, as well as all their books, and packed the suitcases. The last thing to go in, immediately under the lid, was "the wonder", a small round brazier with a hole through the middle which Klara Zakharovna used for baking potatoes and pieces of chicken. There they stood: two suitcases in an empty room.

Klara Zakharovna entrusted her husband's awards and medals to one of her son's comrades, as there remained some uncertainty over the issue.

During the night she woke, firmly convinced she had forgotten something very important. The false leg! She got up, took it and hugged it to her like a little child, lamenting, "Oh, off you went to the holiday home! Oh, you so needed a rest! Oh, now you will rest for ever and ever! How can I live without you? How can I leave you behind?" She cried and cried, hugging the false leg until she fell asleep and forgot everything.

In the morning her son phoned. "How are you, Mum? Bear up. I'm here waiting for you. Life goes on, what else can we do?"

"Yes, yes, my dear, you're quite right, that's what we have to do. I have to leave. Who needs me here? You won't abandon me, will you?"

"How can you think that, Mum! You're in shock, and here you'll get over it and be well again; you'll recover. I'm looking forward to seeing you!" He hung up, although she had much more she wanted to tell him.

A good fifty people turned up at Sheremetievo Airport to see Klara Zakharovna off: relatives, her son's comrades, other people she did not know personally but who asked her to pass on their best wishes to her son.

Just before leaving for the airport, Klara Zakharovna had looked one last time at all the things she had packed, shifted them from one suitcase to the other. She threw out one or two items to make room for the false leg.

Inspecting her luggage, the customs officer was very puzzled. "What's this?"

"My late husband's artificial leg."

The official took the leg, examined it from every angle, rapped his knuckles on the metal parts, weighed it up and departed, telling Klara Zakharovna to wait there. She was moved to one side so as not to be in the way of the other passengers, who were mostly foreigners.

The crowd seeing her off became agitated, none of them knowing about the false leg. They discussed the situation among themselves: "What's going on there? Why are they upsetting an old woman?"

"She's not trying to take out anything dodgy?"

"No chance! Nothing but old rubbish. They just want to be

unpleasant to her…"

Time went by. The officer did not reappear. The queue of people checking in and going through customs control came to an end. Finally the customs officer emerged with the artificial leg. He proceeded unhurriedly to the counter. "This way, please," he called. He put the leg down next to a suitcase and fingered through dresses and shoes wrapped in newspaper. "Go through, citizen."

Klara Zakharovna tried to close the suitcase, but her neat packing had been undone and the lid would not close because the foot of the leg was sticking out awkwardly She removed the leg, snapped the suitcase shut, and her luggage immediately floated away through a black flap. She proceeded to boarding.

She was carrying the false leg in her arms and, when she turned to take her leave, that was what she waved at them.

A Murky Business

Bella Levina emigrated from Kiev to Israel many years ago, even before apartments were privatised. In Israel she was a prey to nostalgia.

When her husband died, and her children moved from Israel to America, Bella began writing to relatives and friends in Ukraine asking them to take her in. Her communications always ended the same way: "I am all alone here, as if that is my fate." People replied sympathetically, but nobody seemed keen to invite her to come and stay with them permanently. In spite of that, Bella came back.

She arrived in the winter, and people said she had done that intentionally: who would be so hard-hearted as to send an old woman out into the cold? Most probably, though, Bella had overlooked the fact of winter, having simply forgotten about the cold while living in foreign climes. So she ended up staying for three months first with one set of relatives, then with another.

People were not unkind to her, but hinted it was time for her to be making long-term arrangements about where she was going to stay. Bella had some savings, her children in America were phoned, and relatives in Kiev chipped in. In the end she was able to afford a little one-room apartment in Brovary in the Kiev suburbs.

People donated furniture they had been going to move to the dacha in the summer, they re-wallpapered the apartment for her to make it more welcoming, brought Bella to Brovary and wished her all the best.

There Bella lived, not pestering anyone with phone calls, not asking for help, and only occasionally, tactfully, reminding them of her existence. Her children in America sent money regularly and she did not have to stint. Cheese, sausage – no problem. She could afford medication. Everybody relaxed.

One and a half years had passed when Bella suddenly told her relatives she intended to move again. She wanted to go back to Oster where she was born. Three generations of her family were buried there (if we are talking about before 1941). Her grandfather and grandmother, and many other family members who left it too late to evacuate in 1941, were in a communal grave. All in all, as Bella had developed such a burning desire to live in the proximity of the dead, it might have seemed simplest for her just to go straight to the cemetery. That was a bit unkind, of course.

It would be no problem to sell the apartment in Brovary and buy a house in Oster, but Oster was nothing like it had been. Now it was the back of beyond. Additionally, she would have to draw water outside the house, and the toilet too would be outside. There were no shops. It was little more than a village.

Bella had all this pointed out to her, but would hear nothing of it.

"It's only an hour from Kiev: what sort of backwater is that? Why are you trying to scare me with an outside toilet? Bah! Everywhere is on the mains now, and money will get you any utility. I'm not asking for support, I'm confronting you with a fact."

Bella phoned her children in America and told them she was moving back to Oster, and as soon as she was settled she would let them know the new address. Her children pretended to agree to wait for that, but rushed to phone their relatives in Kiev to find out if their mother had lost her marbles. They replied that it was impossible to tell. On the one hand, she was eighty years old, on the other she was alert and all her organs seemed to be functioning just fine.

After several more conversations explaining to her what was what, Bella appeared to relent and everything went quiet. Her relatives relaxed again. For a month there were no phone calls. They went to see her in Brovary, rang, knocked: no answer. They broke down the door and found everything in the apartment in perfect order, with the newspapers stacked in a neat pile. The schedule of radio and TV programmes from two weeks previously was marked in different inks. They looked in the wardrobe and found her clothes and suitcases were missing, and in there, on a pile of clothes under which Bella kept her money, they found a note.

"I've left. Don't worry. Bella. 5 June 2004."

They notified the police: a missing woman, etc., etc. The police were reluctant to act. An extremely old lady was missing. She was probably not all there. She had said she was going back to her birthplace? That's what they always do. They go there, then they come back. Her relatives needed to keep a closer eye on her, not come wasting everyone's time with reports of missing persons. The police did, however, accept their report, although it was plainly just to get rid of them.

One of Bella's relatives went to Oster. Where should he start looking? He walked through the streets for a while and finally saw an old man of about ninety, wearing a cap and looking like he might be a Jew. The relative began asking him about the Grobmans (Bella's maiden name). The old man remembered them immediately and offered to show where they lived before the war.

"Why are you interested in the Grobmans? There's been none of them living these many long years," the old man muttered.

"There are none of them living here, but Bella Grobman is alive. You haven't seen her, then?"

The old man stared at this interloper in amazement, but made no comment. "That's their house. Well built, eh? It'll be standing a hundred years from now. During the war the Germans had their headquarters here. It was damaged a bit when our troops were advancing, but not too badly. Beylka's great-grandfather built it, and because of this house her father met his end. Didn't want to abandon it. They say that's where the Germans killed him. Right in the doorway. That's Gottlieb's distinction, you could say: the first Jew to be killed in Oster. Three days later they shot the rest, organised killing… by the Desna, in the ravine. But he had been saying, for one thing they're a civilised nation, and for another, Leyba will fix an exchange, like in the First World War. Leyba was his son, Beylka's elder brother. He volunteered as soon as they made the announcement. But Beylka was with her father. Her mother died back in 1936, she died young. Gottlieb had a bad limp. Just before the war it got really bad, his leg not working. So that's how he and Beylka, the two of them, stayed behind.

Well, why go on. War is war, isn't that right?"

"So what are you telling me? All through the war Bella was here? How was that? Did she join the partisans?"

"What's your link with her, then?" the old man asked, suddenly suspicious.

"I'm a relative. Here's the problem. Bella Gottliebovna has disappeared. She emigrated to Israel, then came back to Kiev, and now she's disappeared. We think she's come here, back to where she was born, you know? And here I am, looking for her."

"Could you show me your identification documents?" the old man asked.

"Of course, of course! But our surnames are different. My wife is her second cousin once removed."

The old man carefully took the passport with its trident symbol and perused the blue and yellow pages at great length.

"Well, who knows if you're a relative or not. Anyway, it makes no difference. I think you must be looking for a different Bella. This one," he nodded towards the Grobmans' house, "has long been in her grave."

"Actually, no. It's the Bella Gottliebovna Grobman who was born in 1925. She said her family lived here for three generations. Her father was in charge of state procurements and played the tambourine. Her grandfather, Yankel, was a blacksmith and played the violin, at weddings. And her uncle, Meir, I believe, would down a tumbler of vodka and crush the glass in his fist."

"All correct. Except it wasn't a tumblerful he drank and crushed but a shot glass he drank and then munched as a snack. That's true. Absolutely. And Beylka was their youngest. I told you, she's dead, and so she is." Without saying goodbye, the old man turned and marched off as fast as his legs would carry

349

him.

Bella's relative was left standing in the road, baffled as to where to go or what to do next. It was impossible to imagine that Bella, if she had come to Oster, would not have gone to her old house. He knocked at the door. A woman holding a baby in her arms opened it.

"Excuse me, have you had a visit from a woman, very old, recently? Her name is Bella Gottliebovna. Interesting-looking, hair dyed dark auburn. A bit plump, wears glasses?"

"Naebuddy's been in. An' who're you? An' wha's she?" the lady of the house enquired. "Come in. Ye'll be frae Kiev I dinna doot. Come through, come through, hen. I'll pour ye some kvass."

Bella's relative went through. Over the kvass he got talking to the woman, told her about Bella and her travels, and about the old man he had met in the street.

"Oh, that'd be oor Chaim. A bit touched in the heid, he is. He'll yatter an yammer. Ye've no tae heed 'im. He'll just upset ye."

"Well, yes. I don't suppose you could tell me where the old Jewish cemetery is?"

The woman explained how to get there. "There's nae a newer ain. Only the auld. We've almost nae Jews left. Chaim is one, and there's a couple more auld men yet."

"Never mind, never mind. I'll go and take a look. Just for the sake of it. Since I've come all this way."

At the cemetery Bella's relative walked back and forth, reading the names on the monuments and blackened wooden plaques, looking for Grobmans but not finding any. He sat down on a bench to rest.

"Ah, there ye are. I saw someone come in the railings but where ye went I couldnae see. Good day to you. I'm the watchman here. Might ye care to make a donation tae the Jewish community? Just a couple of hryvnias, if ye can. I'm the watchman. Keep an eye on the place, to top up my pension. Illya Moiseyevich Kamsky," the watchman introduced himself, holding out his cap like a beggar.

Bella's relative put three hryvnia and some small change in the cap. The watchman scooped them up, slipped them into his jacket pocket and looked in an attentive and business-like manner at this visitor. "So, who would ye be looking for?" The watchman straightened his jacket lapel, which was sagging under the weight of his medals.

"Grobman."

"Ah, the Grobmans... I'll tak' ye there. Kinsfolk of yours are they?"

"Yes, they are."

"There's a lot of Grobmans here, both from before the war and the others. Should I show you them all?"

"Please," Bella's relative sighed.

They visited them all and, tired, sat down on a large bench under a willow. "Well, I've shown ye everything. It's been a bit of an excursion. Are ye well pleased?"

"Yes. Thank you. Tell me, though, Bella Grobman, the youngest daughter of Gottlieb Grobman, wouldn't have been here recently by any chance?"

The watchman hesitated. "Would ye be sure she's still in this world?"

The relative nodded.

"Well, well. Beylka will no' be coming back here if she knows what's guid for her. Not while I, and Chaim and Sunka Ovrutsky are alive. After we, the last survivors, are dead she might turn up."

"Chaim talked to me about Bella, but I didn't really

351

understand. He's convinced she died immediately after the war, but she is alive. Where was she during the war? With the partisans?"

"With the partisans? Well, maybe so. In the war, ye see, people here were badly frightened. The news we were getting… ye'll understand what it was like. People said this and that. But she was a beauty, she was, quite some beauty. That whole family, the Grobmans, they all deserved to be painted in a picture." The watchman glanced briefly at the relative. "You wouldn't be from abroad? Writing a book? Making a film?"

"This is not about a movie! I'm looking for Bella, she's a missing person!" The relative ran through the history of Bella's comings and goings for the watchman. He was unsurprised.

"U-huh. She always had a high opinion o' herself… And then recently, ten years ago or so, we had people come all the way from America, making a film about the Jews, they were. How they questioned us, all but interrogation it was. Paid us, though, they did. Well, Oster before the war, that was quite something! A big Jewish town! Seventy per cent of us Jews, there was. And mind you, we didnae say a word to the Americans about Beylka." The watchman looked pointedly at the relative, "I can tell you, being as how you're her kinsman. Want to know?"

The relative nodded.

"Just before the occupation there was a lot of Jews still living in Oster. There's nobody warned them to get away, nobody organised any warning. Before the Germans got here refugees from the west said they were shooting absolutely all Jews. People didn't believe it. They thought they would be treated the same as Ukrainians and Russians. But that they would be picked out specially, no, nobody believed that. They had their livelihoods here, of course, their homes. And if you had a fine house, and furniture, how could you just leave? So Gottlieb stayed. Beylka didn't want to abandon him. We young lads went straight to the front as Young Communist League volunteers. Away we went, and then what happened here…

"All the Jews who had stayed they shot, every last one. My people, everyone, in the ravine by the river. After the liberation they were all reburied in a common grave. We thought Beylka was in there too.

"And then when people started coming back from the front, I came, Chaim, Sunka Ovrutsky, other comrades, we gathered the Jewish community. People had come back from evacuation. Those in the army had not been demobilised then, only those who were wounded. And a lot of Oster people who had been here under the Germans were Ukrainians. We talked about the situation after the occupation. And what was the situation? Half of Oster had worked for the Germans as policemen, and there they were sitting among us. And everyone knew who had done what. The district authorities gave a speech, condemning individuals. They said, 'We are one family, like it's written.' They said, 'You, comrades, if you know of any collaborators, speak out. You have nothing to fear any more.'

"Well, those who had done the shooting themselves, the women told us, were executed by our troops as soon as they came to liberate us. The law of war. So there were none of those. But the ones who had not done too much, they were sitting with us, in the old synagogue, which was now the club.

"Beylka had showed up before that meeting. About where she had been or how she had saved her skin she said not a word. The women tried so hard to get something out of her but she admitted nothing. "I did what everybody did," was all she would say. Others by the end of the war were haggard and terrible but she was just very thin and her face was as pretty as ever. But then, in all her beauty, she stands up (she was used to being a YCL activist). I can see it now, I remember every word:

"'We have all suffered grievously. My father was murdered by the accursed Germans, my brother fell on the field of honour at the front. I'll say nothing about my own grief. All of us have our family members here in the grave, solely because they were Jews. The Ukrainian people also suffered grievously, although they were not summarily executed. We have been talking about those who worked for the Germans' police force. Certainly no Jews worked for the Polizei because they were shot on the spot and not given that option. Well, everybody had children, everybody wanted to live. There's no bringing back the dead.'

"When she had finished, she sat down. What had she said? Who had she been saying it to? What for? How could she bring herself to say those things? All hell was let loose: *gevalt!* Then Sunka Ovrutsky came on his crutches and started firing his pistol. He yelled, 'Let me put a bullet into this pal of the Polizei. She's worse than Fanny Kaplan!'

"Beylka was going to talk back but everyone piled into her, punching and punching. How they beat her! The authorities had to pull them off, and the militia. Beylka was lying on the floor covered in blood. They poured water over her, she got up and left. Nobody went to comfort her. Nobody."

The watchman stopped talking. After a long pause, he said, "Well, how do you like that?"

"Yes…"

"What do you mean, yes? Tell me if you like it or not!"

The relative said nothing.

"And after something like that you're telling me she'll be coming back here? We thought she had done away with herself, chucked herself in the Desna. Nobody laid eyes on her after that day, but you say she's alive! Hasn't killed herself, the vermin!"

The watchman jumped up and began bending the fingers on his fist, starting with his thumb:

"Chaim is alive, I am alive. Sunka Ovrutsky is alive but has one foot in the grave. We are the Jewish community. We will not have her here!" After bending his second finger, the watchman sat down again, keeping them open as if about to make a rude gesture.

"So many years have passed. Why do you…"

"And what about the fact that every Jew in Oster was shot except for her? So she's alive. Well, who knows, maybe she was with the partisans, but all the partisans got killed and she was still alive to go talking that shit!" The watchman was not looking at Bella's relative but shouting into the air. "What were we fighting at the front for? Why were our people being shot? So that afterwards we could talk the way Beylka was talking?"

"Calm yourself, calm yourself," Bella's relative urged him.

"It's not out of malice I feel like this. I just want things to be right." The watchman straightened his medals and drew himself up to his full height.

"And where is Gottlieb Grobman buried? I don't think you showed me his grave." The relative had to throw back his head in order to see the old man's face.

"Gottlieb? His neighbour, Khomchikha, buried him. The same night that they shot him, in her own Orthodox cemetery. She was too afraid to bring him here. Told me she gave him a decent burial, wrapped in cloth, in clean hessian. I wouldn't be able to find the grave now, and Khomchikha died long ago. While she was alive it didn't seem decent to move him here. She did her best, took a risk. And then, after she died, people were still angry because of Beylka. So Gottlieb is in the Orthodox cemetery to this day."

The watchman straightened his pockets and went ahead, showing the way out. "One towny decided to get by without me. He lost his way! Ended up yelling 'A-oo, A-oo,' like someone stuck in the forest!"

Bella's relative went back to Kiev with nothing to report. The metropolitan police department sent enquiries to Oster but got no joy. No, she did not reappear. No one saw her again.

If Bella is not found, after seven years she can legally be presumed dead.

Translated by Arch Tait

Dedalus Celebrating Women's Literature
2018 – 2028

In 2018 Dedalus celebrates the centenary of women getting the vote in the UK with a programme of women's fiction. In 1918, Parliament passed an act granting the vote to women over the age of thirty who were householders, the wives of householders, occupiers of property with an annual rent of £5, and graduates of British universities. About 8.4 million women gained the vote. It was a big step forward but it was not until the Equal Franchise Act of 1928 that women over twenty-one were able to vote and women finally achieved the same voting rights as men. This act increased the number of women eligible to vote to 15 million. Dedalus' aim is to publish six titles each year for the next ten years, most of which will be translations from other European languages, as we commemorate this important milestone.

Titles published so far:

The Prepper Room – Karen Duve
Slav Sisters: The Dedalus Book of Russian Women's Literature – edited by Natasha Perova
Take Six: Six Portuguese Women Writers – edited by Margaret Jull Costa

Forthcoming titles include:

Baltic Belles: The Dedalus Book of Estonian Women's Literature – edited by Elle-Mari Talivee
The Price of Dreams – Margherita Giacobino
Cleopatra goes to Prison – Claudia Durastanti